AGATHA CHRISTIE

Collected Works

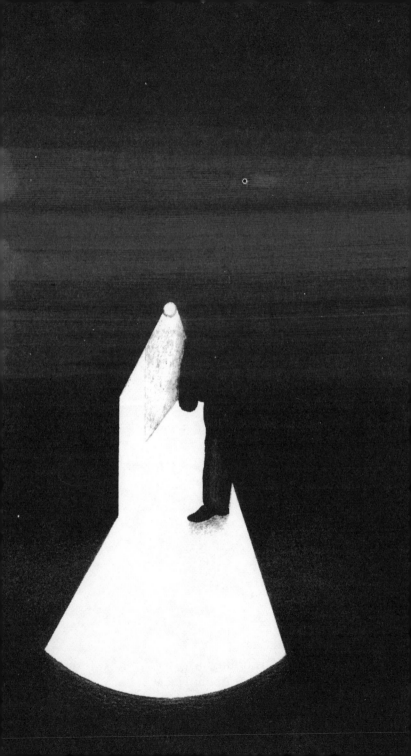

AGATHA CHRISTIE

A Murder is Announced

After the Funeral

Distributed by
Omniprose Ltd., Scarborough, Ontario

Published by arrangement with
William Collins Sons & Co. Ltd.

A Murder Is Announced © Agatha Christie 1950
After The Funeral © Agatha Christie 1953
©Illustrations, Edito-Service S.A., Geneva, 1976; 1975

Original illustrations by
TINA MERCIE &
REYNALD SCHMID

I.S.B.N.: 84-599-0316-8

A Murder is Announced

To
RALPH *and* **ANNE NEWMAN**
at whose house I first tasted
"Delicious Death!"

CONTENTS

I	A Murder is Announced	1
II	Breakfast at Little Paddocks	15
III	At 6.30 p.m.	23
IV	The Royal Spa Hotel	37
V	Miss Blacklock and Miss Bunner	46
VI	Julia, Mitzi and Patrick	59
VII	Among Those Present	68
VIII	Enter Miss Marple	84
IX	Concerning a Door	101
X	Pip and Emma	110
XI	Miss Marple Comes to Tea	123
XII	Morning Activities in Chipping Cleghorn	128
XIII	Morning Activities in Chipping Cleghorn (*continued*)	141
XIV	Excursion into the Past	157
XV	Delicious Death	167
XVI	Inspector Craddock Returns	177
XVII	The Album	183

XVIII	The Letters	192
XIX	Reconstruction of the Crime	207
XX	Miss Marple is Missing	221
XXI	Three Women	234
XXII	The Truth	249
XXIII	Evening at the Vicarage	252
	Epilogue	278

CHAPTER I

A MURDER IS ANNOUNCED

BETWEEN 7.30 and 8.30 every morning except Sundays, Johnnie Butt made the round of the village of Chipping Cleghorn on his bicycle, whistling vociferously through his teeth, and alighting at each house or cottage to shove through the letter-box such morning papers as had been ordered by the occupants of the house in question from Mr. Totman, stationer, of the High Street. Thus, at Colonel and Mrs. Easterbrook's he delivered *The Times* and the *Daily Graphic*; at Mrs. Swettenham's he left *The Times* and the *Daily Worker*; at Miss Hinchliffe and Miss Murgatroyd's he left the *Daily Telegraph* and the *News Chronicle*; at Miss Blacklock's he left the *Telegraph*, *The Times* and the *Daily Mail*.

At all these houses, and indeed at practically every house in Chipping Cleghorn, he delivered every Friday a copy of the *North Benham News and Chipping Cleghorn Gazette*, known locally simply as "*the Gazette*."

Thus, on Friday mornings, after a hurried glance at the headlines in the daily paper (*International situation critical! U.N.O. meets to-day! Bloodhounds seek blonde typist's killer! Three collieries idle. Twenty-three die of food poisoning in Seaside Hotel, etc.*) most of the inhabitants of Chipping Cleghorn eagerly opened the *Gazette* and plunged into the local news. After a cursory glance at Correspondence (in which the passionate hates and feuds of rural life found full play) nine out of ten subscribers then turned to the PERSONAL column. Here were grouped together higgledy piggledy articles

1

for Sale or Wanted, frenzied appeals for Domestic Help, innumerable insertions regarding dogs, announcements concerning poultry and garden equipment; and various other items of an interesting nature to those living in the small community of Chipping Cleghorn.

This particular Friday, October 29th—was no exception to the rule——

II

Mrs. Swettenham, pushing back the pretty little grey curls from her forehead, opened *The Times*, looked with a lack lustre eye at the left hand centre page, decided that, as usual, if there *was* any exciting news *The Times* had succeeded in camouflaging it in an impeccable manner; took a look at the Births, Marriages and Deaths, particularly the latter; then, her duty done, she put aside *The Times* and eagerly seized the *Chipping Cleghorn Gazette*.

When her son Edmund entered the room a moment later, she was already deep in the Personal Column.

" Good morning, dear," said Mrs. Swettenham. " The Smedleys are selling their Daimler. 1935—that's rather a long time ago, isn't it ?"

Her son grunted, poured himself out a cup of coffee, helped himself to a couple of kippers, sat down at the table and opened the *Daily Worker* which he propped up against the toast rack.

" *Bull mastiff puppies*," read out Mrs. Swettenham. " I really don't know how people manage to feed big dogs nowadays—I really *don't* . . . H'm, Selina Lawrence is advertising for a cook again. I could tell her it's just a waste of time advertising in these days. She hasn't put her address, only a box number—that's *quite*

2

fatal—I could have told her so—servants simply insist on knowing where they are going. They like a good address . . . *False teeth*—I can't think why false teeth are so popular. *Best prices paid . . . Beautiful bulbs. Our special selection.* They sound rather cheap . . . Here's a girl wants an '*Interesting post—Would travel.*' I dare say! Who wouldn't? . . . *Dachshunds* . . . I've never really cared for dachshunds myself—I don't mean because they're *German*, because we've got over all that—I just don't care for them, that's all.—Yes, Mrs. Finch?"

The door had opened to admit the head and torso of a grim-looking female in an aged velvet beret.

"Good morning, Mum," said Mrs. Finch. "Can I clear?"

"Not yet. We haven't finished," said Mrs. Swetten‐ham. "Not quite finished," she added ingratiatingly.

Casting a look at Edmund and his paper, Mrs. Finch sniffed, and withdrew.

"I've only just begun," said Edmund, just as his mother remarked:

"I do wish you wouldn't read that horrid paper, Edmund. Mrs. Finch doesn't like it *at all.*"

"I don't see what my political views have to do with Mrs. Finch."

"And it isn't," pursued Mrs. Swettenham, "as though you *were* a worker. You don't do any work at all."

"That's not in the least true," said Edmund indig‐nantly. "I'm writing a book."

"I meant *real* work," said Mrs. Swettenham. "And Mrs. Finch does matter. If she takes a dislike to us and won't come, who else could we get?"

"Advertise in the *Gazette*," said Edmund, grinning.

"I've just told you that's no use. Oh dear me, nowa‐days unless one has an old Nannie in the family, who

3

will go into the kitchen and do everything, one is simply *sunk*."

"Well, why haven't we an old Nannie? How remiss of you not to have provided me with one? What were you thinking about?"

"You had an *ayah*, dear."

"No foresight," murmured Edmund.

Mrs. Swettenham was once more deep in the Personal Column.

"*Second-hand Motor Mower for sale.* Now I wonder ... Goodness, what a *price*! ... More Dachshunds ... '*Do write or communicate desperate Woggles.*' What silly nicknames people have ... *Cocker Spaniels* ... Do you remember darling Susie, Edmund? She really was *human*. Understood every word you said to her ... *Sheraton sideboard for Sale. Genuine family antique. Mrs. Lucas, Dayas Hall* ... What a liar that woman is! Sheraton indeed ... !"

Mrs. Swettenham sniffed and then continued her reading.

"*All a mistake, darling. Undying love. Friday as usual—J.* ... I suppose they've had a lovers' quarrel—or do you think it's a code for burglars? ... *More* Dachshunds! Really, I do think people have gone a little crazy about breeding Dachshunds. I mean, there *are* other dogs. Your Uncle Simon used to breed Manchester Terriers. Such graceful little things. I do like dogs with *legs* ... *Lady going abroad will sell her navy two piece suiting* ... no measurements or price given. ... *A marriage is announced*—no, a *murder* ... *What?* ... *Well*, I never! Edmund, *Edmund*, listen to this ... *A murder is announced and will take place on Friday, October 29th at Little Paddocks at 6.30 p.m. Friends please accept this, the only intimation.* What an extraordinary thing? *Edmund!*"

4

" What's that?" Edmund looked up from his newspaper.

" Friday, October 29th . . . Why, that's *to-day*."

" Let me see." Her son took the paper from her.

" But what does it mean?" Mrs. Swettenham asked with lively curiosity.

Edmund Swettenham rubbed his nose doubtfully.

" Some sort of party, I suppose. The Murder Game— that kind of thing."

" Oh," said Mrs. Swettenham doubtfully. " It seems a very odd way of doing it. Just sticking it in the advertisements like that. Not at all like Letitia Blacklock who always seems to me such a sensible woman."

" Probably got up by the bright young things she has in the house."

" It's very short notice. To-day. Do you think we're just supposed to go?"

" It says ' Friends, please accept this, the only intimation?' " her son pointed out.

" Well, I think these new fangled ways of giving invitations are very tiresome," said Mrs. Swettenham decidedly.

" All right, Mother, you needn't go."

" No," agreed Mrs. Swettenham.

There was a pause.

" Do you really *want* that last piece of toast, Edmund?"

" I should have thought my being properly nourished mattered more than letting that old hag clear the table."

" Sh, dear, she'll *hear* you . . . Edmund, what happens at a Murder Game?"

" I don't know, exactly . . . They pin pieces of paper upon you, or something . . . No, I think you draw them out of a hat. And somebody's the victim and somebody else is a detective—and then they turn the lights out and

5

somebody taps you on the shoulder and then you scream and lie down and sham dead."

" It sounds quite exciting."

" Probably a beastly bore. I'm not going."

" Nonsense, Edmund," said Mrs. Swettenham resolutely. " *I'm* going and *you're* coming with me. That's *settled*!"

III

" Archie," said Mrs. Easterbrook to her husband, " listen to *this*."

Colonel Easterbrook paid no attention, because he was already snorting with impatience over an article in *The Times*.

" Trouble with these fellows is," he said, " that none of them knows the first thing about India! Not the first thing!"

" I know, dear, I know."

" If they did, they wouldn't write such piffle."

" Yes, I know. Archie, do listen. *A murder is announced and will take place on Friday, October 29th* (that's to-day) *at Little Paddocks at 6.30 p.m. Friends please accept this, the only intimation.*"

She paused triumphantly. Colonel Easterbrook looked at her indulgently but without much interest.

" Murder Game," he said.

" Oh."

" That's all it is. Mind you," he unbent a little, " it can be very good fun if it's well done. But it needs good organising by someone who knows the ropes. You draw lots. One person's the murderer, nobody knows who. Lights out. Murderer chooses his victim. The victim has to count twenty before he screams. Then the person who's chosen to be the detective takes charge. Questions

6

everybody. Where they were, what they were doing, tries to trip the real fellow up. Yes, it's a good game—if the detective—er—knows something about police work."

" Like you, Archie. You had all those interesting cases to try in your district."

Colonel Easterbrook smiled indulgently and gave his moustache a complacent twirl.

" Yes, Laura," he said. " I dare say I could give them a hint or two."

And he straightened his shoulders.

" Miss Blacklock ought to have asked you to help her in getting the thing up."

The Colonel snorted.

" Oh, well, she's got that young cub staying with her. Expect this is his idea. Nephew or something. Funny idea, though, sticking it in the paper."

" It was in the Personal Column. We might never have seen it. I suppose it *is* an invitation, Archie?"

" Funny kind of invitation. I can tell you one thing. They can count *me* out."

" Oh, Archie," Mrs. Easterbrook's voice rose in a shrill wail.

" Short notice. For all they know I might be busy."

" But you're not, are you, darling?" Mrs. Easterbrook lowered her voice persuasively. " And I do think, Archie, that you really *ought* to go—just to help poor Miss Blacklock out. I'm sure she's counting on you to make the thing a success. I mean, you know so much about police work and procedure. The whole thing will fall flat if you don't go and help to make it a success. After all, one must be *neighbourly*."

Mrs. Easterbrook put her synthetic blonde head on one side and opened her blue eyes very wide.

" Of course, if you put it like that, Laura . . ." Colonel Easterbrook twirled his grey moustache again, importantly, and looked with indulgence on his fluffy little wife. Mrs. Easterbrook was at least thirty years younger than her husband.

"If you put it like *that*, Laura," he said.

"I really do think it's your *duty*, Archie," said Mrs. Easterbrook solemnly.

IV

The *Chipping Cleghorn Gazette* had also been delivered at Boulders, the picturesque three cottages knocked into one inhabited by Miss Hinchliffe and Miss Murgatroyd.

"Hinch?"

"What is it, Murgatroyd?"

"Where are you?"

"Henhouse."

"Oh."

Paddling gingerly through the long wet grass, Miss Amy Murgatroyd approached her friend. The latter, attired in corduroy slacks and battledress tunic was conscientiously stirring in handfuls of balancer meal to a repellently steaming basin full of cooked potato peelings and cabbage stumps.

She turned her head with its short man-like crop and weatherbeaten countenance toward her friend.

Miss Murgatroyd, who was fat and amiable, wore a checked tweed skirt and a shapeless pullover of brilliant royal blue. Her curly bird's nest of grey hair was in a good deal of disorder and she was slightly out of breath.

"In the *Gazette*," she panted. "Just listen—what can it *mean*? *A murder is announced . . . and will take place on Friday, October 29th at Little Paddocks at 6.30 p.m. Friends please accept this, the only intimation.*"

8

She paused, breathless, as she finished reading, and awaited some authoritative pronouncement.

"Daft," said Miss Hinchliffe.

"Yes, but what do you think it *means*?"

"Means a drink, anyway," said Miss Hinchliffe.

"You think it's a sort of invitation?"

"We'll find out what it means when we get there," said Miss Hinchliffe. "Bad sherry, I expect. You'd better get off the grass, Murgatroyd. You've got your bedroom slippers on still. They're soaked."

"Oh, dear." Miss Murgatroyd looked down ruefully at her feet. "How many eggs to-day?"

"Seven. That damned hen's still broody. I must get her into the coop."

"It's a funny way of putting it, don't you think?" Amy Murgatroyd asked, reverting to the notice in the *Gazette*. Her voice was slightly wistful.

But her friend was made of sterner and more single-minded stuff. She was intent on dealing with recalcitrant poultry and no announcement in a paper, however enigmatic, could deflect her.

She squelched heavily through the mud and pounced upon a speckled hen. There was a loud and indignant squawking.

"Give me ducks every time," said Miss Hinchliffe. "*Far* less trouble . . ."

v

"Oo, scrumptious!" said Mrs. Harmon across the breakfast table to her husband, the Rev. Julian Harmon, "there's going to be a murder at Miss Blacklock's."

"A murder?" said her husband, slightly surprised. "When?"

9

" This afternoon . . . at least, this evening. 6.30. Oh, bad luck, darling, you've got your preparations for confirmation then. It *is* a shame. And you do so love murders ! "

" I don't really know what you're talking about, Bunch ? "

Mrs. Harmon, the roundness of whose form and face had early led to the soubriquet of " Bunch " being substituted for her baptismal name of Diana, handed the *Gazette* across the table.

" There. All among the second-hand pianos, and the old teeth."

" What a very extraordinary announcement."

" Isn't it ? " said Bunch happily. " You wouldn't think that Miss Blacklock cared about murders and games and things, would you ? I suppose it's the young Simmonses put her up to it—though I should have thought Julia Simmons would find murders rather crude. Still, there it is, and I do think, darling, it's a *shame* you can't be there. Anyway, I'll go and tell you all about it, though it's rather wasted on me, because I don't really like games that happen in the dark. They frighten me, and I *do* hope I shan't have to be the one who's murdered. If someone suddenly puts a hand on my shoulder and whispers, ' You're dead,' I know my heart will give such a big bump that perhaps it really *might* kill me ! Do you think that's likely ? "

" No, Bunch. I think you're going to live to be an old, old woman—with me."

" And die on the same day and be buried in the same grave. That would be lovely."

Bunch beamed from ear to ear at this agreeable prospect.

" You seem very happy, Bunch ? " said her husband, smiling.

10

"Who'd *not* be happy if they were me?" demanded Bunch, rather confusedly. "With you and Susan and Edward, and all of you fond of me and not caring if I'm stupid . . . And the sun shining! And this lovely big house to live in!"

The Rev. Julian Harmon looked round the big bare dining-room and assented doubtfully.

"Some people would think it was the last straw to have to live in this great rambling draughty place."

"Well, I like big rooms. All the nice smells from outside can get in and stay there. And you can be untidy and leave things about and they don't clutter you."

"No labour saving devices or central heating? It means a lot of work for you, Bunch."

"Oh, Julian, it doesn't. I get up at half-past six and light the boiler and rush around like a steam engine, and by eight it's all done. And I keep it nice, don't I? With beeswax and polish and big jars of autumn leaves. It's not really harder to keep a big house clean than a small one. You go round with mops and things much quicker, because your behind isn't always bumping into things like it is in a small room. And I like sleeping in a big cold room—it's so cosy to snuggle down with just the tip of your nose telling you what it's like up above. And whatever size of house you live in, you peel the same amount of potatoes and wash up the same amount of plates and all that. Think how nice it is for Edward and Susan to have a big empty room to play in where they can have railways and dolls' tea-parties all over the floor and never have to put them away? And then it's nice to have extra bits of the house that you can let people have to live in. Jimmy Symes and Johnnie Finch— they'd have had to live with their in-laws otherwise. And you know, Julian, it isn't nice living with your in-laws. You're devoted to Mother, but you wouldn't

really have liked to start our married life living with her
and Father. And I shouldn't have liked it, either. I'd
have gone on feeling like a little girl."

Julian smiled at her.

" You're rather like a little girl still, Bunch."

Julian Harmon himself had clearly been a model
designed by Nature for the age of sixty. He was still about
twenty-five years short of achieving Nature's purpose.

" I know I'm stupid——"

" You're not stupid, Bunch. You're very clever."

"No, I'm not. I'm not a bit intellectual. Though I
do try . . . And I really love it when you talk to me
about books and history and things. I think perhaps it
wasn't an awfully good idea to read aloud Gibbon to me
in the evenings, because if it's been a cold wind out, and
it's nice and hot by the fire, there's something about
Gibbon that does, rather, make you go to sleep."

Julian laughed.

" But I do love listening to you, Julian. Tell me the
story again about the old vicar who preached about
Ahasuerus."

" You know that by heart, Bunch."

" Just tell it me again. *Please.*"

Her husband complied.

" It was old Scrymgour. Somebody looked into his
church one day. He was leaning out of the pulpit and
preaching fervently to a couple of old charwomen. He
was shaking his finger at them and saying, ' Aha ! I
know what you are thinking. *You* think that the Great
Ahasuerus of the First Lesson was Artaxerxes the Second.
But he *wasn't* !' And then with enormous triumph, ' He
was Artaxerxes the *Third.*' "

It had never struck Julian Harmon as a particularly
funny story himself, but it never failed to amuse Bunch.

Her clear laugh floated out.

"The old pet!" she exclaimed. "I think you'll be exactly like that some day, Julian."

Julian looked rather uneasy.

"I know," he said with humility. "I do feel very strongly that I can't always get the proper simple approach."

"I shouldn't worry," said Bunch, rising and beginning to pile the breakfast plates on a tray. "Mrs. Butt told me yesterday that Butt, who never went to church and used to be practically the local atheist, comes every Sunday now on purpose to hear you preach."

She went on, with a very fair imitation of Mrs. Butt's super-refined voice:

"'And Butt was saying only the other day, Madam, to Mr. Timkins from Little Worsdale, that we'd got real *culture* here in Chipping Cleghorn. *Not* like Mr. Goss, at Little Worsdale, who talks to the congregation as though they were children who hadn't had any education. Real culture, Butt said, that's what *we've* got. Our Vicar's a highly educated gentleman—Oxford, not Milchester, and he gives us the full benefit of his education. All about the Romans and the Greeks he knows, and the Babylonians and the Assyrians, too. And even the Vicarage cat, Butt says, is called after an Assyrian king!' So there's glory for you," finished Bunch triumphantly. "Goodness, I must get on with things or I shall never get done. Come along, Tiglath Pileser, you shall have the herring bones."

Opening the door and holding it dexterously ajar with her foot, she shot through with the loaded tray, singing in a loud and not particularly tuneful voice, her own version of a sporting song.

"*It's a fine murdering day,* (sang Bunch)
And as balmy as May
And the sleuths from the village are gone,"

13

A rattle of crockery being dumped in the sink drowned the next lines, but as the Rev. Julian Harmon left the house, he heard the final triumphant assertion:

" *And we'll all go a'murdering to-day!* "

14

CHAPTER II

BREAKFAST AT LITTLE PADDOCKS

AT LITTLE PADDOCKS also, breakfast was in progress.

Miss Blacklock, a woman of sixty odd, the owner of the house, sat at the head of the table. She wore country tweeds—and with them, rather incongruously, a choker necklace of large false pearls. She was reading Lane Norcott in the *Daily Mail*. Julia Simmons was languidly glancing through the *Telegraph*. Patrick Simmons was checking up on the crossword in *The Times*. Miss Dora Bunner was giving her attention wholeheartedly to the local weekly paper.

Miss Blacklock gave a subdued chuckle, Patrick muttered : " *Adherent*—not *adhesive*—that's where I went wrong."

Suddenly a loud cluck, like a startled hen, came from Miss Bunner.

" Letty—*Letty*—have you seen this? Whatever *can* it mean?"

" What's the matter, Dora?"

" The most extraordinary advertisement. It says Little Paddocks quite distinctly. But whatever can it *mean*?"

" If you'd let me see, Dora dear——"

Miss Bunner obediently surrendered the paper into Miss Blacklock's outstretched hand, pointing to the item with a tremulous forefinger.

" Just look, Letty."

15

Miss Blacklock looked. Her eyebrows went up. She threw a quick scrutinising glance round the table. Then she read the advertisement out loud.

"*A murder is announced and will take place on Friday, October 29th at Little Paddocks at 6.30 p.m. Friends please accept this, the only intimation.*"

Then she said sharply: "Patrick, is this your idea?"

Her eyes rested searchingly on the handsome devil-may-care face of the young man at the other end of the table.

Patrick Simmons' disclaimer came quickly.

"No, indeed, Aunt Letty. Whatever put that idea into your head? Why should I know anything about it?"

"I wouldn't put it past you," said Miss Blacklock grimly. "I thought it might be your idea of a joke."

"A joke? Nothing of the kind."

"And you, Julia?"

Julia, looking bored, said: "Of course not."

Miss Bunner murmured: "Do you think Mrs. Haymes——" and looked at an empty place where someone had breakfasted earlier.

"Oh, I don't think our Phillipa would try and be funny," said Patrick. "She's a serious girl, she is."

"But what's the idea, anyway?" said Julia, yawning. "What does it mean?"

Miss Blacklock said slowly, "I suppose—it's some silly sort of hoax."

"But why?" Dora Bunner exclaimed. "What's the point of it? It seems a very stupid sort of joke. And in very bad taste."

Her flabby cheeks quivered indignantly, and her short-sighted eyes sparkled with indignation.

16

Miss Blacklock smiled at her.

"Don't work yourself up over it, Bunny," she said. "It's just somebody's idea of humour, but I wish I knew whose."

"It says to-day," pointed out Miss Bunner. "To-day at 6.30 p.m. What do you think is going to happen?"

"*Death!*" said Patrick in sepulchral tones. "Delicious Death."

"Be quiet, Patrick," said Miss Blacklock as Miss Bunner gave a little yelp.

"I only meant the special cake that Mitzi makes," said Patrick apologetically. "You know we *always* call it Delicious Death."

Miss Blacklock smiled a little absentmindedly.

Miss Bunner persisted : "But Letty, what do you really think——"

Her friend cut across the words with reassuring cheerfulness.

"I know one thing that will happen at 6.30," she said dryly. "We'll have half the village up here, agog with curiosity. I'd better make sure we've got some sherry in the house."

II

"You *are* worried, aren't you, Lotty?"

Miss Blacklock started. She had been sitting at her writing-table, absentmindedly drawing little fishes on the blotting paper. She looked up into the anxious face of her old friend.

She was not quite sure what to say to Dora Bunner. Bunny, she knew, mustn't be worried or upset. She was silent for a moment or two, thinking.

17

She and Dora Bunner had been at school together. Dora then had been a pretty fair-haired, blue-eyed rather stupid girl. Her being stupid hadn't mattered, because her gaiety and high spirits and her prettiness had made her an agreeable companion. She ought, her friend thought, to have married some nice Army officer, or a country solicitor. She had so many good qualities—affection, devotion, loyalty. But life had been unkind to Dora Bunner. She had had to earn her living. She had been painstaking but never competent at anything she undertook.

The two friends had lost sight of each other. But six months ago a letter had come to Miss Blacklock, a rambling, pathetic letter. Dora's health had given way. She was living in one room, trying to subsist on her old age pension. She endeavoured to do needlework, but her fingers were stiff with rheumatism. She mentioned their schooldays—since then life had driven them apart—but could—possibly—her old friend help?

Miss Blacklock had responded impulsively. Poor Dora, poor pretty silly fluffy Dora. She had swooped down upon Dora, had carried her off, had installed her at Little Paddocks with the comforting fiction that " the house-work is getting too much for me. I need someone to help me run the house." It was not for long—the doctor had told her that—but sometimes she found poor old Dora a sad trial. She muddled everything, upset the temperamental foreign " help," miscounted the laundry, lost bills and letters—and sometimes reduced the competent Miss Blacklock to an agony of exasperation. Poor old muddle-headed Dora, so loyal, so anxious to help, so pleased and proud to think she was of assistance—and, alas, so completely unreliable.

She said sharply :

18

" Don't, Dora. You know I asked you——"

" Oh," Miss Bunner looked guilty. " I know. I forgot. But—but you *are*, aren't you?"

" Worried? No. At least," she added truthfully, " not exactly. You mean about that silly notice in the *Gazette*?"

" Yes—even if it's a joke, it seems to me it's a—a spiteful sort of joke."

" Spiteful?"

" Yes. It seems to me there's *spite* there somewhere. I mean—it's not a *nice* kind of joke."

Miss Blacklock looked at her friend. The mild eyes, the long obstinate mouth, the slightly upturned nose. Poor Dora, so maddening, so muddleheaded, so devoted and such a problem. A dear fussy old idiot and yet, in a queer way, with an instinctive sense of values.

" I think you're right, Dora," said Miss Blacklock. " It's not a nice joke."

" I don't like it at all," said Dora Bunner with un-suspected vigour. " It frightens me." She added, sud-denly : " And it frightens *you*, Letitia."

" Nonsense," said Miss Blacklock with spirit.

" It's *dangerous*. I'm sure it is. Like those people who send you bombs done up in parcels."

" My dear, it's just some silly idiot trying to be funny."

" But it *isn't* funny."

It wasn't really very funny . . . Miss Blacklock's face betrayed her thoughts, and Dora cried triumphantly, " You see. You think so, too!"

" But Dora, my dear——"

She broke off. Through the door there surged a tem-pestuous young woman with a well developed bosom heaving under a tight jersey. She had on a dirndl skirt of a bright colour and had greasy dark plaits wound

19

round and round her head. Her eyes were dark and flashing.

She said gustily :

" I can speak to you, yes, please, no ?"

Miss Blacklock sighed.

" Of course, Mitzi, what is it ?"

Sometimes she thought it would be preferable to do the entire work of the house as well as the cooking rather than be bothered with the eternal nerve storms of her refugee " lady help."

" I tell you at once—it is in order, I hope ? I give you my notices and I *go*—I go at *once* !"

" For what reason ? Has somebody upset you ?"

" Yes, I am upset," said Mitzi dramatically. " I do not wish to die ! Already in Europe I escape. My family they all die—they are all killed—my mother, my little brother, my so sweet little niece—all, all they are killed. But me I run away—I hide. I get to England. I work. I do work that never—never would I do in my own country—I——"

" I know all that," said Miss Blacklock crisply. It was, indeed, a constant refrain on Mitzi's lips. " But why do you want to leave *now* ?"

" Because again they come to kill me !"

" Who do ?"

" My enemies. The Nazis ! Or perhaps this time it is the Bolsheviks. They find out I am here. They come to kill me. I have read it—yes—it is in the newspaper !"

" Oh, you mean in the *Gazette* ?"

" *Here*, it is written here." Mitzi produced the *Gazette* from where she had been holding it behind her back. " See—here it says a *murder*. At Little Paddocks. That is here, is it not ? This evening at 6.30. Ah ! I do not wait to be murdered—*no*."

20

" But why should this apply to *you*? It's—we think it is a joke."

" A *joke*? It is not a joke to murder someone?"

" No, of course not. But my dear child, if anyone wanted to murder you, they wouldn't advertise the fact in the paper, would they?"

" You do not think they would?" Mitzi seemed a little shaken. "You think, perhaps, they do not mean to murder anyone at all? Perhaps it is *you* they mean to murder, Miss Blacklock."

" I certainly can't believe anyone wants to murder me," said Miss Blacklock lightly. "And really, Mitzi, I don't see why anyone should want to murder you. After all, why should they?"

" Because they are bad peoples . . . Very bad peoples. I tell you, my mother, my little brother, my so sweet niece . . ."

" Yes, yes." Miss Blacklock stemmed the flow, adroitly: "But I cannot really believe *anyone* wants to murder you, Mitzi. Of course, if you want to go off like this at a moment's notice, I cannot possibly stop you. But I think you will be very silly if you do."

She added firmly, as Mitzi looked doubtful :

" We'll have that beef the butcher sent stewed for lunch. It looks very tough."

" I make you a goulash, a special goulash."

" If you prefer to call it that, certainly. And perhaps you could use up that rather hard bit of cheese in making some cheese straws. I think some people may come in this evening for drinks."

" This evening? What do you mean, this evening?"

" At half-past six."

" But that is the time in the paper. Who should come then? *Why* should they come?"

" They're coming to the funeral," said Miss Blacklock

21

with a twinkle. "That'll do now, Mitzi. I'm busy. Shut the door after you," she added firmly.

"And that's settled *her* for the moment," she said as the door closed behind a puzzled-looking Mitzi.

"You are so efficient, Letty," said Miss Bunner admiringly.

22

CHAPTER III

AT 6.30 P.M.

"WELL, here we are, all set," said Miss Blacklock She looked round the double drawing-room with an appraising eye. The rose-patterned chintzes—the two bowls of bronze chrysanthemums, the small vase of violets and the silver cigarette-box on a table by the wall, the tray of drinks on the centre table.

Little Paddocks was a medium-sized house built in the early Victorian style. It had a long shallow veranda and green shuttered windows. The long, narrow drawing-room which lost a good deal of light owing to the veranda roof had originally had double doors at one end leading into a small room with a bay window. A former generation had removed the double doors and replaced them with portiéres of velvet. Miss Blacklock had dispensed with the portiéres so that the two rooms had become definitely one. There was a fireplace each end, but neither fire was lit although a gentle warmth pervaded the room.

" You've had the central heating lit," said Patrick.

Miss Blacklock nodded.

" It's been so misty and damp lately. The whole house felt clammy. I got Evans to light it before he went."

" The precious precious coke?" said Patrick mockingly.

" As you say, the precious coke. But otherwise there would have been the even more precious coal. You know the Fuel Office won't even let us have the little bit that's due to us each week—not unless we can say definitely that we haven't got any other means of cooking."

" I suppose there was once heaps of coke and coal for

23

everybody?" said Julia with the interest of one hearing about an unknown country.

"Yes, and cheap, too."

"And anyone could go and buy as much as they wanted, without filling in anything, and there wasn't any shortage? There was lots of it there?"

"All kinds and qualities—and *not* all stones and slates like what we get nowadays."

"It must have been a wonderful world," said Julia, with awe in her voice.

Miss Blacklock smiled. "Looking back on it, *I* certainly think so. But then I'm an old woman. It's natural for me to prefer my own times. But you young things oughtn't to think so."

"I needn't have had a job then," said Julia. "I could just have stayed at home and done the flowers, and written notes. . . . Why did one write notes and who were they to?"

"All the people that you now ring up on the telephone," said Miss Blacklock with a twinkle. "I don't believe you even know *how* to write, Julia."

"Not in the style of that delicious 'Complete Letter Writer' I found the other day. Heavenly! It told you the correct way of refusing a proposal of marriage from a widower."

"I doubt if you would have enjoyed staying at home as much as you think," said Miss Blacklock. "There were duties, you know." Her voice was dry. "However, I don't really know much about it. Bunny and I," she smiled affectionately at Dora Bunner, "went into the labour market early."

"Oh, we did, we did *indeed*," agreed Miss Bunner. "Those naughty, naughty children. I'll never forget them. Of course, Letty was clever. She was a business woman, secretary to a big financier."

The door opened and Phillipa Haymes came in. She was tall and fair and placid looking. She looked round the room in surprise.

"Hallo," she said. "Is it a party? Nobody told me."

"Of course," cried Patrick. "Our Phillipa doesn't know. The only woman in Chipping Cleghorn who doesn't, I bet."

Phillipa looked at him inquiringly.

"Here you behold," said Patrick dramatically, waving a hand, "the scene of a murder!"

Phillipa Haymes looked faintly puzzled.

"Here," Patrick indicated the two big bowls of chrysanthemums, "are the funeral wreaths and these dishes of cheese straws and olives represent the funeral baked meats."

Phillipa looked inquiringly at Miss Blacklock.

"Is it a joke?" she asked. "I'm always terribly stupid at seeing jokes."

"It's a very nasty joke," said Dora Bunner with energy. "I don't like it at all."

"Show her the advertisement," said Miss Blacklock. "I *must* go and shut up the ducks. It's dark. They'll be in by now."

"Let me do it," said Phillipa.

"Certainly not, my dear. You've finished your day's work."

"I'll do it, Aunt Letty," offered Patrick.

"No, you won't," said Miss Blacklock with energy. "Last time you didn't latch the door properly."

"I'll do it, Letty dear," cried Miss Bunner. "Indeed, I should love to. I'll just slip on my goloshes—and now where did I put my cardigan?"

But Miss Blacklock, with a smile, had already left the room.

"It's no good, Bunny," said Patrick. "Aunt Letty's

25

so efficient that she can never bear anybody else to do things for her. She really much prefers to do everything herself."

"She loves it," said Julia.

"I didn't notice you making any offers of assistance," said her brother.

Julia smiled lazily.

"You've just said Aunt Letty likes to do things herself," she pointed out. "Besides," she held out a well-shaped leg in a sheer stocking, "I've got my best stockings on."

"Death in silk stockings!" declaimed Patrick.

"Not silk—nylons, you idiot."

"That's not nearly such a good title."

"Won't somebody please tell me," cried Phillipa, plaintively, "why there is all this insistence on death?"

Everybody tried to tell her at once—nobody could find the *Gazette* to show her because Mitzi had taken it into the kitchen.

Miss Blacklock returned a few minutes later.

"There," she said briskly, "*that's* done." She glanced at the clock. "Twenty-past six. Somebody ought to be here soon—unless I'm entirely wrong in my estimate of my neighbours."

"I don't see why anybody should come," said Phillipa, looking bewildered.

"Don't you, dear? . . . I dare say you wouldn't. But most people are rather more inquisitive than you are."

"Phillipa's attitude to life is that she just isn't interested," said Julia, rather nastily.

Phillipa did not reply.

Miss Blacklock was glancing round the room. Mitzi had put the sherry and three dishes containing olives, cheese straws and some little fancy pastries on the table in the middle of the room.

26

"You might move that tray—or the whole table if you like—round the corner into the bay window in the other room, Patrick, if you don't mind. After all, I am *not* giving a party! *I* haven't asked anyone. And I don't intend to make it obvious that I expect people to turn up."

"You wish, Aunt Letty, to disguise your intelligent anticipation?"

"Very nicely put, Patrick. Thank you, my dear boy."

"Now we can all give a lovely performance of a quiet evening at home," said Julia, "and be quite surprised when somebody drops in."

Miss Blacklock had picked up the sherry bottle. She stood holding it uncertainly in her hand.

Patrick reassured her.

"There's quite half a bottle there. It ought to be enough."

"Oh, yes—yes . . ." She hesitated. Then, with a slight flush, she said:

"Patrick, would you mind . . . there's a new bottle in the cupboard in the pantry. . . . Bring it and a corkscrew. I—*we*—might as well have a new bottle. This—this has been opened some time."

Patrick went on his errand without a word. He returned with the new bottle and drew the cork. He looked up curiously at Miss Blacklock as he placed it on the tray.

"Taking things seriously, aren't you, darling?" he asked gently.

"Oh," cried Dora Bunner, shocked. "Surely, Letty, you can't imagine——"

"Hush," said Miss Blacklock quickly. "That's the bell. You see, my intelligent anticipation is being justified."

11

Mitzi opened the door of the drawing-room and admitted Colonel and Mrs. Easterbrook. She had her own methods of announcing people.

" Here is Colonel and Mrs. Easterbrook to see you," she said conversationally.

Colonel Easterbrook was very bluff and breezy to cover some slight embarrassment.

" Hope you don't mind us dropping in," he said. (A subdued gurgle came from Julia.) " Happened to be passing this way—eh what? Quite a mild evening. Notice you've got your central heating on. We haven't started ours yet."

" Aren't your chrysanthemums *lovely*?" gushed Mrs. Easterbrook. " *Such* beauties!"

" They're rather scraggy, really," said Julia.

Mrs. Easterbrook greeted Phillipa Haymes with a little extra cordiality to show that she *quite* understood that Phillipa was not really an agricultural labourer.

" How is Mrs. Lucas's garden getting on?" she asked. " Do you think it will ever be straight again? Completely neglected all through the war—and then only that dreadful old man Ashe who simply did nothing but sweep up a few leaves and put in a few cabbage plants."

" It's yielding to treatment," said Phillipa. " But it will take a little time."

Mitzi opened the door again and said :

" Here are the ladies from Boulders."

" 'Evening," said Miss Hinchliffe, striding over and taking Miss Blacklock's hand in her formidable grip. " I said to Murgatroyd : ' Let's just drop in at Little Paddocks!' I wanted to ask you how your ducks are laying."

28

"The evenings do draw in so quickly now, don't they?" said Miss Murgatroyd to Patrick in a rather fluttery way. "What lovely chrysanthemums!"

"Scraggy!" said Julia.

"Why can't you be co-operative?" murmured Patrick to her in a reproachful aside.

"You've got your central heating on," said Miss Hinchliffe. She said it accusingly. "Very early."

"The house gets so damp this time of year," said Miss Blacklock.

Patrick signalled with his eyebrows: "Sherry yet?" and Miss Blacklock signalled back: "Not yet."

She said to Colonel Easterbrook:

"Are you getting any bulbs from Holland this year?"

The door again opened and Mrs. Swettenham came in rather guiltily, followed by a scowling and uncomfortable Edmund.

"Here we are!" said Mrs. Swettenham gaily, gazing round her with frank curiosity. Then, feeling suddenly uncomfortable, she went on: "I just thought I'd pop in and ask you if by any chance you wanted a kitten, Miss Blacklock? Our cat is just——"

"About to be brought to bed of the progeny of a ginger tom," said Edmund. "The result will, I think, be frightful. Don't say you haven't been warned!"

"She's a very good mouser," said Mrs. Swettenham hastily. And added: "What *lovely* chrysanthemums!"

"You've got your central heating on, haven't you?" asked Edmund, with an air of originality.

"Aren't people just like gramophone records?" murmured Julia.

"I don't like the news," said Colonel Easterbrook to Patrick, buttonholing him fiercely. "I don't like it at all. If you ask me, war's inevitable—absolutely inevitable."

"I never pay any attention to news," said Patrick.

29

Once more the door opened and Mrs. Harmon came in.

Her battered felt hat was stuck on the back of her head in a vague attempt to be fashionable and she had put on a rather limp frilly blouse instead of her usual pullover.

"Hallo, Miss Blacklock," she exclaimed, beaming all over her round face. "I'm not too late, am I? When does the murder begin?"

III

There was an audible series of gasps. Julia gave an approving little giggle, Patrick crinkled up his face and Miss Blacklock smiled at her latest guest.

"Julian is just frantic with rage that he can't be here," said Mrs. Harmon. "He *adores* murders. That's really why he preached such a good sermon last Sunday—I suppose I oughtn't to say it was a good sermon as he's my husband—but it really was good, didn't you think? —so much better than his usual sermons. But as I was saying it was all because of *Death Does the Hat Trick*. Have you read it? The girl at Boots' kept it for me specially. It's simply *baffling*. You keep thinking you know—and then the whole thing switches round—and there are a lovely lot of murders, four or five of them. Well, I left it in the study when Julian was shutting himself up there to do his sermon, and he just picked it up and simply *could not* put it down! And consequently he had to write his sermon in a frightful hurry and had to just put down what he wanted to say very simply— without any scholarly twists and bits and learned refer- ences—and naturally it was heaps better. Oh, dear, I'm

30

talking too much. But do tell me, when is the murder going to begin?"

Miss Blacklock looked at the clock on the mantelpiece.

" If it's going to begin," she said cheerfully, " it ought to begin soon. It's just a minute to the half hour. In the meantime, have a glass of sherry."

Patrick moved with alacrity through the archway. Miss Blacklock went to the table by the archway where the cigarette-box was.

" I'd love some sherry," said Mrs. Harmon. " But what do you mean by *if*?"

" Well," said Miss Blacklock. " I'm as much in the dark as you are. I don't know what——"

She stopped and turned her head as the little clock on the mantelpiece began to chime. It had a sweet silvery bell-like tone. Everybody was silent and nobody moved. They all stared at the clock.

It chimed a quarter—and then the half. As the last note died away all the lights went out.

I V

Delighted gasps and feminine squeaks of appreciation were heard in the darkness. " It's beginning," cried Mrs. Harmon in an ecstasy. Dora Bunner's voice cried out plaintively, " Oh, I don't like it!" Other voices said, " How terribly terribly frightening!" " It gives me the creeps." " Archie, where are you?" " What do I have to *do*?" " Oh, dear—did I step on your foot? I'm so sorry."

Then, with a crash the door swung open. A powerful flashlight played rapidly round the room. A man's hoarse nasal voice, reminiscent to all of pleasant afternoons at the cinema directed the company crisply to :

" Stick 'em up!

" Stick 'em up, I tell you!" the voice barked.

Delightedly, hands were raised willingly above heads.

" Isn't it wonderful?" breathed a female voice. " I'm *so* thrilled."

And then, unexpectedly, a revolver spoke. It spoke twice. The ping of two bullets shattered the complacency of the room. Suddenly the game was no longer a game. Somebody screamed. . . .

The figure in the doorway whirled suddenly round, it seemed to hesitate, a third shot rang out, it crumpled and then it crashed to the ground. The flashlight dropped and went out.

There was darkness once again. And gently, with a little Victorian protesting moan, the drawing-room door, as was its habit when not propped open, swung gently to and latched with a click.

v

Inside the drawing-room there was pandemonium. Various voices spoke at once. " Lights." " Can't you find the switch?" " Who's got a lighter?" " Oh, I don't like it, I don't *like* it." " But those shots were *real*!" " It was a *real* revolver he had." " Was it a burglar?" " Oh, Archie, I want to get out of here." " Please, has somebody got a lighter?"

And then, almost at the same moment, two lighters clicked and burned with small steady flames.

Everybody blinked and peered at each other. Startled face looked into startled face. Against the wall by the archway Miss Blacklock stood with her hand up to her face. The light was too dim to show more than that something dark was trickling over her fingers.

32

Colonel Easterbrook cleared his throat and rose to the occasion.

" Try the switches, Swettenham," he ordered.

Edmund, near the door, obediently jerked the switch up and down.

" Off at the main, or a fuse," said the Colonel. " Who's making that awful row?"

A female voice had been screaming steadily from somewhere beyond the closed door. It rose now in pitch and with it came the sound of fists hammering on a door.

Dora Bunner, who had been sobbing quietly, called out :

" It's Mitzi. Somebody's murdering Mitzi. . . ."

Patrick muttered : " No such luck."

Miss Blacklock said : " We must get candles. Patrick, will you———"

The Colonel was already opening the door. He and Edmund, their lighters flickering, stepped into the hall. They almost stumbled over a recumbent figure there.

" Seems to have knocked him out," said the Colonel. " Where's that woman making that hellish noise?"

" In the dining-room," said Edmund.

The dining-room was just across the hall. Someone was beating on the panels and howling and screaming.

" She's locked in," said Edmund, stooping down. He turned the key and Mitzi came out like a bounding tiger.

The dining-room light was still on. Silhouetted against it Mitzi presented a picture of insane terror and continued to scream. A touch of comedy was introduc(' hv the fact that she had been engaged in cleaning silver ana was still holding a chamois leather and a large fish slice.

" Be quiet, Mitzi," said Miss Blacklock.

" Stop it," said Edmund, and as Mitzi showed no disposition to stop screaming, he leaned forward and gave her a sharp slap on the cheek. Mitzi gasped and hiccupped into silence.

" Get some candles," said Miss Blacklock. " In the kitchen cupboard. Patrick, you know where the fusebox is?"

" The passage behind the scullery? Right, I'll see what I can do."

Miss Blacklock had moved foward into the light thrown from the dining-room and Dora Bunner gave a sobbing gasp. Mitzi let out another full-blooded scream.

" The blood, the *blood*!" she gasped. " You are shot —Miss Blacklock, you bleed to death."

" Don't be so stupid," snapped Miss Blacklock. " I'm hardly hurt at all. It just grazed my ear."

" But Aunt Letty," said Julia, " the blood."

And indeed Miss Blacklock's white blouse and pearls and her hand were a horrifyingly gory sight.

" Ears always bleed," said Miss Blacklock. " I remember fainting in the hairdresser's when I was a child. The man had only just snipped my ear. There seemed to be a basin of blood at once. But we *must* have some light."

" I get the candles," said Mitzi.

Julia went with her and they returned with several candles stuck into saucers.

" Now let's have a look at our malefactor," said the Colonel. " Hold the candles down low, will you, Swettenham? As many as you can."

" I'll come the other side," said Phillipa.

With a steady hand she took a couple of saucers. Colonel Easterbrook knelt down.

The recumbent figure was draped in a roughly-made black cloak with a hood to it. There was a black mask over the face and he wore black cotton gloves. The hood had slipped back disclosing a ruffled fair head.

Colonel Easterbrook turned him over, felt the pulse,

34

the heart . . . then drew away his fingers with an exclamation of distaste, looking down on them. They were sticky and red.

" Shot himself," he said.

" Is he badly hurt?" asked Miss Blacklock.

" H'm. I'm afraid he's dead . . . May have been suicide—or he may have tripped himself up with that cloak thing and the revolver went off as he fell. If I could see better——"

At that moment, as though by magic, the lights came on again.

With a queer feeling of unreality those inhabitants of Chipping Cleghorn who stood in the hall of Little Paddocks realised that they stood in the presence of violent and sudden death. Colonel Easterbrook's hand was stained red. Blood was still trickling down Miss Blacklock's neck over her blouse and coat, and the grotesquely sprawled figure of the intruder lay at their feet. . . .

Patrick, coming from the dining-room, said, " It seemed to be just one fuse gone . . ." He stopped.

Colonel Easterbrook tugged at the small black mask.

" Better see who the fellow is," he said. " Though I don't suppose it's anyone we know. . . ."

He detached the mask. Necks were craned forward. Mitzi hiccupped and gasped, but the others were very quiet.

" He's quite young," said Mrs. Harmon with a note of pity in her voice.

And suddenly Dora Bunner cried out excitedly :

" Letty, Letty, it's the young man from the Spa Hotel in Medenham Wells. The one who came out here and wanted you to give him money to get back to Switzerland and you refused. I suppose the whole thing was just a pretext—to spy out the house. . . . Oh, dear—he might easily have killed you. . . ."

Miss Blacklock, in command of the situation, said incisively:

"Phillipa, take Bunny into the dining-room and give her a half glass of brandy. Julia dear, just run up to the bathroom and bring me the sticking plaster out of the bathroom cupboard—it's so messy bleeding like a pig. Patrick, will you ring up the police at once?"

CHAPTER IV

THE ROYAL SPA HOTEL

GEORGE RYDESDALE, Chief Constable of Middle-shire, was a quiet man. Of medium height, with shrewd eyes under rather bushy brows, he was in the habit of listening rather than talking. Then, in his unemotional voice, he would give a brief order—and the order was obeyed.

He was listening now to Detective-Inspector Dermot Craddock. Craddock was now officially in charge of the case. Rydesdale had recalled him last night from Liverpool where he had been sent to make certain inquiries in connection with another case. Rydesdale had a good opinion of Craddock. He not only had brains and imagination, he had also, which Rydesdale appreciated even more, the self-discipline to go slow, to check and examine each fact, and to keep an open mind until the very end of a case.

"Constable Legg took the call, sir," Craddock was saying. "He seems to have acted very well, with prompt-itude and presence of mind. And it can't have been easy. About a dozen people all trying to talk at once, including one of those Mittel Europas who go off at the deep end at the mere sight of a policeman. Made sure she was going to be locked up, and fairly screamed the place down."

"Deceased has been identified?"

"Yes, sir. Rudi Scherz. Swiss Nationality. Employed at the Royal Spa Hotel, Medenham Wells, as a recep-tionist. If you agree, sir, I thought I'd take the Royal

Spa Hotel first, and go out to Chipping Cleghorn afterwards. Sergeant Fletcher is out there now. He'll see the bus people and then go on to the house."

Rydesdale nodded approval.

The door opened, and the Chief Constable looked up.

" Come in, Henry," he said. " We've got something here that's a little out of the ordinary."

Sir Henry Clithering, ex-Commissioner of Scotland Yard, came in with slightly raised eyebrows. He was a tall, distinguished-looking elderly man.

" It may appeal to even your blasé palate," went on Rydesdale.

" I was never blasé," said Sir Henry indignantly.

" The latest idea," said Rydesdale, " is to advertise one's murders beforehand. Show Sir Henry that advertisement, Craddock."

" The *North Benham News and Chipping Cleghorn Gazette*," said Sir Henry. " Quite a mouthful." He read the half-inch of print indicated by Craddock's finger. " H'm, yes, somewhat unusual."

" Any line on who inserted this advertisement?" asked Rydesdale.

" By the description, sir, it was handed in by Rudi Scherz himself—on Wednesday."

" Nobody questioned it? The person who accepted it, didn't think it odd?"

" The adenoidal blonde who receives the advertisements is quite incapable of thinking, I should say, sir. She just counted the words and took the money."

" What was the idea?" asked Sir Henry.

" Get a lot of the locals curious," suggested Rydesdale. " Get them all together at a particular place at a particular time, then hold them up and relieve them of their spare cash and valuables. As an idea, it's not without originality."

38

" What sort of a place is Chipping Cleghorn?" asked Sir Henry.

"A large sprawling picturesque village. Butcher, baker, grocer, quite a good antique shop—two tea-shops. Self-consciously a beauty spot. Caters for the motoring tourist. Also highly residential. Cottages formerly lived in by agricultural labourers now converted and lived in by elderly spinsters and retired couples. A certain amount of building done round about in Victorian times."

" I know," said Sir Henry. " Nice old Pussies and retired Colonels. Yes, if they noticed that advertisement they'd all come sniffing round at 6.30 to see what was up. Lord, I wish I had my own particular old Pussy here. Wouldn't she like to get her nice ladylike teeth into this. Right up her street it would be."

" Who's your own particular Pussy, Henry? An aunt?"

" No," Sir Henry sighed. " She's no relation." He said reverently: " She's just the finest detective God ever made. Natural genius cultivated in a suitable soil."

He turned upon Craddock.

" Don't you despise the old Pussies in this village of yours, my boy," he said. " In case this turns out to be a high powered mystery, which I don't suppose for a moment it will, remember that an elderly unmarried woman who knits and gardens is streets ahead of any detective sergeant. She can tell you what might have happened and what ought to have happened and even what actually *did* happen! And she can tell you *why* it happened!"

" I'll bear that in mind, sir," said Detective-Inspector Craddock in his most formal manner, and nobody would have guessed that Dermot Eric Craddock was actually Sir Henry's godson and was on easy and intimate terms with his godfather.

Rydesdale gave a quick outline of the case to his friend.

"They'd all turn up at 6.30, I grant you that," he said. "But would that Swiss fellow know they would? And another thing, would they be likely to have much loot on them to be worth the taking?"

"A couple of old-fashioned brooches, a string of seed pearls—a little loose change, perhaps a note or two—not more," said Sir Henry, thoughtfully. "Did this Miss Blacklock keep much money in the house?"

"She says not, sir. Five pounds odd, I understand."

"Mere chicken feed," said Rydesdale.

"What you're getting at," said Sir Henry, "is that this fellow liked to playact—it wasn't the loot, it was the fun of playing and acting the hold-up. Cinema stuff? Eh? It's quite possible. How did he manage to shoot himself?"

Rydesdale drew a paper towards him.

"Preliminary medical report. The revolver was discharged at close range—singeing . . . h'm . . . nothing to show whether accident or suicide. Could have been done deliberately, or he could have tripped and fallen and the revolver which he was holding close to him could have gone off. . . . Probably the latter." He looked at Craddock. "You'll have to question the witnesses very carefully and make them say exactly what they saw."

Detective-Inspector Craddock said sadly : "They'll all have seen something different."

"It's always interested me," said Sir Henry, "what people do see at a moment of intense excitement and nervous strain. What they do see and, even more interesting, what they don't see."

"Where's the report on the revolver?"

"Foreign make—(fairly common on the Continent)—

40

Scherz did not hold a permit for it—and did not declare it on coming into England."

"Bad lad," said Sir Henry.

"Unsatisfactory character all round. Well, Craddock, go and see what you can find out about him at the Royal Spa Hotel."

II

At the Royal Spa Hotel, Inspector Craddock was taken straight to the Manager's office.

The Manager, Mr. Rowlandson, a tall florid man with a hearty manner, greeted Inspector Craddock with expansive geniality.

"Glad to help you in any way we can, Inspector," he said. "Really a most surprising business. I'd never have credited it—never. Scherz seemed a very ordinary, pleasant young chap—not at all my idea of a hold-up man."

"How long has he been with you, Mr. Rowlandson?"

"I was looking that up just before you came. A little over three months. Quite good credentials, the usual permits, etc."

"And you found him satisfactory?"

Without seeming to do so, Craddock marked the infinitesimal pause before Rowlandson replied.

"Quite satisfactory."

Craddock made use of a technique he had found efficacious before now.

"No, no, Mr. Rowlandson," he said, gently shaking his head. "That's not really quite the case, is it?"

"We-ll——" The Manager seemed slightly taken aback.

"Come now, there was something wrong. What was it?"

41

"That's just it. I don't know."

"But you *thought* there was something wrong?"

"Well—yes—I did. . . . But I've nothing really to go upon. I shouldn't like my conjectures to be written down and quoted against me."

Craddock smiled pleasantly.

"I know just what you mean. You needn't worry. But I've got to get some idea of what this fellow, Scherz, was like. You suspected him of—what?"

Rowlandson said, rather reluctantly:

"Well, there was trouble, once or twice, about the bills. Items charged that oughtn't to have been there."

"You mean you suspected that he charged up certain items which didn't appear in the hotel records, and that he pocketed the difference when the bill was paid?"

"Something like that. . . . Put it at the best, there was gross carelessness on his part. Once or twice quite a big sum was involved. Frankly, I got our accountant to go over his books suspecting that he was—well, a wrong 'un, but though there were various mistakes and a good deal of slipshod method, the actual cash was quite correct. So I came to the conclusion that I must be mistaken."

"Supposing you hadn't been wrong? Supposing Scherz had been helping himself to various small sums here and there, he could have covered himself, I suppose, by making good the money?"

"Yes, if he *had* the money. But people who help themselves to 'small sums' as you put it—are usually hard up for those sums and spend them offhand."

"So, if he wanted money to replace missing sums, he would have had to get money—by a hold-up or other means?"

"Yes. I wonder if this is his first attempt. . . ."

"Might be. It was certainly a very amateurish one.

42

Is there anyone else he could have got money from? Any women in his life?"

"One of the waitresses in the Grill. Her name's Myrna Harris."

"I'd better have a talk with her."

III

Myrna Harris was a pretty girl with a glorious head of red hair and a pert nose.

She was alarmed and wary, and deeply conscious of the indignity of being interviewed by the police.

"I don't know a thing about it, sir. Not a thing," she protested. "If I'd known what he was like I'd never have gone out with Rudi at all. Naturally, seeing as he worked in Reception here, I thought he was all right. Naturally I did. What I say is the hotel ought to be more careful when they employ people—especially foreigners. Because you never know where you are with foreigners. I suppose he might have been in with one of these gangs you read about?"

"We think," said Craddock, "that he was working quite on his own."

"Fancy—and him so quiet and respectable. You'd never think. Though there have been things missed—now I come to think of it. A diamond brooch—and a little gold locket, I believe. But I never dreamed that it could have been Rudi."

"I'm sure you didn't," said Craddock. "Anyone might have been taken in. You knew him fairly well?"

"I don't know that I'd say *well*."

"But you were friendly?"

"Oh, we were friendly—that's all, just friendly. Noth-

43

ing serious at all. I'm always on my guard with foreigners, anyway. They've often got a way with them, but you never know, do you? Some of those Poles during the war! And even some of the Americans! Never let on they're married men until it's too late. Rudi talked big and all that—but I always took it with a grain of salt."

Craddock seized on the phrase.

"Talked big, did he? That's very interesting, Miss Harris. I can see you're going to be a lot of help to us. In what way did he talk big?"

"Well, about how rich his people were in Switzerland —and how important. But that didn't go with his being as short of money as he was. He always said that because of the money regulation he couldn't get money from Switzerland over here. That might be, I suppose, but his things weren't expensive. His clothes, I mean. They weren't really class. I think, too, that a lot of the stories he used to tell me were so much hot air. About climbing in the Alps, and saving people's lives on the edge of a glacier. Why, he turned quite giddy just going along the edge of Boulter's Gorge. Alps, indeed!"

"You went out with him a good deal?"

"Yes—well—yes, I did. He had awfully good manners and he knew how to—to look after a girl. The best seats at the pictures, always. And even flowers he'd buy me, sometimes. And he was just a lovely dancer—lovely."

"Did he mention this Miss Blacklock to you at all?"

"She comes in and lunches here sometimes, doesn't she? And she's stayed here once. No I don't think Rudi ever mentioned her. I didn't know he knew her."

"Did he mention Chipping Cleghorn?"

He thought a faintly wary look came into Myrna Harris's eyes but he couldn't be sure.

"I don't think so. . . . I think he did once ask about buses—what time they went—but I can't remember if that was Chipping Cleghorn or somewhere else. It wasn't just lately."

He couldn't get more out of her. Rudi Scherz had seemed just as usual. She hadn't seen him the evening before. She'd no idea—no idea *at all*—she stressed the point, that Rudi Scherz was a crook.

And probably, Craddock thought, that was quite true.

CHAPTER V

MISS BLACKLOCK AND MISS BUNNER

LITTLE PADDOCKS was very much as Detective-Inspector Craddock had imagined it to be. He noted ducks and chickens and what had been until lately an attractive herbaceous border and in which a few late Michaelmas daisies showed a last dying splash of purple beauty. The lawn and the paths showed signs of neglect.

Summing up, Detective-Inspector Craddock thought : " Probably not much money to spend on gardeners— fond of flowers and a good eye for planning and massing a border. House needs painting. Most houses do, nowadays. Pleasant little property."

As Craddock's car stopped before the front door, Sergeant Fletcher came round the side of the house. Sergeant Fletcher looked like a guardsman, with an erect military bearing, and was able to impart several different meanings to the one monosyllable : " Sir."

" So there you are, Fletcher."

" Sir," said Sergeant Fletcher.

" Anything to report ?"

" We've finished going over the house, sir. Scherz doesn't seem to have left any fingerprints anywhere. He wore gloves, of course. No signs of any of the doors or windows being forced to effect an entrance. He seems to have come out from Medenham on the bus, arriving here at six o'clock. Side door of the house was locked at 5.30, I understand. Looks as though he must have walked in through the front door. Miss Blacklock states that that door isn't usually locked until the house is shut up for the night. The maid, on the other hand, states that the front door was locked all the afternoon—but she'd say anything. Very temperamental you'll find her. Mittel Europa refugee of some kind."

" Difficult, is she?"

" Sir!" said Sergeant Fletcher, with intense feeling.

Craddock smiled.

Fletcher resumed his report.

" Lighting system is quite in order everywhere. We haven't spotted yet how he operated the lights. It was just the one circuit went. Drawing-room and hall. Of course, nowadays the wall brackets and lamps wouldn't all be on one fuse—but this is an old-fashioned installation and wiring. Don't see how he could have tampered with the fuse-box because it's out by the scullery and he'd have had to go through the kitchen, so the maid would have seen him."

" Unless she was in it with him?"

" That's very possible. Both foreigners—and I wouldn't trust her a yard—not a yard."

Craddock noticed two enormous frightened black eyes peering out of a window by the front door. The face, flattened against the pane, was hardly visible.

" That her there?"

" That's right, sir."

The face disappeared.

Craddock rang the front-door bell.

After a long wait the door was opened by a good-looking young woman with chestnut hair and a bored expression.

" Detective-Inspector Craddock," said Craddock.

The young woman gave him a cool stare out of very attractive hazel eyes and said:

47

"Come in. Miss Blacklock is expecting you."

The hall, Craddock noted, was long and narrow and seemed almost incredibly full of doors.

The young woman threw open a door on the left, and said : " Inspector Craddock, Aunt Letty. Mitzi wouldn't go to the door. She's shut herself up in the kitchen and she's making the most marvellous moaning noises. I shouldn't think we'd get *any* lunch."

She added in an explanatory manner to Craddock : " She doesn't like the police," and withdrew, shutting the door behind her.

Craddock advanced to meet the owner of Little Paddocks.

He saw a tall active-looking woman of about sixty. Her grey hair had a slight natural wave and made a distinguished setting for an intelligent, resolute face. She had keen grey eyes and a square determined chin. There was a surgical dressing on her left ear. She wore no make-up and was plainly dressed in a well-cut tweed coat and skirt and pullover. Round the neck of the latter she wore, rather unexpectedly, a set of old-fashioned cameos—a Victorian touch which seemed to hint at a sentimental streak not otherwise apparent.

Close beside her, with an eager round face and untidy hair escaping from a hair net, was a woman of about the same age whom Craddock had no difficulty in recognising as the " Dora Bunner—companion " of Constable Legg's notes—to which the latter had added an off-the-record commentary of " Scatty !"

Miss Blacklock spoke in a pleasant well-bred voice.

" Good morning, Inspector Craddock. This is my friend, Miss Bunner, who helps me run the house. Won't you sit down? You won't smoke, I suppose?"

" Not on duty, I'm afraid, Miss Blacklock."

"What a shame!"

Craddock's eyes took in the room with a quick, practised glance. Typical Victorian double drawing-room. Two long windows in this room, built out bay window in the other . . . chairs . . . sofa . . . centre table with a big bowl of chrysanthemums—another bowl in window —all fresh and pleasant without much originality. The only incongruous note was a small silver vase with dead violets in it on a table near the archway into the further room. Since he could not imagine Miss Blacklock tolerating dead flowers in a room, he imagined it to be the only indication that something out of the way had occurred to distract the routine of a well-run household.

He said:

"I take it, Miss Blacklock, that this is the room in which the—incident occurred?"

"Yes."

"And you should have seen it last night," Miss Bunner exclaimed. "Such a *mess*. Two little tables knocked over, and the leg off one—people barging about in the dark—and someone put down a lighted cigarette and burnt one of the best bits of furniture. People—young people especially, are so careless about these things. . . . Luckily none of the china got broken——"

Miss Blacklock interrupted gently but firmly:

"Dora, all these things, vexatious as they may be, are only trifles. It will be best, I think, if we just answer Inspector Craddock's questions."

"Thank you, Miss Blacklock. I shall come to what happened last night, presently. First of all I want you to tell me when you first saw the dead man—Rudi Scherz."

"Rudi Scherz?" Miss Blacklock looked slightly surprised. "Is that his name? Somehow, I thought . . . Oh, well, it doesn't matter. My first encounter with him

49

was when I was in Medenham Spa for a day's shopping about—let me see, about three weeks ago. We—Miss Bunner and I—were having lunch at the Royal Spa Hotel. As we were just leaving after lunch, I heard my name spoken. It was this young man. He said: ' It is Miss Blacklock, is it not?' And went on to say that perhaps I did not remember him, but that he was the son of the proprietor of the Hotel des Alpes at Montreux where my sister and I had stayed for nearly a year during the war."

" The Hotel des Alpes, Montreux," noted Craddock. " And did you remember him, Miss Blacklock?"

" No, I didn't. Actually I had no recollection of ever having seen him before. These boys at hotel reception desks all look exactly alike. We had had a very pleasant time at Montreux and the proprietor there had been extremely obliging, so I tried to be as civil as possible and said I hoped he was enjoying being in England, and he said, yes, that his father had sent him over for six months to learn the hotel business. It all seemed quite natural."

" And your next encounter?"

" About—yes, it must have been ten days ago, he suddenly turned up here. I was very surprised to see him. He apologised for troubling me, but said I was the only person he knew in England. He told me that he urgently needed money to return to Switzerland as his mother was dangerously ill."

" But Letty didn't give it to him," Miss Bunner put in breathlessly.

" It was a thoroughly fishy story," said Miss Blacklock, with vigour. " I made up my mind that he was definitely a wrong 'un. That story about wanting the money to return to Switzerland was *nonsense*. His father could easily have wired for arrangements to have been made

50

in this country. These hotel people are all in with each other. I suspected that he'd been embezzling money or something of that kind." She paused and said dryly: "In case you think I'm hardhearted, I was secretary for many years to a big financier and one becomes wary about appeals for money. I know simply all the hard luck stories there are.

"The only thing that did surprise me," she added thoughtfully, "was that he gave in so easily. He went away at once without any more argument. It's as though he had never expected to get the money."

"Do you think now, looking back on it, that his coming was really by way of a pretext to spy out the land?"

Miss Blacklock nodded her head vigorously.

"That's exactly what I do think—now. He made certain remarks as I let him out—about the rooms. He said, 'You have a very nice dining-room (which of course it isn't—it's a horrid dark little room) just as an excuse to look inside. And then he sprang forward and unfastened the front door, said, 'Let me.' I think now he wanted to have a look at the fastening. Actually, like most people round here, we never lock the front door until it gets dark. *Anyone* could walk in."

"And the side door? There is a side door to the garden, I understand?"

"Yes. I went out through it to shut up the ducks not long before the people arrived."

"Was it locked when you went out?"

Miss Blacklock frowned.

"I can't remember. . . . I think so. I certainly locked it when I came in."

"That would be about quarter-past six?"

"Somewhere about then."

"And the front door?"

51

" That's not usually locked until later."

" Then Scherz could have walked in quite easily that way. Or he could have slipped in whilst you were out shutting up the ducks. He'd already spied out the lie of the land and had probably noted various places of concealment—cupboards, etc. Yes, that all seems quite clear."

" I beg your pardon, it isn't at all clear," said Miss Blacklock. " Why on earth should anyone take all that elaborate trouble to come and burgle this house and stage that silly sort of hold-up?"

" Do you keep much money in the house, Miss Blacklock?"

" About five pounds in that desk there, and perhaps a pound or two in my purse."

" Jewellery?"

" A couple of rings and brooches and the cameos I'm wearing. You must agree with me, Inspector, that the whole thing's absurd."

" It wasn't burglary at all," cried Miss Bunner. " I've told you so, Letty, all along. It was *revenge*! Because you wouldn't give him that money! He deliberately shot at you—twice."

" Ah," said Craddock. " We'll come now to last night. What happened exactly, Miss Blacklock? Tell me in your own words as nearly as you can remember."

Miss Blacklock reflected a moment.

" The clock struck," she said. " The one on the mantelpiece. I remember saying that if anything were going to happen it would have to happen soon. And then the clock struck. We all listened to it without saying anything. It chimes, you know. It chimed the two quarters and then, quite suddenly, the lights went out."

" What lights were on?"

"The wall brackets in here and the further room. The standard lamp and the two small reading lamps weren't on."

"Was there a flash first, or a noise when the lights went out?"

"I don't think so."

"I'm sure there *was* a flash," said Dora Bunner. "*And* a crackling noise. Dangerous!"

"And then, Miss Blacklock?"

"The door opened——"

"Which door? There are two in the room."

"Oh, this door in here. The one in the other room doesn't open. It's a dummy. The door opened and there he was—a masked man with a revolver. It just seemed too fantastic for words, but of course at the time I just thought it was a silly joke. He said something—I forget what——"

"Hands up or I shoot!" supplied Miss Bunner, dramatically.

"Something like that," said Miss Blacklock, rather doubtfully.

"And you all put your hands up?"

"Oh, *yes*," said Miss Bunner. "We all did. I mean, it was *part* of it."

"*I* didn't," said Miss Blacklock, crisply. "It seemed so utterly silly. And I was annoyed by the whole thing."

"And then?"

"The flashlight was right in my eyes. It dazzled me. And then, quite incredibly, I heard a bullet whizz past me and hit the wall by my head. Somebody shrieked and then I felt a burning pain in my ear and heard the second report."

"It was *terrifying*," put in Miss Bunner.

"And what happened next, Miss Blacklock?"

"It's difficult to say—I was so staggered by the pain

53

and the surprise. The—the figure turned away and seemed to stumble and then there was another shot and his torch went out and everybody began pushing and calling out. All banging into each other."

"Where were you standing, Miss Blacklock?"

"She was over by the table. She'd got that vase of violets in her hand," said Miss Bunner breathlessly.

"I was over here," Miss Blacklock went over to the small table by the archway. "Actually it was the cigarette-box I'd got in my hand."

Inspector Craddock examined the wall behind her. The two bullet holes showed plainly. The bullets themselves had been extracted and had been sent for comparison with the revolver.

He said quietly:

"You had a very near escape, Miss Blacklock."

"He did shoot at her," said Miss Bunner. "Deliberately at her! I saw him. He turned the flash round on everybody until he found her and then he held it right at her and just fired at her. He meant to kill you, Letty."

"Dora dear, you've just got that into your head from mulling the whole thing over and over."

"He shot at you," repeated Dora stubbornly. "He meant to shoot you and when he'd missed, he shot himself. I'm certain that's the way it was!"

"I don't think he meant to shoot himself for a minute," said Miss Blacklock. "He wasn't the kind of man who shoots himself."

"You tell me, Miss Blacklock, that until the revolver was fired you thought the whole business was a joke?"

"Naturally. What else could I think it was?"

"Who do you think was the author of this joke?"

"You thought Patrick had done it at first," Dora Bunner reminded her.

54

" Patrick?" asked the Inspector sharply.

" My young cousin, Patrick Simmons," Miss Blacklock continued sharply, annoyed with her friend. " It did occur to me when I saw this advertisement that it might be some attempt at humour on his part, but he denied it absolutely."

" And then you were worried, Letty," said Miss Bunner. " You *were* worried, although you pretended not to be. And you were quite right to be worried. It said a murder is announced—and it *was* announced—*your* murder! And if the man hadn't missed, you *would* have been murdered. And then where should we all be?"

Dora Bunner was trembling as she spoke. Her face was puckered up and she looked as though she were going to cry.

Miss Blacklock patted her on the shoulder.

" It's all right, Dora dear—don't get excited. It's so bad for you. Everything's quite all right. We've had a nasty experience, but it's over now." She added, " You must pull yourself together for my sake, Dora. I rely on you, you know, to keep the house going. Isn't it the day for the laundry to come?"

" Oh, dear me, Letty, how *fortunate* you reminded me! I wonder if they'll return that missing pillowcase. I must make a note in the book about it. I'll go and see to it at once."

" And take those violets away," said Miss Blacklock. " There's nothing I hate more than dead flowers."

" What a pity. I picked them fresh yesterday. They haven't lasted at all—oh, dear, I must have forgotten to put any water in the vase. Fancy that! I'm always forgetting things. Now I must go and see about the laundry. They might be here any moment."

She bustled away, looking quite happy again.

"She's not very strong," said Miss Blacklock, "and excitements are bad for her. Is there anything more you want to know, Inspector?"

"I just want to know exactly how many people make up your household here and something about them."

"Yes, well in addition to myself and Dora Bunner, I have two young cousins living here at present, Patrick and Julia Simmons."

"Cousins? Not a nephew and niece?"

"No. They call me Aunt Letty, but actually they are distant cousins. Their mother was my second cousin."

"Have they always made their home with you?"

"Oh, dear no, only for the last two months. They lived in the South of France before the war. Patrick went into the Navy and Julia, I believe, was in one of the Ministries. She was at Llandudno. When the war was over their mother wrote and asked me if they could possibly come to me as paying guests—Julia is training as a dispenser in Milchester General Hospital, Patrick is studying for an engineering degree at Milchester University. Milchester, as you know, is only fifty minutes by bus, and I was very glad to have them here. This house is really too large for me. They pay a small sum for board and lodging and it all works out very well." She added with a smile, "I like having somebody young about the place."

"Then there is a Mrs. Haymes, I believe?"

"Yes. She works as an assistant gardener at Dayas Hall, Mrs. Lucas's place. The cottage there is occupied by the old gardener and his wife and Mrs. Lucas asked if I could billet her here. She's a very nice girl. Her husband was killed in Italy, and she has a boy of eight who is at a prep school and whom I have arranged to have here in the holidays."

" And by way of domestic help?"

" A jobbing gardener comes in on Tuesdays and Fridays. A Mrs. Huggins from the village comes up five mornings a week and I have a foreign refugee with a most unpronounceable name as a kind of lady cook help. You will find Mitzi rather difficult, I'm afraid. She has a kind of persecution mania."

Craddock nodded. He was conscious in his own mind of yet another of Constable Legg's invaluable commentaries. Having appended the word " Scatty " to Dora Bunner, and " All right " to Letitia Blacklock, he had embellished Mitzi's record with the one word " Liar."

As though she had read his mind Miss Blacklock said :

" Please don't be too prejudiced against the poor thing because she's a liar. I do really believe that, like so many liars, there is a real substratum of truth behind her lies. I mean that though, to take an instance, her atrocity stories have grown and grown until every kind of unpleasant story that has ever appeared in print has happened to her or her relations personally, she did have a bad shock initially and did see one, at least, of her relations killed. I think a lot of these displaced persons feel, perhaps justly, that their claim to our notice and sympathy lies in their atrocity value and so they exaggerate and invent."

She added : " Quite frankly, Mitzi is a maddening person. She exasperates and infuriates us all, she is suspicious and sulky, is perpetually having ' feelings ' and thinking herself insulted. But in spite of it all, I really am sorry for her." She smiled. " And also, when she wants to, she can cook very nicely."

" I'll try not to ruffle her more than I can help," said Craddock soothingly. " Was that Miss Julia Simmons who opened the door to me?"

"Yes. Would you like to see her now? Patrick has gone out. Phillipa Haymes you will find working at Dayas Hall."

"Thank you, Miss Blacklock. I'd like to see Miss Simmons now if I may."

CHAPTER VI

JULIA, MITZI AND PATRICK

JULIA, when she came into the room, and sat down in the chair vacated by Letitia Blacklock, had an air of composure that Craddock for some reason found annoying. She fixed a limpid gaze on him and waited for his questions.

Miss Blacklock had tactfully left the room.

" Please tell me about last night, Miss Simmons."

" Last night?" murmured Julia with a blank stare. " Oh, we all slept like logs. Reaction, I suppose."

" I mean last night from six o'clock onwards."

" Oh, I see. Well, a lot of tiresome people came——"

" They were?"

She gave him another limpid stare.

" Don't you know all this already?"

" I'm asking the questions, Miss Simmons," said Craddock pleasantly.

" My mistake. I always find repetitions so dreary. Apparently you don't. . . . Well, there was Colonel and Mrs. Easterbrook, Miss Hinchliffe and Miss Murgatroyd, Mrs. Swettenham and Edmund Swettenham, and Mrs. Harmon, the Vicar's wife. They arrived in that order, and if you want to know what they said—they all said the same things in turn. ' I see you've got your central heating on ' and ' What *lovely* chrysanthemums !' "

Craddock bit his lip. The mimicry was good.

" The exception was Mrs. Harmon. She's rather a pet. She came in with her hat falling off and her shoelaces

59

untied and she asked straight out when the murder was going to happen? It embarrassed everybody because they'd all been pretending they'd dropped in by chance. Aunt Letty said in her dry way that it was due to happen quite soon. And then that clock chimed and just as it finished, the lights went out, the door was flung open and a masked figure said, ' Stick 'em up, guys,' or something like that. It was exactly like a bad film. Really quite ridiculous. And then he fired two shots at Aunt Letty and suddenly it wasn't ridiculous any more."

" Where was everybody when this happened?"

" When the lights went out? Well, just standing about, you know. Mrs. Harmon was sitting on the sofa— Hinch (that's Miss Hinchliffe) had taken up a manly stance in front of the fireplace."

" You were all in this room, or the far room?"

" Mostly, I think, in this room. Patrick had gone into the other to get the sherry. I think Colonel Easterbrook went after him, but I don't really know. We were—well —as I said, just standing about."

" Where were you yourself?"

" I think I was over by the window. Aunt Letty went to get the cigarettes."

" On that table by the archway?"

" Yes—and then the lights went out and the bad film started."

" The man had a powerful torch. What did he do with it?"

" Well, he shone it on us. Horribly dazzling. It just made you blink."

" I want you to answer this very carefully, Miss Simmons. Did he hold the torch steady, or did he move it about?"

Julia considered. Her manner was now definitely less weary.

" He moved it," she said slowly. " Like a spotlight in a dance hall. It was full in my eyes and then it went on round the room and then the shots came. Two shots."

" And then?"

" He whirled round—and Mitzi began to scream like a siren from somewhere and his torch went out and there was another shot. And then the door closed (it does, you know, slowly, with a whining noise—quite uncanny) and there we were all in the dark, not knowing what to do, and poor Bunny squealing like a rabbit and Mitzi going all out across the hall."

" Would it be your opinion that the man shot himself deliberately, or do you think he stumbled and the revolver went off accidentally?"

" I haven't the faintest idea. The whole thing was so stagey. Actually I thought it was still some silly joke—until I saw the blood from Letty's ear. But even if you were actually going to fire a revolver to make the thing more real, you'd be careful to fire it well above someone's head, wouldn't you?"

" You would indeed. Do you think he could see clearly who he was firing at? I mean, was Miss Blacklock clearly outlined in the light of the torch?"

" I've no idea. I wasn't looking at her. I was looking at the man."

" What I'm getting at is—do you think the man was deliberately aiming at her—at her in particular, I mean?"

Julia seemed a little startled by the idea.

" You mean deliberately picking on Aunt Letty? Oh, I shouldn't think so. . . . After all, if he wanted to take a pot shot at Aunt Letty, there would be heaps of more suitable opportunities. There would be no point in collecting all the friends and neighbours just to make it more difficult. He could have shot her from behind a hedge in the good old Irish fashion any day of the week, and probably got away with it."

And that, thought Craddock, was a very complete reply to Dora Bunner's suggestion of a deliberate attack on Letitia Blacklock.

He said with a sigh, " Thank you, Miss Simmons. I'd better go and see Mitzi now."

" Mind her fingernails," warned Julia. " She's a tartar!"

II

Craddock, with Fletcher in attendance, found Mitzi in the kitchen. She was rolling pastry and looked up suspiciously as he entered.

Her black hair hung over her eyes; she looked sullen, and the purple jumper and brilliant green skirt she wore were not becoming to her pasty complexion.

" What do you come in my kitchen for, Mr. Policeman? You are police, yes? Always, always there is persecution—ah! I should be used to it by now. They say it is different here in England, but no, it is just the same. You come to torture me, yes, to make me say things, but I shall say *nothing*. You will tear off my fingernails, and put lighted matches on my skin—oh, yes, and worse than that. But I will not speak, do you hear? I shall say nothing—nothing at all. And you will send me away to a concentration camp, and I shall not care."

Craddock looked at her thoughtfully, selecting what was likely to be the best method of attack. Finally he sighed and said :

" O.K. then, get your hat and coat."

" What is that you say?" Mitzi looked startled.

" Get your hat and coat and come along. I haven't

got my nail-pulling apparatus and the rest of the bag of tricks with me. We keep all that down at the station. Got the handcuffs handy, Fletcher?"

" Sir!" said Sergeant Fletcher with appreciation.

" But I do not want to come," screeched Mitzi, backing away from him.

" Then you'll answer civil questions civilly. If you like, you can have a solicitor present."

" A lawyer? I do not like a lawyer. I do not want a lawyer."

She put the rolling pin down, dusted her hands on a cloth and sat down.

" What do you want to know?" she asked sulkily.

" I want your account of what happened here last night."

" You know very well what happened."

" I want your account of it."

" I tried to go away. Did she tell you that? When I saw that in the paper saying about murder. I wanted to go away. She would not let me. She is very hard—not at all sympathetic. She made me stay. But I knew—*I* knew what would happen. *I* knew I should be murdered."

" Well, you weren't murdered, were you?"

" No," admitted Mitzi grudgingly.

" Come now, tell me what happened."

" I was nervous. Oh, I was nervous. All that evening. I hear things. People moving about. Once I think someone is in the hall moving stealthily—but it is only that Mrs. Haymes coming in through the side door (so as not to dirty the front steps, *she* says. Much *she* cares!). She is a Nazi herself, that one, with her fair hair and her blue eyes, so superior and looking at me and thinking that I—I am only dirt——"

" Never mind Mrs. Haymes."

63

"Who does she think *she* is? Has she had expensive university education like I have? Has she a degree in Economics? No, she is just a paid labourer. She digs and mows grass and is paid so much every Saturday. Who is she to call herself a lady?"

"Never mind Mrs. Haymes, I said. Go on."

"I take the sherry and the glasses, and the little pastries that I have made so nice into the drawing-room. Then the bell rings and I answer the door. Again and again I answer the door. It is degrading—but I do it. And then I go back into the pantry and I start to polish the silver, and I think it will be very handy, that, because if someone comes to kill me, I have there close at hand the big carving knife, all sharp."

"Very foresighted of you."

"And then, suddenly—I hear shots. I think : ' It has come—it is happening.' I run through the dining-room (the other door—it will not open) I stand a moment to listen and then there comes another shot and a big thud, out there in the hall, and I turn the door handle, but it is locked outside. I am shut in there like a rat in a trap. And I go mad with fear. I scream and I scream and I beat upon the door. And at last—at last—they turn the key and let me out. And then I bring candles, many many candles—and the lights go on, and I see blood—blood! Ach, Gott in Himmel, the blood! It is not the first time I have seen blood. My little brother—I see him killed before my eyes—I see blood in the street—people shot, dying—I——"

"Yes," said Inspector Craddock. "Thank you very much."

"And now," said Mitzi dramatically, "you can arrest me and take me to prison !"

"Not to-day," said Inspector Craddock.

III

As Craddock and Fletcher went through the hall to the front door it was flung open and a tall handsome young man almost collided with them.

" Sleuths, as I live," cried the young man.

" Mr. Patrick Simmons?"

" Quite right, Inspector. You're the Inspector, aren't you, and the other's the Sergeant?"

" You are quite right, Mr. Simmons. Can I have a word with you, please?"

" I am innocent, Inspector. I swear I am innocent."

" Now then, Mr. Simmons, don't play the fool. I've a good many other people to see and I don't want to waste time. What's this room? Can we go in here?"

" It's the so-called study—but nobody studies."

" I was told that you were studying?" said Craddock.

" I found I couldn't concentrate on mathematics, so I came home."

In a businesslike manner Inspector Craddock demanded full name, age, details of war service.

" And now, Mr. Simmons, will you describe what happened last night?"

" We killed the fatted calf, Inspector. That is, Mitzi set her hand to making savoury pastries, Aunt Letty opened a new bottle of sherry——"

Craddock interrupted.

" A new bottle? Was there an old one?"

" Yes. Half full. But Aunt Letty didn't seem to fancy it."

" Was she nervous, then?"

" Oh, not really. She's extremely sensible. It was old

65

Bunny, I think, who had put the wind up her—prophesying disaster all day."

"Miss Bunner was definitely apprehensive, then?"

"Oh, yes, she enjoyed herself thoroughly."

"She took the advertisement seriously?"

"It scared her into fits."

"Miss Blacklock seems to have thought, when she first read that advertisement, that you had had something to do with it. Why was that?"

"Ah, sure, I get blamed for everything round here!"

"You *didn't* have anything to do with it, did you, Mr. Simmons?"

"Me? Never in the world."

"Had you ever seen or spoken to this Rudi Scherz?"

"Never seen him in my life."

"It was the kind of joke you might have played, though?"

"Who's been telling you that? Just because I once made Bunny an apple-pie bed—and sent Mitzi a postcard saying the Gestapo was on her track——"

"Just give me your account of what happened."

"I'd just gone into the small drawing-room to fetch the drinks when, Hey Presto, the lights went out. I turned round and there's a fellow standing in the doorway saying, 'Stick your hands up,' and everybody gasping and squealing, and just when I'm thinking—can I rush him? he starts firing a revolver and then crash down he goes and his torch goes out and we're in the dark again, and Colonel Easterbrook starts shouting orders in his barrack-room voice. 'Lights,' he says, and will my lighter go on? No, it won't as is the way of those cussed inventions."

"Did it seem to you that the intruder was definitely aiming at Miss Blacklock?"

"Ah, how could I tell? I should say he just loosed off

66

his revolver for the fun of the thing—and then found, maybe, he'd gone too far."

" And shot himself?"

" It could be. When I saw the face of him, he looked like the kind of little pasty thief who might easily lose his nerve."

" And you're sure you had never seen him before?"

" Never."

" Thank you, Mr. Simmons. I shall want to interview the other people who were here last night. Which would be the best order in which to take them?"

" Well, our Phillipa—Mrs. Haymes—works at Dayas Hall. The gates of it are nearly opposite this gate. After that, the Swettenhams are the nearest. Anyone will tell you."

CHAPTER VII

AMONG THOSE PRESENT

DAYAS HALL had certainly suffered during the war years. Couch grass grew enthusiastically over what had once been an asparagus bed, as evidenced by a few waving tufts of asparagus foliage. Groundsel, bindweed and other garden pests showed every sign of vigorous growth.

A portion of the kitchen garden bore evidence of having been reduced to discipline and here Craddock found a sour-looking old man leaning pensively on a spade.

"It's Mrs. 'Aymes you want? I couldn't say where you'd find 'er. 'As 'er own ideas, she 'as, about what she'll do. Not one to take advice. I could show her—show 'er willing—but what's the good, won't listen these young ladies won't! Think they know everything because they've put on breeches and gone for a ride on a tractor. But it's *gardening* that's needed here. And that isn't learned in a day. *Gardening*, that's what this place needs."

"It looks as though it does," said Craddock.

The old man chose to take this remark as an aspersion.

"Now look here, mister, what do you suppose I can do with a place this size? Three men and a boy, that's what it used to 'ave. And that's what it wants. There's not many men could put in the work on it that I do. 'Ere sometimes I am till eight o'clock at night. Eight o'clock."

"What do you work by? An oil lamp."

" Naterally I don't mean this time o' year. Naterally.
Summer evenings I'm talking about."

" Oh," said Craddock, " I'd better go and look for
Mrs. Haymes."

The rustic displayed some interest.

" What are you wanting 'er for? Police, aren't you?
She been in trouble, or is it the do there was up to Little
Paddocks? Masked men bursting in and holding up a
roomful of people with a revolver. An' that sort of thing
wouldn't 'ave 'appened afore the war. Deserters, that's
what it is. Desperate men roaming the countryside. Why
don't the military round 'em up?"

" I've no idea," said Craddock. " I suppose this hold-
up caused a lot of talk?"

" That it did. What's us coming to? That's what Ned
Barker said. Comes of going to the pictures so much, he
said. But Tom Riley he says it comes of letting these
furriners run about loose. And depend on it, he says,
that girl as cooks up there for Miss Blacklock and 'as
such a nasty temper—*she's* in it, he said. She's a com-
munist or worse, he says, and we don't like that sort 'ere.
And Marlene, who's behind the bar, you understand, she
will 'ave it that there must be something very valuable
up at Miss Blacklock's. Not that you'd think it, she
says, for I'm sure Miss Blacklock goes about as plain as
plain, except for them great rows of false pearls she
wears. And then she says—Supposin' as them pearls is
real, and Florrie (what's old Bellamy's daughter) *she*
says, ' Nonsense,' she says—' *noovo ar*—that's what they
are—costume jewellery,' she says. Costume jewellery—
that's a fine way of labelling a string of false pearls.
Roman pearls; the gentry used to call 'em once—and
Parisian diamonds—my wife was a lady's maid and I
know. But what does it all mean—just glass! I suppose
it's ' costume jewellery ' that young Miss Simmons wears

—gold ivy leaves and dogs and such like. 'Tisn't often you see a real bit of gold nowadays—even wedding rings they make of this grey plattinghum stuff. Shabby, I call it—for all that it costs the earth."

Old Ashe paused for breath and then continued :

" ' Miss Blacklock don't keep much money in the 'ouse, that I do know,' says Jim Huggins, speaking up. He should know, for it's his wife as goes up and does for 'em at Little Paddocks, and she's a woman as knows most of what's going on. Nosey, if you take me."

" Did he say what Mrs. Huggins' view was?"

" That Mitzi's mixed up in it, that's what she thinks. Awful temper she 'as, and the airs she gives herself! Called Mrs. Huggins a working woman to her face the other morning."

Craddock stood a moment, checking over in his orderly mind the substance of the old gardener's remarks. It gave him a good cross-section of rural opinion in Chipping Cleghorn, but he didn't think there was anything to help him in his task. He turned away and the old man called after him grudgingly :

" Maybe you'd find her in the apple orchard. She's younger than I am for getting the apples down."

And sure enough in the apple orchard Craddock found Phillipa Haymes. His first view was a pair of nice legs encased in breeches sliding easily down the trunk of a tree. Then Phillipa, her face flushed, her fair hair ruffled by the branches, stood looking at him in a startled fashion.

" Make a good Rosalind," Craddock thought automatically, for Detective-Inspector Craddock was a Shakespeare enthusiast and had played the part of the melancholy Jaques with great success in a performance of *As You Like It* for the Police Orphanage.

A moment later he amended his view. Phillipa Haymes

was too wooden for Rosalind, her fairness and her impass-
ivity were intensely English, but English of the twentieth
rather than of the sixteenth century. Well-bred, unemotional English, without a sparkle of mischief.

" Good morning, Mrs. Haymes. I'm sorry if I startled
you. I'm Detective-Inspector Craddock of the Middle-
shire Police. I wanted to have a word with you."

" About last night?"

" Yes."

" Will it take long? Shall we——"

She looked about her rather doubtfully.

Craddock indicated a fallen tree trunk.

" Rather informal," he said pleasantly, " but I don't
want to interrupt your work longer than necessary."

" Thank you."

" It's just for the record. You came in from work at
what time last night?"

" At about half-past five. I'd stayed about twenty
minutes later in order to finish some watering in the
greenhouse."

" You came in by which door?"

" The side door. One cuts across by the ducks and the
henhouse from the drive. It saves you going round, and
besides it avoids dirtying up the front porch. I'm in
rather a mucky state sometimes."

" You always come in that way?"

" Yes."

" The door was unlocked?"

" Yes. During the summer it's usually wide open.
This time of the year it's shut but not locked. We all go
out and in a good deal that way. I locked it when I
came in."

" Do you always do that?"

" I've been doing it for the last week. You see, it gets
dark at six. Miss Blacklock goes out to shut up the ducks

71

and the hens sometime in the evening, but she very often goes out through the kitchen door."

"And you are quite sure you did lock the side door this time?"

"I really am quite sure about that."

"Quite so, Mrs. Haymes. And what did you do when you came in?"

"Kicked off my muddy footwear and went upstairs and had a bath and changed. Then I came down and found that a kind of party was in progress. I hadn't known anything about this funny advertisement until then."

"Now please describe just what occurred when the hold-up happened."

"Well, the lights went out suddenly——"

"Where were you?"

"By the mantelpiece. I was searching for my lighter which I thought I had put down there. The lights went out—and everybody giggled. Then the door was flung open and this man shone a torch on us and flourished a revolver and told us to put our hands up."

"Which you proceeded to do?"

"Well, I didn't, actually. I thought it was just fun, and I was tired and I didn't think I needed really to put them up."

"In fact you were bored by the whole thing?"

"I was, rather. And then the revolver went off. The shots sounded deafening and I was really frightened. The torch went whirling round and dropped and went out, and then Mitzi started screaming. It was just like a pig being killed."

"Did you find the torch very dazzling?"

"No, not particularly. It was quite a strong one, though. It lit up Miss Bunner for a moment and she looked quite like a turnip ghost—you know, all white

72

and staring with her mouth open and her eyes starting out of her head."

" The man moved the torch?"

" Oh, yes, he played it all round the room."

" As though he were looking for someone?"

" Not particularly, I should say."

" And after that, Mrs. Haymes?"

Phillipa Haymes frowned.

" Oh, it was all a terrible muddle and confusion. Edmund Swettenham and Patrick Simmons switched on their lighters and they went out into the hall and we followed, and someone opened the dining-room door—the lights hadn't fused there—and Edmund Swettenham gave Mitzi a terrific slap on the cheek and brought her out of her screaming fit, and after that it wasn't so bad."

" You saw the body of the dead man?"

" Yes."

" Was he known to you? Had you ever seen him before?"

" Never."

" Have you any opinion as to whether his death was accidental, or do you think he shot himself deliberately?"

" I haven't the faintest idea."

" You didn't see him when he came to the house previously?"

" No. I believe it was in the middle of the morning and I shouldn't have been there. I'm out all day."

" Thank you, Mrs. Haymes. One thing more. You haven't any valuable jewellery? Rings, bracelets, anything of that kind?"

Phillipa shook her head.

" My engagement ring—a couple of brooches."

" And as far as you know, there was nothing of particular value in the house?"

"No. I mean there is some quite nice silver—but nothing out of the ordinary."

"Thank you, Mrs. Haymes."

II

As Craddock retraced his steps through the kitchen garden he came face to face with a large red-faced lady, carefully corseted.

"Good morning," she said belligerently. "What do you want here?"

"Mrs. Lucas? I am Detective-Inspector Craddock."

"Oh, that's who you are. I beg your pardon. I don't like strangers forcing their way into my garden wasting the gardeners' time. But I quite understand you have to do your duty."

"Quite so."

"May I ask if we are to expect a repetition of that outrage last night at Miss Blacklock's? Is it a gang?"

"We are satisfied, Mrs. Lucas, that it was *not* the work of a gang."

"There are far too many robberies nowadays. The police are getting slack." Craddock did not reply. "I suppose you've been talking to Phillipa Haymes?"

"I wanted her account as an eye-witness."

"You couldn't have waited until one o'clock, I suppose? After all, it would be fairer to question her in *her* time, rather than in *mine* . . ."

"I'm anxious to get back to headquarters."

"Not that one expects consideration nowadays. Or a decent day's work. On duty late, half an hour's pottering. A break for elevenses at ten o'clock. No work done at all the moment the rain starts. When you want the lawn mown there's always something wrong with the

74

mower. And off duty five or ten minutes before the proper time."

" I understood from Mrs. Haymes that she left here at twenty minutes past five yesterday instead of five o'clock."

" Oh, I dare say she did. Give her her due, Mrs. Haymes is quite keen on her work, though there have been days when I have come out here and not been able to find her anywhere. She is a lady by birth, of course, and one feels it's one's duty to do something for these poor young war widows. Not that it isn't very inconvenient. Those long school holidays and the arrangement is that she has extra time off then. I told her that there are really excellent camps nowadays where children can be sent and where they have a delightful time and enjoy it far more than wandering about with their parents. They need practically not come home at all in the summer holidays."

" But Mrs. Haymes didn't take kindly to that idea?"

" She's as obstinate as a mule, that girl. Just the time of year when I want the tennis court mowed and marked nearly every day. Old Ashe gets the lines crooked. But *my* convenience is never considered!"

" I presume Mrs. Haymes takes a smaller salary than is usual."

" Naturally. What else could she expect?"

" Nothing, I'm sure," said Craddock. " Good morning, Mrs. Lucas."

III

" It was dreadful," said Mrs. Swettenham happily. " Quite—quite—dreadful, and what I say is that they ought to be far more careful what advertisements they accept at the *Gazette* office. At the time, when I read it, I thought it was very odd. I said so, didn't I, Edmund?"

"Do you remember just what you were doing when the lights went out, Mrs. Swettenham?" asked the Inspector.

"How that reminds me of my old Nannie! *Where was Moses when the light went out?* The answer, of course, was 'In the Dark.' Just like us yesterday evening. All standing about and wondering what was going to happen. And then, you know, the *thrill* when it suddenly went pitch black. And the door opening—just a dim figure standing there with a revolver and that blinding light and a menacing voice saying 'Your money or your life!' Oh, I've never enjoyed anything so much. And then a minute later, of course, it was all *dreadful*. *Real* bullets, just *whistling* past our ears! It must have been just like the Commandos in the war."

"Whereabouts were you standing or sitting at the time, Mrs. Swettenham?"

"Now let me see, where was I? Who was I talking to, Edmund?"

"I really haven't the least idea, Mother."

"Was it Miss Hinchliffe I was asking about giving the hens cod liver oil in the cold weather? Or was it Mrs. Harmon—no, she'd only just arrived. I think I was just saying to Colonel Easterbrook that I thought it was really very dangerous to have an atom research station in England. It ought to be on some lonely island in case the radio-activity gets loose."

"You don't remember if you were sitting or standing?"

"Does it really matter, Inspector? I was somewhere over by the window or near the mantelpiece, because I know I was *quite* near the clock when it struck. Such a thrilling moment! Waiting to see if anything might be going to happen."

" You describe the light from the torch as blinding. Was it turned full on to you?"

" It was right in my eyes. I couldn't see a thing."

" Did the man hold it still, or did he move it about, from person to person?"

" Oh, I don't really know. Which did he do, Edmund?"

" It moved rather slowly over us all, so as to see what we were all doing, I suppose, in case we should try and rush him."

"And where exactly in the room were *you*, Mr. Swettenham?"

" I'd been talking to Julia Simmons. We were both standing up in the middle of the room—the long room."

" Was everyone in that room, or was there anyone in the far room?"

"Phillipa Haymes had moved in there, I think. She was over by that far mantelpiece. I think she was looking for something."

" Have you any idea as to whether the third shot was suicide or an accident?"

" I've no idea at all. The man seemed to swerve round very suddenly and then crumple up and fall—but it was all very confused. You must realise that you couldn't really see anything. And then that refugee girl started yelling the place down."

" I understand it was you who unlocked the dining-room door and let her out?"

" Yes."

" The door was definitely locked on the outside?"

Edmund looked at him curiously.

" Certainly it was. Why, you don't imagine——"

" I just like to get my facts quite clear. Thank you, Mr. Swettenham."

IV

Inspector Craddock was forced to spend quite a long time with Colonel and Mrs. Easterbrook. He had to listen to a long disquisition on the psychological aspect of the case.

"The psychological approach—that's the only thing nowadays," the Colonel told him. "You've got to understand your criminal. Now the whole set-up here is quite plain to a man who's had the wide experience that I have. Why does this fellow put that advert in? Psychology. He wants to advertise himself—to focus attention on himself. He's been passed over, perhaps despised as a foreigner by the other employees at the Spa Hotel. A girl has turned him down, perhaps. He wants to rivet her attention on him. Who is the idol of the cinema nowadays—the gangster—the tough guy? Very well, he will be a tough guy. Robbery with violence. A mask? A revolver? But he wants an audience—he must have an audience. So he arranges for an audience. And then, at the supreme moment, his part runs away with him—he's more than a burglar. He's a killer. He shoots—blindly——"

Inspector Craddock caught gladly at a word:

"You say ' blindly,' Colonel Easterbrook. You didn't think that he was firing deliberately at one particular object—at Miss Blacklock, that is to say?"

"No, no. He just loosed off, as I say, blindly. And that's what brought him to himself. The bullet hit some-one—actually it was only a graze, but he didn't know that. He comes to himself with a bang. All this—this make-believe he's been indulging in—is *real*. He's shot at someone—perhaps killed someone. . . . It's all up with him. And so in blind panic he turns the revolver on himself."

Colonel Easterbrook paused, cleared his throat appreciatively and said in a satisfied voice, " Plain as a pikestaff, that's what it is, plain as a pikestaff."

" It really is wonderful," said Mrs. Easterbrook, " the way you know exactly what happened, Archie."

Her voice was warm with admiration.

Inspector Craddock thought it was wonderful, too, but he was not quite so warmly appreciative.

" Exactly where were you in the room, Colonel Easterbrook, when the actual shooting business took place?"

" I was standing with my wife—near a centre table with some flowers on it."

" I caught hold of your arm, didn't I, Archie, when it happened? I was simply scared to death. I just had to hold on to you."

" Poor little kitten," said the Colonel playfully.

v

The Inspector ran Miss Hinchliffe to earth by a pigsty.

" Nice creatures, pigs," said Miss Hinchliffe, scratching a wrinkled pink back. " Coming on well, isn't he? Good bacon round about Christmas time. Well, what do you want to see me about? I told your people last night I hadn't the least idea who the man was. Never seen him anywhere in the neighbourhood snooping about or anything of that sort. Our Mrs. Mopp says he came from one of the big hotels in Medenham Wells. Why didn't he hold up someone there if he wanted to? Get a much better haul."

That was undeniable—Craddock proceeded with his inquiries.

"Where were you exactly when the incident took place?"

"Incident! Reminds me of my A.R.P. days. Saw some incidents then, I can tell you. Where was I when the shooting started? That what you want to know?"

"Yes."

"Leaning up against the mantelpiece hoping to God someone would offer me a drink soon," replied Miss Hinchliffe promptly.

"Do you think that the shots were fired blindly, or aimed carefully at one particular person?"

"You mean aimed at Letty Blacklock? How the devil should I know? Damned hard to sort out what your impressions really were or what really happened after it's all over. All I know is the lights went out, and that torch went whirling round dazzling us all, and then the shots were fired and I thought to myself, 'If that damned young fool Patrick Simmons is playing his jokes with a loaded revolver somebody will get hurt.'"

"You thought it was Patrick Simmons?"

"Well, it seemed likely. Edmund Swettenham is intellectual and writes books and doesn't care for horse-play, and old Colonel Easterbrook wouldn't think that sort of thing funny. But Patrick's a wild boy. However, I apologise to him for the idea."

"Did your friend think it might be Patrick Simmons?"

"Murgatroyd? You'd better talk to her yourself. Not that you'll get any sense out of her. She's down the orchard. I'll yell for her if you like."

Miss Hinchliffe raised her stentorian voice in a powerful bellow:

"Hi-youp, Murgatroyd . . ."

"Coming . . ." floated back a thin cry.

"Hurry up—Polieece," bellowed Miss Hinchliffe.

Miss Murgatroyd arrived at a brisk trot very much out

of breath. Her skirt was down at the hem and her hair was escaping from an inadequate hair net. Her round, good-natured face beamed.

" Is it Scotland Yard?" she asked breathlessly. " I'd no idea. Or I wouldn't have left the house."

" We haven't called in Scotland Yard yet, Miss Murgatroyd. I'm Inspector Craddock from Milchester."

" Well, that's very nice, I'm sure," said Miss Murgatroyd vaguely. " Have you found any clues?"

" Where were you at the time of the crime, that's what he wants to know, Murgatroyd?" said Miss Hinchliffe. She winked at Craddock.

" Oh, dear," gasped Miss Murgatroyd. " Of course. I ought to have been prepared. *Alibis*, of course. Now, let me see, I was just with everybody else."

" You weren't with me," said Miss Hinchliffe.

" Oh, dear, Hinch, wasn't I? No, of course, I'd been admiring the chrysanthemums. Very poor specimens, really. And then it all happened—only I didn't really know it had happened—I mean I didn't know that anything like that had happened. I didn't imagine for a moment that it was a real revolver—and all so awkward in the dark, and that dreadful screaming. I got it all wrong, you know. I thought *she* was being murdered— I mean the refugee girl. I thought she was having her throat cut across the hall somewhere. I didn't know it was *him*—I mean, I didn't even know there was a man. It was really just a voice, you know, saying, ' Put them up, please.' "

" ' Stick 'em up! ' " Miss Hinchliffe corrected. " And no suggestion of ' please ' about it."

" It's so terrible to think that until that girl started screaming I was actually enjoying myself. Only being in the dark was very awkward and I got a knock on my corn. Agony, it was. Is there anything more you want to know, Inspector?"

"No," said Inspector Craddock, eyeing Miss Murgatroyd speculatively. "I don't really think there is."

Her friend gave a short bark of laughter.

"He's got you taped, Murgatroyd."

"I'm sure, Hinch," said Miss Murgatroyd, "that I'm only too willing to say anything I can."

"He doesn't want that," said Miss Hinchliffe.

She looked at the Inspector. "If you're doing this geographically I suppose you'll go to the Vicarage next. You might get something there. Mrs. Harmon looks as vague as they make them—but I sometimes think she's got brains. Anyway, she's got something."

As they watched the Inspector and Sergeant Fletcher stalk away, Amy Murgatroyd said breathlessly:

"Oh, Hinch, was I very awful? I do get so flustered!"

"Not at all." Miss Hinchliffe smiled. "On the whole, I should say you did very well."

V I

Inspector Craddock looked round the big shabby room with a sense of pleasure. It reminded him a little of his own Cumberland home. Faded chintz, big shabby chairs, flowers and books strewn about, and a spaniel in a basket. Mrs. Harmon, too, with her distraught air, and her general disarray and her eager face he found sympathetic.

But she said at once, frankly, "I shan't be any help to you. Because I shut my eyes. I hate being dazzled. And then there were shots and I screwed them up tighter than ever. And I did wish, oh, I did wish, that it had been a *quiet* murder. I don't like bangs."

" So you didn't see anything." The Inspector smiled at her. " But you heard——?"

"Oh, my goodness yes, there was plenty to *hear*. Doors opening and shutting, and people saying silly things and gasping and old Mitzi screaming like a steam engine—and poor Bunny squealing like a trapped rabbit. And everyone pushing and falling over everyone else. However, when there really didn't seem to be any more bangs coming, I opened my eyes. Everyone was out in the hall then, with candles. And then the lights came on and suddenly it was all as usual—I don't mean really as usual, but we were ourselves again, not just—people in the dark. People in the dark are quite different, aren't they?"

" I think I know what you mean, Mrs. Harmon."

Mrs. Harmon smiled at him.

" And there he was," she said. " A rather weaselly-looking foreigner—all pink and surprised looking—lying there dead—with a revolver beside him. It didn't—oh, it didn't seem to make *sense*, somehow."

It did not make sense to the Inspector, either. . . .

The whole business worried him.

CHAPTER VIII

ENTER MISS MARPLE

CRADDOCK laid the typed transcript of the various interviews before the Chief Constable. The latter had just finished reading the wire received from the Swiss Police.

"So he had a police record all right," said Rydesdale. "H'm—very much as one thought."

"Yes, sir."

"Jewellery . . . h'm, yes . . . falsified entries . . . yes . . . cheque . . . Definitely a dishonest fellow."

"Yes, sir—in a small way."

"Quite so. And small things lead to large things."

"I wonder, sir."

The Chief Constable looked up.

"Worried, Craddock?"

"Yes, sir."

"Why? It's a straightforward story. Or isn't it? Let's see what all these people you've been talking to have to say."

He drew the report towards him and read it through rapidly.

"The usual thing—plenty of inconsistencies and contradictions. Different people's accounts of a few moments of stress never agree. But the main picture seems clear enough."

"I know, sir—but it's an unsatisfactory picture. If you know what I mean—it's the wrong picture."

"Well, let's take the facts. Rudi Scherz took the 5.20

84

bus from Medenham to Chipping Cleghorn arriving there at six o'clock. Evidence of conductor and two passengers. From the bus stop he walked away in the direction of Little Paddocks. He got into the house with no particular difficulty—probably through the front door. He held up the company with a revolver, he fired two shots, one of which slightly wounded Miss Blacklock, he then killed himself with a third shot, whether accidentally or deliberately there is not sufficient evidence to show. The reasons *why* he did all this are profoundly unsatisfactory, I agree. But *why* isn't really a question we are called upon to answer. A Coroner's jury may bring it in suicide—or accidental death. Whichever verdict it is, it's the same as far as we're concerned. We can write finis."

" You mean we can always fall back upon Colonel Easterbrook's psychology," said Craddock gloomily.

Rydesdale smiled.

" After all, the Colonel's probably had a good deal of experience," he said. " I'm pretty sick of the psychological jargon that's used so glibly about everything nowadays—but we can't really rule it out."

" I still feel the picture's all wrong, sir."

" Any reason to believe that somebody in the set-up at Chipping Cleghorn is lying to you?"

Craddock hesitated.

" I think the foreign girl knows more than she lets on. But that may be just prejudice on my part."

" You think she might possibly have been in it with this fellow? Let him into the house? Put him up to it?"

" Something of the kind. I wouldn't put it past her. But that surely indicates that there really was something valuable, money or jewellery, in the house, and that doesn't seem to have been the case. Miss Blacklock negatived it quite decidedly. So did the others. That

85

leaves us with the proposition that there was something valuable in the house that nobody knew about———"

" Quite a best seller plot."

" I agree it's ridiculous, sir. The only other point is Miss Bunner's certainty that it was a definite attempt by Scherz to murder Miss Blacklock."

" Well, from what you say—and from her statement, this Miss Bunner———"

" Oh, I agree, sir," Craddock put in quickly, " she's an utterly unreliable witness. Highly suggestible. Anyone could put a thing into her head—but the interesting thing is that this is quite her own theory—no one *has* suggested it to her. Everybody else negatives it. For once she's *not* swimming with the tide. It definitely *is* her own impression."

" And why should Rudi Scherz want to kill Miss Blacklock?"

" There you are, sir. I don't know. Miss Blacklock doesn't know—unless she's a much better liar than I think she is. Nobody knows. So presumably it isn't true."

He sighed.

" Cheer up, Craddock," said the Chief Constable. " I'm taking you off to lunch with Sir Henry and myself. The best that the Royal Spa Hotel in Medenham Wells can provide."

" Thank you, sir." Craddock looked slightly surprised.

" You see, we received a letter———" He broke off as Sir Henry Clithering entered the room. " Ah, there you are, Henry."

Sir Henry, informal this time, said, " 'Morning, Dermot."

" I've got something for you, Henry," said the Chief Constable."

" What's that?"

" Authentic letter from an old Pussy. Staying at the

Royal Spa Hotel. Something she thinks we might like to know in connection with this Chipping Cleghorn business."

"The old Pussies," said Sir Henry triumphantly. "What did I tell you? They hear everything. They see everything. And, unlike the famous adage, they speak all evil. What's this particular one got hold of?"

Rydesdale consulted the letter.

"Writes just like my old grandmother," he complained. "Spiky. Like a spider in the ink bottle, and all underlined. A good deal about how she hopes it won't be taking up our valuable time, but might possibly be of some slight assistance, etc., etc. What's her name? Jane —something—Murple—no, Marple, Jane Marple."

"Ye Gods and Little Fishes," said Sir Henry, "can it be? George, it's my own particular, one and only, four starred Pussy. The super Pussy of all old Pussies. And she has managed somehow to be at Medenham Wells, instead of peacefully at home in St. Mary Mead, just at the right time to be mixed up in a murder. Once more a murder is announced—for the benefit and enjoyment of Miss Marple."

"Well, Henry," said Rydesdale sardonically. "I'll be glad to see your paragon. Come on! We'll lunch at the Royal Spa and we'll interview the lady. Craddock, here, is looking highly sceptical."

"Not at all, sir," said Craddock politely.

He thought to himself that sometimes his godfather carried things a bit far.

II

Miss Jane Marple was very nearly, if not quite, as Craddock had pictured her. She was far more benignant

87

than he had imagined and a good deal older. She seemed indeed very old. She had snow white hair and a pink crinkled face and very soft innocent blue eyes, and she was heavily enmeshed in fleecy wool. Wool round her shoulders in the form of a lacy cape and wool that she was knitting and which turned out to be a baby's shawl.

She was all incoherent delight and pleasure at seeing Sir Henry, and became quite flustered when introduced to the Chief Constable and Detective-Inspector Craddock.

"But really, Sir Henry, how fortunate . . . how very fortunate. So long since I have seen you. . . . Yes, my rheumatism. Very bad of late. Of course I couldn't have afforded this hotel (really fantastic what they charge nowadays) but Raymond—my nephew, Raymond West, you may remember him——?"

"Everyone knows *his* name."

"Yes, the dear boy has been so successful with his clever books—he prides himself upon never writing about anything pleasant. The dear boy insisted on paying all my expenses. And his dear wife is making a name for herself too, as an artist. Mostly jugs of dying flowers and broken combs on windowsills. I never dare tell her, but I still admire Blair Leighton and Alma Tadema. Oh, but I'm chattering. And the Chief Constable himself—indeed I never expected—so afraid I shall be taking up his time——"

"Completely ga-ga," thought the disgusted Detective-Inspector Craddock.

"Come into the Manager's private room," said Rydesdale. "We can talk better there."

When Miss Marple had been disentangled from her wool, and her spare knitting pins collected, she accompanied them, fluttering and protesting, to Mr. Rowlandson's comfortable sitting-room.

"Now, Miss Marple, let's hear what you have to tell us," said the Chief Constable.

Miss Marple came to the point with unexpected brevity.

"It was a cheque," she said. "He altered it."

"He?"

"The young man at the desk here, the one who is supposed to have staged that hold-up and shot himself."

"He altered a cheque, you say?"

Miss Marple nodded.

"Yes. I have it here." She extracted it from her bag and laid it on the table. "It came this morning with my others from the Bank. You can see it was for seven pounds, and he altered it to seventeen. A stroke in front of the 7, and *teen* added after the word seven with a nice artistic little blot just blurring the whole word. Really very nicely done. A certain amount of *practice*, I should say. It's the same ink, because I wrote the cheque actually at the desk. I should think he'd done it quite often before, wouldn't you?"

"He picked the wrong person to do it to, this time," remarked Sir Henry.

Miss Marple nodded agreement.

"Yes. I'm afraid he would never have gone very far in crime. I was quite the wrong person. Some busy young married woman, or some girl having a love affair —that's the kind who write cheques for all sorts of different sums and don't really look through their passbooks carefully. But an old woman who has to be careful of the pennies, and who has formed habits—that's quite the wrong person to choose. Seventeen pounds is a sum I *never* write a cheque for. Twenty pounds, a round sum, for the monthly wages and books. And as for my personal expenditure, I usually cash seven—it used to be five, but everything has gone up so."

89

"And perhaps he reminded you of someone?" prompted Sir Henry, mischief in his eye.

Miss Marple smiled and shook her head at him.

"You are very naughty, Sir Henry. As a matter of fact he *did*. Fred Tyler, at the fish shop. Always slipped an extra 1 in the shillings column. Eating so much fish as we do nowadays, it made a long bill, and lots of people never added it up. Just ten shillings in his pocket every time, not much but enough to get himself a few neckties and take Jessie Spragge (the girl in the draper's) to the pictures. Cut a splash, that's what these young fellows want to do. Well, the very first week I was here, there was a mistake in my bill. I pointed it out to the young man and he apologised very nicely and looked very much upset, but I thought to myself then : 'You've got a shifty eye, young man.'

"What I mean by a shifty eye," continued Miss Marple, "is the kind that looks very straight at you and never looks away or blinks."

Craddock gave a sudden movement of appreciation. He thought to himself " Jim Kelly to the life " remembering a notorious swindler he had helped to put behind bars not long ago.

"Rudi Scherz was a thoroughly unsatisfactory character," said Rydesdale. "He's got a police record in Switzerland, we find."

"Made the place too hot for him, I suppose, and came over here with forged papers?" said Miss Marple.

"Exactly," said Rydesdale.

"He was going about with the little red-haired waitress from the dining-room," said Miss Marple. "Fortunately I don't think her heart's affected at all. She just liked to have someone a bit ' different,' and he used to give her flowers and chocolates which the English boys don't do much. Has she told you all she knows?" she asked,

90

turning suddenly to Craddock. " Or not quite all yet?"

" I'm not absolutely sure," said Craddock cautiously.

" I think there's a little to come," said Miss Marple. " She's looking very worried. Brought me kippers instead of herrings this morning, and forgot the milk jug. Usually she's an excellent waitress. Yes, she's worried. Afraid she might have to give evidence or something like that. But I expect "—her candid blue eyes swept over the manly proportions and handsome face of Detective-Inspector Craddock with truly feminine Victorian appreciation—" that *you* will be able to persuade her to tell you all she knows."

Detective-Inspector Craddock blushed and Sir Henry chuckled.

" It might be important," said Miss Marple. " He may have told her who it was."

Rydesdale stared at her.

" Who what was?"

" I express myself so badly. Who it was who put him up to it, I mean."

" So you think someone put him up to it?"

Miss Marple's eyes widened in surprise.

" Oh, but surely—I mean . . . Here's a personable young man—who filches a little bit here and a little bit there—alters a small cheque, perhaps helps himself to a small piece of jewellery if it's left lying around, or takes a little money from the till—all sorts of small petty thefts. Keeps himself going in ready money so that he can dress well, and take a girl about—all that sort of thing. And then suddenly he goes off, with a revolver, and holds up a room full of people, and shoots at someone. He'd *never* have done a thing like that—not for a moment! He wasn't that kind of person. It doesn't make *sense*."

Craddock drew in his breath sharply. That was what Letitia Blacklock had said. What the Vicar's wife had said. What he himself felt with increasing force. *It didn't make sense.* And now Sir Henry's old Pussy was saying it, too, with complete certainty in her fluting old lady's voice.

"Perhaps you'll tell us, Miss Marple," he said, and his voice was suddenly aggressive, "what did happen, then?"

She turned on him in surprise.

"But how should I know what happened? There was an account in the paper—but it says so little. One can make conjectures, of course, but one has no accurate information."

"George," said Sir Henry. "Would it be very unorthodox if Miss Marple were allowed to read the notes of the interviews Craddock had with these people at Chipping Cleghorn."

"It may be unorthodox," said Rydesdale, "but I've not got where I am by being orthodox. She can read them. I'd be curious to hear what she has to say."

Miss Marple was all embarrassment.

"I'm afraid you've been listening to Sir Henry. Sir Henry is always too kind. He thinks too much of any little observations I may have made in the past. Really, I have no gifts—no gifts at all—except perhaps a certain knowledge of human nature. People, I find, are apt to be far too trustful. I'm afraid that I have a tendency always to believe the *worst*. Not a nice trait. But so often justified by subsequent events."

"Read these," said Rydesdale, thrusting the typewritten sheets upon her. "They won't take you long. After all, these people are your kind—you must know a lot of people like them. You may be able to spot something that we haven't. The case is just going to be closed. Let's have an amateur's opinion on it before we shut up the files. I don't mind telling you that Craddock here isn't satisfied. He says, like you, that it doesn't make sense."

There was silence whilst Miss Marple read. She put the typewritten sheets down at last.

" It's very interesting," she said with a sigh. " All the different things that people say—and think. The things they see—or think that they see. And all so complex, nearly all so trivial and if one thing isn't trivial, it's so hard to spot which one—like a needle in a haystack."

Craddock felt a twinge of disappointment. Just for a moment or two, he had wondered if Sir Henry might be right about this funny old lady. She might have put her finger on something—old people were often very sharp. He'd never, for instance, been able to conceal anything from his own great aunt Emma. She had finally told him that his nose twitched when he was about to tell a lie.

But just a few fluffy generalities, that was all that Sir Henry's famous Miss Marple could produce. He felt annoyed with her and said rather curtly :

" The truth of the matter is that the facts are indisputable. Whatever conflicting details these people give, they all saw one thing. They saw a masked man with a revolver and a torch open the door and hold them up, and whether they think he said ' Stick 'em up ' or ' Your money or your life,' or whatever phrase is associated with a hold-up in their minds, they *saw* him."

" But surely," said Miss Marple gently. " They couldn't —actually—have seen anything at all. . . ."

Craddock caught his breath. She'd got it ! She was sharp, after all. He was testing her by that speech of his, but she hadn't fallen for it. It didn't actually make any difference to the facts, or to what happened, but she'd realised, as he'd realised, that those people who had seen a masked man holding them up couldn't really have *seen* him at all.

" If I understand rightly," Miss Marple had a pink flush on her cheeks, her eyes were bright and pleased as a child's, " there wasn't any light in the hall outside— and not on the landing upstairs either?"

" That's right," said Craddock.

" And so, if a man stood in the doorway and flashed a powerful torch into the room, *nobody could see anything but the torch*, could they?"

" No, they couldn't. I tried it out."

" And so when some of them say they saw a masked man, etc., they are really, though they don't realise it, recapitulating from what they saw *afterwards*—when the lights came on. So it really all fits in very well, doesn't it, on the assumption that Rudi Scherz was the— I think, ' fall guy ' is the expression I mean?"

Rydesdale stared at her in such surprise that she grew pinker still.

" I may have got the term wrong," she murmured. " I am not very clever about Americanisms—and I understand they change very quickly. I got it from one of Mr. Dashiel Hammett's stories. (I understand from my nephew Raymond that he is considered at the top of the tree in what is called the ' tough ' style of literature.) A ' *fall guy*,' if I understand it rightly, means someone who will be blamed for a crime really committed by someone else. This Rudi Scherz seems to me exactly the right type for that. Rather stupid really, you know, but full of cupidity and probably extremely credulous."

Rydesdale said, smiling tolerantly :

" Are you suggesting that he was persuaded by someone to go out and take pot shots at a room full of people? Rather a tall order."

" I think he was told that it was a *joke*," said Miss

94

Marple. "He was paid for doing it, of course. Paid, that is, to put an advertisement in the newspaper, to go out and spy out the household premises, and then, on the night in question, he was to go there, assume a mask and a black cloak and throw open a door, brandishing a torch, and cry ' Hands up !' "

"And fire off a revolver?"

"No, no," said Miss Marple. "He never had a revolver."

"But everyone says——" began Rydesdale, and stopped.

"Exactly," said Miss Marple. "Nobody could possibly have *seen* a revolver even if he had one. And I don't think he had. I think that after he'd called ' Hands up ' somebody came up quietly behind him in the darkness and fired those two shots over his shoulder. It frightened him to death. He swung round and as he did so, that other person shot him and then let the revolver drop beside him. . . ."

The three men looked at her. Sir Henry said softly :

"It's a possible theory."

"But who is Mr. X. who came up in the darkness?" asked the Chief Constable.

Miss Marple coughed.

"You'll have to find out from Miss Blacklock who wanted to kill her."

Good for old Dora Bunner, thought Craddock. Instinct against intelligence every time.

"So you think it was a deliberate attempt on Miss Blacklock's life," asked Rydesdale.

"It certainly has that appearance," said Miss Marple. "Though there are one or two difficulties. But what I was really wondering about was whether there mightn't be a short cut. I've no doubt that whoever arranged this with Rudi Scherz took pains to tell him to keep his mouth shut about it, and perhaps he did keep his mouth shut, but if he talked to anybody it would probably be to that girl, Myrna Harris. And he may—he just may—have dropped some hint as to the kind of person who'd suggested the whole thing."

"I'll see her now," said Craddock, rising.

Miss Marple nodded.

"Yes, do, Inspector Craddock. I'll feel happier when you have. Because once she's told you anything she knows she'll be much safer."

"Safer? ... Yes, I see."

He left the room. The Chief Constable said doubtfully, but tactfully:

"Well, Miss Marple, you've certainly given us something to think about."

III

"I'm sorry about it, I am really," said Myrna Harris. "It's ever so nice of you not to be ratty about it. But you see Mum's the sort of person who fusses like anything. And it did look as though I'd—what's the phrase—been an accessory before the fact" (the words ran glibly off her tongue). "I mean, I was afraid you'd never take my word for it that I only thought it was just a bit of fun."

Inspector Craddock repeated the reassuring phrases with which he had broken down Myrna's resistance.

"I will. I'll tell you *all* about it. But you will keep me out of it if you can because of Mum? It all started with Rudi breaking a date with me. We were going to the pictures that evening and then he said he wouldn't be able to come and I was a bit stand-offish with him about it—because after all, it had been his idea and I

96

don't fancy being stood up by a foreigner. And he said it wasn't his fault, and I said that was a likely story, and then he said he'd got a bit of a lark on that night—and that he wasn't going to be out of pocket by it and how would I fancy a wrist-watch? So I said, what do you mean by a lark? And he said not to tell anyone, but there was to be a party somewhere and he was to stage a sham hold-up. Then he showed me the advertisement he'd put in and I had to laugh. He was a bit scornful about it all. Said it was kid's stuff really—but that was just like the English. They never really grew up—and of course, I said what did he mean by talking like that about Us—and we had a bit of an argument, but we made it up. Only you can understand, can't you, sir, that when I read all about it, and it hadn't been a joke at all and Rudi had shot someone and then shot himself —why, I didn't know *what* to do. I thought if I said I knew about it beforehand, it would look as though I were in on the whole thing. But it really did seem like a joke when he told me about it. I'd have sworn he meant it that way. I didn't even know he'd got a re-volver. He never said anything about taking a revolver with him."

Craddock comforted her and then asked the most important question.

" Who did he say it was who had arranged this party?"

But there he drew a blank.

" He never said who it was that was getting him to do it. I suppose nobody was, really. It was all his own doing."

" He didn't mention a name? Did he say he—or she?"

" He didn't say anything except that it was going to be a scream. ' I shall laugh to see all their faces.' That's what he said."

97

He hadn't had long to laugh, Craddock thought.

IV

"It's only a theory," said Rydesdale as they drove back to Medenham. "Nothing to support it, nothing at all. Put it down as old maid's vapourings and let it go, eh?"

"I'd rather not do that, sir."

"It's all very improbable. A mysterious X appearing suddenly in the darkness behind our Swiss friend. Where did he come from? Who was he? Where had he been?"

"He could have come in through the side door," said Craddock, "just as Scherz came. Or," he added slowly, "he could have come from the kitchen."

"*She* could have come from the kitchen, you mean?"

"Yes, sir, it's a possibility. I've not been satisfied about that girl all along. She strikes me as a nasty bit of goods. All that screaming and hysterics—it could have been put on. She could have worked on this young fellow, let him in at the right moment, rigged the whole thing, shot him, bolted back into the dining-room, caught up her bit of silver and her chamois and started her screaming act."

"Against that we have the fact that—er—what's his name—oh, yes, Edmund Swettenham, definitely says the key was turned on the outside of the door, and that he turned it to release her. Any other door into that part of the house?"

"Yes, there's a door to the back stairs and kitchen just under the stairs, but it seems the handle came off three weeks ago and nobody's come to put it on yet. In the meantime you can't open the door. I'm bound to say that story seems correct. The spindle and the two handles were on a shelf outside the door in the hall and they were thickly coated with dust, but of course a professional would have ways of opening that door all right."

"Better look up the girl's record. See if her papers are in order. But it seems to me the whole thing is very theoretical."

Again the Chief Constable looked inquiringly at his subordinate. Craddock replied quietly :

"I know, sir, and of course if you think the case ought to be closed, it must be. But I'd appreciate it if I could work on it for just a little longer."

Rather to his surprise the Chief Constable said quietly and approvingly :

"Good lad."

"There's the revolver to work on. If this theory is correct, it wasn't Scherz's revolver and certainly nobody so far has been able to say that Scherz ever had a revolver."

"It's a German make."

"I know, sir. But this country's absolutely full of continental makes of guns. All the Americans brought them back and so did our chaps. You can't go by that."

"True enough. Any other lines of inquiry?"

"There's got to be a motive. If there's anything in this theory at all, it means that last Friday's business wasn't a mere joke and wasn't an ordinary hold-up, it was a cold-blooded attempt at murder. *Somebody tried to murder Miss Blacklock.* Now *why?* It seems to me that if anyone knows the answer to that it must be Miss Blacklock herself."

"I understand she rather poured cold water on that idea?"

"She poured cold water on the idea that *Rudi Scherz* wanted to murder her. And she was quite right. And there's another thing, sir."

99

" Yes?"

" Somebody might try again."

" That would certainly prove the truth of the theory," said the Chief Constable dryly. " By the way, look after Miss Marple, won't you?"

" Miss Marple? Why?"

" I gather she is taking up residence at the Vicarage in Chipping Cleghorn and coming into Medenham Wells twice a week for her treatments. It seems that Mrs. What'shername is the daughter of an old friend of Miss Marple's. Good sporting instincts, that old bean. Oh, well, I suppose she hasn't much excitement in her life and sniffing round after possible murderers gives her a kick."

" I wish she wasn't coming," said Craddock seriously.

" Going to get under your feet?"

" Not that, sir, but she's a nice old thing. I shouldn't like anything to happen to her . . . always supposing, I mean, that there's anything *in* this theory."

CHAPTER IX

CONCERNING A DOOR

"I'M sorry to bother you again, Miss Blacklock——"

"Oh, it doesn't matter. I suppose, as the inquest was adjourned for a week, you're hoping to get more evidence?"

Detective-Inspector Craddock nodded.

"To begin with, Miss Blacklock, Rudi Scherz was not the son of the proprietor of the Hotel des Alpes at Montreux. He seems to have started his career as an orderly in a hospital at Berne. A good many of the patients missed small pieces of jewellery. Under another name he was a waiter at one of the small winter sports places. His speciality there was making out duplicate bills in the restaurant with items on one that didn't appear on the other. The difference, of course, went into his pocket. After that he was in a department store in Zürich. Their losses from shoplifting were rather above the average whilst he was with them. It seems likely that the shoplifting wasn't entirely due to customers."

"He was a picker up of unconsidered trifles, in fact?" said Miss Blacklock dryly. "Then I was right in thinking that I had not seen him before?"

"You were quite right—no doubt you were pointed out to him at the Royal Spa Hotel and he pretended to recognise you. The Swiss police had begun to make his own country rather too hot for him, and he came over here with a very nice set of forged papers and took a job at the Royal Spa."

"Quite a good hunting ground," said Miss Blacklock

dryly. " It's extremely expensive and very well-off people stay there. Some of them are careless about their bills, I expect."

" Yes," said Craddock. " There were prospects of a satisfactory harvest."

Miss Blacklock was frowning.

" I see all that," she said. " But why come to Chipping Cleghorn? What does he think we've got here that could possibly be better than the rich Royal Spa Hotel?"

" You stick to your statement that there's nothing of especial value in the house?"

" Of course there isn't. *I* should know. I can assure you, Inspector, we've not got an unrecognised Rembrandt or anything like that."

" Then it looks, doesn't it, as though your friend, Miss Bunner were right? He came here to attack *you*."

(" There, Letty, what did I tell you!"

" Oh, nonsense, Bunny.")

" But is it nonsense?" said Craddock. " I think, you know, that it's true."

Miss Blacklock stared very hard at him.

" Now, let's get this straight. You really believe that this young man came out here—having previously arranged by means of an advertisement that half the village would turn up agog at that particular time——"

" But he mayn't have meant *that* to happen," interrupted Miss Bunner eagerly. " It may have been just a horrid sort of warning—to *you*, Letty—that's how I read it at the time—' *A murder is announced* '—I felt in my bones that it was sinister—if it had all gone as planned he would have shot you and got away—and how would anyone have ever known who it was?"

" That's true enough," said Miss Blacklock. " But——"

" I knew that advertisement wasn't a joke, Letty. I said so. And look at Mitzi—*she* was frightened, too!"

" Ah," said Craddock, " Mitzi. I'd like to know rather more about that young woman."

" Her permit and papers are quite in order."

" I don't doubt that," said Craddock dryly. " Scherz's papers appeared to be quite correct, too."

" But why should this Rudi Scherz want to murder me? That's what you don't attempt to explain, Inspector Craddock."

" There may have been someone behind Scherz," said Craddock slowly. " Have you thought of that?"

He used the words metaphorically though it flashed across his mind that if Miss Marple's theory was correct, the words would also be true in a literal sense. In any case they made little impression on Miss Blacklock, who still looked sceptical.

" The point remains the same," she said. " Why on earth should anyone want to murder *me*?"

" It's the answer to that that I want *you* to give me, Miss Blacklock."

" Well, I can't! That's flat. I've no enemies. As far as I'm aware I've always lived on perfectly good terms with my neighbours. I don't know any guilty secrets about anyone. The whole idea is ridiculous! And if what you're hinting is that Mitzi has something to do with this, that's absurd, too. As Miss Bunner has just told you she was frightened to death when she saw that advertisement in the *Gazette*. She actually wanted to pack up and leave the house then and there."

" That may have been a clever move on her part. She may have known you'd press her to stay."

" Of course, if you've made up your mind about it, you'll find an answer to everything. But I can assure you that if Mitzi had taken an unreasoning dislike to me, she might conceivably poison my food, but I'm sure she wouldn't go in for all this elaborate rigmarole.

" The whole idea's absurd. I believe you police have got an anti-foreigner complex. Mitzi may be a liar but she's *not* a cold-blooded murderer. Go and bully her if you must. But when she's departed in a whirl of indignation, or shut herself up howling in her room, I've a good mind to make *you* cook the dinner. Mrs. Harmon is bringing some old lady who is staying with her to tea this afternoon and I wanted Mitzi to make some little cakes —but I suppose you'll upset her completely. Can't you *possibly* go and suspect somebody else?"

11

Craddock went out to the kitchen. He asked Mitzi questions that he had asked her before and received the same answers.

Yes, she had locked the front door soon after four o'clock. No, she did not always do so, but that afternoon she had been nervous because of " that dreadful advertisement." It was no good locking the side door because Miss Blacklock and Miss Bunner went out that way to shut up the ducks and feed the chickens and Mrs. Haymes usually came in that way from work.

" Mrs. Haymes says she locked the door when she came in at 5.30."

" Ah, and you believe her—oh, yes, you believe her. . . ."

" Do you think we shouldn't believe her?"

" What does it matter what I think? You will not believe *me*."

" Supposing you give us a chance. You think Mrs. Haymes didn't lock that door?"

" I thinking she was very careful not to lock it."

" What do you mean by that?" asked Craddock.

"That young man, he does not work alone. No, he knows *where* to come, he knows that *when* he comes a door will be left open for him—oh, very conveniently open!"

"What are you trying to say?"

"What is the use of what I say? You will not listen. You say I am a poor refugee girl who tells lies. You say that a fair-haired English lady, oh, no, *she* does not tell lies—she is so British—so honest. So you believe her and not me. But I could tell you. Oh, yes, I could tell you!"

She banged down a saucepan on the stove.

Craddock was in two minds whether to take notice of what might be only a stream of spite.

"We note everything we are told," he said.

"I shall not tell you anything at all. Why should I? You are all alike. You persecute and despise poor refugees. If I say to you that when, a week before, that young man come to ask Miss Blacklock for money and she sends him away, as you say, with a flea in the ear—if I tell you that after that I hear him talking with Mrs. Haymes—yes, out there in the summerhouse—all you say is that I make it up!"

And so you probably are making it up, thought Craddock. But he said aloud:

"You couldn't hear what was said out in the summerhouse."

"There you are wrong," screamed Mitzi triumphantly. "I go out to get nettles—it makes very nice vegetables, nettles. They do not think so, but I cook it and not tell them. And I hear them talking in there. He say to her 'But where can I hide?' And she say 'I will show you' —and then she say, 'At a quarter-past six,' and I think, 'Ach so! That is how you behave, my fine lady! After you come back from work, you go out to meet a man. You bring him into the house.' Miss Blacklock, I think,

105

she will not like that. She will turn you out. I will watch, I think, and listen and then I will tell Miss Black-lock. But I understand now I was wrong. It was not love she planned with him, it was to rob and to murder. But you will say I make all this up. Wicked Mitzi, you will say. I will take her to prison."

Craddock wondered. She might be making it up. But possibly she might not. He asked cautiously:

"You are sure it was this Rudi Scherz she was talking to?"

"Of course I am sure. He just leave and I see him go from the drive across to the summerhouse. And presently," said Mitzi defiantly, "I go out to see if there are any nice young green nettles."

Would there, the Inspector wondered, be any nice young green nettles in October? But he appreciated that Mitzi had had to produce a hurried reason for what had undoubtedly been nothing more than plain snooping.

"You didn't hear any more than what you have told me?"

Mitzi looked aggrieved.

"That Miss Bunner, the one with the long nose, she call and call me. Mitzi! Mitzi! So I have to go. Oh, she is irritating. Always interfering. Says she will teach me to cook. *Her* cooking! It tastes, yes, everything she does, of water, water, *water*!"

"Why didn't you tell me this the other day?" asked Craddock sternly.

"Because I did not remember—I did not think. . . . Only afterwards do I say to myself, it was planned then —planned with *her*."

"You are quite sure it was Mrs. Haymes?"

"Oh, yes, I am sure. Oh, yes, I am very sure. She is a thief, that Mrs. Haymes. A thief and the associate of thieves. What she gets for working in the garden, it is not enough for such a fine lady, no. She has to rob Miss Blacklock who has been kind to her. Oh, she is bad, bad, bad, that one!"

"Supposing," said the Inspector, watching her closely, "that someone was to say that *you* had been seen talking to Rudi Scherz?"

The suggestion had less effect than he had hoped for. Mitzi merely snorted and tossed her head.

"If anyone say they see me talking to him, that is lies, lies, lies, lies," she said contemptuously. "To tell lies about anyone, that is easy, but in England you have to prove them true. Miss Blacklock tell me that, and it is true, is it not? I do not speak with murderers and thieves. And no English policeman shall say I do. And how can I do cooking for lunch if you are here, talk, talk, talk? Go out of my kitchens, please. I want now to make a very careful sauce."

Craddock went obediently. He was a little shaken in his suspicions of Mitzi. Her story about Phillipa Haymes had been told with great conviction. Mitzi might be a liar (he thought she was), but he fancied that there might be some substratum of truth in this particular tale. He resolved to speak to Phillipa on the subject. She had seemed to him when he questioned her a quiet, well-bred young woman. He had had no suspicion of her.

Crossing the hall, in his abstraction, he tried to open the wrong door. Miss Bunner, descending the staircase, hastily put him right.

"Not that door," she said. "It doesn't open. The next one to the left. Very confusing, isn't it. So many doors."

"There are a good many," said Craddock, looking up and down the narrow hall.

Miss Bunner amiably enumerated them for him.

"First the door to the cloakroom, and then the cloaks

107

cupboard door and then the dining-room—that's on that side. And on this side, the dummy door that you were trying to get through and then there's the drawing-room door proper, and then the china cupboard door and the door of the little flower room, and at the end the side door. Most confusing. Especially these two being so near together. I've often tried the wrong one by mistake. We used to have the hall table against it, as a matter of fact, but then we moved it along against the wall there."

Craddock had noted, almost mechanically, a thin line horizontally across the panels of the door he had been trying to open. He realised now it was the mark where the table had been. Something stirred vaguely in his mind as he asked, "Moved? How long ago?"

In questioning Dora Bunner there was fortunately no need to give a reason for any question. Any query on any subject seemed perfectly natural to the garrulous Miss Bunner who delighted in the giving of information, however trivial.

"Now let me see, really quite recently—ten days or a fortnight ago."

"Why was it moved?"

"I really can't remember. Something to do with the flowers. I think Phillipa did a big vase—she arranges flowers quite beautifully—all autumn colouring and twigs and branches, and it was so big it caught your hair as you went past, and so Phillipa said, ' Why not move the table along and anyway the flowers would look much better against the bare wall than against the panels of the door.' Only we had to take down ' Wellington at Waterloo.' Not a print I'm really very fond of. We put it under the stairs."

"It's not really a dummy, then?" Craddock asked, looking at the door.

"Oh, no, it's a *real* door, if that's what you mean. It's

the door of the small drawing-room, but when the rooms were thrown into one, one didn't need two doors, so this one was fastened up."

"Fastened up?" Craddock tried it again, gently. "You mean it's nailed up? Or just locked?"

"Oh, locked, I think, and bolted too."

He saw the bolt at the top and tried it. The bolt slid back easily—too easily. . . .

"When was it last open?" he asked Miss Bunner.

"Oh, years and years ago, I imagine. It's never been opened since I've been here, I know that."

"You don't know where the key is?"

"There are a lot of keys in the hall drawer. It's probably among those."

Craddock followed her and looked at a rusty assortment of old keys pushed far back in the drawer. He scanned them and selected one that looked different from the rest and went back to the door. The key fitted and turned easily. He pushed and the door slid open noiselessly.

"Oh, do be careful," cried Miss Bunner. "There may be something resting against it inside. We never open it."

"Don't you?" said the Inspector.

His face now was grim. He said with emphasis:

"This door's been opened quite recently, Miss Bunner. The lock's been oiled and the hinges."

She stared at him, her foolish face agape.

"But who could have done that?" she asked.

"That's what I mean to find out," said Craddock grimly. He thought—"X from outside? No—X was here—in this house—X was in the drawing-room that night. . . ."

109

CHAPTER X

PIP AND EMMA

MISS BLACKLOCK listened to him this time with more attention. She was an intelligent woman, as he had known, and she grasped the implications of what he had to tell her.

"Yes," she said quietly. "That does alter things. . . . No one had any right to meddle with that door. Nobody *has* meddled with it to my knowledge."

"You see what it means," the Inspector urged. "When the lights went out, *anybody in this room the other night* could have slipped out of that door, come up behind Rudi Scherz and fired at you."

"Without being seen or heard or noticed?"

"Without being seen or heard or noticed. Remember when the lights went out people moved, exclaimed, bumped into each other. And after that all that could be seen was the blinding light of the electric torch."

Miss Blacklock said slowly, "And you believe that one of those people—one of my nice commonplace neighbours—slipped out and tried to murder me? *Me?* But *why?* For goodness' sake, why?"

"I've a feeling that you *must* know the answer to that question, Miss Blacklock."

"But I don't, Inspector. I can assure you, I don't."

"Well, let's make a start. Who gets your money if you were to die?"

Miss Blacklock said rather reluctantly:

"Patrick and Julia. I've left the furniture in this

110

house and a small annuity to Bunny. Really, I've not much to leave. I had holdings in German and Italian securities which became worthless, and what with taxation, and the lower percentages that are now paid on invested capital, I can assure you I'm not worth murdering—I put most of my money into an annuity about a year ago."

"Still, you *have* some income, Miss Blacklock, and your nephew and niece would come into it."

"And so Patrick and Julia would plan to murder me? I simply don't believe it. They're not desperately hard up or anything like that."

"Do you know that for a fact?"

"No. I suppose I only know it from what they've told me. . . . But I really refuse to suspect them. *Some*day I *might* be worth murdering, but not now."

"What do you mean by someday you might be worth murdering, Miss Blacklock?" Inspector Craddock pounced on the statement.

"Simply that one day—possibly quite soon—I *may* be a very rich woman."

"That sounds interesting. Will you explain?"

"Certainly. You may not know it, but for more than twenty years I was secretary to and closely associated with Randall Goedler."

Craddock was interested. Randall Goedler had been a big name in the world of finance. His daring speculations and the rather theatrical publicity with which he surrounded himself had made him a personality not quickly forgotten. He had died, if Craddock remembered rightly, in 1937 or 1938.

"He's rather before your time, I expect," said Miss Blacklock. "But you've probably heard of him."

"Oh, yes. He was a millionaire, wasn't he?"

"Oh, several times over—though his finances fluctuated. He always risked most of what he made on some new *coup*."

She spoke with a certain animation, her eyes brightened by memory.

"Anyway he died a very rich man. He had no children. He left his fortune in trust for his wife during her lifetime and after her death to me absolutely."

A vague memory stirred in the Inspector's mind.

IMMENSE FORTUNE TO COME TO FAITHFUL SECRETARY —something of that kind.

"For the last twelve years or so," said Miss Blacklock with a slight twinkle, "*I've* had an excellent motive for murdering Mrs. Goedler—but that doesn't help you, does it?"

"Did—excuse me for asking this—did Mrs. Goedler resent her husband's disposition of his fortune?"

Miss Blacklock was now looking frankly amused.

"You needn't be so very discreet. What you really mean is, was I Randall Goedler's mistress? No, I wasn't. I don't think Randall ever gave me a sentimental thought, and I certainly didn't give him one. He was in love with Belle (his wife), and remained in love with her until he died. I think in all probability it was gratitude on his part that prompted his making his will. You see, Inspector, in the very early days, when Randall was still on an insecure footing, he came very near to disaster. It was a question of just a few thousands of actual cash. It was a big *coup*, and a very exciting one; daring, as all his schemes were; but he just hadn't got that little bit of cash to tide him over. I came to the rescue. I had a little money of my own. I believed in Randall. I sold every penny I had out and gave it to him. It did the trick. A week later he was an immensely wealthy man.

"After that, he treated me more or less as a junior

partner. Oh! they were exciting days." She sighed. "I enjoyed it all thoroughly. Then my father died, and my only sister was left a hopeless invalid. I had to give it all up and go and look after her. Randall died a couple of years later. I had made quite a lot of money during our association and I didn't really expect him to leave me anything, but I was very touched, yes, and very proud to find that if Belle predeceased me (and she was one of those delicate creatures whom everyone always says won't live long) I was to inherit his entire fortune. I think really the poor man didn't know who to leave it to. Belle's a dear, and she was delighted about it. She's really a very sweet person. She lives up in Scotland. I haven't seen her for years—we just write at Christmas. You see, I went with my sister to a sanatorium in Switzerland just before the war. She died of consumption out there."

She was silent for a moment or two, then said:

"I only came back to England just over a year ago."

"You said you might be a rich woman very soon. . . . How soon?"

"I heard from the nurse attendant who looks after Belle Goedler that Belle is sinking rapidly. It may be— only a few weeks."

She added sadly:

"The money won't mean much to me now. I've got quite enough for my rather simple needs. Once I should have enjoyed playing the markets again—but now . . . Oh, well, one grows old. Still, you do see, Inspector, don't you, that if Patrick and Julia wanted to kill me for a financial reason they'd be crazy not to wait for another few weeks."

"Yes, Miss Blacklock, but what happens if you should predecease Mrs. Goedler. Who does the money go to then?"

113

" D'you know, I've never really thought. Pip and Emma, I suppose. . . ."

Craddock stared and Miss Blacklock smiled.

" Does that sound rather crazy? I believe, if I predecease Belle, the money would go to the legal offspring —or whatever the term is—of Randall's only sister, Sonia. Randall had quarrelled with his sister. She married a man whom he considered a crook and worse."

" And was he a crook?"

" Oh, definitely, I should say. But I believe a very attractive person to women. He was a Greek or a Roumanian or something—what was his name now—Stamfordis, Dmitri Stamfordis."

" Randall Goedler cut his sister out of his will when she married this man?"

" Oh, Sonia was a very wealthy woman in her own right. Randall had already settled packets of money on her, as far as possible in a way so that her husband couldn't touch it. But I believe that when the lawyers urged him to put in someone in case I predeceased Belle, he reluctantly put down Sonia's offspring, simply because he couldn't think of anyone else and he wasn't the sort of man to leave money to charities."

" And there were children of the marriage?"

" Well, there are Pip and Emma." She laughed. " I know it sounds ridiculous. All I know is that Sonia wrote once to Belle after her marriage, telling her to tell Randall that she was extremely happy and that she had just had twins and was calling them Pip and Emma. As far as I know she never wrote again. But Belle, of course, may be able to tell you more."

Miss Blacklock had been amused by her own recital. The Inspector did not look amused.

" It comes to this," he said. " If you had been killed the other night, there are presumably at least two people

114

in the world who would have come into a very large fortune. You are wrong, Miss Blacklock, when you say that there is no one who has a motive for desiring your death. There are two people, at least, who are vitally interested. How old would this brother and sister be?"

Miss Blacklock frowned.

" Let me see . . . 1922 . . . no—it's difficult to remember. . . . I suppose about twenty-five or twenty-six." Her face had sobered. " But you surely don't think——"

" I think somebody shot at you with the intent to kill you. I think it possible that that same person or persons might try again. I would like you, if you will, to be very *very* careful, Miss Blacklock. One murder has been arranged and did not come off. I think it possible that another murder may be arranged very soon."

II

Phillipa Haymes straightened her back and pushed back a tendril of hair from her damp forehead. She was cleaning a flower border.

" Yes, Inspector?"

She looked at him inquiringly. In return he gave her a rather closer scrutiny than he had done before. Yes, a good-looking girl, a very English type with her pale ash-blonde hair and her rather long face. An obstinate chin and mouth. Something of repression—of tautness about her. The eyes were blue, very steady in their glance, and told you nothing at all. The sort of girl, he thought, who would keep a secret well.

" I'm sorry always to bother you when you're at work, Mrs. Haymes," he said, " but I didn't want to wait until you came back for lunch. Besides, I thought it might be easier to talk to you here, away from Little Paddocks."

" Yes, Inspector?"

No emotion and little interest in the voice. But was there a note of wariness—or did he imagine it?

" A certain statement has been made to me this morning. This statement concerns you."

Phillipa raised her eyebrows very slightly.

"You told me, Mrs. Haymes, that this man, Rudi Scherz, was quite unknown to you?"

" Yes."

" That when you saw him there, dead, it was the first time you had set eyes on him. Is that so?"

" Certainly. I had never seen him before."

" You did not, for instance, have a conversation with him in the summerhouse of Little Paddocks?"

" In the *summer*house?"

He was almost sure he caught a note of fear in her voice.

" Yes, Mrs. Haymes."

" *Who* says so?"

" I am told that you had a conversation with this man, Rudi Scherz, and that he asked you where he could hide and you replied that you would show him, and that a time, a quarter-past six, was definitely mentioned. It would be a quarter-past six, roughly, when Scherz would get here from the bus stop on the evening of the hold-up."

There was a moment's silence. Then Phillipa gave a short scornful laugh. She looked amused.

" I don't know who told you that," she said. " At least I can guess. It's a very silly, clumsy story—spiteful, of course. For some reason Mitzi dislikes me even more than she dislikes the rest of us."

" You deny it?"

" Of course it's not true. . . . I never met or saw Rudi Scherz in my life, and I was nowhere near the house that morning. I was over here, working."

116

Inspector Craddock said very gently :
" Which morning?"

There was a momentary pause. Her eyelids flickered.
" Every morning. I'm here every morning. I don't
get away until one o'clock."

She added scornfully:
" It's no good listening to what Mitzi tells you. She
tells lies all the time."

" And that's that," said Craddock when he was walking
away with Sergeant Fletcher. " Two young women
whose stories flatly contradict each other. Which one
am I to believe?"

" Everyone seems to agree that this foreign girl tells
whoppers," said Fletcher. " It's been my experience in
dealing with aliens that lying comes more easy than
truth telling. Seems to be clear she's got a spite against
this Mrs. Haymes."

" So, if you were me, you'd believe Mrs. Haymes?"

" Unless you've got reason to think otherwise, sir."

And Craddock hadn't, not really—only the remembrance of a pair of over-steady blue eyes and the glib
enunciation of the words *that morning*. For to the best
of his recollection he hadn't said whether the interview
in the summerhouse had taken place in the morning or
the afternoon.

Still, Miss Blacklock, or if not Miss Blacklock, certainly
Miss Bunner, might have mentioned the visit of the
young foreigner who had come to cadge his fare back to
Switzerland. And Phillipa Haymes might have therefore
assumed that the conversation was supposed to have
taken place on that particular morning.

But Craddock still thought that there had been a note
of fear in her voice as she asked :
" In the *summer*house?"

He decided to keep an open mind on the subject.

III

It was very pleasant in the Vicarage garden. One of those sudden spells of autumn warmth had descended upon England. Inspector Craddock could never remember if it was St. Martin's or St. Luke's Summer, but he knew that it was very pleasant—and also very enervating. He sat in a deck chair provided for him by an energetic Bunch, just on her way to a Mothers' Meeting, and, well protected with shawls and a large rug round her knees, Miss Marple sat knitting beside him. The sunshine, the peace, the steady click of Miss Marple's knitting needles, all combined to produce a soporific feeling in the Inspector. And yet, at the same time, there was a nightmarish feeling at the back of his mind. It was like a familiar dream where an undertone of menace grows and finally turns Ease into Terror. . . .

He said abruptly, " You oughtn't to be here."

Miss Marple's needles stopped clicking for a moment. Her placid china blue eyes regarded him thoughtfully.

She said, " I know what you mean. You're a very conscientious boy. But it's perfectly all right. Bunch's father (he was vicar of our parish, a very fine scholar) and her mother (who is a most remarkable woman—real spiritual power) are very old friends of mine. It's the most natural thing in the world that when I'm at Medenham I should come on here to stay with Bunch for a little."

" Oh, perhaps," said Craddock. " But—but don't snoop around. . . . I've a feeling—I have really—that it isn't *safe*."

Miss Marple smiled a little.

118

"But I'm afraid," she said, "that we old women always do snoop. It would be very odd and much more noticeable if I didn't. Questions about mutual friends in different parts of the world and whether they remember so and so, and do they remember who it was that Lady Somebody's daughter married? All that helps, doesn't it?"

"Helps?" said the Inspector, rather stupidly.

"Helps to find out if people are who they say they are," said Miss Marple.

She went on:

"Because that's what's worrying you, isn't it? And that's really the particular way the world has changed since the war. Take this place, Chipping Cleghorn, for instance. It's very much like St. Mary Mead where I live. Fifteen years ago one *knew* who everybody was. The Bantrys in the big house—and the Hartnells and the Price Ridleys and the Weatherbys. . . . They were people whose fathers and mothers and grandfathers and grandmothers, or whose aunts and uncles, had lived there before them. If somebody new came to live there, they brought letters of introduction, or they'd been in the same regiment or served on the same ship as someone there already. If anybody new—really new—really a stranger—came, well, they stuck out—everybody wondered about them and didn't rest till they found out."

She nodded her head gently:

"But it's not like that any more. Every village and small country place is full of people who've just come and settled there without any ties to bring them. The big houses have been sold, and the cottages have been converted and changed. And people just come—and all you know about them is what they say of themselves. They've come, you see, from all over the world. People from India and Hong Kong and China, and people who used to live in France and Italy in little cheap places and odd islands. And people who've made a little money and can afford to retire. But nobody *knows* any more who anyone is. You can have Benares brassware in your house and talk about *tiffin* and *chota Hazri*—and you can have pictures of Taormina and talk about the English church and the library—like Miss Hinchliffe and Miss Murgatroyd. You can come from the South of France, or have spent your life in the East. People take you at your own valuation. They don't wait to call until they've had a letter from a friend saying that the So-and-So's are delightful people and she's known them all their lives."

And that, thought Craddock, was exactly what *was* oppressing him. He didn't *know*. They were just faces and personalities and they were backed up by ration books and identity cards—nice neat identity cards with numbers on them, without photographs or fingerprints. Anbody who took the trouble could have a suitable identity card—and partly because of that, the subtler links that had held together English social rural life had fallen apart. In a town nobody expected to know his neighbour. In the country now nobody knew his neighbour either, though possibly he still thought he did. . . .

Because of the oiled door, Craddock knew that there had been somebody in Letitia Blacklock's drawing-room who was not the pleasant friendly country neighbour he or she pretended to be. . . .

And because of that he was afraid for Miss Marple who was frail and old and who noticed things. . . .

He said : " We can, to a certain extent, check up on these people. . . ." But he knew that that wasn't so easy. India and China and Hong Kong and the South of France . . . It wasn't as easy as it would have been fifteen years ago. There were people, as he knew only too well, who were going about the country with borrowed identities—borrowed from people who had met sudden death by " incidents " in the cities. There were organisations who bought up identities, who faked identity and ration cards—there were a hundred small rackets springing into being. You *could* check up—but it would take time—and time was what he hadn't got, because Randall Goedler's widow was very near death.

It was then that, worried and tired, lulled by the sunshine, he told Miss Marple about Randall Goedler and about Pip and Emma.

" Just a couple of names," he said. " Nicknames at that! They mayn't exist. They may be respectable citizens living in Europe somewhere. On the other hand one, or both, of them may be here in Chipping Cleghorn."

Twenty-five years old approximately—Who filled that description? He said, thinking aloud :

" That nephew and niece of hers—or cousins or whatever they are . . . I wonder when she saw them last——"

Miss Marple said gently : " I'll find out for you, shall I?"

" Now, please, Miss Marple, don't——"

" It will be quite simple, Inspector, you really need not worry. And it won't be noticeable if I do it, because, you see, it won't be official. If there is anything wrong you don't want to put them on their guard."

Pip and Emma, thought Craddock, Pip and Emma? He was getting obsessed by Pip and Emma. That attractive dare-devil young man, the good-looking girl with the cool stare. . . .

He said : " I may find out more about them in the next forty-eight hours. I'm going up to Scotland. Mrs. Goedler, if she's able to talk, may know a good deal more about them."

" I think that's a very wise move." Miss Marple hesitated. " I hope," she murmured, " that you have warned Miss Blacklock to be careful?"

" I've warned her, yes. And I shall leave a man here to keep an unobtrusive eye on things."

He avoided Miss Marple's eye which said plainly enough that a policeman keeping an eye on things would be little good if the danger was in the family circle. . . .

" And remember," said Craddock, looking squarely at her, " I've warned you."

" I assure you, Inspector," said Miss Marple, " that I can take care of myself."

CHAPTER XI

MISS MARPLE COMES TO TEA

IF LETITIA BLACKLOCK seemed slightly absent-minded when Mrs. Harmon came to tea and brought a guest who was staying with her, Miss Marple, the guest in question, was hardly likely to notice the fact since it was the first time she had met her.

The old lady was very charming in her gentle gossipy fashion. She revealed herself almost at once to be one of those old ladies who have a constant preoccupation with burglars.

"They can get in anywhere, my dear," she assured her hostess, "absolutely *anywhere* nowadays. So many new American methods. I myself pin my faith to a very old-fashioned device. *A cabin hook and eye.* They can pick locks and draw back bolts but a brass hook and eye defeats them. Have you ever tried that?"

"I'm afraid we're not very good at bolts and bars," said Miss Blacklock cheerfully. "There's really nothing much to burgle."

"A chain on the front door," Miss Marple advised. "Then the maid need only open it a crack and see who is there and they can't force their way in."

"I expect Mitzi, our Mittel European, would love that."

"The hold-up you had must have been very, very frightening," said Miss Marple. "Bunch has been telling me all about it."

"I was scared stiff," said Bunch.

123

"It was an alarming experience," admitted Miss Blacklock.

"It really seems like Providence that the man tripped himself up and shot himself. These burglars are so *violent* nowadays. How did he get in?"

"Well, I'm afraid we don't lock our doors much."

"Oh, Letty," exclaimed Miss Bunner. "I forgot to tell you the Inspector was most peculiar this morning. He insisted on opening the second door—you know—the one that's never been opened—the one over there. He hunted for the key and everything and said the door had been oiled. But I can't see why because——"

Too late she got Miss Blacklock's signal to be quiet, and paused open-mouthed.

"Oh, Lotty, I'm so—sorry—I mean, oh, I *do* beg your pardon, Letty—oh, dear, how stupid I am."

"It doesn't matter," said Miss Blacklock, but she was annoyed. "Only I don't think Inspector Craddock wants that talked about. I didn't know you had been there when he was experimenting, Dora. You do understand, don't you, Mrs. Harmon?"

"Oh, yes," said Bunch. "We won't breathe a word, will we, Aunt Jane. But I wonder *why* he——"

She relapsed into thought. Miss Bunner fidgeted and looked miserable, bursting out at last: "I always say the wrong thing—Oh, dear, I'm nothing but a trial to you, Letty."

Miss Blacklock said quickly, "You're my great comfort, Dora. And anyway in a small place like Chipping Cleghorn, there aren't really any secrets."

"Now that is very true," said Miss Marple. "I'm afraid, you know, that things do get round in the most extraordinary way. Servants, of course, and yet it can't only be that, because one has so few servants nowadays. Still, there are the daily women and perhaps they are worse, because they go to everybody in turn and pass the news round."

"Oh!" said Bunch Harmon suddenly. "I've got it! Of course, if that door could open too, someone might have gone out of here in the dark and done the hold-up —only of course they didn't—because it was the man from the Royal Spa Hotel. Or wasn't it? . . . No, I don't see after all . . ." she frowned.

"Did it all happen in this room then?" asked Miss Marple, adding apologetically: "I'm afraid you must think me sadly *curious*, Miss Blacklock—but it really is so very exciting—just like something one reads about in the paper—and actually to have happened to someone one knows . . . I'm just longing to hear all about it and to picture it all, if you know what I mean——"

Immediately Miss Marple received a confused and voluble account from Bunch and Miss Bunner—with occasional emendations and corrections from Miss Blacklock.

In the middle of it Patrick came in and good-naturedly entered into the spirit of the recital—going so far as to enact himself the part of Rudi Scherz.

"And Aunt Letty was there—in the corner by the archway . . . Go and stand there, Aunt Letty."

Miss Blacklock obeyed, and then Miss Marple was shown the actual bullet holes.

"What a marvellous—what a providential escape," she gasped.

"I was just going to offer my guests cigarettes——" Miss Blacklock indicated the big silver box on the table.

"People are so careless when they smoke," said Miss Bunner disapprovingly. "Nobody really respects good furniture as they used to do. Look at the horrid burn somebody made on this beautiful table by putting a cigarette down on it. *Disgraceful.*"

Miss Blacklock sighed.

"Sometimes, I'm afraid, one thinks too much of one's possessions."

"But it's such a lovely table, Letty."

Miss Bunner loved her friend's possessions with as much fervour as though they had been her own. Bunch Harmon had always thought it was a very endearing trait in her. She showed no sign of envy.

"It is a lovely table," said Miss Marple politely. "And what a very pretty china lamp on it."

Again it was Miss Bunner who accepted the compliment as though she and not Miss Blacklock was the owner of the lamp.

"Isn't it delightful? Dresden. There is a pair of them. The other's in the spare room, I think."

"You know where everything in this house is, Dora—or you think you do," said Miss Blacklock, good-humouredly. "You care far more about my things than I do."

Miss Bunner flushed.

"I *do* like nice things," she said. Her voice was half defiant—half wistful.

"I must confess," said Miss Marple, "that my own few possessions are very dear to me, too—so many *memories*, you know. It's the same with photographs. People nowadays have so few photographs about. Now I like to keep all the pictures of my nephews and nieces as babies—and then as children—and so on."

"You've got a horrible one of me, aged three," said Bunch. "Holding a fox terrier and squinting."

"I expect your aunt has many photographs of you," said Miss Marple, turning to Patrick.

"Oh, we're only distant cousins," said Patrick.

"I believe Elinor did send me one of you as a baby, Pat," said Miss Blacklock. "But I'm afraid I didn't keep it. I'd really forgotten how many children she'd had or what their names were until she wrote me about you two being over here."

"Another sign of the times," said Miss Marple. "Nowadays one so often doesn't know one's younger relations *at all*. In the old days, with all the big family reunions, that would have been impossible."

"I last saw Pat and Julia's mother at a wedding thirty years ago," said Miss Blacklock. "She was a very pretty girl."

"That's why she has such handsome children," said Patrick with a grin.

"You've got a marvellous old album," said Julia. "Do you remember, Aunt Letty, we looked through it the other day. The hats!"

"And how smart we thought ourselves," said Miss Blacklock with a sigh.

"Never mind, Aunt Letty," said Patrick, "Julia will come across a snapshot of herself in about thirty years' time—and won't she think she looks a guy!"

"Did you do that on purpose?" said Bunch, as she and Miss Marple were walking home. "Talk about photographs I mean?"

"Well, my dear, it *is* interesting to know that Miss Blacklock didn't know either of her two young relatives by sight. . . . Yes—I think Inspector Craddock will be interested to hear that."

127

CHAPTER XII

MORNING ACTIVITIES IN CHIPPING
CLEGHORN

EDMUND SWETTENHAM sat down rather precariously on a garden roller.

" Good morning, Phillipa," he said.

" Hallo."

" Are you very busy?"

" Moderately."

" What are you doing?"

" Can't you see?"

" No. I'm not a gardener. You seem to be playing with earth in some fashion."

" I'm pricking out winter lettuce."

" Pricking out? What a curious term! Like pinking. Do you know what pinking is? I only learnt the other day. I always thought it was a term for professional duelling."

" Do you want anything particular?" asked Phillipa coldly.

" Yes. I want to see you."

Phillipa gave him a quick glance.

" I wish you wouldn't come here like this. Mrs. Lucas won't like it."

" Doesn't she allow you to have followers?"

" Don't be absurd."

" Followers. That's another nice word. It describes my attitude perfectly. Respectful—at a distance—but firmly pursuing."

" Please go away, Edmund. You've no business to come here."

128

"You're wrong," said Edmund triumphantly. "I *have* business here. Mrs. Lucas rang up my mamma this morning and said she had a good many vegetable marrows."

"Masses of them."

"And would we like to exchange a pot of honey for a vegetable marrow or so."

"That's not a fair exchange at all! Vegetable marrows are quite unsaleable at the moment—everybody has such a lot."

"Naturally. That's why Mrs. Lucas rang up. Last time, if I remember rightly, the exchange suggested was some skim milk—*skim* milk, mark you—in exchange for some lettuces. It was then very early in the season for lettuces. They were about a shilling each."

Phillipa did not speak.

Edmund tugged at his pocket and extracted a pot of honey.

"So here," he said, "is my alibi. Used in a loose and quite indefensible meaning of the term. If Mrs. Lucas pops her bust round the door of the potting shed, I'm here in quest of vegetable marrows. There is absolutely no question of dalliance."

"I see."

"Do you ever read Tennyson?" inquired Edmund conversationally.

"Not very often."

"You should. Tennyson is shortly going to make a come-back in a big way. When you turn on your wireless in the evening it will be the *Idyls of the King* you will hear and not interminable Trollope. I always thought the Trollope pose was the most unbearable affectation. Perhaps a little of Trollope, but not to drown in him. But speaking of Tennyson, have you read 'Maud'?"

129

" Once, long ago."

" It's got some points about it." He quoted softly:
" ' Faultily faultless, icily regular, splendidly null.' That's
you, Phillipa."

" Hardly a compliment !"

" No, it wasn't meant to be. I gather Maud got under
the poor fellow's skin just like you've got under mine."

" Don't be absurd, Edmund."

" Oh, hell, Phillipa, why are you like you are? What
goes on behind your splendidly regular features? What
do you think? What do you *feel*? Are you happy, or
miserable, or frightened, or what? There must be
something."

Phillipa said quietly.

" What I feel is my own business."

" It's mine, too. I want to make you talk. I want to
know what goes on in that quiet head of yours. I've a
right to know. I have really. I didn't want to fall in
love with you. I wanted to sit quietly and write my book.
Such a nice book, all about how miserable the world is.
It's frightfully easy to be clever about how miserable
everybody is. And it's all a habit, really. Yes, I've suddenly become convinced of that. After reading a life of
Burne Jones."

Phillipa had stopped pricking out. She was staring at
him with a puzzled frown.

" What has Burne Jones got to do with it?"

" Everything. When you've read all about the Pre-
Raphaelites you realise just what fashion is. They were
all terrifically hearty and slangy and jolly, and laughed
and joked, and everything was fine and wonderful. That
was fashion, too. They weren't any happier or heartier
than we are. And we're not any more miserable than
they were. It's all fashion, I tell you. After the last war,
we went in for sex. Now it's all frustration. None of it

matters. Why are we talking about all this? I started out to talk about *us*. Only I got cold feet and shied off. Because you won't help me."

" What do you want me to do?"

" *Talk!* Tell me things. Is it your husband? Do you adore him and he's dead and so you've shut up like a clam? Is that it? All right, you adored him, and he's dead. Well, other girls' husbands are dead—lots of them—and some of the girls loved their husbands. They tell you so in bars, and cry a bit when they're drunk enough, and then want to go to bed with you so that they'll feel better. It's one way of getting over it, I suppose. You've got to get over it, Phillipa. You're young —and you're extremely lovely—and I love you like Hell. Talk about your damned husband, tell me about him."

" There's nothing to tell. We met and got married."

" You must have been very young."

" Too young."

" Then you weren't happy with him? Go *on*, Phillipa."

" There's nothing to go on about. We were married. We were as happy as most people are, I suppose. Harry was born. Ronald went overseas. He—he was killed in Italy."

" And now there's Harry?"

" And now there's Harry."

" I like Harry. He's a really nice kid. He likes me. We get on. What about it, Phillipa? Shall we get married? You can go on gardening and I can go on writing my book and in the holidays we'll leave off working and enjoy ourselves. We can manage, with tact, not to have to live with Mother. She can fork out a bit to support her adored son. I sponge, I write tripey books, I have defective eyesight and I talk too much. That's the worst. Will you try it?"

Phillipa looked at him. She saw a tall rather solemn

131

young man with an anxious face and large spectacles. His sandy head was rumpled and he was regarding her with a reassuring friendliness.

" No," said Phillipa.

" Definitely no?"

" Definitely no."

" Why?"

" You don't know anything about me."

" Is that all?"

" No, you don't know anything about anything."

Edmund considered.

" Perhaps not," he admitted. " But who does? Phillipa, my adored one——" He broke off.

A shrill and prolonged yapping was rapidly approaching.

" *Pekes in the high hall garden,* (said Edmund)
When twilight was falling (only it's eleven a.m.)
Phil, Phil, Phil, Phil,
They were crying and calling

" Your name doesn't lend itself to the rhythm, does it? Sounds like an ' Ode to a Fountain Pen.' Have you got another name?"

" Joan. *Please* go away. That's Mrs. Lucas."

" *Joan, Joan, Joan, Joan.* Better, but still not good. *When greasy Joan the pot doth keel*—that's not a nice picture of married life, either."

" Mrs. Lucas is——"

" Oh, *hell!*" said Edmund. " Get me a blasted vegetable marrow."

11

Sergeant Fletcher had the house at Little Paddocks to himself.

132

It was Mitzi's day off. She always went by the eleven o'clock bus into Medenham Wells. By arrangement with Miss Blacklock, Sergeant Fletcher had the run of the house. She and Dora Bunner had gone down to the village.

Fletcher worked fast. Someone in the house had oiled and prepared that door, and whoever had done it, had done it in order to be able to leave the drawing-room unnoticed as soon as the lights went out. That ruled out Mitzi who wouldn't have needed to use the door.

Who was left? The neighbours, Fletcher thought, might also be ruled out. He didn't see how they could have found an opportunity to oil and prepare the door. That left Patrick and Julia Simmons, Phillipa Haymes, and possibly Dora Bunner. The young Simmons were in Milchester. Phillipa Haymes was at work. Sergeant Fletcher was free to search out any secrets he could. But the house was disappointingly innocent. Fletcher, who was an expert on electricity could find nothing suggestive in the wiring or appurtenances of the electric fixtures to show how the lights had been fused. Making a rapid survey of the household bedrooms he found an irritating normality. In Phillipa Haymes' room were photographs of a small boy with serious eyes, an earlier photo of the same child, a pile of schoolboy letters, a theatre programme or two. In Julia's room there was a drawer full of snapshots of the South of France. Bathing photos, a villa set amidst mimosa. Patrick's held some souvenirs of Naval days. Dora Bunner's held few personal possessions and they seemed innocent enough.

And yet, thought Fletcher, someone in the house must have oiled that door.

His thoughts broke off at a sound below stairs. He went quickly to the top of the staircase and looked down.

Mrs. Swettenham was crossing the hall. She had a basket on her arm. She looked into the drawing-room, crossed the hall and went into the dining-room. She came out again without the basket.

Some faint sound that Fletcher made, a board that creaked unexpectedly under his feet, made her turn her head. She called up:

" Is that you, Miss Blacklock?"

" No, Mrs. Swettenham, it's me," said Fletcher.

Mrs. Swettenham gave a faint scream.

"Oh! how you startled me. I thought it might be another burglar."

Fletcher came down the stairs.

" This house doesn't seem very well protected against burglars," he said. " Can anybody always walk in and out just as they like?"

" I just brought up some of my quinces," explained Mrs. Swettenham. " Miss Blacklock wants to make quince jelly and she hasn't got a quince tree here. I left them in the dining-room."

Then she smiled.

" Oh, I see, you mean how did I get in? Well, I just came in through the side door. We all walk in and out of each other's houses, Sergeant. Nobody dreams of locking a door until it's dark. I mean it would be so awkward, wouldn't it, if you brought things and couldn't get in to leave them? It's not like the old days when you rang a bell and a servant always came to answer it." Mrs. Swettenham sighed. " In India, I remember," she said mournfully, " we had eighteen servants—eighteen. Not counting the *ayah*. Just as a matter of course. And at home, when I was a girl, we always had three— although Mother always felt it was terribly poverty stricken not to be able to afford a kitchen-maid. I must say that I find life very odd nowadays, Sergeant, though

I know one mustn't complain. So much worse for the miners always getting psittiscosis (or is that parrot disease?) and having to come out of the mines and try to be gardeners though they don't know weeds from spinach."

She added, as she tripped towards the door, " I mustn't keep you. I expect you're very busy. Nothing else is going to happen, is it?"

" Why should it, Mrs. Swettenham?"

" I just wondered, seeing you here. I thought it might be a *gang*. You'll tell Miss Blacklock about the quinces, won't you?"

Mrs. Swettenham departed. Fletcher felt like a man who has received an unexpected jolt. He had been assuming—erroneously, he now perceived—that it must have been someone in the house who had done the oiling of the door. He saw now that he was wrong. An outsider had only to wait until Mitzi had departed by bus and Letitia Blacklock and Dora Bunner were both out of the house. Such an opportunity must have been simplicity itself. That meant that he couldn't rule out anybody who had been in the drawing-room that night.

III

" Murgatroyd."

" Yes, Hinch?"

" I've been doing a bit of thinking?"

" Have you, Hinch?"

" Yes, the great brain has been working. You know, Murgatroyd, the whole set-up the other evening was decidedly fishy."

" Fishy?"

"Yes. Tuck your hair up, Murgatroyd, and take this trowel. Pretend it's a revolver."

"Oh," said Miss Murgatroyd, nervously.

"All right. It won't bite you. Now come along to the kitchen door. You're going to be the burglar. You stand *here*. Now you're going into the kitchen to hold up a lot of nit-wits. Take the torch. Switch it on."

"But it's broad daylight!"

"Use your imagination, Murgatroyd. Switch it on."

Miss Murgatroyd did so, rather clumsily, shifting the trowel under one arm while she did so.

"Now then," said Miss Hinchliffe, "off you go. Remember the time you played Hermia in *A Midsummer Night's Dream* at the Women's Institute? Act. Give it all you've got. 'Stick 'em up!' Those are your lines—and don't ruin them by saying 'Please.' "

Obediently, Miss Murgatroyd raised her torch, flourished the trowel and advanced on the kitchen door.

Transferring the torch to her right hand she swiftly turned the handle and stepped forward, resuming the torch in her left hand.

"Stick 'em up!" she fluted, adding vexedly: "Dear me, this is very difficult, Hinch."

"Why?"

"The door. It's a swing door, it keeps coming back and I've got both hands full."

"Exactly," boomed Miss Hinchliffe. "And the drawing-room door at Little Paddocks always swings to. It isn't a swing door like this, but it won't stay open. That's why Letty Blacklock bought that absolutely delectable heavy glass doorstop from Elliot's in the High Street. I don't mind saying I've never forgiven her for getting in ahead of me there. I was beating the old brute down from eight guineas to six pound ten, and then Blacklock comes along and buys the damned thing. I'd never seen

136

as attractive a doorstop, you don't often get those glass bubbles in that big size."

" Perhaps the burglar put the doorstop against the door to keep it open," suggested Miss Murgatroyd.

" Use your common sense, Murgatroyd. What does he do? Throw the door open, say ' excuse me a moment,' stoop and put the stop into position and then resume business by saying ' Hands up?' Try holding the door with your shoulder."

" It's still very awkward," complained Miss Murgatroyd.

" Exactly," said Miss Hinchliffe. " A revolver, a torch and a door to hold open—a bit too much, isn't it? So what's the answer?"

Miss Murgatroyd did not attempt to supply an answer. She looked inquiringly and admiringly at her masterful friend and waited to be enlightened.

" We know he'd got a revolver, because he fired it," said Miss Hinchliffe. " And we know he had a torch because we all saw it—that is unless we're all the victims of mass hypnotism like explanations of the Indian Rope trick (what a bore that old Easterbrook is with his Indian stories) so the question is, did someone hold that door open for him?"

" But who could have done that?"

" Well, you could have for one, Murgatroyd. As far as I remember, you were standing directly behind it when the lights went out." Miss Hinchliffe laughed heartily. " Highly suspicious character, aren't you, Murgatroyd? But who'd think it to look at you. Here, give me that trowel—thank heavens it isn't really a revolver. You'd have shot yourself by now!"

IV

" It's a most extraordinary thing," muttered Colonel Easterbrook. " Most extraordinary. Laura."

" Yes, darling?"

" Come into my dressing-room a moment."

" What is it, darling?"

Mrs. Easterbrook appeared through the open door.

" Remember my showing you that revolver of mine?"

" Oh, yes, Archie, a nasty horrid black thing."

" Yes. Hun souvenir. Was in this drawer, wasn't it?"

" Yes, it was."

" Well, it's not there now."

" Archie, how *extraordinary*!"

" You haven't moved it or anything?"

" Oh, no, I'd never dare to touch the horrid thing."

" Think old mother wha.'sername did?"

" Oh, I shouldn't think so, for a minute. Mrs. Butt would never do a thing like that. Shall I ask her?"

" No—no, better not. Don't want to start a lot of talk. Tell me, do you remember when it was I showed it to you?"

" Oh, about a week ago. You were grumbling about your collars and the laundry and you opened this drawer wide and there it was at the back and I asked you what it was."

" Yes, that's right. About a week ago. You don't remember the date?"

Mrs. Easterbrook considered, eyelids down over her eyes, a shrewd brain working.

" Of course," she said. " It was Saturday. The day we were to have gone in to the pictures, but we didn't."

" H'm—sure it wasn't before that? Wednesday? Thursday or even the week before that again?"

"No, dear," said Mrs. Easterbrook. " I remember *quite* distinctly. It was Saturday the 30th. It just seems a long time because of all the trouble there's been. And I can tell you *how* I remember. It's because it was the day after the hold-up at Miss Blacklock's. Because when I saw your revolver it reminded me of the shooting the night before."

" Ah," said Colonel Easterbrook, " then that's a great load off my mind."

" Oh, Archie, why?"

" Just because if that revolver had disappeared before the shooting—well, it might possibly have been my revolver that was pinched by that Swiss fellow."

" But how would he have known you had one?"

" These gangs have a most extraordinary communication service. They get to know everything about a place and who lives there."

" What a lot you do know, Archie."

" Ha. Yes. Seen a thing or two in my time. Still as you definitely remember seeing my revolver *after* the hold-up—well, that settles it. The revolver that Swiss fellow used can't have been mine, can it?"

" Of course it can't."

" A great relief. I should have had to go to the police about it. And they ask a lot of awkward questions. Bound to. As a matter of fact I never took out a licence for it. Somehow, after a war, one forgets these peacetime regulations. I looked on it as a war souvenir, not as a firearm."

" Yes, I see. Of course."

" But all the same—where on earth can the damned thing be?"

" Perhaps Mrs. Butt took it. She's always seemed

quite honest, but perhaps she felt nervous after the hold-up and thought she'd like to—to have a revolver in the house. Of course, she'll never admit doing that. I shan't even ask her. She might get offended. And what should we do then? This is such a big house—I simply couldn't——"

"Quite so," said Colonel Easterbrook. "Better not say anything."

140

CHAPTER XIII

MORNING ACTIVITIES IN CHIPPING CLEGHORN
(continued)

MISS MARPLE came out of the Vicarage gate and walked down the little lane that led into the main street.

She walked fairly briskly with the aid of the Rev. Julian Harmon's stout ashplant stick.

She passed the Red Cow and the butcher's and stopped for a brief moment to look into the window of Mr. Elliot's antique shop. This was cunningly situated next door to the Bluebird Tearooms and Café so that rich motorists, after stopping for a nice cup of tea and somewhat euphemistically named " Home Made Cakes " of a bright saffron colour, could be tempted by Mr. Elliot's judiciously planned shop window.

In this antique bow frame, Mr. Elliot catered for all tastes. Two pieces of Waterford glass reposed on an impeccable wine cooler. A walnut bureau, made up of various bits and pieces proclaimed itself a Genuine Bargain and on a table, in the window itself, were a nice assortment of cheap doorknockers and quaint pixies, a few chipped bits of Dresden, a couple of sad-looking bead necklaces, a mug with " A Present from Tunbridge Wells " on it, and some tit-bits of Victorian silver.

Miss Marple gave the window her rapt attention, and Mr. Elliot, an elderly obese spider, peeped out of his web to appraise the possibilities of this new fly.

But just as he decided that the charms of the Present from Tunbridge Wells were about to be too much for the

141

lady who was staying at the Vicarage (for of course Mr. Elliot, like everybody else, knew exactly who she was), Miss Marple saw out of the corner of her eye Miss Dora Bunner entering the Bluebird Café, and immediately decided that what she needed to counteract the cold wind was a nice cup of morning coffee.

Four or five ladies were already engaged in sweetening their morning shopping by a pause for refreshment. Miss Marple, blinking a little in the gloom of the interior of the Bluebird, and hovering artistically, was greeted by the voice of Dora Bunner at her elbow.

"Oh, good morning, Miss Marple. Do sit down here. I'm all alone."

"Thank you."

Miss Marple subsided gratefully on to the rather angular little blue-painted arm-chair which the Bluebird affected.

"Such a sharp wind," she complained. "And I can't walk very fast because of my rheumatic leg."

"Oh, I know. I had sciatica one year—and really, most of the time I was in *agony*."

The two ladies talked rheumatism, sciatica and neuritis for some moments with avidity. A sulky-looking girl in a pink overall with a flight of bluebirds down the front of it took their order for coffee and cakes with a yawn and an air of weary patience.

"The cakes," Miss Bunner said in a conspiratorial whisper, "are really *quite* good here."

"I was so interested in that very pretty girl I met as we were coming away from Miss Blacklock's the other day," said Miss Marple. "I think she said she does gardening. Or is she on the land? Hynes—was that her name?"

"Oh, yes, Phillipa Haymes. Our 'Lodger,' as we call her." Miss Bunner laughed at her own humour.

"Such a nice quiet girl. A *lady*, if you know what I mean."

"I wonder now. I knew a Colonel Haymes—in the Indian cavalry. Her father perhaps?"

"She's *Mrs.* Haymes. A widow. Her husband was killed in Sicily or Italy. Of course, it might be *his* father."

"I wondered, perhaps, if there might be a little romance on the way?" Miss Marple suggested roguishly. "With that tall young man?"

"With Patrick, do you mean? Oh, I don't——"

"No, I meant a young man with spectacles. I've seen him about."

"Oh, of course, Edmund Swettenham. Sh! That's his mother, Mrs. Swettenham, over in the corner. I don't know, I'm sure. You think he admires her? He's such an odd young man—says the most disturbing things sometimes. He's supposed to be *clever*, you know," said Miss Bunner with frank disapproval.

"Cleverness isn't everything," said Miss Marple, shaking her head. "Ah, here is our coffee."

The sulky girl deposited it with a clatter. Miss Marple and Miss Bunner pressed cakes on each other.

"I was so interested to hear you were at school with Miss Blacklock. Yours is indeed an old friendship."

"Yes, indeed." Miss Bunner sighed. "Very few people would be as loyal to their old friends as dear Miss Blacklock is. Oh, dear, those days seem a long time ago. Such a pretty girl and enjoyed life so much. It all seemed so *sad*."

Miss Marple, though with no idea of what had seemed so sad, sighed and shook her head.

"Life is indeed hard," she murmured.

"*And sad affliction bravely borne,*" murmured Miss Bunner, her eyes suffusing with tears. "I always think

143

of that verse. True patience; true resignation. Such courage and patience *ought* to be rewarded, that is what I say. What I feel is that *nothing* is too good for dear Miss Blacklock, and whatever good things come to her, she truly *deserves* them."

" Money," said Miss Marple, " can do a lot to ease one's path in life."

She felt herself safe in this observation since she judged that it must be Miss Blacklock's prospects of future affluence to which her friend referred.

The remark, however, started Miss Bunner on another train of thought.

" Money!" she exclaimed with bitterness. " I don't believe, you know, that until one has really experienced it, one can know what money, or rather the lack of it, *means*."

Miss Marple nodded her white head sympathetically.

Miss Bunner went on rapidly, working herself up, and speaking with a flushed face :

" I've heard people say so often ' I'd rather have flowers on the table than a meal without them.' But how many meals have those people ever missed? They don't know what it is—nobody knows who hasn't been through it—to be really *hungry*. Bread, you know, and a jar of meat paste, and a scrape of margarine. Day after day, and how one longs for a good plate of meat and two vegetables. And the *shabbiness*. Darning one's clothes and hoping it won't show. And applying for jobs and always being told you're too old. And then perhaps getting a job and after all one isn't strong enough. One faints. And you're back again. It's the *rent*—always the *rent*—that's *got* to be paid—otherwise you're out in the street. And in these days it leaves so little over. One's old age pension doesn't go far—indeed it doesn't."

144

"I know," said Miss Marple gently. She looked with compassion at Miss Bunner's twitching face.

"I wrote to Letty. I just happened to see her name in the paper. It was a luncheon in aid of Milchester Hospital. There it was in black and white, Miss Letitia Blacklock. It brought the past back to me. I hadn't heard of her for years and years. She'd been secretary, you know, to that very rich man, Goedler. She was always a clever girl—the kind that gets on in the world. Not so much looks—as *character*. I thought—well, I thought—perhaps she'll remember me—and she's one of the people I *could* ask for a little help. I mean someone you've known as a girl—been at school with—well, they do *know* about you—they know you're not just a—begging letter writer——"

Tears came into Dora Bunner's eyes.

"And then Lotty came and took me away—said she needed someone to help her. Of course, I was very surprised—*very* surprised—but then newspapers do get things wrong. How kind she was—and how *sympathetic*. And remembering all the old days so well . . . I'd do anything for her—I really would. And I try *very* hard, but I'm afraid sometimes I muddle things—my head's not what it was. I make mistakes. And I forget and say foolish things. She's very patient. What's so nice about her is that she always pretends that I *am* useful to her. That's real kindness, isn't it?"

Miss Marple said gently: "Yes, that's real kindness."

"I used to worry, you know, even after I came to Little Paddocks—about what would become of me if—if anything were to happen to Miss Blacklock. After all, there are so many accidents—these motors dashing about—one never knows, does one? But naturally I never *said* anything—but she must have guessed. Suddenly, one day she told me that she'd left me a small annuity

145

in her will—and—what I value far more—all her beautiful furniture. I was quite *overcome* . . . But she said
nobody else would value it as I should—and that is quite
true—I can't bear to see some lovely piece of china
smashed—or wet glasses put down on a table and leaving
a mark. I do really look after her things. Some people
—some people especially, are so terribly careless—and
sometimes worse than careless!

"I'm not really as stupid as I look," Miss Bunner
continued with simplicity. "I can see, you know, when
Letty's being imposed upon. Some people—I won't
name names—but they take *advantage*. Dear Miss
Blacklock is, perhaps, just a shade too *trusting*."

Miss Marple shook her head.

"*That's* a mistake."

"Yes, it is. You and I, Miss Marple, know the world.
Dear Miss Blacklock——" She shook her head.

Miss Marple thought that as the secretary of a big
financier Miss Blacklock might be presumed to know the
world too. But probably what Dora Bunner meant was
that Letty Blacklock had always been comfortably off,
and that the comfortably off do not know the deeper
abysses of human nature.

"That Patrick!" said Miss Bunner with a suddenness
and an asperity that made Miss Marple jump. "Twice,
at least, to my knowledge, he's got money out of her.
Pretending he's hard up. Run into debt. All that sort of
thing. She's far too generous. All she said to me when
I remonstrated with her was: 'The boy's young, Dora.
Youth is the time to have your fling.'"

"Well, that's true enough," said Miss Marple. "Such
a handsome young man, too."

"Handsome is as handsome does," said Dora Bunner.
"Much too fond of poking fun at people. And a lot of
going on with girls. I expect. I'm just a figure of fun to

146

him—that's all. He doesn't seem to realise that people have their feelings."

"Young people *are* rather careless that way," said Miss Marple.

Miss Bunner leaned forward suddenly with a mysterious air.

"You won't breathe a word, will you, my dear?" she demanded. "But I can't help feeling that he *was* mixed up in this dreadful business. I think he knew that young man—or else Julia did. I daren't hint at such a thing to dear Miss Blacklock—at least I did, and she just snapped my head off. And, of course, it's *awkward*—because he's her nephew—or at any rate her *cousin*—and if the Swiss young man shot himself Patrick might be held morally responsible, mightn't he? If he'd put him up to it, I mean. I'm really terribly confused about the whole thing. Everyone making such a fuss about that other door into the drawing-room. That's another thing that worries me—the detective saying it had been oiled. Because you see, I saw——"

She came to an abrupt stop.

Miss Marple paused to select a phrase.

"Most difficult for you," she said sympathetically. "Naturally you wouldn't want anything to get round to the police."

"That's just it," Dora Bunner cried. "I lie awake at nights and worry . . . because, you see, I came upon Patrick in the shrubbery the other day. I was looking for eggs—one hen lays out—and there he was holding a feather and a cup—an oily cup. And he jumped most guiltily when he saw me and he said: 'I was just wondering what this was doing here.' Well, of course, he's a quick thinker. I should say he thought that up quickly when I startled him. And how did he come to find a thing like that in the shrubbery unless he was looking for

147

it, knowing perfectly well it was there. Of course, I didn't *say* anything."

"No, no, of course not."

"But I gave him a *look*, if you know what I mean."

Dora Bunner stretched out her hand and bit abstractedly into a lurid salmon coloured cake.

"And then another day I happened to overhear him having a very curious conversation with Julia. They seemed to be having a kind of quarrel. He was saying: 'If I thought you had anything to do with a thing like that!' and Julia (she's always so calm, you know) said: 'Well, little brother, what would you do about it?' And then, *most* unfortunately, I trod on that board that always squeaks, and they saw me. So I said, quite gaily: 'You two having a quarrel?' and Patrick said, 'I'm warning Julia not to go in for these black market deals.' Oh, it was all very slick, but I don't believe they were talking about anything of the sort! And if you ask me, I believe Patrick had tampered with that lamp in the drawing-room—to make the lights go out, because I remember distinctly that it was the shepherdess—*not* the shepherd. And the next day——"

She stopped and her face grew pink. Miss Marple turned her head to see Miss Blacklock, standing behind them—she must just have come in.

"Coffee and gossip, Bunny?" said Miss Blacklock with quite a shade of reproach in her voice. "Good morning, Miss Marple. Cold, isn't it?"

"We were just talking," said Miss Bunner, hurriedly. "So many rules and regulations nowadays. One really doesn't know where one is."

The doors flew open with a clang and Bunch Harmon came into the Bluebird with a rush.

"Hallo," she said, "am I too late for coffee?"

148

"No, dear," said Miss Marple. "Sit down and have a cup."

"We must get home," said Miss Blacklock. "Done your shopping, Bunny?"

Her tone was indulgent once more, but her eyes still held a slight reproach.

"Yes—yes, thank you, Letty. I must just pop into the chemists' in passing and get some aspirin and some corn-plasters."

As the doors of the Bluebird swung to behind them, Bunch asked:

"What were you talking about?"

Miss Marple did not reply at once. She waited whilst Bunch gave the order, then she said:

"Family solidarity is a very strong thing. Very strong. Do you remember some famous case—I really can't remember what it was. They said the husband poisoned his wife. In a glass of wine. Then, at the trial, the daughter said she'd drunk half her mother's glass—so that knocked the case against her father to pieces. They do say—but that may be just rumour—that she never spoke to her father or lived with him again. Of course, a father is one thing—and a nephew or a distant cousin is another. But still there it is—no one wants a member of their own family hanged, do they?"

"No," said Bunch, considering. "I shouldn't think they would."

Miss Marple leaned back in her chair. She murmured under her breath, "People are really very alike, everywhere."

"Who am I like?"

"Well, really, dear, you are very much like yourself. I don't know that you remind me of anyone in particular. Except perhaps——"

"Here it comes," said Bunch.

"I was just thinking of a parlourmaid of mine, dear."

"A parlourmaid? I should make a terrible parlour-maid."

"Yes, dear, so did she. She was no good at all at waiting at table. Put everything on the table crooked, mixed up the kitchen knives with the dining-room ones, and her cap (this was a long time ago, dear) her cap was *never* straight."

Bunch adjusted her hat automatically.

"Anything else?" she demanded anxiously.

"I kept her because she was so pleasant to have about the house—and because she used to make me laugh. I liked the way she said things straight out. Came to me one day, 'Of course, I don't know, m'am,' she says, 'but Florrie, the way she sits down, it's just like a married woman.' And sure enough poor Florrie was in trouble—the gentlemanly assistant at the hairdresser's. Fortunately it was in good time, and I was able to have a little talk with him, and they had a very nice wedding and settled down quite happily. She was a good girl, Florrie, but inclined to be taken in by a gentlemanly appearance."

"She didn't do a murder, did she?" asked Bunch. "The parlourmaid, I mean."

"No, indeed," said Miss Marple. "She married a Baptist Minister and they had a family of five."

"Just like me," said Bunch. "Though I've only got as far as Edward and Susan up to date."

She added, after a minute or two:

"Who are you thinking about now, Aunt Jane?"

"Quite a lot of people, dear, quite a lot of people," said Miss Marple, vaguely.

"In St. Mary Mead?"

"Mostly . . . I was really thinking about Nurse Eller-ton—really an excellent kindly woman. Took care of an old lady, seemed really fond of her. Then the old lady died. And another came and *she* died. Morphia. It all came out. Done in the kindest way, and the shocking thing was that the woman herself really couldn't see that she'd done anything wrong. They hadn't long to live in any case, she said, and one of them had cancer and quite a lot of pain."

"You mean—it was a mercy killing?"

"No, *no*. They signed their money away to her. She liked money, you know. . . .

"And then there was that young man on the liner—Mrs. Pusey at the paper shop, *her* nephew. Brought home stuff he'd stolen and got her to dispose of it. Said it was things that he'd bought abroad. She was quite taken in. And then when the police came round and started asking questions, he tried to bash her on the head, so that she shouldn't be able to give him away. . . . Not a nice young man—but very good-looking. Had two girls in love with him. He spent a lot of money on one of them."

"The nastiest one, I suppose," said Bunch.

"Yes, dear. And there was Mrs. Cray at the wool shop. Devoted to her son, spoilt him, of course. He got in with a very queer lot. Do you remember Joan Croft, Bunch?"

"N-no, I don't think so."

"I thought you might have seen her when you were with me on a visit. Used to stalk about smoking a cigar or a pipe. We had a Bank hold-up once, and Joan Croft was in the Bank at the time. She knocked the man down and took his revolver away from him. She was congratulated on her courage by the Bench."

Bunch listened attentively. She seemed to be learning by heart.

"And——" she prompted.

"That girl at St. Jean des Collines that summer. Such a quiet girl—not so much quiet as silent. Everybody liked her, but they never got to know her much better. . . . We heard afterwards that her husband was a *forger*. It made her feel cut off from people. It made her, in the end, a little queer. Brooding does, you know."

"Any Anglo-Indian Colonels in your reminiscences, darling?"

"Naturally, dear. There was Major Vaughan at The Larches and Colonel Wright at Simla Lodge. Nothing wrong with either of them. But I do remember Mr. Hodgson, the Bank Manager, went on a cruise and married a woman young enough to be his daughter. No idea of where she came from—except what she told him of course."

"And that wasn't true?"

"No, dear, it definitely wasn't."

"Not bad," said Bunch nodding, and ticking people off on her fingers. "We've had devoted Dora, and handsome Patrick, and Mrs. Swettenham and Edmund, and Phillipa Haymes, and Colonel Easterbrook and Mrs. Easterbrook—and if you ask me, I should say you're absolutely right about *her*. But there wouldn't be any reason for her murdering Letty Blacklock."

"Miss Blacklock, of course, might know something about her that she didn't want known."

"Oh, darling, that old Tanqueray stuff? Surely that's dead as the hills."

"It might not be. You see, Bunch, you are not the kind that minds much about what people think of you."

"I see what you mean," said Bunch suddenly. "If you'd been up against it, and then, rather like a shivering stray cat, you'd found a home and a cream and a warm stroking hand and you were called Pretty Pussy and somebody thought the world of you . . . You'd do a lot to keep that . . . Well, I must say, you've presented me with a very complete gallery of people."

" You didn't get them all right, you know," said Miss Marple, mildly.

" Didn't I? Where did I slip up? Julia? *Julia, pretty Juliar is peculiar.*"

" Three and sixpence," said the sulky waitress, materialising out of the gloom.

" And," she added, her bosom heaving beneath the bluebirds, " I'd like to know, Mrs. Harmon, why you call me peculiar. I had an aunt who joined the Peculiar People, but I've always been good Church of England myself, as the late Rev. Hopkinson can tell you."

" I'm terribly sorry," said Bunch. " I was just quoting a song. I didn't mean you at all. I didn't know your name was Julia."

" Quite a coincidence," said the sulky waitress, cheering up. " No offence, I'm sure, but hearing my name, as I thought—well, naturally if you think someone's talking about you, it's only human nature to listen. Thank you."

She departed with her tip.

" Aunt Jane," said Bunch, " don't look so upset. What is it?"

" But surely," murmured Miss Marple. " That couldn't be so. There's no *reason*——"

" Aunt Jane!"

Miss Marple sighed and then smiled brightly.

" It's nothing, dear," she said.

" Did you think you knew who did the murder?" asked Bunch. " Who was it?"

" I don't know at all," said Miss Marple. " I got an idea for a moment—but it's gone. I wish I did know. Time's so short. So terribly short."

"What do you mean short?"

"That old lady up in Scotland may die any moment."

Bunch said, staring:

"Then you really do believe in Pip and Emma. You think it was them—and that they'll try again?"

"Of course they'll try again," said Miss Marple, almost absentmindedly. "If they tried once, they'll try again. If you've made up your mind to murder someone, you don't stop because the first time it didn't come off. Especially if you're fairly sure you're not suspected."

"But if it's Pip and Emma," said Bunch, "there are only two people it *could* be. It *must* be Patrick and Julia. They're brother and sister and they're the only ones who are the right age."

"My dear, it isn't nearly as simple as that. There are all sort of ramifications and combinations. There's Pip's wife if he's married, or Emma's husband. There's their mother—she's an interested party even if she doesn't inherit direct. If Letty Blacklock hasn't seen her for thirty years, she'd probably not recognise her now. One elderly woman is very like another. You remember Mrs. Wotherspoon drew her own and Mrs. Bartlett's Old Age Pension although Mrs. Bartlett had been dead for years. Anyway, Miss Blacklock's shortsighted. Haven't you noticed how she peers at people? And then there's the father. Apparently he was a real bad lot."

"Yes, but he's a foreigner."

"By birth. But there's no reason to believe he speaks broken English and gesticulates with his hands. I dare say he could play the part of—of an Anglo-Indian Colonel as well as anybody else."

"Is *that* what you think?"

"No, I don't. I don't indeed, dear. I just think that there's a great deal of money at stake, a great deal of money. And I'm afraid I know only too well the really terrible things that people will do to lay their hands on a lot of money."

"I suppose they will," said Bunch. "It doesn't really do them any good, does it? Not in the end?"

"No—but they don't usually know that."

"I can understand it." Bunch smiled suddenly, her sweet rather crooked smile. "One feels it would be different for oneself. . . . Even I feel that." She considered: "You pretend to yourself that you'd do a lot of good with all that money. Schemes . . . Homes for Unwanted Children . . . Tired Mothers . . . A lovely rest abroad somewhere for elderly women who have worked too hard. . . ."

Her face grew sombre. Her eyes were suddenly dark and tragic.

"I know what you're thinking," she said to Miss Marple. "You're thinking that I'd be the worst kind. Because I'd kid myself. If you just wanted the money for selfish reasons you'd at any rate *see* what you were like. But once you began to pretend about doing good with it, you'd be able to persuade yourself, perhaps, that it wouldn't very much matter killing someone. . . ."

Then her eyes cleared.

"But I shouldn't," she said. "I shouldn't really kill anyone. Not even if they were old, or ill, or doing a lot of harm in the world. Not even if they were blackmailers or—or absolute *beasts*." She fished a fly carefully out of the dregs of the coffee and arranged it on the table to dry. "Because people like living, don't they? So do flies. Even if you're old and in pain and you can just crawl out in the sun. Julian says those people like living even more than young strong people do. It's harder, he says, for them to die, the struggle's greater. I like living myself—not just being happy and enjoying myself and

155

having a good time. I mean *living*—waking up and feeling, all over me, that I'm *there*—ticking over."

She blew on the fly gently; it waved its legs, and flew rather drunkenly away.

"Cheer up, darling Aunt Jane," said Bunch. "*I'd* never kill anybody."

CHAPTER XIV

EXCURSION INTO THE PAST

AFTER a night in the train, Inspector Craddock alighted at a small station in the Highlands.

It struck him for a moment as strange that the wealthy Mrs. Goedler—an invalid—with a choice of a London house in a fashionable square, an estate in Hampshire, and a villa in the South of France, should have selected this remote Scottish home as her residence. Surely she was cut off here from many friends and distractions. It must be a lonely life—or was she too ill to notice or care about her surroundings?

A car was waiting to meet him. A big old-fashioned Daimler with an elderly chauffeur driving it. It was a sunny morning and the inspector enjoyed the twenty mile drive, though he marvelled anew at this preference for isolation. A tentative remark to the chauffeur brought partial enlightenment.

" It's her own home as a girl. Ay, she's the last of the family. And she and Mr. Goedler were always happier here than anywhere, though it wasn't often he could get away from London. But when he did they enjoyed themselves like a couple of bairns."

When the grey walls of the old keep came in sight, Craddock felt that time was slipping backwards. An elderly butler received him, and after a wash and a shave, he was shown into a room with a huge fire burning in the grate, and breakfast was served to him.

After breakfast, a tall middle-aged woman in nurse's

157

dress, with a pleasant and competent manner, came in and introduced herself as Sister McClelland.

" I have my patient all ready for you, Mr. Craddock. She is, indeed, looking forward to seeing you."

" I'll do my best not to excite her," Craddock promised.

" I had better warn you of what will happen. You will find Mrs. Goedler apparently quite normal. She will talk and enjoy talking and then—quite suddenly—her powers will fail. Come away at once, then, and send for me. She is, you see, kept almost entirely under the influence of morphia. She drowses most of the time. In preparation for your visit, I have given her a strong stimulant. As soon as the effect of the stimulant wears off, she will relapse into semi-consciousness."

" I quite understand, Miss McClelland. Would it be in order for you to tell me exactly what the state of Mrs. Goedler's health is?"

" Well, Mr. Craddock, she is a dying woman. Her life cannot be prolonged for more than a few weeks. To say that she should have been dead years ago would strike you as odd, yet it is the truth. What has kept Mrs. Goedler alive is her intense enjoyment and love of being alive. That sounds, perhaps, an odd thing to say of someone who has lived the life of an invalid for many years and has not left her home here for fifteen years, but it is true. Mrs. Goedler has never been a strong woman—but she has retained to an astonishing degree the will to live." She added with a smile, " She is a very charming woman, too, as you will find."

Craddock was shown into a large bedroom where a fire was burning and where an old lady lay in a large canopied bed. Though she was only about seven or eight years older than Letitia Blacklock, her fragility made her seem older than her years.

Her white hair was carefully arranged, a froth of pale

blue wool enveloped her neck and shoulders. There were lines of pain on the face, but lines of sweetness, too. And there was, strangely enough, what Craddock could only describe as a roguish twinkle in her faded blue eyes.

" Well, this is interesting," she said. " It's not often I receive a visit from the police. I hear Letitia Blacklock wasn't much hurt by this attempt on her? How is my dear Blackie?"

" She's very well, Mrs. Goedler. She sent you her love."

" It's a long time since I've seen her. . . . For many years now, it's been just a card at Christmas. I asked her to come up here when she came back to England after Charlotte's death, but she said it would be painful after so long and perhaps she was right. . . . Blackie always had a lot of sense. I had an old school friend to see me about a year ago, and Lor!"—she smiled—" we bored each other to death. After we'd finished all the ' Do you remembers?' there wasn't anything to say. Most embarrassing."

Craddock was content to let her talk before pressing his questions. He wanted, as it were, to get back into the past, to get the feel of the Goedler-Blacklock ménage.

" I suppose," said Belle shrewdly, " that you want to ask about the money? Randall left it all to go to Blackie after my death. Really, of course, Randall never dreamed that I'd outlive him. He was a big strong man, never a day's illness, and I was always a mass of aches and pains and complaints and doctors coming and pulling long faces over me."

" I don't think complaints would be the right word, Mrs. Goedler."

The old lady chuckled.

" I didn't mean it in the complaining sense. I've never been too sorry for myself. But it was always taken for granted that I, being the weakly one, would go first. It

159

didn't work out that way. No—it didn't work out that way. . . ."

"Why, exactly, did your husband leave his money the way he did?"

"You mean, why did he leave it to Blackie? Not for the reason you've probably been thinking." The roguish twinkle was very apparent. "What minds you policemen have! Randall was never in the least in love with her and she wasn't with him. Letitia, you know, has really got a man's mind. She hasn't any feminine feelings or weaknesses. I don't believe she was ever in love with any man. She was never particularly pretty and she didn't care for clothes. She used a little make-up in deference to prevailing custom, but not to make herself look prettier." There was pity in the old voice as she went on : "She never knew any of the fun of being a woman."

Craddock looked at the frail little figure in the big bed with interest. Belle Goedler, he realised, *had* enjoyed— still enjoyed—being a woman. She twinkled at him.

"I've always thought," she said, "it must be terribly dull to be a man."

Then she said thoughtfully :

"I think Randall looked on Blackie very much as a kind of younger brother. He relied on her judgment which was always excellent. She kept him out of trouble more than once, you know."

"She told me that she came to his rescue once with money?"

"That, yes, but I meant more than that. One can speak the truth after all these years. Randall couldn't really distinguish between what was crooked and what wasn't. His conscience wasn't sensitive. The poor dear really didn't know what was just smart—and what was dishonest. Blackie kept him straight. That's one thing about Letitia Blacklock, she's absolutely dead straight.

160

She would never do anything that was dishonest. She's a very fine character, you know. I've always admired her. They had a terrible girlhood, those girls. The father was an old country doctor—terrifically pig-headed and narrow-minded—the complete family tyrant. Letitia broke away, came to London, and trained herself as a chartered accountant. The other sister was an invalid, there was a deformity of kinds and she never saw people or went out. That's why when the old man died, Letitia gave up everything to go home and look after her sister. Randall was wild with her—but it made no difference. If Letitia thought a thing was her duty she'd do it. And you couldn't move her."

"How long was that before your husband died?"

"A couple of years, I think. Randall made his will before she left the firm, and he didn't alter it. He said to me: 'We've no one of our own.' (Our little boy died, you know, when he was two years old.) 'After you and I are gone, Blackie had better have the money. She'll play the markets and make 'em sit up.'

"You see," Belle went on, "Randall enjoyed the whole money-making game so much—it wasn't just the money—it was the adventure, the risks, the excitement of it all. And Blackie liked it too. She had the same adventurous spirit and the same judgment. Poor darling, she'd never had any of the usual fun—being in love, and leading men on and teasing them—and having a home and children and all the real fun of life."

Craddock thought it was odd, the real pity and indulgent contempt felt by this woman, a woman whose life had been hampered by illness, whose only child had died, whose husband had died, leaving her to a lonely widowhood, and who had been a hopeless invalid for years.

She nodded her head at him.

161

" I know what you're thinking. But I've *had* all the things that make life worthwhile—they may have been taken from me—but I have had them. I was pretty and gay as a girl, I married the man I loved, and he never stopped loving me . . . My child died, but I had him for two precious years . . . I've had a lot of physical pain —but if you have pain, you know how to enjoy the exquisite pleasure of the times when pain stops. And everyone's been kind to me, always. . . . I'm a lucky woman, really."

Craddock seized upon an opening in her former remarks.

" You said just now, Mrs. Goedler, that your husband left his fortune to Miss Blacklock because he had no one else to leave it to. But that's not strictly true, is it? He had a sister."

" Oh, Sonia. But they quarrelled years ago and made a clean break of it."

" He disapproved of her marriage?"

" Yes, she married a man called—now what was his name——?"

" Stamfordis."

" That's it. Dmitri Stamfordis. Randall always said he was a crook. The two men didn't like each other from the first. But Sonia was wildly in love with him and quite determined to marry him. And I really never saw why she shouldn't. Men have such odd ideas about these things. Sonia wasn't a mere girl—she was twenty-five, and she knew exactly what she was doing. He was a crook, I dare say—I mean really a crook. I believe he had a criminal record—and Randall always suspected the name he was passing under here wasn't his own. Sonia knew all that. The point was, which of course Randall couldn't appreciate, that Dmitri was really a wildly attractive person to women. And he was just as much in love with Sonia as she was with him. Randall insisted that he was just marrying her for her money— but that wasn't true. Sonia was very handsome, you know. And she had plenty of spirit. If the marriage had turned out badly, if Dmitri had been unkind to her or unfaithful to her, she would just have cut her losses and walked out on him. She was a rich woman and could do as she chose with her life."

" The quarrel was never made up?"

" No. Randall and Sonia never had got on very well. She resented his trying to prevent the marriage. She said, ' Very well. You're quite impossible! This is the last you hear of me!' "

" But it was not the last you heard of her?"

Belle smiled.

" No, I got a letter from her about eighteen months afterwards. She wrote from Budapest, I remember, but she didn't give an address. She told me to tell Randall that she was extremely happy and that she'd just had twins."

" And she told you their names?"

Again Belle smiled. " She said they were born just after midday—and she intended to call them Pip and Emma. That may have been just a joke, of course."

" Didn't you hear from her again?"

" No. She said she and her husband and the babies were going to America on a short stay. I never heard any more. . . ."

" You don't happen, I suppose, to have kept that letter?"

" No, I'm afraid not. . . . I read it to Randall and he just grunted : ' She'll regret marrying that fellow one of these days.' That's all he ever said about it. We really forgot about her. She went right out of our lives. . . ."

" Nevertheless Mr. Goedler left his estate to her children in the event of Miss Blacklock predeceasing you?"

"Oh, that was my doing. I said to him, when he told me about the will: 'And suppose Blackie dies before I do?' He was quite surprised. I said, 'Oh, I know Blackie is as strong as a horse and I'm a delicate creature —but there's such a thing as accidents, you know, and there's such a thing as creaking gates . . .' And he said, 'There's no one—absolutely no one.' I said, 'There's Sonia.' And he said at once, 'And let that fellow get hold of my money? No—indeed!' I said, 'Well, her children then. Pip and Emma, and there may be lots more by now'—and so he grumbled, but he did put it in."

"And from that day to this," Craddock said slowly, "you've heard nothing of your sister-in-law or her children?"

"Nothing—they may be dead—they may be—anywhere."

They may be in Chipping Cleghorn, thought Craddock.

As though she read his thoughts, a look of alarm came into Belle Goedler's eyes. She said, "Don't let them hurt Blackie. Blackie's *good*—really good—you mustn't let harm come to——"

Her voice trailed off suddenly. Craddock saw the sudden grey shadows round her mouth and eyes.

"You're tired," he said. "I'll go."

She nodded.

"Send Mac to me," she whispered. "Yes, tired . . ." She made a feeble motion of her hand. "Look after Blackie . . . Nothing must happen to Blackie . . . look after her. . . ."

"I'll do my very best, Mrs. Goedler." He rose and went to the door.

Her voice, a thin thread of sound, followed him . . .

164

" Not long now—until I'm dead—dangerous for her—Take care . . ."

Sister McClelland passed him as he went out. He said, uneasily :

" I hope I haven't done her harm."

" Oh, I don't think so, Mr. Craddock. I told you she would tire quite suddenly."

Later, he asked the nurse :

" The only thing I hadn't time to ask Mrs. Goedler was whether she had any old photographs? If so, I wonder——"

She interrupted him.

" I'm afraid there's nothing of that kind. All her personal papers and things were stored with their furniture from the London house at the beginning of the war. Mrs. Goedler was desperately ill at the time. Then the storage depository was blitzed. Mrs. Goedler was very upset at losing so many personal souvenirs and family papers. I'm afraid there's nothing of that kind."

So that was that, Craddock thought.

Yet he felt his journey had not been in vain. Pip and Emma, those twin wraiths, were not quite wraiths.

Craddock thought, " Here's a brother and sister brought up somewhere in Europe. Sonia Goedler was a rich woman at the time of her marriage, but money in Europe hasn't remained money. Queer things have happened to money during these war years. And so there are two young people, the son and daughter of a man who had a criminal record. Suppose they came to England, more or less penniless. What would they do? Find out about any rich relatives. Their uncle, a man of vast fortune is dead. Possibly the first thing they'd do would be to look up that uncle's will. See if by any chance money had been left to them or to their mother. So they go to Somerset House and learn the contents of his will, and then, perhaps, they learn of the existence of Miss Letitia Blacklock. Then they make inquiries about Randall Goedler's widow. She's an invalid, living up in Scotland, and they find out she hasn't long to live. *If this Letitia Blacklock dies before her*, they will come into a vast fortune. What then?"

Craddock thought, " They wouldn't go to Scotland. They'd find out where Letitia Blacklock is living now. And they'd go there—but not as themselves . . . They'd go together—or separately? Emma . . . I wonder? . . . Pip and Emma . . . I'll eat my hat if Pip, or Emma, or both of them, aren't in Chipping Cleghorn now. . . ."

166

CHAPTER XV

DELICIOUS DEATH

IN the kitchen at Little Paddocks, Miss Blacklock was giving instructions to Mitzi.

"Sardine sandwiches as well as the tomato ones. And some of those little scones you make so nicely. And I'd like you to make that special cake of yours."

"Is it a party then, that you want all these things?"

"It's Miss Bunner's birthday, and some people will be coming to tea."

"At her age one does not have birthdays. It is better to forget."

"Well, she doesn't want to forget. Several people are bringing her presents—and it will be nice to make a little party of it."

"That is what you say last time—and see what happened!"

Miss Blacklock controlled her temper.

"Well, it won't happen this time."

"How do you know what may happen in this house? All day long I shiver and at night I lock my door and I look in the wardrobe to see no one is hidden there."

"That ought to keep you nice and safe," said Miss Blacklock, coldly.

"The cake that you want me to make, it is the——"
Mitzi uttered a sound that to Miss Blacklock's English ear sounded like Schwitzebzr or alternatively like cats spitting at each other.

"That's the one. The rich one."

"Yes. It is rich. For it have I *nothing*! Impossible to make such a cake. I need for it chocolate and much butter, and sugar and raisins."

"You can use this tin of butter that was sent us from America. And some of the raisins we were keeping for Christmas, and here is a slab of chocolate and a pound of sugar."

Mitzi's face suddenly burst into radiant smiles.

"So, I make him for you good—good," she cried, in an ecstasy. "It will be rich, rich, of a melting richness! And on top I will put the icing—chocolate icing—I make him so nice—and write on it *Good Wishes*. These English people with their cakes that tastes of sand, never *never*, will they have tasted such a cake. Delicious, they will say—delicious——"

Her face clouded again.

"Mr. Patrick. He called it Delicious Death. My cake! I will not have my cake called that!"

"It was a compliment really," said Miss Blacklock. "He meant it was worth dying to eat such a cake."

Mitzi looked at her doubtfully.

"Well, I do not like that word—*death*. They are not dying because they eat my cake, no, they feel much much better. . . ."

"I'm sure we all shall."

Miss Blacklock turned away and left the kitchen with a sigh of relief at the successful ending of the interview. With Mitzi one never knew.

She ran into Dora Bunner outside.

"Oh, Letty, shall I run in and tell Mitzi just how to cut the sandwiches?"

"No," said Miss Blacklock, steering her friend firmly into the hall. "She's in a good mood now and I don't want her disturbed."

"But I could just show her——"

168

"Please don't show her *anything*, Dora. These central Europeans don't *like* being shown. They hate it."

Dora looked at her doubtfully. Then she suddenly broke into smiles.

"Edmund Swettenham just rang up. He wished me many happy returns of the day and said he was bringing me a pot of honey as a present this afternoon. Isn't it kind? I can't imagine how he knew it was my birthday."

"Everybody seems to know. You must have been talking about it, Dora."

"Well, I did just happen to mention that to-day I should be fifty-nine——"

"You're sixty-four," said Miss Blacklock with a twinkle.

"And Miss Hinchliffe said, 'You don't look it. What age do you think *I* am?' Which was rather awkward because Miss Hinchliffe always looks so peculiar that she might be any age. She said she was bringing me some eggs, by the way. I said our hens hadn't been laying very well, lately."

"We're not doing so badly out of your birthday," said Miss Blacklock. "Honey, eggs—a magnificent box of chocolates from Julia——"

"I don't know where she gets such things."

"Better not ask. Her methods are probably strictly illegal."

"And your lovely brooch." Miss Bunner looked down proudly at her bosom on which was pinned a small diamond leaf.

"Do you like it? I'm glad. I never cared for jewellery."

"I love it."

"Good. Let's go and feed the ducks."

169

11

"Ha," cried Patrick dramatically, as the party took their places round the dining-room table. "What do I see before me? *Delicious Death*."

"Hush," said Miss Blacklock. "Don't let Mitzi hear you. She objects to your name for her cake very much."

"Nevertheless, Delicious Death it is! Is it Bunny's birthday cake?"

"Yes, it is," said Miss Bunner. "I really am having the most wonderful birthday."

Her cheeks were flushed with excitement and had been ever since Colonel Easterbrook had handed her a small box of sweets and declaimed with a bow, "Sweets to the Sweet!"

Julia had turned her head away hurriedly, and had been frowned at by Miss Blacklock.

Full justice was done to the good things on the tea table and they rose from their seats after a round of crackers.

"I feel slightly sick," said Julia. "It's that cake. I remember I felt just the same last time."

"It's worth it," said Patrick.

"These foreigners certainly understand confectionery," said Miss Hinchliffe. "What they can't make is a plain boiled pudding."

Everybody was respectfully silent, though it seemed to be hovering on Patrick's lips to ask if anyone really *wanted* a plain boiled pudding.

"Got a new gardener?" asked Miss Hinchliffe of Miss Blacklock as they returned to the drawing-room.

170

"No, why?"

"Saw a man snooping round the henhouse. Quite a decent-looking Army type."

"Oh, *that*," said Julia. "That's our detective."

Mrs. Easterbrook dropped her handbag.

"Detective?" she exclaimed. "But—but—why?"

"I don't know," said Julia. "He prowls about and keeps an eye on the house. He's protecting Aunt Letty, I suppose."

"Absolute nonsense," said Miss Blacklock. "I can protect myself, thank you."

"But surely it's all over now," cried Mrs. Easterbrook. "Though I meant to ask you, why did they adjourn the inquest?"

"Police aren't satisfied," said her husband. "That's what that means."

"But aren't satisfied of what?"

Colonel Easterbrook shook his head with the air of a man who could say a good deal more if he chose. Edmund, who disliked the Colonel, said, "The truth of it is, we're all under suspicion."

"But suspicion of *what*?" repeated Mrs. Easterbrook.

"Never mind, kitten," said her husband.

"Loitering with intent," said Edmund. "The intent being to commit murder upon the first opportunity."

"Oh, don't, please don't, Mr. Swettenham." Dora Bunner began to cry. "I'm sure nobody here could possibly want to kill dear, dear Letty."

There was a moment of horrible embarrassment. Edmund turned scarlet, murmured, "Just a joke." Phillipa suggested in a high clear voice that they might listen to the six o'clock news and the suggestion was received with enthusiastic assent.

Patrick murmured to Julia: "We need Mrs. Harmon here. She'd be sure to say in that high clear voice of

171

hers, ' But I suppose somebody *is* still waiting for a good chance to murder you, Miss Blacklock?' "

" I'm glad she and that old Miss Marple couldn't come," said Julia. " That old woman is the prying kind. And a mind like a sink, I should think. Real Victorian type."

Listening to the news led easily into a pleasant discussion on the horrors of atomic warfare. Colonel Easterbrook said that the real menace to civilisation was undoubtedly Russia, and Edmund said that he had several charming Russian friends—which announcement was coldly received.

The party broke up with renewed thanks to the hostess.

" Enjoy yourself, Bunny?" asked Miss Blacklock, as the last guest was sped.

" Oh, I did. But I've got a terrible headache. It's the excitement, I think."

" It's the cake," said Patrick. " I feel a bit liverish myself. And you've been nibbling chocolates all the morning."

" I'll go and lie down, I think," said Miss Bunner. " I'll take a couple of aspirins and try and have a nice sleep."

" That would be a very good plan," said Miss Blacklock.

Miss Bunner departed upstairs.

" Shall I shut up the ducks for you, Aunt Letty?"

Miss Blacklock looked at Patrick severely.

" If you'll be sure to latch that door properly."

" I will. I swear I will."

" Have a glass of sherry, Aunt Letty," said Julia. " As my old nurse used to say, ' It will settle your stomach.' A revolting phrase—but curiously apposite at this moment."

172

" Well, I dare say it might be a good thing. The truth is one isn't used to rich things. Oh, Bunny, how you made me jump. What is it?"

" I can't find my aspirin," said Miss Bunner disconsolately.

" Well, take some of mine, dear, they're by my bed."

" There's a bottle on my dressing-table," said Phillipa.

" Thank you—thank you very much. If I can't find mine—but I know I've got it *somewhere*. A new bottle. Now where could I have put it?"

" There's heaps in the bathroom," said Julia impatiently. " This house is chock full of aspirin."

" It vexes me to be so careless and mislay things," replied Miss Bunner, retreating up the stairs again.

" Poor old Bunny," said Julia, holding up her glass. " Do you think we ought to have given her some sherry?"

" Better not, I think," said Miss Blacklock. " She had a lot of excitement to-day, and it isn't really good for her. I'm afraid she'll be the worse for it to-morrow. Still, I really do think she has enjoyed herself!"

" She's loved it," said Phillipa.

" Let's give Mitzi a glass of sherry," suggested Julia. " Hi, Pat," she called as she heard him entering the side door, " fetch Mitzi."

So Mitzi was brought in and Julia poured her out a glass of sherry.

" Here's to the best cook in the world," said Patrick.

Mitzi was gratified—but felt nevertheless that a protest was due.

" That is not so. I am not really a cook. In my country I do intellectual work."

" Then you're wasted," said Patrick. " What's intellectual work compared to a *chef d'oeuvre* like Delicious Death?"

" Oo—I say to you I do not like——"

"Never mind what you like, my girl," said Patrick. "That's my name for it and here's to it. Let's all drink to Delicious Death and to hell with the after effects."

III

"Phillipa, my dear, I want to talk to you."

"Yes, Miss Blacklock?"

Phillipa Haymes looked up in slight surprise.

"You're not worrying about anything, are you?"

"Worrying?"

"I've noticed that you've looked worried lately. There isn't anything wrong, is there?"

"Oh no, Miss Blacklock. What should there be?"

"Well—I wondered. I thought, perhaps, that you and Patrick——?"

"Patrick?" Phillipa looked really surprised.

"It's not so, then. Please forgive me if I've been impertinent. But you've been thrown together a lot— and although Patrick is my cousin, I don't think he's the type to make a satisfactory husband. Not for some time to come, at all events."

Phillipa's face had frozen into a hard immobility.

"I shan't marry again," she said.

"Oh, yes, you will someday, my child. You're young. But we needn't discuss that. There's no other trouble. You're not worried about—money, for instance?"

"No, I'm quite all right."

"I know you get anxious sometimes about your boy's education. That's why I want to tell you something. I drove into Milchester this afternoon to see Mr. Bedding-feld, my lawyer. Things haven't been very settled lately and I thought I would like to make a new will—in view of certain eventualities. Apart from Bunny's legacy, everything goes to you, Phillipa."

"What?" Phillipa spun round. Her eyes stared. She looked dismayed, almost frightened.

"But I don't want it—really I don't . . . Oh, I'd rather not . . . And anyway, why? Why to *me*?"

"Perhaps," said Miss Blacklock in a peculiar voice, "because there's no one else."

"But there's Patrick and Julia."

"Yes, there's Patrick and Julia." The odd note in Miss Blacklock's voice was still there.

"They are your relations."

"Very distant ones. They have no claim on me."

"But I—I haven't either—I don't know what you think . . . Oh, I don't want it."

Her gaze held more hostility than gratitude. There was something almost like fear in her manner.

"I know what I'm doing, Phillipa. I've become fond of you—and there's the boy . . . You won't get very much if I should die now—but in a few weeks' time it might be different."

Her eyes met Phillipa's steadily.

"But you're not going to die!" Phillipa protested.

"Not if I can avoid it by taking due precautions."

"Precautions?"

"Yes. Think it over . . . And don't worry any more."

She left the room abruptly. Phillipa heard her speaking to Julia in the hall.

Julia entered the drawing-room a few moments later. There was a slightly steely glitter in her eyes.

"Played your cards rather well, haven't you, Phillipa? I see you're one of those quiet ones . . . a dark horse."

"So you heard——"

"Yes, I heard. I rather think I was meant to hear."

"What do you mean?"

175

"Our Letty's no fool . . . Well, anyway, you're all right, Phillipa. Sitting pretty, aren't you?"

"Oh, Julia—I didn't mean—I never meant——"

"Didn't you? Of course you did. You're fairly up against things, aren't you? Hard up for money. But just remember this—if anyone bumps off Aunt Letty now, *you'll* be suspect No. 1."

"But I shan't be. It would be idiotic if I killed her now when—if I waited——"

"So you *do* know about old Mrs. Whatshername dying up in Scotland? I wondered . . . Phillipa, I'm beginning to believe you're a very dark horse indeed."

"I don't want to do you and Patrick out of anything."

"Don't you, my dear? I'm sorry—but I don't believe you."

176

CHAPTER XVI

INSPECTOR CRADDOCK RETURNS

INSPECTOR CRADDOCK had had a bad night on his night journey home. His dreams had been less dreams than nightmares. Again and again he was racing through the grey corridors of an old-world castle in a desperate attempt to get somewhere, or to prevent something, in time. Finally he dreamt that he awoke. An enormous relief surged over him. Then the door of his compartment slid slowly open, and Letitia Blacklock looked in at him with blood running down her face, and said reproachfully: " Why didn't you save me? You could have if you'd tried."

This time he really awoke.

Altogether, the inspector was thankful finally to reach Milchester. He went straight away to make his report to Rydesdale who listened carefully.

" It doesn't take us much further," he said. " But it confirms what Miss Blacklock told you. Pip and Emma —h'm, I wonder."

" Patrick and Julia Simmons are the right age, sir. If we could establish that Miss Blacklock hadn't seen them since they were children——"

With a very faint chuckle, Rydesdale said : " Our ally, Miss Marple, has established that for us. Actually Miss Blacklock had never seen either of them at all until two months ago."

" Then, surely, sir——"

" It's not so easy as all that, Craddock. We've been checking up. On what we've got, Patrick and Julia seem

definitely to be out of it. His Naval record is genuine—
quite a good record bar a tendency to ' insubordination.'
We've checked with Cannes, and an indignant Mrs.
Simmons says of course her son and daughter are at
Chipping Cleghorn with her cousin Letitia Blacklock. So
that's that!"

" And Mrs. Simmons *is* Mrs. Simmons?"

" She's been Mrs. Simmons for a very long time, that's
all I can say," said Rydesdale dryly.

" That seems clear enough. Only—those two fitted.
Right age. Not known to Miss Blacklock, personally. If
we wanted Pip and Emma—well, there they were."

The Chief Constable nodded thoughtfully, then he
pushed across a paper to Craddock.

" Here's a little something we've dug up on Mrs.
Easterbrook."

The Inspector read with lifted eyebrows.

" Very interesting," he remarked. " Hoodwinked that
old ass pretty well, hasn't she? It doesn't tie in with this
business though, as far as I can see."

" Apparently not."

" And here's an item that concerns Mrs. Haymes."

Again Craddock's eyebrows rose.

" I think I'll have another talk with the lady," he said.

" You think this information might be relevant?"

" I think it might be. It would be a long shot, of
course. . . ."

The two men were silent for a moment or two.

" How has Fletcher got on, sir?"

" Fletcher has been exceedingly active. He's made a
routine search of the house by agreement with Miss
Blacklock—but he didn't find anything significant. Then
he's been checking up on who could have had the opportunity of oiling that door. Checking who was up at
the house on the days that that foreign girl was out. A

little more complicated than we thought, because it appears she goes for a walk most afternoons. Usually down to the village where she has a cup of coffee at the Bluebird. So that when Miss Blacklock and Miss Bunner are out—which is most afternoons—they go blackberry-ing—the coast is clear."

"And the doors are always left unlocked?"

"They used to be. I don't suppose they are now."

"What are Fletcher's results? Who's known to have been in the house when it was left empty?"

"Practically the whole lot of them."

Rydesdale consulted a page in front of him.

"Miss Murgatroyd was there with a hen to sit on some eggs. (Sounds complicated but that's what she says.) Very flustered about it all and contradicts herself, but Fletcher thinks that's temperamental and not a sign of guilt."

"Might be," Craddock admitted. "She flaps."

"Then Mrs. Swettenham came up to fetch some horse meat that Miss Blacklock had left for her on the kitchen table, because Miss Blacklock had been in to Milchester in the car that day and always gets Mrs. Swettenham's horse meat for her. That makes sense to you?"

Craddock considered.

"Why didn't Miss Blacklock leave the horse meat when she passed Mrs. Swettenham's house on her way back from Milchester?"

"I don't know, but she didn't. Mrs. Swettenham says she (Miss B.) always leaves it on the kitchen table, and she (Mrs. S.) likes to fetch it when Mitzi isn't there because Mitzi is sometimes so rude."

"Hangs together quite well. And the next?"

"Miss Hinchliffe. Says she wasn't there at all lately. But she was. Because Mitzi saw her coming out of the side door one day and so did a Mrs. Butt (she's one of the locals). Miss H. then admitted she might have been there but had forgotten. Can't remember what she went for. Says she probably just dropped in."

"That's rather odd."

"So was her manner, apparently. Then there's Mrs. Easterbrook. She was exercising the dear dogs out that way and she just popped in to see if Miss Blacklock would lend her a knitting pattern but Miss Blacklock wasn't in. She says she waited a little."

"Just so. Might be snooping round. Or might be oiling a door. And the Colonel?"

"Went there one day with a book on India that Miss Blacklock had expressed a desire to read."

"Had she?"

"Her account is that she tried to get out of having to read it, but it was no use."

"And that's fair enough," sighed Craddock. "If anyone is really determined to lend you a book, you never can get out of it!"

"We don't know if Edmund Swettenham was up there. He's extremely vague. Said he did drop in occasionally on errands for his mother, but thinks not lately."

"In fact, it's all inconclusive."

"Yes."

Rydesdale said, with a slight grin :

"Miss Marple has also been active. Fletcher reports that she had morning coffee at the Bluebird. She's been to sherry at Boulders, and to tea at Little Paddocks. She's admired Mrs. Swettenham's garden—and dropped in to see Colonel Easterbrook's Indian curios."

"She may be able to tell us if Colonel Easterbrook's a pukka Colonel or not."

"She'd know, I agree—he seems all right. We'd have to check with the Far Eastern Authorities to get certain identification."

" And in the meantime "—Craddock broke off—" do you think Miss Blacklock would consent to go away?"

" Go away from Chipping Cleghorn?"

" Yes. Take the faithful Bunner with her, perhaps, and leave for an unknown destination. Why shouldn't she go up to Scotland and stay with Belle Goedler. It's a pretty unget-at-able place."

" Stop there and wait for her to die? I don't think she'd do that. I don't think any nice-natured woman would like that suggestion."

" If it's a matter of saving her life——"

" Come now, Craddock, it isn't quite so easy to bump someone off as you seem to think."

" Isn't it, sir?"

" Well—in one way—it's easy enough I agree. Plenty of methods. Weed-killer. A bash on the head when she's out shutting up the poultry, a pot shot from behind a hedge. All quite simple. But to bump someone off and not be suspected of bumping them off—that's not quite so easy. And they must realise by now that they're all under observation. The original carefully planned scheme failed. Our unknown murderer has got to think up something else."

" I know that, sir. But there's the time element to consider. Mrs. Goedler's a dying woman—she might pop off any minute. That means that our murderer can't afford to wait."

" True."

" And another thing, sir. He—or she—must know that we're checking up on everybody."

" And that takes time," said Rydesdale with a sigh. " It means checking with the East, with India. Yes, it's a long tedious business."

" So that's another reason for—hurry. I'm sure, sir, that the danger is very real. It's a very large sum that's at stake. If Belle Goedler dies——"

He broke off as a constable entered.

" Constable Legg on the line from Chipping Cleghorn, sir."

" Put him through here."

Inspector Craddock, watching the Chief Constable, saw his features harden and stiffen.

"Very good," barked Rydesdale. " Detective-Inspector Craddock will be coming out immediately."

He put the receiver down.

" Is it——" Craddock broke off.

Rydesdale shook his head.

" No," he said. " It's Dora Bunner. She wanted some aspirin. Apparently she took some from a bottle beside Letitia Blacklock's bed. There were only a few tablets left in the bottle. She took two and left one. The doctor's got that one and is sending it to be analysed. He says it's definitely *not* aspirin."

" She's dead?"

" Yes, found dead in her bed this morning. Died in her sleep, doctor says. He doesn't think it was natural though her health was in a bad state. Narcotic poisoning, that's his guess. Autopsy's fixed for to-night."

" Aspirin tablets by Letitia Blacklock's bed. The clever clever devil. Patrick told me Miss Blacklock threw away a half bottle of sherry—opened a new one. I don't suppose she'd have thought of doing that with an open bottle of aspirin. Who had been in the house this time—within the last day or two? The tablets can't have been there long."

Rydesdale looked at him.

" All our lot were there yesterday," he said. " Birthday party for Miss Bunner. Any of them could have nipped upstairs and done a neat little substitution. Or of course anyone living in the house could have done it any time."

CHAPTER XVII

THE ALBUM

STANDING by the Vicarage gate, well wrapped up, Miss Marple took the note from Bunch's hand.

"Tell Miss Blacklock," said Bunch, "that Julian is terribly sorry he can't come up himself. He's got a parishioner dying out at Locke Hamlet. He'll come up after lunch if Miss Blacklock would like to see him. The note's about the arrangements for the funeral. He suggests Wednesday if the inquest's on Tuesday. Poor old Bunny. It's so typical of her, somehow, to get hold of poisoned aspirin meant for someone else. Good-bye, darling. I hope the walk won't be too much for you. But I've simply got to get that child to hospital at once."

Miss Marple said the walk wouldn't be too much for her, and Bunch rushed off.

Whilst waiting for Miss Blacklock, Miss Marple looked round the drawing-room, and wondered just exactly what Dora Bunner had meant that morning in the Bluebird by saying that she believed Patrick had "tampered with the lamp" to "make the lights go out." What lamp? And how had he "tampered" with it?

She must, Miss Marple decided, have meant the small lamp that stood on the table by the archway. She had said something about a shepherdess or a shepherd—and this was actually a delicate piece of Dresden china, a shepherd in a blue coat and pink breeches holding what had originally been a candlestick and had now been adapted to electricity. The shade was of plain vellum and a little too big so that it almost masked the figure.

What else was it that Dora Bunner had said? "I remember distinctly that it was the shepherdess. And the next day——" Certainly it was a shepherd now.

Miss Marple remembered that when she and Bunch had come to tea, Dora Bunner had said something about the lamp being one of a *pair*. Of course—a shepherd and a shepherdess. And it had been the shepherdess on the day of the hold-up—and the next morning it had been the *other* lamp—the lamp that was here now, the shepherd. The lamps had been changed over during the night. And Dora Bunner had had reason to believe (or had believed without reason) that it was Patrick who had changed them.

Why? Because, if the original lamp were examined, it would show just how Patrick had managed to "make the lights go out." How had he managed? Miss Marple looked earnestly at the lamp in front of her. The flex ran along the table over the edge and was plugged into the wall. There was a small pear-shaped switch half-way along the flex. None of it suggested anything to Miss Marple because she knew very little about electricity.

Where was the shepherdess lamp? she wondered. In the "spare room" or thrown away, or—where was it Dora Bunner had come upon Patrick Simmons with a feather and an oily cup? In the shrubbery? Miss Marple made up her mind to put all these points to Inspector Craddock.

At the very beginning Miss Blacklock had leaped to the conclusion that her nephew Patrick had been behind the insertion of that advertisement. That kind of instinctive belief was often justified, or so Miss Marple believed. Because, if you knew people fairly well, you knew the kind of things they thought of . . .

Patrick Simmons . . .

A handsome young man. An engaging young man. A

young man whom women liked, both young women and old women. The kind of man, perhaps, that Randall Goedler's sister had married. Could Patrick Simons be " Pip "? But he'd been in the Navy during the war. The police could soon check up on that.

Only—sometimes—the most amazing impersonations *did* happen.

You could get away with a great deal if you had enough audacity . . .

The door opened and Miss Blacklock came in. She looked, Miss Marple thought, many years older. All the life and energy had gone out of her.

" I'm very sorry, disturbing you like this," said Miss Marple. " But the Vicar had a dying parishioner and Bunch had to rush a sick child to hospital. The Vicar wrote you a note."

She held it out and Miss Blacklock took it and opened it.

" Do sit down, Miss Marple," she said. " It's very kind of you to have brought this."

She read the note through.

" The Vicar's a very understanding man," she said quietly. " He doesn't offer one fatuous consolation . . . Tell him that these arrangements will do very well. Her —her favourite hymn was *Lead Kindly Light*."

Her voice broke suddenly.

Miss Marple said gently :

" I am only a stranger, but I am so very very sorry."

And suddenly, uncontrollably, Letitia Blacklock wept. It was a piteous overmastering grief, with a kind of hopelessness about it. Miss Marple sat quite still.

Miss Blacklock sat up at last. Her face was swollen and blotched with tears.

" I'm sorry," she said. " It—it just came over me. What I've lost. She—she was the only link with the past, you see. The only one who—who *remembered*. Now that she's gone I'm quite alone."

"I know what you mean," said Miss Marple. "One *is* alone when the last one who *remembers* is gone. I have nephews and nieces and kind friends—but there's no one who knew me as a young girl—no one who belongs to the old days. I've been alone for quite a long time now."

Both women sat silent for some moments.

"You understand very well," said Letitia Blacklock. She rose and went over to her desk. "I must write a few words to the Vicar." She held the pen rather awkwardly and wrote slowly.

"Arthritic," she explained. "Sometimes I can hardly write at all."

She sealed up the envelope and addressed it.

"If you wouldn't mind taking it, it would be very kind."

Hearing a man's voice in the hall she said quickly:

"That's Inspector Craddock."

She went to the mirror over the fireplace and applied a small powder puff to her face.

Craddock came in with a grim, angry face.

He looked at Miss Marple with disapprobation.

"Oh," he said. "So *you're* here."

Miss Blacklock turned from the mantelpiece.

"Miss Marple kindly came up with a note from the Vicar."

Miss Marple said in a flurried manner:

"I am going at once—at once. Please don't let me hamper you in *any* way."

"Were you at the tea party here yesterday afternoon?"

Miss Marple said, nervously:

"No—no, I wasn't. Bunch drove me over to call on some friends."

"Then there's nothing you can tell me." Craddock

held the door open in a pointed manner, and Miss Marple scuttled out in a somewhat abashed fashion.

"Nosey Parkers, these old women," said Craddock.

"I think you're being unfair to her," said Miss Blacklock. "She really did come with a note from the Vicar."

"I bet she did."

"I don't think it was idle curiosity."

"Well, perhaps you're right, Miss Blacklock, but my own diagnosis would be a severe attack of Nosey Parkeritis. . . ."

"She's a very harmless old creature," said Miss Blacklock.

"Dangerous as a rattlesnake if you only knew," the Inspector thought grimly. But he had no intention of taking anyone into his confidence unnecessarily. Now that he knew definitely there was a killer at large, he felt that the less said the better. He didn't want the next person bumped off to be Jane Marple.

Somewhere—a killer . . . Where?

"I won't waste time offering sympathy, Miss Blacklock," he said. "As a matter of fact I feel pretty bad about Miss Bunner's death. We ought to have been able to prevent it."

"I don't see what you could have done."

"No—well, it wouldn't have been easy. But now we've got to work fast. Who's doing this, Miss Blacklock? Who's had two shots at killing you, and will probably, if we don't work fast enough, soon have another?"

Letitia Blacklock shivered. "I don't know, Inspector —I don't know *at all*!"

"I've checked up with Mrs. Goedler. She's given me all the help she can. It wasn't very much. There are just a few people who would definitely profit by your death. First Pip and Emma. Patrick and Julia Simmons are the right age, but their background seems clear enough. Anyway, we can't concentrate on these two alone. Tell me, Miss Blacklock, would you recognise Sonia Goedler if you saw her?"

"Recognise Sonia? Why, of course——" she stopped suddenly. "No," she said slowly, "I don't know that I would. It's a long time. Thirty years . . . She'd be an elderly woman now."

"What was she like when you remember her?"

"Sonia?" Miss Blacklock considered for some moments. "She was rather small, dark . . ."

"Any special peculiarities? Mannerisms?"

"No—no, I don't think so. She was gay—very gay."

"She mayn't be so gay now," said the Inspector. "Have you got a photograph of her?"

"Of Sonia? Let me see—not a proper photograph. I've got some old snapshots—in an album somewhere—at least I think there's one of her."

"Ah. Can I have a look at it?"

"Yes, of course. Now where did I put that album?"

"Tell me, Miss Blacklock, do you consider it remotely possible that Mrs. Swettenham might be Sonia Goedler?"

"*Mrs. Swettenham?*" Miss Blacklock looked at him in lively astonishment. "But her husband was in the Government Service—in India first, I think, and then in Hong Kong."

"What you mean is, that that's the story she's told you. You don't, as we say in the Courts, know it of your own knowledge, do you?"

"No," said Miss Blacklock slowly. "When you put it like that, I don't . . . But Mrs. Swettenham? Oh, it's absurd!"

"Did Sonia Goedler ever do any acting? Amateur theatricals?"

"Oh, yes. She was good."

"There you are! Another thing, Mrs. Swettenham

A MURDER IS ANNOUNCED

wears a wig. At least," the Inspector corrected himself,
" Mrs. Harmon says she does."

" Yes—yes, I suppose it might be a wig. All those little
grey curls. But I still think it's absurd. She's really very
nice and exceedingly funny sometimes."

" Then there's Miss Hinchliffe and Miss Murgatroyd.
Could either of them be Sonia Goedler?"

" Miss Hinchliffe is too tall. She's as tall as a man."

" Miss Murgatroyd then?"

" Oh, but—oh, no, I'm sure Miss Murgatroyd couldn't
be Sonia."

" You don't see very well, do you, Miss Blacklock?"

" I'm short-sighted, is that what you mean?"

" Yes. What I'd like to see is a snapshot of this Sonia
Goedler, even if it's a long time ago and not a good likeness. We're trained, you know, to pick out resemblances,
in a way no amateur can ever do."

" I'll try and find it for you."

" Now?"

" What, at once?"

" I'd prefer it."

" Very well. Now, let me see. I saw that album when
we were tidying a lot of books out of the cupboard. Julia
was helping me. She laughed, I remember, at the
clothes we used to wear in those days . . . The books we
put in the shelf in the drawing-room. Where did we put
the albums and the big bound volumes of the Art Jour-
nal? What a wretched memory I have! Perhaps Julia
will remember. She's at home to-day."

" I'll find her."

The Inspector departed on his quest. He did not find
Julia in any of the downstairs rooms. Mitzi, asked where
Miss Simmons was, said crossly that it was not her
affair.

" Me! I stay in my kitchen and concern myself with

the lunch. And nothing do I eat that I have not cooked myself. Nothing, do you hear?"

The Inspector called up the stair " Miss Simmons," and getting no response, went up.

He met Julia face to face just as he turned the corner of the landing. She had just emerged from a door that showed behind it a small twisty staircase.

" I was up in the attic," she explained. " What is it?"

Inspector Craddock explained.

" Those old photograph albums? Yes, I remember them quite well. We put them in the big cupboard in the study, I think. I'll find them for you."

She led the way downstairs and pushed open the study door. Near the window there was a large cupboard. Julia pulled it open and disclosed a heterogeneous mass of objects.

" Junk," said Julia. " All junk. But elderly people simply will *not* throw things away."

The Inspector knelt down and took a couple of old-fashioned albums from the bottom shelf.

" Are these they?"

" Yes."

Miss Blacklock came in and joined them.

" Oh, so *that's* where we put them. I couldn't remember."

Craddock had the books on the table and was turning the pages.

Women in large cartwheel hats, women with dresses tapering down to their feet so that they could hardly walk. The photos had captions neatly printed underneath them, but the ink was old and faded.

" It would be in this one," said Miss Blacklock. " On about the second or third page. The other book is after Sonia had married and gone away." She turned a page. " It ought to be here." She stopped.

There were several empty spaces on the page. Craddock bent down and deciphered the faded writing. "Sonia . . . Self . . . R.G." A little farther along, "Sonia and Belle on beach." And again on the opposite page, "Picnic at Skeyne." He turned over another page, "Charlotte, Self, Sonia. R.G."

Craddock stood up. His lips were grim.

"*Somebody has removed these photographs*—not long ago, I should say."

"There weren't any blank spaces when we looked at them the other day. Were there, Julia?"

"I didn't look very closely—only at some of the dresses. But no . . . you're right, Aunt Letty, there *weren't* any blank spaces."

Craddock looked grimmer still.

"Somebody," he said, "has removed every photo of Sonia Goedler from this album."

CHAPTER XVIII

THE LETTERS

" SORRY to worry you again, Mrs. Haymes."

" It doesn't matter," said Phillipa coldly.

" Shall we go into this room here?"

" The study? Yes, if you like, Inspector. It's very cold. There's no fire."

" It doesn't matter. It's not for long. And we're not so likely to be overheard here."

" Does that matter?"

" Not to me, Mrs. Haymes. It might to you."

" What do you mean?"

" I think you told me, Mrs. Haymes, that your husband was killed fighting in Italy?"

" Well?"

" Wouldn't it have been simpler to have told me the truth—that he was a deserter from his regiment."

He saw her face grow white, and her hands close and unclose themselves.

She said bitterly :

" Do you have to rake up *everything*?"

Craddock said dryly :

" We expect people to tell us the truth about themselves."

She was silent. Then she said :

" Well?"

" What do you mean by ' Well?', Mrs. Haymes?"

" I mean, what are you going to do about it? Tell everybody? Is that necessary—or fair—or kind?"

" Does nobody know?"

" Nobody here. Harry "—her voice changed—" my son, he doesn't know. I don't want him to know. I don't want him to know—ever."

" Then let me tell you that you're taking a very big risk, Mrs. Haymes. When the boy is old enough to understand, tell him the truth. If he finds out by himself some day—it won't be good for him. If you go on stuffing him up with tales of his father dying like a hero———"

" I don't do that. I'm not completely dishonest. I just don't talk about it. His father was—killed in the war. After all, that's what it amounts to—for us."

" But your husband is still alive?"

" Perhaps. How should I know?"

" When did you see him last, Mrs. Haymes?"

Phillipa said quickly:

" I haven't seen him for years."

" Are you quite sure that's true? You didn't, for instance, see him about a fortnight ago?"

" What are you suggesting?"

" It never seemed to me very likely that you met Rudi Scherz in the summerhouse here. But Mitzi's story was very emphatic. I suggest, Mrs. Haymes, that the man you came back from work to meet that morning was your husband."

" I didn't meet anybody in the summerhouse."

" He was hard up for money, perhaps, and you supplied him with some?"

" I've not seen him, I tell you. I didn't meet anybody in the summerhouse."

" Deserters are often rather desperate men. They often take part in robberies, you know. Hold-ups. Things of that kind. *And they have foreign revolvers very often that they've brought back from abroad.*"

193

"I don't know where my husband is. I haven't seen him for years."

"Is that your last word, Mrs. Haymes?"

"I've nothing else to say."

II

Craddock came away from his interview with Phillipa Haymes feeling angry and baffled.

"Obstinate as a mule," he said to himself angrily.

He was fairly sure that Phillipa was lying, but he hadn't succeeded in breaking down her obstinate denials.

He wished he knew a little more about ex-Captain Haymes. His information was meagre. An unsatisfactory Army record, but nothing to suggest that Haymes was likely to turn criminal.

And anyway Haymes didn't fit in with the oiled door.

Someone in the house had done that, or someone with easy access to it.

He stood looking up the staircase, and suddenly he wondered what Julia had been doing up in the attic. An attic, he thought, was an unlikely place for the fastidious Julia to visit.

What had she been doing up there?

He ran lightly up to the first floor. There was no one about. He opened the door out of which Julia had come and went up the narrow stairs to the attic.

There were trunks there, old suitcases, various broken articles of furniture, a chair with a leg off, a broken china lamp, part of an old dinner service.

He turned to the trunks and opened the lid of one.

Clothes. Old-fashioned, quite good quality women's

clothes. Clothes belonging, he supposed, to Miss Blacklock, or to her sister who had died.

He opened another trunk.

Curtains.

He passed to a small attaché-case. It had papers in it
and letters. Very old letters, yellowed with time.

He looked at the outside of the case which had the
initials C.L.B. on it. He deduced correctly that it had
belonged to Letitia's sister Charlotte. He unfolded one
of the letters. It began *Dearest Charlotte. Yesterday
Belle felt well enough to go for a picnic. R.G. also took
a day off. The Asvogel flotation has gone splendidly,
R.G. is terribly pleased about it. The Preference shares
are at a premium.*

He skipped the rest and looked at the signature :

Your loving sister, Letitia.

He picked up another.

*Darling Charlotte. I wish you would sometimes make
up your mind to see people. You do exaggerate, you
know. It isn't nearly as bad as you think. And people
really don't mind things like that. It's not the disfigurement you think it is.*

He nodded his head. He remembered Belle Goedler
saying that Charlotte Blacklock had a disfigurement or
deformity of some kind. Letitia had, in the end, resigned
her job, to go and look after her sister. These letters all
breathed the anxious spirit of her affection and love for
an invalid. She had written her sister, apparently, long
accounts of everyday happenings, of any little detail that
she thought might interest the sick girl. And Charlotte
had kept these letters. Occasionally odd snapshots had
been enclosed.

Excitement suddenly flooded Craddock's mind. Here,
it might be, he would find a clue. In these letters there
would be written down things that Letitia Blacklock

herself had long forgotten. Here was a faithful picture of the past and somewhere amongst it, there might be a clue that would help him to identify the unknown. Photographs, too. There might, just possibly, be a photograph of Sonia Goedler here that the person who had taken the other photos out of the album did not know about.

Inspector Craddock packed the letters up again, carefully, closed the case, and started down the stairs.

Letitia Blacklock, standing on the landing below, looked at him in amazement.

" Was that you up in the attic? I heard footsteps. I couldn't imagine who——"

" Miss Blacklock, I have found some letters here, written by you to your sister Charlotte many years ago. Will you allow me to take them away and read them?"

She flushed angrily.

" Must you do a thing like that? Why? What good can they be to you?"

" They might give me a picture of Sonia Goedler, of her character—there may be some allusion—some incident—that will help."

" They are private letters, Inspector."

" I know."

" I suppose you will take them anyway . . . You have the power to do so, I suppose, or you can easily get it. Take them—take them! But you'll find very little about Sonia. She married and went away only a year or two after I began to work for Randall Goedler."

Craddock said obstinately :

" There may be *something*." He added, " We've got to try everything. I assure you the danger is very real."

She said, biting her lips :

" I know. Bunny is dead—from taking an aspirin tablet that was meant for me. It may be Patrick, or

Julia, or Phillipa, or Mitzi next—somebody young with their life in front of them. Somebody who drinks a glass of wine that is poured out for me, or eats a chocolate that is sent to me. Oh! take the letters—take them away. And afterwards burn them. They don't mean anything to anyone but me and Charlotte. It's all over —gone—past. Nobody remembers now . . ."

Her hand went up to the choker of false pearls she was wearing. Craddock thought how incongruous it looked with her tweed coat and skirt.

She said again:

" Take the letters."

III

It was the following afternoon that the Inspector called at the Vicarage.

It was a dark gusty day.

Miss Marple had her chair pulled close to the fire and was knitting. Bunch was on hands and knees, crawling about the floor, cutting out material to a pattern.

She sat back and pushed a mop of hair out of her eyes, looking up expectantly at Craddock.

" I don't know if it's a breach of confidence," said the Inspector, addressing himself to Miss Marple, " but I'd like you to look at this letter."

He explained the circumstances of his discovery in the attic.

" It's rather a touching collection of letters," he said. " Miss Blacklock poured out everything in the hopes of sustaining her sister's interest in life and keeping her health good. There's a very clear picture of an old father in the background—old Dr. Blacklock. A real old pig-headed bully, absolutely set in his ways, and convinced that everything he thought and said was right. Probably killed thousands of patients through obstinacy. He wouldn't stand for any new ideas or methods."

" I don't really know that I blame him there," said Miss Marple. " I always feel that the young doctors are only too anxious to experiment. After they've whipped out all our teeth, and administered quantities of very peculiar glands, and removed bits of our insides, they then confess that nothing can be done for us. I really prefer the old-fashioned remedy of big black bottles of medicine. After all, one can always pour those down the sink."

She took the letter that Craddock handed her.

He said : " I want you to read it because I think that that generation is more easily understood by you than by me. I don't know really quite how these people's minds worked."

Miss Marple unfolded the fragile paper.

Dearest Charlotte,

I've not written for two days because we've been having the most terrible domestic complications. Randall's sister Sonia (you remember her? She came to take you out in the car that day? How I wish you would go out *more*), Sonia has declared her intention of marrying one, Dmitri Stamfordis. I have only seen him once. Very attractive—not to be trusted, I should say. R.G. raves against him and says he is a crook and a swindler. Belle, bless her, just smiles and lies on her sofa. Sonia, who though she looks so impassive has really a terrific temper, is simply wild with R.G. I really thought yesterday she was going to murder him !

I've done my best. I've talked to Sonia and I've

talked to R.G. and I've got them both into a more reasonable frame of mind and then they come together and it all starts over again! You've no idea how *tiring* it is. R.G. has been making enquiries— and it does really seem as though this Stamfordis man was thoroughly undesirable.

In the meantime business is being neglected. I carry on at the office and in a way it's rather fun because R.G. gives me a free hand. He said to me yesterday : " Thank Heaven, there's one sane person in the world. You're never likely to fall in love with a crook, Blackie, are you?" I said I didn't think I was likely to fall in love with anybody. R.G. said : " Let's start a few new hares in the City." He's really rather a mischievous devil sometimes and he sails terribly near the wind. " You're quite determined to keep me on the straight and narrow path aren't you, Blackie?" he said the other day. And I shall too! I can't understand how people can't *see* when a thing's dishonest—but R.G. really and truly *doesn't*. He only knows what is actually against the law.

Belle only laughs at all this. She thinks the fuss about Sonia is all nonsense. " Sonia has her own money," she said. " Why shouldn't she marry this man if she wants to?" I said it might turn out to be a terrible mistake and Belle said, " It's never a mistake to marry a man you want to marry—even if you regret it." And then she said, " I suppose Sonia doesn't want to break with Randall because of money. Sonia's very fond of money."

No more now. How is father? I won't say Give him my love. But you can if you think it's better to do so. Have you seen more people? You really must not be *morbid*, darling.

199

Sonia asks to be remembered to you. She has just come in and is closing and unclosing her hands like an angry cat sharpening its claws. I think she and R.G. have had another row. Of course Sonia can be *very* irritating. She stares you down with that cool stare of hers.

Lots of love, darling, and buck up. This iodine treatment may make a lot of difference. I've been inquiring about it and it really does seem to have good results.

Your loving sister,
Letitia

Miss Marple folded the letter and handed it back. She looked abstracted.

" Well, what do you think about her?" Craddock urged. " What picture do you get of her?"

" Of Sonia? It's difficult, you know, to see anyone through another person's mind . . . Determined to get her own way—that, definitely, I think. And wanting the best of two worlds . . ."

" *Closing and unclosing her hands like an angry cat,*" murmured Craddock. " You know, that reminds me of someone . . ."

He frowned.

" Making inquiries . . ." murmured Miss Marple.

" If we could get hold of the result of those inquiries," said Craddock.

" Does that letter remind you of anything in St. Mary Mead?" asked Bunch rather indistinctly since her mouth was full of pins.

" I really can't say it does, dear . . . Dr. Blacklock is, perhaps, a little like Mr. Curtiss the Wesleyan Minister. He wouldn't let his child wear a plate on her teeth. Said it was the Lord's Will if her teeth stuck out. ' After all,'

I said to him, 'you do trim your beard and cut your hair. It might be the Lord's Will that your hair should grow out.' He said that was quite different. So like a man. But that doesn't help us with our present problem."

"We've never traced that revolver, you know. It wasn't Rudi Scherz. If I knew who had had a revolver in Chipping Cleghorn——"

"Colonel Easterbrook has one," said Bunch. "He keeps it in his collar drawer."

"How do you know, Mrs. Harmon?"

"Mrs. Butt told me. She's my daily. Or rather, my twice weekly. Being a military gentleman, she said, he'd naturally have a revolver and very handy it would be if burglars were to come along."

"When did she tell you this?"

"Ages ago. About six months ago, I should think."

"Colonel Easterbrook?" murmured Craddock.

"It's like those pointer things at fairs, isn't it?" said Bunch, still speaking through a mouthful of pins. "Go round and round and stop at something different every time."

"You're telling me!" said Craddock and groaned.

"Colonel Easterbrook was up at Little Paddocks to leave a book there one day. He could have oiled that door then. He was quite straightforward about being there though. Not like Miss Hinchliffe."

Miss Marple coughed gently. "You must make allowances for the times we live in, Inspector," she said.

Craddock looked at her, uncomprehendingly.

"After all," said Miss Marple, "you *are* the Police, aren't you? People can't say everything they'd like to say to the Police, can they?"

"I don't see why not," said Craddock. "Unless they've got some criminal matter to conceal."

"She means butter," said Bunch, crawling actively round a table leg to anchor a floating bit of paper. "Butter and corn for hens, and sometimes cream—and sometimes, even, a side of bacon."

"Show him that note from Miss Blacklock," said Miss Marple. "It's some time ago now, but it reads like a first-class mystery story."

"What have I done with it. Is this the one you mean, Aunt Jane?"

Miss Marple took it and looked at it.

"Yes," she said with satisfaction. "That's the one."

She handed it to the Inspector.

"*I have made inquiries—Thursday is the day,*" Miss Blacklock had written. "*Any time after three. If there is any for me leave it in the usual place.*"

Bunch spat out her pins and laughed. Miss Marple was watching the Inspector's face.

The Vicar's wife took it upon herself to explain.

"Thursday is the day one of the farms round here makes butter. They let anybody they like have a bit. It's usually Miss Hinchliffe who collects it. She's very much in with all the farmers—because of her pigs, I think. But it's all a bit hush-hush, you know, a kind of local scheme of barter. One person gets butter, and sends along cucumbers, or something like that—and a little something when a pig's killed. And now and then an animal has an accident and has to be destroyed. Oh, you know the sort of thing. Only one can't, very well, say it right out to the Police. Because I suppose quite a lot of this barter is illegal—only nobody really knows because it's all so complicated. But I expect Hinch had slipped into Little Paddocks with a pound of butter or something and had put it in the *usual place.* That's a flour bin under the dresser, by the way. It doesn't have flour in it."

A MURDER IS ANNOUNCED

Craddock sighed.

"I'm glad I came here to you ladies," he said.

"There used to be clothing coupons, too," said Bunch. "Not usually bought—that wasn't considered honest. No money passes. But people like Mrs. Butt or Mrs. Finch or Mrs. Huggins like a nice woollen dress or a winter coat that hasn't seen too much wear, and they pay for it with coupons instead of money."

"You'd better not tell me any more," said Craddock. "It's all against the law."

"Then there oughtn't to be such silly laws," said Bunch, filling her mouth up with pins again. "I don't do it, of course, because Julian doesn't like me to, so I don't. But I know what's going on, of course."

A kind of despair was coming over the Inspector.

"It all sounds so pleasant and ordinary," he said. "Funny and petty and simple. And yet one woman and a man have been killed, and another woman may be killed before I can get anything definite to go on. I've left off worrying about Pip and Emma for the moment. I'm concentrating on Sonia. I wish I knew what she looked like. There was a snapshot or two in with these letters, but none of the snaps could have been of her."

"How do you know it couldn't have been her? Do you know what she looked like?"

"She was small and dark, Miss Blacklock said."

"Really," said Miss Marple, "that's *very* interesting."

"There was one snap that reminded me vaguely of someone. A tall fair girl with her hair all done up on top of her head. I don't know who she could have been. Anyway, it can't have been Sonia. Do you think Mrs. Swettenham could have been dark when she was a girl?"

203

"Not very dark," said Bunch. "She's got blue eyes."

"I hoped there might be a photo of Dmitri Stamfordis —but I suppose that was too much to hope for . . . Well "—he took up the letter—" I'm sorry this doesn't suggest anything to you, Miss Marple."

"Oh! but it does," said Miss Marple. "It suggests a good deal. Just read it through again, Inspector—especially where it says that Randall Goedler was making inquiries about Dmitri Stamfordis."

Craddock stared at her.

The telephone rang.

Bunch got up from the floor and went out into the hall where, in accordance with the best Victorian traditions, the telephone had originally been placed and where it still was.

She re-entered the room to say to Craddock:

"It's for you."

Slightly surprised, the Inspector went out to the instrument—carefully shutting the door of the living-room behind him.

"Craddock? Rydesdale here."

"Yes, sir."

"I've been looking through your report. In the interview you had with Phillipa Haymes I see she states positively that she hasn't seen her husband since his desertion from the Army?"

"That's right, sir—she was most emphatic. But in my opinion she wasn't speaking the truth."

"I agree with you. Do you remember a case about ten days ago—man run over by a lorry—taken to Milchester General with concussion and a fractured pelvis?"

"The fellow who snatched a child practically from under the wheels of a lorry, and got run down himself?"

"That's the one. No papers of any kind on him and nobody came forward to identify him. Looked as though he might be on the run. He died last night without regaining consciousness. But he's been identified—deserter from the Army—Ronald Haymes, ex-Captain in the South Loamshires."

"Phillipa Haymes' husband?"

"Yes. He'd got an old Chipping Cleghorn bus ticket on him, by the way—and quite a reasonable amount of money."

"So he did get money from his wife? I always thought he was the man Mitzi overheard talking to her in the summerhouse. She denied it flatly, of course. But surely, sir, that lorry accident was before——"

Rydesdale took the words out of his mouth.

"Yes, he was taken to Milchester General on the 28th. The hold-up at Little Paddocks was on the 29th. That lets him out of any possible connection with it. But his wife, of course, knew nothing about the accident. She may have been thinking all along that he *was* concerned in it. She'd hold her tongue—naturally—after all he *was* her husband."

"It was a fairly gallant bit of work, wasn't it, sir?" said Craddock slowly.

"Rescuing that child from the lorry? Yes. Plucky. Don't suppose it was cowardice that made Haymes desert. Well, all that's past history. For a man who'd blotted his copybook, it was a good death."

"I'm glad for her sake," said the Inspector. "And for that boy of theirs."

"Yes, he needn't be too ashamed of his father. And the young woman will be able to marry again now."

Craddock said slowly:

"I was thinking of that, sir. . . . It opens up—possibilities."

" You'd better break the news to her as you're on the spot."

" I will, sir. I'll push along there now. Or perhaps I'd better wait until she's back at Little Paddocks. It may be rather a shock—and there's someone else I rather want to have a word with first."

CHAPTER XIX

RECONSTRUCTION OF THE CRIME

"I'LL put on a lamp by you before I go," said Bunch. "It's so dark in here. There's going to be a storm, I think."

She lifted the small reading lamp to the other side of the table where it would throw light on Miss Marple's knitting as she sat in a wide high-backed chair.

As the flex pulled across the table, Tiglath Pileser the cat, leapt upon it and bit and clawed it violently.

"No, Tiglath Pileser, you mustn't . . . He really is awful. Look, he's nearly bitten it through—it's all frayed. Don't you understand, you idiotic puss, that you may get a nasty electric shock if you do that?"

"Thank you, dear," said Miss Marple, and put out a hand to turn on the lamp.

"It doesn't turn on there. You have to press that silly little switch half-way along the flex. Wait a minute. I'll take these flowers out of the way."

She lifted a bowl of Christmas roses across the table. Tiglath Pileser, his tail switching, put out a mischievous paw and clawed Bunch's arm. She spilled some of the water out of the vase. It fell on the frayed area of flex and on Tiglath Pileser himself, who leapt to the floor with an indignant hiss.

Miss Marple pressed the small pear-shaped switch. Where the water had soaked the frayed flex there was a flash and a crackle.

"Oh, dear," said Bunch. "It's fused. Now I suppose

all the lights in here are off." She tried them. " Yes, they are. So stupid being all on the same thingummibob. And it's made a burn on the table, too. Naughty Tiglath Pileser—it's all his fault. Aunt Jane—what's the matter? Did it startle you?"

" It's nothing, dear. Just something I saw quite suddenly which I ought to have seen before . . ."

" I'll go and fix the fuse and get the lamp from Julian's study."

" No, dear, don't bother. You'll miss your bus. I don't want any more light. I just want to sit quietly and—think about something. Hurry dear, or you won't catch your bus."

When Bunch had gone, Miss Marple sat quite still for about two minutes. The air of the room was heavy and menacing with the gathering storm outside.

Miss Marple drew a sheet of paper towards her.

She wrote first : *Lamp?* and underlined it heavily.

After a moment or two, she wrote another word.

Her pencil travelled down the paper, making brief cryptic notes. . . .

II

In the rather dark living-room of Boulders with its low ceiling and latticed window panes, Miss Hinchliffe and Miss Murgatroyd were having an argument.

" The trouble with you, Murgatroyd," said Miss Hinchliffe, " is that you won't *try*."

" But I tell you, Hinch, I can't remember a thing."

" Now look here, Amy Murgatroyd, we're going to do some constructive thinking. So far we haven't shone on the detective angle. I was quite wrong over that door business. You didn't hold the door open for the murderer after all. You're cleared, Murgatroyd!"

Miss Murgatroyd gave a rather watery smile.

"It's just our luck to have the only silent cleaning woman in Chipping Cleghorn," continued Miss Hinchliffe. "Usually I'm thankful for it, but this time it means we've got off to a bad start. Everybody else in the place knows about that second door in the drawing-room being used—and we only heard about it yesterday——"

"I still don't quite understand how——"

"It's perfectly simple. Our original premises were quite right. You can't hold open a door, wave a torch and shoot with a revolver all at the same time. We kept in the revolver and the torch and cut out the door. Well, we were wrong. It was the revolver we ought to have cut out."

"But he *did* have a revolver," said Miss Murgatroyd. "I saw it. It was there on the floor beside him."

"When he was dead, yes. It's all quite clear. *He* didn't fire that revolver——"

"Then who did?"

"That's what we're going to find out. But whoever did it, the same person put a couple of poisoned aspirin tablets by Letty Blacklock's bed—and thereby bumped off poor Dora Bunner. And that couldn't have been Rudi Scherz, because he's as dead as a doornail. It was someone who was in the room that night of the hold-up and probably someone who was at the birthday party, too. And the only person *that* lets out is Mrs. Harmon."

"You think someone put those aspirins there the day of the birthday party?"

"Why not?"

"But how could they?"

209

"Well, we all went to the lou, didn't we?" said Miss Hinchliffe coarsely. "And I washed my hands in the bathroom because of that sticky cake. And little Sweetie Easterbrook powdered her grubby little face in Blacklock's bedroom, didn't she?"

"Hinch! Do you think *she*——"

"I don't know yet. Rather obvious, if she did. I don't think if you were going to plant some tablets, that you'd want to be seen in the bedroom at all. Oh, yes, there were plenty of opportunities."

"The men didn't go upstairs."

"There are back stairs. After all, if a man leaves the room, you don't follow him to see if he really is going where you think he is going. It wouldn't be delicate! Anyway, don't *argue*, Murgatroyd. I want to get back to the original attempt on Letty Blacklock. Now, to begin with, get the facts firmly into your head, because it's all going to depend upon you."

Miss Murgatroyd looked alarmed.

"Oh, dear, Hinch, you know what a muddle I get into!"

"It's not a question of your brains, or the grey fluff that passes for brains with you. It's a question of *eyes*. It's a question of what you *saw*."

"But I didn't see *anything*."

"The trouble with you is, Murgatroyd, as I said just now, that you won't *try*. Now pay attention. This is what happened. Whoever it is that's got it in for Letty Blacklock was there in that room that evening. He (I say *he* because it's easier, but there's no reason why it should be a man more than a woman except, of course, that men are dirty dogs), well, he has previously oiled that second door that leads out of the drawing-room and which is supposed to be nailed up or something. Don't ask me *when* he did it, because that confuses things.

Actually, by choosing my time, I could walk into any house in Chipping Cleghorn and do anything I liked there for half an hour or so with no one being the wiser. It's just a question of working out where the daily women are and when the occupiers are out and exactly where they've gone and how long they'll be. Just good staff work. Now, to continue. He's oiled that second door. It will open without a sound. Here's the set-up : Lights go out, door A (the regular door) opens with a flourish. Business with torch and hold-up lines. In the meantime, while we're all goggling, X (that's the best term to use) slips quietly out by door B into the dark hall, comes up behind that Swiss idiot, takes a couple of shots at Letty Blacklock and then shoots the Swiss. Drops the revolver, where lazy thinkers like you will assume it's evidence that the Swiss did the shooting, and nips back into the room again by the time that someone gets a lighter going. Got it?"

" Yes—ye-es, but who was it?"

" Well, if *you* don't know, Murgatroyd, nobody does!"

" *Me?*" Miss Murgatroyd fairly twittered in alarm. " But I don't know anything *at all*. I don't *really*, Hinch!"

" Use that fluff of yours you call a brain. To begin with, where was everybody when the lights went out?"

" I don't know."

" Yes, you do. You're maddening, Murgatroyd. You know where *you* were, don't you? You were behind the door."

" Yes—yes, I was. It knocked against my corn when it flew open."

" Why don't you go to a proper chiropodist instead of messing about yourself with your feet. You'll give your-

self blood poisoning one of these days. Come on, now—
you're behind the door. *I'm* standing against the mantelpiece with my tongue hanging out for a drink. Letty
Blacklock is by the table near the archway, getting the
cigarettes. Patrick Simmons has gone through the archway into the small room where Letty Blacklock has had
the drinks put. Agreed?"

" Yes, yes, I remember all that."

" Good, now somebody else followed Patrick into that
room or was just starting to follow him. One of the men.
The annoying thing is that I can't remember whether it
was Easterbrook or Edmund Swettenham. Do you
remember?"

" No, I don't."

" You wouldn't! And there was someone else who
went through to the small room; Phillipa Haymes. I
remember that distinctly because I remember noticing
what a nice flat back she has, and I thought to myself
' that girl would look well on a horse.' I was watching
her and thinking just that. She went over to the mantelpiece in the other room. I don't know what it was she
wanted there, because at that moment the lights went
out.

" So that's the position. In the far drawing-room are
Patrick Simmons, Phillipa Haymes, and *either* Colonel
Easterbrook or Edmund Swettenham—we don't know
which. Now, Murgatroyd, pay attention. The most
probable thing is that it was *one of those three* who did
it. If anyone wanted to get out of that far door, they'd
naturally take care to put themselves in a convenient
place when the lights went out. So, as I say, in all
probability, it's one of those three. And in that case,
Murgatroyd, there's not a thing you can do about
it!"

Miss Murgatroyd brightened perceptibly.

"On the other hand," continued Miss Hinchliffe, "there's the possibility that it *wasn't* one of those three. And that's where you come in, Murgatroyd."

"But how should *I* know anything about it?"

"As I said before, if you don't nobody does."

"But I don't! I really *don't*! I couldn't see anything *at all*!"

"Oh, yes, you could. You're the only person who *could* see. You were standing behind the door. You couldn't look *at* the torch—because the door was between you and it. You were facing the other way, the same way as the torch was pointing. The rest of us were just dazzled. But *you* weren't dazzled."

"No—no, perhaps not, but I didn't *see* anything, the torch went round and round——"

"Showing you *what*? It rested on *faces*, didn't it? And on tables? And on chairs?"

"Yes—yes, it did . . . Miss Bunner, her mouth wide open and her eyes popping out of her head, staring and blinking."

"That's the stuff!" Miss Hinchliffe gave a sigh of relief. "The difficulty there is in making you use that grey fluff of yours! Now then, keep it up."

"But I didn't see any more, I didn't, really."

"You mean you saw an empty room? Nobody standing about? Nobody sitting down?"

"No, of course not *that*. Miss Bunner with her mouth open and Mrs. Harmon was sitting on the arm of a chair. She had her eyes tight shut and her knuckles all doubled up to her face—like a child."

"Good, that's Mrs. Harmon and Miss Bunner. Don't you see yet what I'm getting at? The difficulty is that I don't want to put ideas into your head. But when we've eliminated who you *did* see—we can get on to the important point which is, was there anyone you *didn't* see.

213

Got it? Besides the tables and the chairs and the chrys-anthemums and the rest of it, there were certain people; Julia Simmons, Mrs. Swettenham, Mrs. Easterbrook—*either* Colonel Easterbrook or Edmund Swettenham—Dora Bunner and Bunch Harmon. All right, you saw Bunch Harmon and Dora Bunner. Cross them off. Now *think*, Murgatroyd, *think*, was there one of those people who definitely *wasn't* there?"

Miss Murgatroyd jumped slightly as a branch knocked against the open window. She shut her eyes. She murmured to herself . . .

"The flowers . . . on the table . . . the big arm-chair . . . the torch didn't come round as far as you, Hinch—Mrs. Harmon, yes . . ."

The telephone rang sharply. Miss Hinchliffe went to it.

"Hallo, yes? The station?"

The obedient Miss Murgatroyd, her eyes closed, was reliving the night of the 29th. The torch, sweeping slowly round . . . a group of people . . . the windows . . . the sofa . . . Dora Bunner . . . the wall . . . the table with lamp . . . the archway . . . the sudden spat of the revolver . . .

". . . but that's *extraordinary*!" said Miss Murga-troyd.

"What?" Miss Hinchliffe was barking angrily into the telephone. "Been there since this morning? What time? Damn and blast you, and you only ring me up *now*? I'll set the S.P.C.A. after you. An oversight? Is *that* all you've got to say?"

She banged down the receiver.

"It's that dog," she said. "The red setter. Been at the station since this morning—since this morning at eight o'clock! Without a drop of water! And the idiots only ring me up now. I'm going to get her right away."

She plunged out of the room, Miss Murgatroyd squeaking shrilly in her wake.

" But listen, Hinch, a most extraordinary thing . . . I don't understand it . . ."

Miss Hinchliffe had dashed out of the door and across to the shed which served as a garage.

" We'll go on with it when I come back," she called. " I can't wait for you to come with me. You've got your bedroom slippers on as usual."

She pressed the starter of the car and backed out of the garage with a jerk. Miss Murgatroyd skipped nimbly sideways.

" But listen, Hinch, I *must* tell you——"

" When I come back . . ."

The car jerked and shot forwards. Miss Murgatroyd's voice came faintly after it on a high excited note.

" But, Hinch, *she wasn't there* . . ."

III

Overhead, the clouds had been gathering thick and blue. As Miss Murgatroyd stood looking after the retreating car, the first big drops began to fall.

In an agitated fashion, Miss Murgatroyd plunged across to a line of string on which she had, some hours previously, hung out a couple of jumpers and a pair of woollen combinations to dry.

She was murmuring under her breath :

" Really *most* extraordinary . . . Oh, dear, I shall never get these down in time . . . And they were nearly dry. . . ."

She struggled with a recalcitrant clothes peg, then turned her head as she heard someone approaching.

Then she smiled a pleased welcome.

" Hallo—do go inside, you'll get wet."

" Let me help you."

" Oh, if you don't mind . . . so annoying if they all get soaked again. I really ought to let down the line, but I think I can just reach."

" Here's your scarf. Shall I put it round your neck?"

" Oh, thank you . . . Yes, perhaps . . . If I could just reach this peg . . ."

The woollen scarf was slipped round her neck and then, suddenly, pulled tight . . .

Miss Murgatroyd's mouth opened, but no sound came except a small choking gurgle.

And the scarf was pulled tighter still . . .

I V

On her way back from the station, Miss Hinchliffe stopped the car to pick up Miss Marple who was hurrying along the street.

" Hallo," she shouted. " You'll get very wet. Come and have tea with us. I saw Bunch waiting for the bus. You'll be all alone at the Vicarage. Come and join us. Murgatroyd and I are doing a bit of reconstruction of the crime. I rather think we're just getting somewhere. Mind the dog. She's rather nervous."

" What a beauty."

" Yes, lovely bitch, isn't she? Those fools kept her at the station since this morning without letting me know. I told them off, the lazy b——s. Oh! excuse my language. I was brought up by grooms at home in Ireland."

The little car turned with a jerk into the small back-yard of Boulders.

216

A crowd of eager ducks and fowls encircled the two ladies as they descended.

"Curse Murgatroyd," said Miss Hinchliffe, "she hasn't given 'em their corn."

"Is it difficult to get corn?" Miss Marple inquired.

Miss Hinchliffe winked.

"I'm in with most of the farmers," she said.

Shooing away the hens, she escorted Miss Marple towards the cottage.

"Hope you're not too wet?"

"No, this is a very good mackintosh."

"I'll light the fire if Murgatroyd hasn't lit it. Hiyah, Murgatroyd? Where is the woman? Murgatroyd! Where's that dog? *She's* disappeared now."

A slow dismal howl came from outside.

"Curse the silly bitch." Miss Hinchliffe tramped to the door and called:

"Hyoup, Cutie—Cutie. Damn' silly name but that's what they called her apparently. We must find her another name. Hiyah, Cutie."

The red setter was sniffing at something lying below the taut string where a row of garments swirled in the wind.

"Murgatroyd's not even had the sense to bring the washing in. Where *is* she?"

Again the red setter nosed at what seemed to be a pile of clothes, and raised her nose high in the air and howled again.

"What's the *matter* with the dog?"

Miss Hinchliffe strode across the grass.

And quickly, apprehensively, Miss Marple ran after her. They stood there, side by side, the rain beating down on them and the older woman's arm went round the younger one's shoulders.

She felt the muscles go stiff and taut as Miss

Hinchliffe stood looking down on the thing lying there, with the blue congested face and the protruding tongue.

"I'll kill whoever did this," said Miss Hinchliffe in a low quiet voice, "if I once get my hands on her . . ."

Miss Marple said questioningly:

"*Her?*"

Miss Hinchliffe turned a ravaged face towards her.

"Yes. I know who it is—near enough . . . That is, it's one of three possibles."

She stood for another moment, looking down at her dead friend, and then turned towards the house. Her voice was dry and hard.

"We must ring up the police," she said. "And while we're waiting for them, I'll tell you. My fault, in a way, that Murgatroyd's lying out there. I made a game of it . . . Murder isn't a game. . . ."

"No," said Miss Marple. "Murder isn't a game."

"You know something about it, don't you?" said Miss Hinchliffe as she lifted the receiver and dialled.

She made a brief report and hung up.

"They'll be here in a few minutes . . . Yes, I heard that you'd been mixed up in this sort of business before . . . I think it was Edmund Swettenham told me so . . . Do you want to hear what we were doing, Murgatroyd and I?"

Succinctly she described the conversation held before her departure for the station.

"She called after me, you know, just as I was leaving . . . That's how I know it's a woman and not a man . . . If I'd waited—if only I'd *listened*! God dammit, the dog could have stopped where she was for another quarter of an hour."

"Don't blame yourself, my dear. That does no good. One can't foresee."

"No, one can't . . . Something tapped against the window, I remember. Perhaps *she* was outside there, then—yes, of course, she must have been . . . coming to the house . . . and there were Murgatroyd and I shouting at each other. Top of our voices . . . She heard . . . She heard it all . . ."

"You haven't told me yet what your friend said."

"Just one sentence! '*She wasn't there.*'"

She paused. "You see? There were three women we hadn't eliminated. Mrs. Swettenham, Mrs. Easterbrook, Julia Simmons. And one of those three—*wasn't there* . . . She wasn't there in the drawing-room because she had slipped out through the other door and was out in the hall."

"Yes," said Miss Marple, "I see."

"It's *one* of those three women. I don't know which. But I'll find out!"

"Excuse me," said Miss Marple. "But did she—did Miss Murgatroyd, I mean, say it exactly as you said it?"

"How d'you mean—as I said it?"

"Oh, dear, how can I explain? You said it like this. *She-wasn't-there.* An equal emphasis on every word. You see, there are three ways you could say it. You could say, '*She* wasn't there.' Very personal. Or again. 'She *wasn't* there.' Confirming some suspicion already held. Or else you could say (and this is nearer to the way you said it just now), 'She wasn't *there* . . .' quite blankly —with the emphasis, if there was emphasis—on the '*there*.'"

"I don't know," Miss Hinchliffe shook her head. "I can't remember . . . How the hell can I remember? I think, yes, surely she'd say '*She* wasn't there'? That would be the natural way, I should think. But I simply don't know. Does it make any difference?"

"Yes," said Miss Marple, thoughtfully. "I think so. It's a very *slight* indication, of course, but I think it *is* an indication. Yes, I should think it makes a lot of difference . . ."

220

CHAPTER XX

MISS MARPLE IS MISSING

THE postman, rather to his disgust, had lately been given orders to make an afternoon delivery of letters in Chipping Cleghorn as well as a morning one.

On this particular afternoon he left three letters at Little Paddocks at exactly ten minutes to five.

One was addressed to Phillipa Haymes in a school-boy's hand; the other two were for Miss Blacklock. She opened them as she and Phillipa sat down at the tea table. The torrential rain had enabled Phillipa to leave Dayas Hall early to-day, since once she had shut up the greenhouses there was nothing more to do.

Miss Blacklock tore open her first letter which was a bill for repairing the kitchen boiler. She snorted angrily.

" Dymond's prices are *preposterous*—quite preposterous. Still, I suppose all the other people are just as bad."

She opened the second letter which was in a hand-writing quite unknown to her.

Dear Cousin Letty (*it said*),

I hope it will be all right for me to come to you on Tuesday? I wrote to Patrick two days ago but he hasn't answered. So I presume it's all right. Mother is coming to England next month and hopes to see you then.

My train arrives at Chipping Cleghorn at 6.15 if that's convenient?

Yours affectionately,

Julia Simmons

Miss Blacklock read the letter once with astonishment pure and simple, and then again with a certain grimness. She looked up at Phillipa who was smiling over her son's letter.

"Are Julia and Patrick back, do you know?"

Phillipa looked up.

"Yes, they came in just after I did. They went upstairs to change. They were wet."

"Perhaps you'd not mind going and calling them."

"Of course, I will."

"Wait a moment—I'd like you to read this."

She handed Phillipa the letter she had received.

Phillipa read it and frowned. "I don't understand . . ."

"Nor do I, quite . . . I think it's about time I did. Call Patrick and Julia, Phillipa."

Phillipa called from the bottom of the stairs:

"Patrick! Julia! Miss Blacklock wants you."

Patrick came running down the stairs and entered the room.

"Don't go, Phillipa," said Miss Blacklock.

"Hallo, Aunt Letty," said Patrick cheerfully. "Want me?"

"Yes, I do. Perhaps you'll give me an explanation of *this*?"

Patrick's face showed an almost comical dismay as he read.

"I meant to telegraph her! What an ass I am!"

"This letter, I presume, is from your sister Julia?"

"Yes—yes, it is."

Miss Blacklock said grimly:

"*Then who, may I ask, is the young woman whom you brought here as Julia Simmons*, and whom I was given to understand was your sister and my cousin?"

"Well—you see—Aunt Letty—the fact of the matter is—I can explain it all—I know I oughtn't to have done

222

it—but it really seemed more of a lark than anything else. If you'll just let me explain——"

"I am waiting for you to explain. *Who is this young woman?*"

"Well, I met her at a cocktail party soon after I got demobbed. We got talking and I said I was coming here and then—well, we thought it might be rather a good wheeze if I brought her along . . . You see, Julia, the real Julia was mad to go on the stage and Mother had seven fits at the idea—however, Julia got a chance to join a jolly good repertory company up in Perth or somewhere and she thought she'd give it a try—but she thought she'd keep Mum calm by letting Mum think that she was here with me studying to be a dispenser like a good little girl."

"I still want to know who this other young woman *is*."

Patrick turned with relief as Julia, cool and aloof, came into the room.

"The balloon's gone up," he said.

Julia raised her eyebrows. Then, still cool, she came forward and sat down.

"O.K.," she said. "That's that. I suppose you're very angry?" She studied Miss Blacklock's face with almost dispassionate interest. "I should be if I were you."

"*Who are you?*"

Julia sighed.

"I think the moment's come when I make a clean breast of things. Here we go. I'm one half of the Pip and Emma combination. To be exact, my christened name is Emma Jocelyn Stamfordis—only Father soon dropped the Stamfordis. I think he called himself De Courcy next.

"My father and mother, let me tell you, split up about three years after Pip and I were born. Each of

223

them went their own way. And they split us up. I was
Father's part of the loot. He was a bad parent on the
whole, though quite a charming one. I had various
desert spells of being educated in convents—when Father
hadn't any money, or was preparing to engage in some
particularly nefarious deal. He used to pay the first
term with every sign of affluence and then depart and
leave me on the nuns' hands for a year or two. In the
intervals, he and I had some very good times together,
moving in cosmopolitan society. However, the war separ-
ated us completely. I've no idea of what's happened to
him. I had a few adventures myself. I was with the
French Resistance for a time. Quite exciting. To cut a
long story short, I landed up in London and began to
think about my future. I knew that Mother's brother
with whom she'd had a frightful row, had died a very
rich man. I looked up his will to see if there was anything for me. There wasn't—not directly, that is to say.
I made a few inquiries about his widow—it seemed she
was quite gaga and kept under drugs and was dying by
inches. Frankly, it looked as though *you* were my best
bet. You were going to come into a hell of a lot of
money and from all I could find out, you didn't seem to
have anyone much to spend it on. I'll be quite frank. It
occurred to me that if I could get to know you in a
friendly kind of way, and if you took a fancy to me—
well, after all, conditions have changed a bit, haven't
they, since Uncle Randall died? I mean any money we
ever had has been swept away in the cataclysm of
Europe. I thought you might pity a poor orphan girl,
all alone in the world, and make her, perhaps a small
allowance."

"Oh, you did, did you?" said Miss Blacklock grimly.

"Yes. Of course, I hadn't seen you then . . . I
visualised a kind of sob stuff approach . . . Then, by a

marvellous stroke of luck, I met Patrick here—and he turned out to be your nephew or your cousin, or something. Well, that struck me as a marvellous chance. I went bullheaded for Patrick and he fell for me in a most gratifying way. The real Julia was all wet about this acting stuff and I soon persuaded her it was her duty to Art to go and fix herself up in some uncomfortable lodgings in Perth and train to be the new Sarah Bernhardt.

"You mustn't blame Patrick too much. He felt awfully sorry for me, all alone in the world—and he soon thought it would be a really marvellous idea for me to come here as his sister and do my stuff."

"And he also approved of your continuing to tell a tissue of lies to the Police?"

"Have a heart, Letty. Don't you see that when that ridiculous hold-up business happened—or rather after it happened—I began to feel I was in a bit of a spot. Let's face it, I've got a perfectly good motive for putting you out of the way. You've only got my word for it now that I wasn't the one who tried to do it. You can't expect me deliberately to go and incriminate myself. Even Patrick got nasty ideas about me from time to time, and if even *he* could think things like that, what on earth would the police think? That Detective-Inspector struck me as a man of singularly sceptical mind. No, I figured out the only thing for me to do was to sit tight as Julia and just fade away when term came to an end.

"How was I to know that fool Julia, the real Julia, would go and have a row with the producer, and fling the whole thing up in a fit of temperament? She writes to Patrick and asks if she can come here, and instead of wiring her 'Keep away' he goes and forgets to do anything at all!" She cast an angry glance at Patrick. "Of all the utter *idiots*!"

She sighed.

225

" You don't know the straits I've been put to in Milchester! Of course, I haven't been to the hospital at all. But I had to go *somewhere*. Hours and hours I've spent in the pictures seeing the most frightful films over and over again."

" *Pip and Emma*," murmured Miss Blacklock. " I never believed, somehow, in spite of what the Inspector said, that they were *real*——"

She looked searchingly at Julia.

" You're Emma," she said. " Where's Pip?"

Julia's eyes, limpid and innocent, met hers.

" I don't know," she said. " I haven't the least idea."

" I think you're lying, Julia. When did you see him last?"

Was there a momentary hesitation before Julia spoke? She said clearly and deliberately :

" I haven't seen him since we were both three years old—when my mother took him away. I haven't seen either him or my mother. I don't know where they are."

" And that's all you have to say?"

Julia sighed.

" I could say I was sorry. But it wouldn't really be true; because actually I'd do the same thing again— though not if I'd known about this murder business, of course."

" Julia," said Miss Blacklock, " (I call you that because I'm used to it). You were with the French Resistance, you say?"

" Yes. For eighteen months."

" Then I suppose you learned to shoot?"

Again those cool blue eyes met hers.

" I can shoot all right. I'm a first-class shot. I didn't shoot at you, Letitia Blacklock, though you've only got my word for that. But I can tell you this, that if *I* had shot at you, I wouldn't have been likely to miss."

11

The sound of a car driving up to the door broke through the tenseness of the moment.

" Who can that be?" asked Miss Blacklock.

Mitzi put a tousled head in. She was showing the whites of her eyes.

" It is the Police come again," she said. " This, it is persecution! Why will they not leave us alone? I will not bear it. I will write to the Prime Minister. I will write to your King."

Craddock's hand put her firmly and not too kindly aside. He came in with such a grim set to his lips that they all looked at him apprehensively. This was a new Inspector Craddock.

He said sternly:

" Miss Murgatroyd has been murdered. She was strangled—not more than an hour ago." His eye singled out Julia. " You—Miss Simmons—where have you been all day?"

Julia said warily:

" In Milchester. I've just got in."

" And you?" The eye went on to Patrick.

" Yes."

" Did you both come back here together?"

" Yes—yes, we did," said Patrick.

" No," said Julia. " It's no good, Patrick. That's the kind of lie that will be found out at once. The bus people know us well. I came back on the earlier bus, Inspector—the one that gets here at four o'clock."

" And what did you do then?"

" I went for a walk."

" In the direction of Boulders?"

" No, I went across the fields."

He stared at her. Julia, her face pale, her lips tense, stared back.

Before anyone could speak, the telephone rang.

Miss Blacklock, with an inquiring glance at Craddock, picked up the receiver.

" Yes. Who? Oh, Bunch. What? No. No, she hasn't. I've no idea . . . Yes, he's here now."

She lowered the instrument and said :

" Mrs. Harmon would like to speak to you, Inspector. Miss Marple has not come back to the Vicarage and Mrs. Harmon is worried about her."

Craddock took two strides forward and gripped the telephone.

" Craddock speaking."

" I'm worried, Inspector." Bunch's voice came through with a childish tremor in it. " Aunt Jane's out somewhere—and I don't know where. And they say that Miss Murgatroyd's been killed. Is it true?"

" Yes, it's true, Mrs. Harmon. Miss Marple was there with Miss Hinchliffe when they found the body."

" Oh, so *that's* where she is." Bunch sounded relieved.

" No—no, I'm afraid she isn't. Not now. She left there about—let me see—half an hour ago. She hasn't got home?"

" No—she hasn't. It's only ten minutes' walk. Where can she be?"

" Perhaps she's called in on one of your neighbours?"

" I've rung them up—*all of them*. She's not there. I'm frightened, Inspector."

" So am I," thought Craddock.

He said quickly :

228

" I'll come round to you—at once."

" Oh, *do*—there's a piece of paper. She was writing on it before she went out. I don't know if it means anything . . . It just seems gibberish to me."

Craddock replaced the receiver.

Miss Blacklock said anxiously :

" Has something happened to Miss Marple? Oh, I hope not."

" I hope not, too." His mouth was grim.

" She's so old—and frail."

" I know."

Miss Blacklock, standing with her hand pulling at the choker of pearls round her neck, said in a hoarse voice :

" It's getting worse and worse. Whoever's doing these things must be mad, Inspector—quite mad . . ."

" I wonder."

The choker of pearls round Miss Blacklock's neck broke under the clutch of her nervous fingers. The smooth white globules rolled all over the room.

Letitia cried out in an anguished tone.

" My pearls—my *pearls*——" The agony in her voice was so acute that they all looked at her in astonishment. She turned, her hand to her throat, and rushed sobbing out of the room.

Phillipa began picking up the pearls.

" I've never seen her so upset over anything," she said. " Of course—she always wears them. Do you think, perhaps, that someone special gave them to her? Randall Goedler, perhaps."

" It's possible," said the Inspector slowly.

" They're not—they couldn't be—*real* by any chance?" Phillipa asked from where, on her knees, she was still collecting the white shining globes.

Taking one in his hand, Craddock was just about to

reply contemptuously, " Real? Of course not !" when he suddenly stifled the words.

After all, *could* the pearls be real?

They were so large, so even, so white that their falseness seemed palpable, but Craddock remembered suddenly a police case where a string of real pearls had been bought for a few shillings in a pawnbroker's shop.

Letitia Blacklock had assured him that there was no jewellery of value in the house. If these pearls were, by any chance, genuine, they must be worth a fabulous sum. And if Randall Goedler had given them to her—then they might be worth any sum you cared to name.

They looked false—they *must* be false, but—if they were real?

Why not? She might herself be unaware of their value. Or she might choose to protect her treasure by treating it as though it were a cheap ornament worth a couple of guineas at most. What would they be worth if real? A fabulous sum . . . Worth doing murder for—*if anybody knew about them*.

With a start, the Inspector wrenched himself away from his speculations. Miss Marple was missing. He must go to the Vicarage.

III

He found Bunch and her husband waiting for him, their faces anxious and drawn.

" She hasn't come back," said Bunch.

" Did she say she was coming back here when she left Boulders?" asked Julian.

" She didn't actually say so," said Craddock slowly,

throwing his mind back to the last time he had seen Jane Marple.

He remembered the grimness of her lips and the severe frosty light in those usually gentle blue eyes.

Grimness, an inexorable determination . . . to do what? To go where?

"She was talking to Sergeant Fletcher when I last saw her," he said. "Just by the gate. And then she went through it and out. I took it she was going straight home to the Vicarage. I would have sent her in the car—but there was so much to attend to, and she slipped away very quietly. Fletcher may know something! Where's Fletcher?"

But Sergeant Fletcher, it seemed, as Craddock learned when he rang up Boulders, was neither to be found there nor had he left any message where he had gone. There was some idea that he had returned to Milchester for some reason.

The Inspector rang up headquarters in Milchester, but no news of Fletcher was to be found there.

Then Craddock turned to Bunch as he remembered what she had told him over the telephone.

"Where's that paper? You said she'd been writing something on a bit of paper."

Bunch brought it to him. He spread it out on the table and looked down on it. Bunch leant over his shoulder and spelled it out as he read. The writing was shaky and not easy to read:

Lamp.

Then came the word "*Violets.*"

Then after a space:

Where is bottle of aspirin?

The next item in this curious list was more difficult to make out. "*Delicious Death,*" Bunch read. "That's Mitzi's cake."

231

"*Making enquiries*," read Craddock.

"Inquiries? What about, I wonder? What's this? *Severe affliction bravely borne* . . . What on earth——!"

"*Iodine*," read the Inspector. "*Pearls*. Ah, pearls."

"And then *Lotty*—no, *Letty*. Her *e*'s look like *o*'s. And then *Berne*. And what's this? *Old Age Pension* . . ."

They looked at each other in bewilderment.

Craddock recapitulated swiftly:

"Lamp. Violets. Where is bottle of aspirin? Delicious Death. Making enquiries. Severe affliction bravely borne. Iodine. Pearls. Letty. Berne. Old Age Pension."

Bunch asked: "Does it mean anything? Anything at all? I can't see any connection."

Craddock said slowly: "I've just a glimmer—but I don't see. It's odd that she should have put down that about pearls."

"What about pearls? What does it mean?"

"Does Miss Blacklock always wear that three tier choker of pearls?"

"Yes, she does. We laugh about it sometimes. They're so dreadfully false looking, aren't they? But I suppose she thinks it's fashionable."

"There might be another reason," said Craddock slowly.

"You don't mean that they're *real*. Oh! they *couldn't* be!"

"How often have you had an opportunity of seeing real pearls of that size, Mrs. Harmon?"

"But they're so glassy."

Craddock shrugged his shoulders.

"Anyway, they don't matter now. It's Miss Marple that matters. We've got to find her."

They'd got to find her before it was too late—but perhaps it was already too late? Those pencilled words showed that she was on the track . . . But that was dangerous—horribly dangerous. And where the hell was Fletcher?

Craddock strode out of the Vicarage to where he'd left his car. Search—that was all he could do—search.

A voice spoke to him out of the dripping laurels.

"Sir!" said Sergeant Fletcher urgently. "*Sir . . .*"

CHAPTER XXI

THREE WOMEN

DINNER was over at Little Paddocks. It had been a silent and uncomfortable meal.

Patrick, uneasily aware of having fallen from grace, only made spasmodic attempts at conversation—and such as he did make were not well received. Phillipa Haymes was sunk in abstraction. Miss Blacklock herself had abandoned the effort to behave with her normal cheerfulness. She had changed for dinner and had come down wearing her necklace of cameos but for the first time fear showed from her darkly circled eyes, and betrayed itself by her twitching hands.

Julia alone, had maintained her air of cynical detachment throughout the evening.

" I'm sorry, Letty," she said, " that I can't pack my bag and go. But I presume the police wouldn't allow it. I don't suppose I'll darken your roof—or whatever the expression is—for long. I should imagine that Inspector Craddock will be round with a warrant and the handcuffs any moment. In fact, I can't imagine why something of the kind hasn't happened already."

" He's looking for the old lady—for Miss Marple," said Miss Blacklock.

" Do you think she's been murdered, too?" Patrick asked with scientific curiosity. " But why? What could she know?"

" I don't know," said Miss Blacklock dully. " Perhaps Miss Murgatroyd told her something."

" If she's been murdered too," said Patrick, " there

seems to be logically only one person who could have done it."

" Who?"

" Hinchliffe, of course," said Patrick triumphantly. " That's where she was last seen alive—at Boulders. My solution would be that she never left Boulders."

" My head aches," said Miss Blacklock in a dull voice. She pressed her fingers to her forehead. " Why should Hinch murder Miss Marple? It doesn't make sense."

" It would if Hinch had really murdered Murgatroyd," said Patrick triumphantly.

Phillipa came out of her apathy to say:

" Hinch wouldn't murder Murgatroyd."

Patrick was in an argumentative mood.

" She might have if Murgatroyd had blundered on something to show that she—Hinch—was the criminal."

" Anyway, Hinch was at the station when Murgatroyd was killed."

" She could have murdered Murgatroyd before she left."

Startling them all, Letitia Blacklock suddenly screamed out:

" Murder, murder, *murder*——! Can't you talk of *anything* else? I'm frightened, don't you understand? I'm frightened. I wasn't before. I thought I could take care of myself . . . But what can you do against a murderer who's waiting—and watching—and biding his time! Oh, God!"

She dropped her head forward on her hands. A moment later she looked up and apologised stiffly.

" I'm sorry. I—I lost control."

" That's all right, Aunt Letty," said Patrick affectionately. " I'll look after you."

" You?" was all Letitia Blacklock said, but the disillusionment behind the word was almost an accusation.

That had been shortly before dinner, and Mitzi had then created a diversion by coming and declaring that she was not going to cook the dinner.

" I do not do anything more in this house. I go to my room. I lock myself in. I stay there until it is daylight. I am afraid—people are being killed—that Miss Murgatroyd with her stupid English face—who would want to kill *her*? Only a maniac! Then it is a maniac that is about! And a maniac does not care *who* he kills. But me, I do not want to be killed! There are shadows in that kitchen—and I hear noises—I think there is some- one out in the yard and then I think I see a shadow by the larder door and then it is footsteps I hear. So I go now to my room and I lock the door and perhaps even I put the chest of drawers against it. And in the morning I tell that cruel hard policeman that I go away from here. And if he will not let me I say: ' I scream and I scream and I scream until you have to let me go!' "

Everybody, with a vivid recollection of what Mitzi could do in the screaming line, shuddered at the threat.

" So I go to my room," said Mitzi, repeating the state- ment once more to make her intentions quite clear. With a symbolic action she cast off the cretonne apron she had been wearing. " Good night, Miss Blacklock. Per- haps in the morning, you may not be alive. So in case that is so, I say good-bye."

She departed abruptly and the door, with its usual gentle little whine, closed softly after her.

Julia got up.

" I'll see to dinner," she said in a matter-of-fact way. " Rather a good arrangement—less embarrassing for you all than having me sit down at table with you. Patrick (since he's constituted himself your protector, Aunt Letty) had better taste every dish first. I don't want to be accused of poisoning you on top of everything else."

So Julia had cooked and served a really excellent meal.
Phillipa had come out to the kitchen with an offer of assistance but Julia had said firmly that she didn't want any help.

" Julia, there's something I want to say——"

" This is no time for girlish confidences," said Julia firmly. " Go on back in the dining-room, Phillipa."

Now dinner was over and they were in the drawing-room with coffee on the small table by the fire—and nobody seemed to have anything to say. They were waiting—that was all.

At 8.30 Inspector Craddock rang up.

" I shall be with you in about a quarter of an hour's time," he announced. " I'm bringing Colonel and Mrs. Easterbrook and Mrs. Swettenham and her son with me."

" But really, Inspector . . . I can't cope with people to-night——"

Miss Blacklock's voice sounded as though she were at the end of her tether.

" I know how you feel, Miss Blacklock. I'm sorry. But this is urgent."

" Have you—found Miss Marple ?"

" No," said the Inspector and rang off.

Julia took the coffee tray out to the kitchen where, to her surprise, she found Mitzi contemplating the piled up dishes and plates by the sink.

Mitzi burst into a torrent of words.

" See what you do in my so nice kitchen ! That frying pan—only, *only* for omelettes do I use it ! And you, what have you used it for ?"

" Frying onions."

" Ruined—*ruined*. It will have now to be *washed* and never—*never*—do I wash my omelette pan. I rub it carefully over with a greasy newspaper, that is all. And

237

this saucepan here that you have used—that one, I use him only for milk——"

"Well, I don't know what pans you use for what," said Julia crossly. "You chose to go to bed and why on earth you've chosen to get up again, I can't imagine. Go away again and leave me to wash up in peace."

"No, I will not let you use my kitchen."

"Oh, Mitzi, you *are* impossible!"

Julia stalked angrily out of the kitchen and at that moment the door bell rang.

"I do not go to the door," Mitzi called from the kitchen. Julia muttered an impolite Continental expression under her breath and stalked to the front door.

It was Miss Hinchliffe.

"'Evening," she said in her gruff voice. "Sorry to barge in. Inspector's rung up, I expect?"

"He didn't tell us you were coming," said Julia, leading the way to the drawing-room.

"He said I needn't come unless I liked," said Miss Hinchliffe. "But I do like."

Nobody offered Miss Hinchliffe sympathy or mentioned Miss Murgatroyd's death. The ravaged face of the tall vigorous woman told its own tale, and would have made any expression of sympathy an impertinence.

"Turn all the lights on," said Miss Blacklock. "And put more coal on the fire. I'm cold—horribly cold. Come and sit here by the fire, Miss Hinchliffe. The Inspector said he would be here in a quarter of an hour. It must be nearly that now."

"Mitzi's come down again," said Julia.

"Has she? Sometimes I think that girl's mad—quite mad. But then perhaps we're all mad."

"I've no patience with this saying that all people who commit crimes are mad," barked Miss Hinchliffe. "Horribly and intelligently sane—that's what I think a criminal is!"

The sound of a car was heard outside and presently Craddock came in with Colonel and Mrs. Easterbrook and Edmund and Mrs. Swettenham.

They were all curiously subdued.

Colonel Easterbrook said in a voice that was like an echo of his usual tones :

" Ha! A good fire."

Mrs. Easterbrook wouldn't take off her fur coat and sat down close to her husband. Her face, usually pretty and rather vapid, was like a little pinched weasel face. Edmund was in one of his furious moods and scowled at everybody. Mrs. Swettenham made what was evidently a great effort, and which resulted in a kind of parody of herself.

" It's awful—isn't it?" she said conversationally. " Everything, I mean. And really the less one says, the better. Because one doesn't know *who next*—like the Plague. Dear Miss Blacklock, don't you think you ought to have a little brandy? Just half a wineglass even? I always think there's nothing like brandy—such a wonderful stimulant. I—it seems so terrible of us—forcing our way in here like this, but Inspector Craddock *made us* come. And it seems so terrible—she hasn't been found, you know. That poor old thing from the Vicarage, I mean. Bunch Harmon is nearly frantic. Nobody knows *where* she went instead of going home. She didn't come to us. I've not even seen her to-day. And I should know if she *had* come to the house because I was in the drawing-room—at the back, you know, and Edmund was in his study writing—and that's at the front—so if she'd come either way we *should* have seen. And, oh, I do hope and pray that nothing has happened to that dear sweet old thing—all her faculties still and *everything*."

"Mother," said Edmund in a voice of acute suffering, "can't you shut up?"

"I'm sure, dear, I don't want to say a *word*," said Mrs. Swettenham, and sat down on the sofa by Julia.

Inspector Craddock stood near the door. Facing him, almost in a row, were the three women. Julia and Mrs. Swettenham on the sofa. Mrs. Easterbrook on the arm of her husband's chair. He had not brought about this arrangement, but it suited him very well.

Miss Blacklock and Miss Hinchliffe were crouching over the fire. Edmund stood near them. Phillipa was far back in the shadows.

Craddock began without preamble.

"You all know that Miss Murgatroyd's been killed," he began. "We've reason to believe that the person who killed her was a woman. And for certain other reasons we can narrow it down still more. I'm about to ask certain ladies here to account for what they were doing between the hours of four and four-twenty this afternoon. I have already had an account of her movements from—from the young lady who has been calling herself Miss Simmons. I will ask her to repeat that statement. At the same time, Miss Simmons, I must caution you that you need not answer if you think your answers may incriminate you, and anything you say will be taken down by Constable Edwards and may be used as evidence in court."

"You have to say that, don't you?" said Julia. She was rather pale, but still composed. "I repeat that between four and four-thirty I was walking along the field leading down to the brook by Compton Farm. I came back to the road by that field with three poplars in it. I didn't meet anyone as far as I can remember. I did not go near Boulders."

"Mrs. Swettenham?"

Edmund said, " Are you cautioning all of us?"

The Inspector turned to him.

" No. At the moment only Miss Simmons. I have no reason to believe that any other statement made will be incriminating, but anyone, of course, is entitled to have a solicitor present and to refuse to answer questions unless he *is* present."

" Oh, but that would be very silly and a complete waste of time," cried Mrs. Swettenham. " I'm sure I can tell you at once exactly what I was doing. That's what you want, isn't it? Shall I begin now?"

" Yes, please, Mrs. Swettenham."

" Now, let me see." Mrs. Swettenham closed her eyes, opened them again. " Of course I had nothing *at all* to do with killing Miss Murgatroyd. I'm sure *everybody* here knows *that*. But I'm a woman of the world, I know quite well that the police have to ask all the most unnecessary questions and write the answers down very carefully, because it's all for what they call ' the record.' That's it, isn't it?" Mrs. Swettenham flashed the question at the diligent Constable Edwards and added graciously, " I'm not going too fast for you, I hope?"

Constable Edwards, a good shorthand writer, but with little social *savoir-faire*, turned red to the ears and replied :

" It's quite all right, madam. Well, perhaps a *little* slower would be better."

Mrs. Swettenham resumed her discourse with emphatic pauses where she considered a comma or a full stop might be appropriate.

" Well, of course it's difficult to say—exactly—because I've not got, really, a very good sense of time. And ever since the war quite half our clocks haven't gone at all, and the ones that do go are often either fast or slow or stop because we haven't wound them up." Mrs. Swettenham paused to let this picture of confused time sink in and then went on earnestly, " What I *think* I was doing at four o'clock was turning the heel of my sock (and for some extraordinary reason I was going round the wrong way—in purl, you know, not plain) but if I *wasn't* doing that, I must have been outside snipping off the dead chrysanthemums—no, that was earlier—before the rain."

" The rain," said the inspector, " started at 4.10 exactly."

" Did it now? That helps a lot. Of course, I was upstairs putting a wash-basin in the passage where the rain always comes through. And it was coming through so fast that I guessed at once that the gutter was stopped up again. So I came down and got my mackintosh and rubber boots. I called Edmund, but he didn't answer, so I thought perhaps he'd got to a very important place in his novel and I wouldn't disturb him, and I've done it quite often myself before. With the broom handle, you know, tied on to that long thing you push up windows with."

" You mean," said Craddock, noting bewilderment on his subordinate's face, " that you were cleaning out the gutter?"

" Yes, it was all choked up with leaves. It took a long time and I got rather wet, but I got it clear at last. And then I went in and got changed and washed—so *smelly*, dead leaves—and then I went into the kitchen and put the kettle on. It was 6.15 by the kitchen clock."

Constable Edwards blinked.

" Which means," finished Mrs. Swettenham triumphantly, " that it was exactly twenty minutes to five."

" Or near enough," she added.

" Did anybody see what you were doing whilst you were out cleaning the gutter?"

" No, indeed," said Mrs. Swettenham, " I'd soon have

roped them in to help if they had! It's a most difficult thing to do single-handed."

"So, by your own statement, you were outside, in a mackintosh and boots, at the time when the rain was coming down, and according to you, you were employed during that time in cleaning out a gutter but you have no one who can substantiate that statement?"

"You can look at the gutter," said Mrs. Swettenham. "It's beautifully clear."

"Did you hear your mother call to you, Mr. Swetten-ham?"

"No," said Edmund. "I was fast asleep."

"Edmund," said his mother reproachfully, "I thought you were *writing*."

Inspector Craddock turned to Mrs. Easterbrook.

"Now, Mrs. Easterbrook?"

"I was sitting with Archie in his study," said Mrs. Easterbrook fixing wide innocent eyes on him. "We were listening to the wireless together, weren't we, Archie?"

There was a pause. Colonel Easterbrook was very red in the face. He took his wife's hand in his.

"You don't understand these things, kitten," he said. "I—well, I must say, Inspector, you've rather sprung this business on us. My wife, you know, has been terribly upset by all this. She's nervous and highly strung and doesn't appreciate the importance of—of taking due consideration before she makes a statement."

"Archie," cried Mrs. Easterbrook reproachfully, "are you going to say you weren't with me?"

"Well, I wasn't, was I, my dear? I mean one's got to stick to the facts. Very important in this sort of inquiry. I was talking to Lampson, the farmer at Croft End, about some chicken netting. That was about a quarter to four. I didn't get home until after the rain had stopped. Just before tea. A quarter to five. Laura was toasting the scones."

" And had *you* been out also, Mrs. Easterbrook?"

The pretty face looked more like a weasel's than ever. Her eyes had a trapped look.

" No—no, I just sat listening to the wireless. I didn't go out. Not then. I'd been out earlier. About—about half-past three. Just for a little walk. Not far."

She looked as though she expected more questions, but Craddock said quietly :

" That's all, Mrs. Easterbrook."

He went on : " These statements will be typed out. You can read them and sign them if they are substantially correct."

Mrs. Easterbrook looked at him with sudden venom.

" Why don't you ask the others where they were? That Haymes woman? And Edmund Swettenham? How do you know he *was* asleep indoors? Nobody saw him."

Inspector Craddock said quietly :

" Miss Murgatroyd, before she died, made a certain statement. On the night of the hold-up here, *someone* was absent from this room. Someone who was supposed to have been in the room all the time. Miss Murgatroyd told her friend the names of the people she *did* see. By a process of elimination, she made the discovery that there was someone she did *not* see."

" Nobody could see anything," said Julia.

" Murgatroyd could," said Miss Hinchliffe, speaking suddenly in her deep voice. " She was over there behind the door, where Inspector Craddock is now. She was the only person who could see anything of what was happening."

" *Aha! That is what you think, is it!*" demanded Mitzi.

244

She made one of her dramatic entrances, flinging open the door and almost knocking Craddock sideways. She was in a frenzy of excitement.

" Ah, you do not ask Mitzi to come in here with the others, do you, you stiff policeman? I am only Mitzi! Mitzi in the kitchen! Let her stay in the kitchen where she belongs! But I tell you that Mitzi, as well as anyone else, and perhaps better, yes, better, can see things. Yes, I see things. I see something the night of the burglary. I see something and I do not quite believe it, and I hold my tongue till now. I think to myself I will not tell what it is I have seen, not yet. I will wait."

" And when everything had calmed down, you meant to ask for a little money from a certain person, eh?" said Craddock.

Mitzi turned on him like an angry cat.

" And why not? Why look down your nose? Why should I not be paid for it if I have been so generous as to keep silence? Especially if some day there will be money—much *much* money. Oh! I have heard things —I know what goes on. I know this Pippemmer—this secret society of which *she* "—she flung a dramatic finger towards Julia—" is an agent. Yes, I would have waited and asked for money—but now I am afraid. I would rather be *safe*. For soon, perhaps, someone will kill *me*. So I will tell what I know."

" All right then," said the Inspector sceptically. " What *do* you know?"

" I tell you." Mitzi spoke solemnly. " On that night I am *not* in the pantry cleaning silver as I say—I am already in the dining-room when I hear the gun go off. I look through the keyhole. The hall it is black, but the gun go off again and the torch it falls—and it swings round as it falls—and I see *her*. I see *her* there close to him, with the gun in her hand. I see Miss Blacklock."

" Me?" Miss Blacklock sat up in astonishment. " You must be mad!"

" But that's impossible," cried Edmund. " Mitzi couldn't have seen Miss Blacklock———"

Craddock cut in and his voice had the corrosive quality of a deadly acid.

" *Couldn't she, Mr. Swettenham? And why not?* Because it *wasn't* Miss Blacklock who was standing there with the gun? It was *you*, wasn't it?"

" I?—of course not—what the *hell*!"

" *You* took Colonel Easterbrook's revolver. *You* fixed up the business with Rudi Scherz—as a good joke. You had followed Patrick Simmons into the far room and when the lights went out, you slipped out through the carefully oiled door. You shot at Miss Blacklock and then you killed Rudi Scherz. A few seconds later you were back in the drawing-room clicking your lighter."

For a moment Edmund seemed at a loss for words, then he spluttered out :

" The whole idea is *monstrous*. Why *me*? What earthly motive had *I* got?"

" If Miss Blacklock dies before Mrs. Goedler, two people inherit, remember. The two we know of as Pip and Emma. Julia Simmons has turned out to be Emma———"

" And you think I'm Pip?" Edmund laughed. " Fantastic—absolutely *fantastic*! I'm about the right age— nothing else. And I can prove to you, you damned fool, that I *am* Edmund Swettenham. Birth certificate, schools, university—everything."

" He isn't Pip." The voice came from the shadows in the corner. Phillipa Haymes came forward, her face pale. " *I'm Pip*, Inspector."

" *You*, Mrs. Haymes?"

" Yes. Everybody seems to have assumed that Pip

was a boy—Julia knew, of course, that her twin was another girl—I don't know why she didn't say so this afternoon——"

"Family solidarity," said Julia. "I suddenly realised who you were. I'd had no idea till that moment."

"I'd had the same idea as Julia did," said Phillipa, her voice trembling a little. "After I—lost my husband and the war was over, I wondered what I was going to do. My mother died many years ago. I found out about my Goedler relations. Mrs. Goedler was dying and at her death the money would go to a Miss Blacklock. I found out where Miss Blacklock lived and I—I came here. I took a job with Mrs. Lucas. I hoped that, since this Miss Blacklock was an elderly woman without relatives, she might, perhaps, be willing to help. Not me, because I could work, but help with Harry's education. After all, it *was* Goedler money and she'd no one particular of her own to spend it on.

"And then," Phillipa spoke faster, it was as though, now her long reserve had broken down, she couldn't get the words out fast enough, "that hold-up happened and I began to be frightened. Because it seemed to me that the only possible person with a motive for killing Miss Blacklock was *me*. I hadn't the least idea who Julia was —we aren't identical twins and we're not much alike to look at. No, it seemed as though I was the only one bound to be suspected."

She stopped and pushed her fair hair back from her face, and Craddock suddenly realised that the faded snapshot in the box of letters must have been a photograph of Phillipa's mother. The likeness was undeniable. He knew too why that mention of closing and unclosing hands had seemed familiar—Phillipa was doing it now.

"Miss Blacklock has been good to me. Very *very* good to me—I didn't try to kill her. I never thought of killing

247

her. But all the same, I'm Pip." She added, "You see, you needn't suspect Edmund any more."

"Needn't I?" said Craddock. Again there was that acid biting tone in his voice. "Edmund Swettenham's a young man who's fond of money. A young man, perhaps, who would like to marry a rich wife. But she wouldn't be a rich wife *unless Miss Blacklock died before Mrs. Goedler*. And since it seemed almost certain that Mrs. Goedler would die before Miss Blacklock, well—he had to do something about it—*didn't you, Mr. Swettenham?*"

"It's a damned lie!" Edmund shouted.

And then, suddenly, a sound rose on the air. It came from the kitchen—a long unearthly shriek of terror.

"That isn't Mitzi!" cried Julia.

"No," said Inspector Craddock, "it's someone who's murdered three people . . ."

CHAPTER XXII

THE TRUTH

WHEN the Inspector turned on Edmund Swettenham, Mitzi had crept quietly out of the room and back to the kitchen. She was running water into the sink when Miss Blacklock entered.

Mitzi gave her a shamefaced sideways look.

"What a liar you are, Mitzi," said Miss Blacklock pleasantly. "Here—that isn't the way to wash up. The silver first, and fill the sink right up. You can't wash up in about two inches of water."

Mitzi turned the taps on obediently.

"You are not angry at what I say, Miss Blacklock?" she asked.

"If I were to be angry at all the lies you tell, I should never be out of a temper," said Miss Blacklock.

"I will go and say to the Inspector that I make it all up, shall I?" asked Mitzi.

"He knows that already," said Miss Blacklock, pleasantly.

Mitzi turned off the taps and as she did so two hands came up behind her head and with one swift movement forced it down into the water-filled sink.

"Only *I* know that you're telling the truth for once," said Miss Blacklock viciously.

Mitzi thrashed and struggled but Miss Blacklock was strong and her hands held the girl's head firmly under water.

Then, from somewhere quite close behind her, Dora Bunner's voice rose piteously on the air :

"*Oh Lotty—Lotty—don't do it . . . Lotty.*"

Miss Blacklock screamed. Her hands flew up in the air, and Mitzi, released, came up choking and spluttering.

Miss Blacklock screamed again and again. For there was no one, except Mitzi, there in the kitchen with her . . .

"*Dora, Dora, forgive me. I had to . . . I had to——*"

She rushed distractedly towards the scullery door—and the bulk of Sergeant Fletcher barred her way, just as Miss Marple stepped, flushed and triumphant, out of the broom cupboard.

"I could always mimic people's voices," said Miss Marple.

"You'll have to come with me, madam," said Sergeant Fletcher. "I was a witness of your attempt to drown this girl. And there will be other charges. I must warn you, Letitia Blacklock——"

"Charlotte Blacklock," corrected Miss Marple. "That's who she is, you know. Under that choker of pearls she always wears you'll find the scar of the operation."

"Operation?"

"Operation for goitre."

Miss Blacklock, quite calm now, looked at Miss Marple.

"So you know all about it?" she said.

"Yes, I've known for some time."

Charlotte Blacklock sat down by the table and began to cry.

"You shouldn't have done that," she said. "Not made Dora's voice come. I loved Dora. I really loved Dora."

Inspector Craddock and the others had crowded in the doorway.

Constable Edwards, who added a knowledge of first-aid and artificial respiration to his other accomplishments, was busy with Mitzi. As soon as Mitzi could speak she was lyrical with self-praise.

" I do that good, do I not? I am clever! And I am brave! Oh, I am brave! Very very nearly was *I* murdered, too. But I am so brave I risk *everything*."

With a rush Miss Hinchliffe thrust aside the others and leapt upon the weeping figure of Charlotte Blacklock by the table.

It took all Sergeant Fletcher's strength to hold her off.

" Now then——" he said. " Now then—no, no, Miss Hinchliffe——"

Between clenched teeth Miss Hinchliffe was muttering :

" Let me get at her. Just let me get at her. It was she who killed Amy Murgatroyd."

Charlotte Blacklock looked up and sniffed.

" I didn't want to kill her. I didn't want to kill anybody—I had to—but it's Dora I mind about—after Dora was dead, I was all alone—ever since she died—I've been alone—oh, Dora—Dora——"

And once again she dropped her head on her hands and wept.

CHAPTER XXIII

EVENING AT THE VICARAGE

MISS MARPLE sat in the tall arm-chair. Bunch was on the floor in front of the fire with her arms round her knees.

The Reverend Julian Harmon was leaning forward and was for once looking more like a schoolboy than a man foreshadowing his own maturity. And Inspector Craddock was smoking his pipe and drinking a whisky and soda and was clearly very much off duty. An outer circle was composed of Julia, Patrick, Edmund and Phillipa.

" I think it's your story, Miss Marple," said Craddock.

" Oh no, my dear boy. I only just helped a little, here and there. *You* were in charge of the whole thing, and conducted it all, and you know so much that I don't."

" Well, tell it together," said Bunch impatiently. " Bit each. Only let Aunt Jane start because I like the muddly way her mind works. When did you first think that the whole thing was a put up job by the Blacklock?"

" Well, my dear Bunch, it's hard to say. Of course, right at the very beginning, it did seem as though the ideal person—or rather the *obvious* person, I should say —to have arranged the hold-up *was* Miss Blacklock herself. She was the only person who was known to have been in contact with Rudi Scherz, and how much easier to arrange something like that when it's your own house. The central heating, for instance. No fires—because that would have meant light in the room. But the only person

252

who could have arranged *not* to have a fire was the mistress of the house herself.

"Not that I thought of all that at the time—it just seemed to me that it was a pity it *couldn't* be as simple as that! Oh, no, I was taken in like everyone else, I thought that someone really did want to kill Letitia Blacklock."

"I think I'd like to get clear first on what really happened," said Bunch. "Did this Swiss boy recognise her?"

"Yes. He'd worked in——"

She hesitated and looked at Craddock.

"In Dr. Adolf Koch's clinic in Berne," said Craddock. "Koch was a world famous specialist on operations for goitre. Charlotte Blacklock went there to have her goitre removed and Rudi Scherz was one of the orderlies. When he came to England he recognised in the hotel a lady who had been a patient and on the spur of the moment he spoke to her. I dare say he mightn't have done that if he'd paused to think, because he left the place under a cloud, but that was sometime after Charlotte had been there, so she wouldn't know anything about it."

"So he never said anything to her about Montreux and his father being a hotel proprietor?"

"Oh, no, she made that up to account for his having spoken to her."

"It must have been a great shock to her," said Miss Marple, thoughtfully. "She felt reasonably safe—and then—the almost impossible mischance of somebody turning up who had known her—not as one of the two Miss Blacklocks—she was prepared for *that*—but definitely as *Charlotte* Blacklock, a patient who'd been operated on for goitre.

"But you wanted to go through it all from the beginning. Well, the beginning, I think—if Inspector Craddock agrees with me—was when Charlotte Blacklock, a pretty, light-hearted, affectionate girl, developed that enlargement of the thyroid gland that's called a goitre. It ruined her life, because she was a very sensitive girl. A girl, too, who had always set a lot of stress on her personal appearance. And girls just at that age in their teens, are particularly sensitive about themselves. If she'd had a mother, or a reasonable father, I don't think she would have got into the morbid state she undoubtedly did get into. She had no one, you see, to take her out of herself, and force her to see people and lead a normal life and not think too much about her infirmity. And, of course, in a different household, she might have been sent for an operation many years earlier.

"But Dr. Blacklock, I think, was an old-fashioned, narrow-minded, tyrannical and obstinate man. He didn't believe in these operations. Charlotte must take it from him that nothing could be done—apart from dosage with iodine and other drugs. Charlotte *did* take it from him, and I think her sister also placed more faith in Dr. Blacklock's powers as a physician than he deserved.

"Charlotte was devoted to her father in a rather weak and soppy way. She thought, definitely, that her father knew best. But she shut herself up more and more as the goitre became larger and more unsightly, and refused to see people. She was actually a kindly, affectionate creature."

"That's an odd description of a murderess," said Edmund.

"I don't know that it is," said Miss Marple. "Weak and kindly people are often very treacherous. And if they've got a grudge against life it saps the little moral strength that they may possess.

"Letitia Blacklock, of course, had quite a different

personality. Inspector Craddock told me that Belle Goedler described her as really *good*—and I think Letitia *was* good. She was a woman of great integrity who found—as she put it herself—a great difficulty in understanding how people couldn't see what was dishonest. Letitia Blacklock, however tempted, would never have contemplated any kind of fraud for a moment.

" Letitia was devoted to her sister. She wrote her long accounts of everything that happened in an effort to keep her sister in touch with life. She was worried by the morbid state Charlotte was getting into.

" Finally Dr. Blacklock died. Letitia, without hesitation, threw up her position with Randall Goedler and devoted herself to Charlotte. She took her to Switzerland to consult authorities there on the possibility of operating. It had been left very late—but as we know the operation was successful. The deformity was gone—and the scar this operation had left was easily hidden by a choker of pearls or beads.

" The war had broken out. A return to England was difficult and the two sisters stayed in Switzerland doing various Red Cross and other work. That's right, isn't it, Inspector?"

" Yes, Miss Marple."

" They got occasional news from England—amongst other things, I expect, they heard that Belle Goedler could not live long. I'm sure it would be only human nature for them both to have planned and talked together of the days ahead when a big fortune would be theirs to spend. One has got to realise, I think, that this prospect meant much more to *Charlotte* than it did to Letitia. For the first time in her life, Charlotte could go about feeling herself a normal woman, a woman at whom no one looked with either repulsion or pity. She was free at last to enjoy life—and she had a whole lifetime, as it were, to crowd into her remaining years. To travel, to have a house and beautiful grounds—to have clothes and jewels, and go to plays and concerts, to gratify every whim—it was all a kind of fairy tale come true to Charlotte.

" And then Letitia, the strong healthy Letitia, got flu which turned to pneumonia and died within the space of a week! Not only had Charlotte lost her sister, but the whole dream existence she had planned for herself was cancelled. I think, you know, that she may have felt almost resentful towards Letitia. Why need Letitia have died, just then, when they had just had a letter saying Belle Goedler could not last long? Just one more month, perhaps, and the money would have been Letitia's—and hers when Letitia died . . .

" Now this is where I think the difference between the two came in. Charlotte didn't really feel that what she suddenly thought of doing was wrong—not really wrong. The money was meant to come to Letitia—it *would* have come to Letitia in the course of a few months—and she regarded herself and Letitia as one.

" Perhaps the idea didn't occur to her until the doctor or someone asked her her sister's Christian name—and then she realised how to nearly everyone they had appeared as the two Miss Blacklocks—elderly, well-bred Englishwomen, dressed much the same, with a strong family resemblance—(and, as I pointed out to Bunch, one elderly woman is *so* like another). Why shouldn't it be Charlotte who had died and *Letitia* who was alive?

" It was an impulse, perhaps, more than a plan. Letitia was buried under Charlotte's name. ' Charlotte ' was dead, ' Letitia ' came to England. All the natural initiative and energy, dormant for so many years, were now in the ascendant. As Charlotte she had played second fiddle. She now assumed the airs of command, the feeling of command that had been Letitia's. They were not really so unlike in mentality—though there was, I think, a big difference *morally.*

"Charlotte had, of course, to take one or two obvious precautions. She bought a house in a part of England quite unknown to her. The only people she had to avoid were a few people in her own native town in Cumberland (where in any case she'd lived as a recluse) and, of course, Belle Goedler who had known Letitia so well that any impersonation would have been out of the question. Handwriting difficulties were got over by the arthritic condition of her hands. It was really very easy because so few people had ever really known Charlotte."

"But supposing she'd met people who'd known Letitia?" asked Bunch. "There must have been plenty of those."

"They wouldn't matter in the same way. Someone might say: 'I came across Letitia Blacklock the other day. She's changed so much I really wouldn't have known her.' But there still wouldn't be any suspicion in their minds that she wasn't Letitia. People *do* change in the course of ten years. *Her* failure to recognise *them* could always be put down to her short-sightedness: and you must remember that she knew every detail of Letitia's life in London—the people she met—the places she went. She'd got Letitia's letters to refer to, and she could quickly have disarmed any suspicion by mention of some incident, or an inquiry after a mutual friend. No, it was recognition as *Charlotte* that was the only thing she had to fear.

"She settled down at Little Paddocks, got to know her neighbours and, when she got a letter asking dear Letitia to be kind, she accepted with pleasure the visit of two young cousins she had never seen. Their acceptance of her as Aunt Letty increased her security.

" The whole thing was going splendidly. And then—
she made her big mistake. It was a mistake that arose
solely from her kindness of heart and her naturally affectionate nature. She got a letter from an old school friend
who had fallen on evil days, and she hurried to the rescue.
Perhaps it may have been partly because she was, in
spite of everything, lonely. Her secret kept her in a way
apart from people. And she had been genuinely fond of
Dora Bunner and remembered her as a symbol of her
own gay carefree days at school. Anyway, on an impulse,
she answered Dora's letter in person. And very surprised
Dora must have been! She'd written to *Letitia* and the
sister who turned up in answer to her letter was *Charlotte*. There was never any question of pretending to be
Letitia to Dora. Dora was one of the few old friends who
had been admitted to see Charlotte in her lonely and
unhappy days.

" And because she knew that Dora would look at the
matter in exactly the same way as she did herself, she
told Dora what she had done. Dora approved wholeheartedly. In her confused muddle-headed mind it
seemed only right that dear Lotty should not be done out
of her inheritance by Letty's untimely death. Lotty
deserved a reward for all the patient suffering she had
borne so bravely. It would have been most unfair if all
that money should have gone to someone nobody had
ever heard of.

" She quite understood that nothing must be allowed
to get out. It was like an extra pound of butter. You
couldn't talk about it but there was nothing wrong about
having it. So Dora came to Little Paddocks—and very
soon Charlotte began to understand that she had made a
terrible mistake. It was not merely the fact that Dora
Bunner, with her muddles and her mistakes and her
bungling, was quite maddening to live with. Charlotte

258

could have put up with that—because she really cared for Dora, and anyway knew from the doctor that Dora hadn't got a very long time to live. But Dora very soon became a real danger. Though Charlotte and Letitia had called each other by their full names, Dora was the kind of person who always uses abbreviations. To her the sisters had always been Letty and Lotty. And though she schooled her tongue resolutely to call her friend Letty —the old name often slipped out. Memories of the past, too, were rather apt to come to her tongue—and Charlotte had constantly to be on the watch to check these forgetful allusions. It began to get on her nerves.

" Still, nobody was likely to pay much attention to Dora's inconsistencies. The real blow to Charlotte's security came, as I say, when she was recognised and spoken to by Rudi Scherz at the Royal Spa Hotel.

" I think that the money Rudi Scherz used to replace his earlier defalcations at the hotel may have come from Charlotte Blacklock. Inspector Craddock doesn't believe —and I don't either—that Rudi Scherz applied to her for money with any idea of blackmail in his head."

" He hadn't the faintest idea he knew anything to blackmail her about," said Inspector Craddock. " He knew that he was quite a personable young man—and he was aware by experience that personable young men sometimes can get money out of elderly ladies if they tell a hard luck story convincingly enough.

" But she may have seen it differently. She may have thought that it was a form of insidious blackmail, that perhaps he suspected something—and that later, if there was publicity in the papers as there might be after Belle Goedler's death, he would realise that in her he had found a gold mine.

" And she was committed to the fraud now. She'd established herself as Letitia Blacklock. With the Bank.

With Mrs. Goedler. The only snag was this rather dubious Swiss hotel clerk, an unreliable character, and possibly a blackmailer. If only he were out of the way— she'd be safe.

" Perhaps she made it all up as a kind of fantasy first. She'd been starved of emotion and drama in her life. She pleased herself by working out the details. How would she go about getting rid of him?

" She made her plan. And at last she decided to act on it. She told her story of a sham hold-up at a party to Rudi Scherz, explained that she wanted a stranger to act the part of the ' gangster,' and offered him a generous sum for his co-operation.

" And the fact that he agreed without any suspicion is what makes me quite certain that Scherz had no idea that he had any kind of hold over her. To him she was just a rather foolish old woman, very ready to part with money.

" She gave him the advertisement to insert, arranged for him to pay a visit to Little Paddocks to study the geography of the house, and showed him the spot where she would meet him and let him into the house on the night in question. Dora Bunner, of course, knew nothing about all this.

" The day came——" He paused.

Miss Marple took up the tale in her gentle voice.

" She must have spent a very miserable day. You see, it still wasn't too late to draw back . . . Dora Bunner told us that Letty was frightened that day and she must have been frightened. Frightened of what she was going to do, frightened of the plan going wrong—but not frightened enough to draw back.

" It had been fun, perhaps, getting the revolver out of Colonel Easterbrook's collar drawer. Taking along eggs, or jam—slipping upstairs in the empty house. It had

260

been fun getting the second door in the drawing-room oiled, so that it would open and shut noiselessly. Fun suggesting the moving of the table outside the door so that Phillipa's flower arrangements would show to better advantage. It may have all seemed like a game. But what was going to happen next definitely wasn't a game any longer. Oh, yes, she was frightened . . . Dora Bunner was right about that."

"All the same, she went through with it," said Craddock. "And it all went according to plan. She went out just after six to 'shut up the ducks,' and she let Scherz in then and gave him the mask and cloak and gloves and the torch. Then, at 6.30, when the clock begins to chime, she's ready by that table near the archway with her hand on the cigarette-box. It's all so natural. Patrick, acting as host, has gone for the drinks. She, the hostess, is fetching the cigarettes. She's judged, quite correctly, that when the clock begins to chime, everyone will look at the clock. They did. Only one person, the devoted Dora, kept her eyes fixed on her friend. And she told us, in her very first statement, exactly what Miss Blacklock did. She said that Miss Blacklock had picked up the vase of violets.

"She'd previously frayed the cord of the lamp so that the wires were nearly bare. The whole thing only took a second. The cigarette-box, the vase and the little switch were all close together. She picked up the violets, spilt the water on the frayed place, and switched on the lamp. Water's a good conductor of electricity. The wires fused."

"Just like the other afternoon at the Vicarage," said Bunch. "That's what startled you so, wasn't it, Aunt Jane?"

"Yes, my dear. I've been puzzling about those lights. I'd realised that there were two lamps, a pair, and that one had been changed for the other—probably during the night."

"That's right," said Craddock. "When Fletcher examined that lamp the next morning it was, like all the others, perfectly in order, no frayed flex or fused wires."

"I'd understood what Dora Bunner meant by saying it had been the shepherdess the night before," said Miss Marple, "but I fell into the error of thinking, as she thought, that *Patrick* had been responsible. The interesting thing about Dora Bunner was that she was quite unreliable in repeating things she had heard—she always used her imagination to exaggerate or distort them, and she was usually wrong in what she *thought*—but she was quite accurate about the things she *saw*. She saw Letitia pick up the violets——"

"And she saw what she described as a flash and a crackle," put in Craddock.

"And of course, when dear Bunch spilt the water from the Christmas roses on to the lamp wire—I realised at once that only Miss Blacklock herself could have fused the lights because only she was near that table."

"I could kick myself," said Craddock. "Dora Bunner even prattled about a burn on the table where someone had 'put their cigarette down'—but nobody had even lit a cigarette . . . And the violets were dead because there was no water in the vase—a slip on Letitia's part—she ought to have filled it up again. But I suppose she thought nobody would notice and as a matter of fact Miss Bunner was quite ready to believe that she herself had put no water in the vase to begin with."

He went on :

"She was highly suggestible, of course. And Miss Blacklock took advantage of that more than once. Bunny's suspicions of Patrick were I think, induced by her."

"Why pick on me?" demanded Patrick in an aggrieved tone.

"It was not, I think, a serious suggestion—but it would keep Bunny distracted from any suspicion that Miss Blacklock might be stage managing the business. Well, we know what happened next. As soon as the lights went and everyone was exclaiming, she slipped out through the previously oiled door and up behind Rudi Scherz who was flashing his torch round the room and playing his part with gusto. I don't suppose he realised for a moment she was there behind him with her gardening gloves pulled on and the revolver in her hand. She waits till the torch reaches the spot she must aim for— the wall near which she is supposed to be standing. Then she fires rapidly twice and as he swings round startled, she holds the revolver close to his body and fires again. She lets the revolver fall by his body, throws her gloves carelessly on the hall table, then back through the other door and across to where she had been standing when the lights went out. She nicked her ear—I don't quite know how——"

"Nail scissors, I expect," said Miss Marple. "Just a snip on the lobe of the ear lets out a lot of blood. That was very good psychology, of course. The actual blood running down over her white blouse made it seem certain that she *had* been shot at, and that it had been a near miss."

"It ought to have gone off quite all right," said Craddock. "Dora Bunner's insistence that Scherz had definitely aimed at Miss Blacklock had its uses. Without meaning it, Dora Bunner conveyed the impression that she'd actually seen her friend wounded. It might have been brought in Suicide or Accidental Death. And the case would have been closed. That it was kept open is due to Miss Marple here."

"Oh, no, no." Miss Marple shook her head energetically. "Any little efforts on my part were quite incidental. It was you who weren't satisfied, Mr. Craddock. It was *you* who wouldn't let the case be closed."

"I wasn't happy about it," said Craddock. "I knew it was all wrong somewhere. But I didn't see *where* it was wrong, till you showed me. And after that Miss Blacklock had a real piece of bad luck. I discovered that that second door had been tampered with. Until that moment, whatever we agreed *might* have happened— we'd nothing to go upon but a pretty theory. But that oiled door was *evidence*. And I hit upon it by pure chance—by catching hold of a handle by mistake."

"I think you were *led* to it, Inspector," said Miss Marple. "But then I'm old-fashioned."

"So the hunt was up again," said Craddock. "But this time with a difference. We were looking now for someone with a motive to kill Letitia Blacklock."

"And there *was* someone with a motive, and Miss Blacklock knew it," said Miss Marple. "I think she recognised Phillipa almost at once. Because Sonia Goedler seems to have been one of the very few people who had been admitted to Charlotte's privacy. And when one is old (you wouldn't know this yet, Mr. Craddock) one has a much better memory for a face you've seen when you were young than you have for anyone you've only met a year or two ago. Phillipa must have been just about the same age as her mother was when Charlotte remembered her, and she was very like her mother. The odd thing is that I think Charlotte was very pleased to recognise Phillipa. She became very fond of Phillipa and I think, unconsciously, it helped to stifle any qualms of conscience she may have had. She told herself that when she inherited the money, she was going to look after Phillipa. She would treat her as a daughter. Phillipa and Harry should live with her. She felt quite happy and beneficent about it. But once the Inspector began asking questions and finding out about 'Pip and Emma' Charlotte became very uneasy. She didn't want to make a scapegoat of Phillipa. Her whole idea had been to make the business look like a hold-up by a young criminal and his accidental death. But now, with the discovery of the oiled door, the whole viewpoint was changed. And, except for Phillipa, there wasn't (as far as *she* knew, for she had absolutely no idea of Julia's identity) anyone with the least possible motive for wishing to kill her. She did her best to shield Phillipa's identity. She was quick-witted enough to tell you when you asked her, that Sonia was small and dark and she took the old snapshots out of the album, so that you shouldn't notice any resemblance, at the same time as she removed snapshots of Letitia herself."

"And to think I suspected Mrs. Swettenham of being Sonia Goedler," said Craddock disgustedly.

"My poor Mamma," murmured Edmund. "A woman of blameless life—or so I have always believed."

"But of course," Miss Marple went on. "It was Dora Bunner who was the real danger. Every day Dora got more forgetful and more talkative. I remember the way Miss Blacklock looked at her the day we went to tea there. Do you know why? Dora had just called her Lotty again. It seemed to us a mere harmless slip of the tongue. But it frightened Charlotte. And so it went on. Poor Dora could not stop herself talking. That day we had coffee together in the Bluebird, I had the oddest impression that Dora was talking about *two* people, not one—and so, of course, she was. At one moment she spoke of her friend as not pretty but having so much character—but almost at the same moment she described her as a pretty light-hearted girl. She'd talk of Letty as

265

so clever and so successful—and then say what a sad life she'd had, and then there was that quotation about stern affliction bravely borne—which really didn't seem to fit Letitia's life at all. Charlotte must, I think, have overheard a good deal that morning she came into the café. She certainly must have heard Dora mention about the lamp having been changed—about its being the shepherd and not the shepherdess. And she realised then what a very real danger to her security poor devoted Dora Bunner was.

" I'm afraid that that conversation with me in the café really sealed Dora's fate—if you'll excuse such a melodramatic expression. But I think it would have come to the same in the end . . . Because life couldn't be safe for Charlotte while Dora Bunner was alive. She loved Dora—she didn't want to kill Dora—but she couldn't see any other way. And, I expect (like Nurse Ellerton that I was telling you about, Bunch) she persuaded herself that it was really almost a *kindness*. Poor Bunny—not long to live anyway and perhaps a painful end. The queer thing is that she did her best to make Bunny's last day a happy day. The birthday party—and the special cake . . ."

" Delicious Death," said Phillipa with a shudder.

" Yes—yes, it was rather like that . . . she tried to give her friend a delicious death . . . The party, and all the things she liked to eat, and trying to stop people saying things to upset her. And then the tablets, whatever they were, in the aspirin bottle by her own bed so that Bunny, when she couldn't find the new bottle of aspirin she'd just bought, would go there to get some. And it would look, as it did look, that the tablets had been meant for *Letitia* . . .

" And so Bunny died in her sleep, quite happily, and Charlotte felt safe again. But she missed Dora Bunner—

266

she missed her affection and her loyalty, the missed being able to talk to her about the old days . . . She cried bitterly the day I came up with that note from Julian— and her grief was quite genuine. She'd killed her own dear friend . . ."

" That's horrible," said Bunch. " Horrible."

" But it's very human," said Julian Harmon. " One forgets how human murderers are."

" I know," said Miss Marple. " Human. And often very much to be pitied. But very dangerous, too. Especially a weak kindly murderer like Charlotte Blacklock. Because, once a weak person gets *really* frightened, they get savage with terror and they've no self-control at all."

" Murgatroyd?" said Julian.

" Yes, poor Miss Murgatroyd. Charlotte must have come up to the cottage and heard them rehearsing the murder. The window was open and she listened. It had never occurred to her until that moment that there was anyone else who could be a danger to her. Miss Hinchliffe was urging her friend to remember what she'd seen and until that moment Charlotte hadn't realised that anyone could have seen anything at all. She'd assumed that everybody would automatically be looking at Rudi Scherz. She must have held her breath outside the window and listened. Was it going to be all right? And then, just as Miss Hinchliffe rushed off to the station Miss Murgatroyd got to a point which showed that she had stumbled on the truth. She called after Miss Hinchliffe : ' She wasn't *there* . . .'

" I asked Miss Hinchliffe, you know, if that was the way she said it . . . Because if she'd said ' *She* wasn't there ' it wouldn't have meant the same thing."

" Now that's too subtle a point for me," said Craddock.

Miss Marple turned her eager pink and white face to him.

" Just think what's going on in Miss Murgatroyd's mind . . . One does see things, you know, and not know one sees them. In a railway accident once, I remember noticing a large blister of paint at the side of the carriage. I could have *drawn* it for you afterward. And once, when there was a fly-bomb in London—splinters of glass everywhere—and the shock—but what I remember best is a woman standing in front of me who had a big hole half-way up the leg of her stockings and the stockings didn't match. So when Miss Murgatroyd stopped thinking and just tried to remember what she *saw*, she remembered a good deal.

" She started, I think, near the mantelpiece, where the torch must have hit first—then it went along the two windows and there were people in between the windows and her. Mrs. Harmon with her knuckles screwed into her eyes for instance. She went on in her mind following the torch past Miss Bunner with her mouth open and her eyes staring—past a blank wall and a table with a lamp and a cigarette-box. And then came the shots—and quite suddenly she remembered a most incredible thing. She'd seen the wall where, later, there were the two bullet holes, the wall where Letitia Blacklock had been standing when she was shot, and at the moment when the revolver went off and Letty was shot, *Letty hadn't been there* . . .

" You see what I mean now? She'd been thinking of the three women Miss Hinchliffe had told her to think about. If one of them hadn't been there, it would have been the *personality* she'd have fastened upon. She'd have said—in effect—' *That's* the one! *She* wasn't there!' But it was a *place* that was in her mind—a place where someone should have been—but the place wasn't

268

filled—there wasn't anybody there. The place was there —but the person wasn't. And she couldn't take it in all at once. 'How extraordinary, Hinch,' she said. 'She wasn't *there*.' . . . So that could only mean Letitia Blacklock . . ."

"But you knew before that, didn't you?" said Bunch. "When the lamp fused. When you wrote down those things on the paper."

"Yes, my dear. It all came together then, you see— all the various isolated bits—and made a coherent pattern."

Bunch quoted softly:

"*Lamp?* Yes. *Violets?* Yes. *Bottle of Aspirin*. You meant that Bunny had been going to buy a new bottle that day, and so she ought not to have needed to take Letitia's?"

"Not unless her own bottle had been taken or hidden. It had to appear as though Letitia Blacklock was the one meant to be killed."

"Yes, I see. And then 'Delicious Death.' The cake— but more than the cake. The whole party set-up. A happy day for Bunny before she died. Treating her rather like a dog you were going to destroy. That's what I find the most horrible thing of all—the sort of—of spurious kindness."

"She *was* quite a kindly woman. What she said at the last in the kitchen was quite true. 'I didn't want to kill anybody.' What she wanted was a great deal of money that didn't belong to her! And before that desire —(and it had become a kind of obsession—the money was to pay her back for all the suffering life had inflicted on her)—everything else went to the wall. People with a grudge against the world are always dangerous. They seem to think life owes them something. I've known many an invalid who has suffered far worse and been

cut off from life much more than Charlotte Blacklock—
and they've managed to lead happy contented lives. It's
what's in *yourself* that makes you happy or unhappy.
But, oh dear, I'm afraid I'm straying away from what
we were talking about. Where were we?"

"Going over your list," said Bunch. "What did you
mean by ' Making enquiries?' Inquiries about what?"

Miss Marple shook her head playfully at Inspector
Craddock.

"You ought to have seen that, Inspector Craddock.
You showed me that letter from Letitia Blacklock to her
sister. It had the word ' enquiries ' in it twice—each time
spelt with an *e*. But in the note I asked Bunch to show
you, Miss Blacklock had written ' inquiries ' with an *i*.
People don't often alter their spelling as they get older.
It seemed to me very significant."

"Yes," Craddock agreed. "I ought to have spotted
that."

Bunch was continuing. "*Severe affliction bravely
borne*. That's what Bunny said to you in the café and of
course Letitia hadn't had any affliction. *Iodine*. That
put you on the track of goitre?"

"Yes, dear. Switzerland, you know, and Miss Blacklock giving the impression that her sister had died of
consumption. But I remembered then that the greatest
authorities on goitre and the most skilful surgeons operating on it are Swiss. And it linked up with those really
rather preposterous pearls that Letitia Blacklock always
wore. Not really her *style*—but just right for concealing
the scar."

"I understand now her agitation the night the string
broke," said Craddock. "It seemed at the time quite
disproportionate."

"And after that, it *was* Lotty you wrote not Letty as
we thought," said Bunch.

"Yes, I remembered that the sister's name was Charlotte, and that Dora Bunner had called Miss Blacklock Lotty once or twice—and that each time she did so, she had been very upset afterwards."

"And what about Berne and Old Age Pension?"

"Rudi Scherz had been an orderly in a hospital in Berne."

"And Old Age Pension."

"Oh, my dear Bunch, I mentioned that to you in the Bluebird though I didn't really see the application then. How Mrs. Wotherspoon drew Mrs. Bartlett's Old Age Pension as well as her own—though Mrs. Bartlett had been dead for years—simply because one old woman is so like another old woman—yes, it all made a pattern and I felt so worked up I went out to cool my head a little and think what could be done about proving all this. Then Miss Hinchliffe picked me up and we found Miss Murgatroyd . . ."

Miss Marple's voice dropped. It was no longer excited and pleased. It was quiet and remorseless.

"I knew then something had *got* to be done. Quickly! But there still wasn't any *proof*. I thought out a possible plan and I talked to Sergeant Fletcher."

"And I have had Fletcher on the carpet for it!" said Craddock. "He'd no business to go agreeing to your plans without reporting first to me."

"He didn't like it, but I talked him into it," said Miss Marple. "We went up to Little Paddocks and I got hold of Mitzi."

Julia drew a deep breath and said, "I can't imagine how you ever got her to do it."

"I worked on her, my dear," said Miss Marple. "She thinks far too much about herself anyway, and it will be good for her to have done something for others. I flattered her up, of course, and said I was sure if she'd

271

been in her own country she'd have been in the Resistance movement, and she said, 'Yes, indeed.' And I said I could see she had got just the temperament for that sort of work. She was brave, didn't mind taking risks, and could act a part. I told her stories of deeds done by girls in the Resistance movements, some of them true, and some of them, I'm afraid, invented. She got tremendously worked up!"

"Marvellous," said Patrick.

"And then I got her to agree to do her part. I rehearsed her till she was word perfect. Then I told her to go upstairs to her room and not come down until Inspector Craddock came. The worst of these excitable people is that they're apt to go off half-cocked and start the whole thing before the time."

"She did it very well," said Julia.

"I don't quite see the point," said Bunch. "Of course, I wasn't there——" she added apologetically.

"The point was a little complicated—and rather touch and go. The idea was that Mitzi whilst admitting, as though casually, that blackmail *had* been in her mind, was now so worked up and terrified that she was willing to come out with the truth. She'd seen, through the keyhole of the dining-room, Miss Blacklock in the hall with a revolver behind Rudi Scherz. She'd seen, that is, *what had actually taken place.* Now the only danger was that Charlotte Blacklock might have realised that, as the key was in the keyhole, Mitzi couldn't possibly have seen anything at all. But I banked on the fact that you don't think of things like that when you've just had a bad shock. All she could take in was that Mitzi had seen her."

Craddock took over the story.

"But—and this was essential—I pretended to receive this with scepticism, and I made an immediate attack as though unmasking my batteries at last, upon someone

272

who had not been previously suspected. I accused Edmund——"

"And very nicely *I* played *my* part," said Edmund. "Hot denial. All according to plan. What wasn't according to plan, Phillipa, my love, was you throwing in your little chirp and coming out into the open as ' Pip.' Neither the Inspector nor I had any idea you were Pip. *I* was going to be Pip! It threw us off our stride for the moment, but the Inspector made a masterly comeback and made some perfectly filthy insinuations about my wanting a rich wife which will probably stick in your subconscious and make irreparable trouble between us one day."

"I don't see why that was necessary?"

"Don't you? It meant that, *from Charlotte Black-lock's point of view*, the only person who suspected or knew the truth, was *Mitzi*. The suspicions of the police were elsewhere. They had treated Mitzi for the moment as a liar. But if Mitzi were to persist, they might listen to her and take her seriously. So Mitzi had got to be silenced."

"Mitzi went straight out of the room and back to the kitchen—just like I had told her," said Miss Marple. "Miss Blacklock came out after her almost immediately. Mitzi was apparently alone in the kitchen. Sergeant Fletcher was behind the scullery door. And I was in the broom cupboard in the kitchen. Luckily I'm very thin."

Bunch looked at Miss Marple.

"What did you expect to happen, Aunt Jane?"

"One of two things. Either Charlotte would offer Mitzi money to hold her tongue—and Sergeant Fletcher would be a witness to that offer, or else—or else I thought she'd try to kill Mitzi."

"But she couldn't hope to get away with *that*? She'd have been suspected at once."

273

" Oh, my dear, she was past reasoning. She was just a snapping terrified cornered rat. Think what had happened that day. The scene between Miss Hinchliffe and Miss Murgatroyd. Miss Hinchliffe driving off to the station. As soon as she comes back Miss Murgatroyd will explain that Letitia Blacklock wasn't in the room that night. There's just a few minutes in which to make sure Miss Murgatroyd can't tell anything. No time to make a plan or set a stage. Just crude murder. She greets the poor woman and strangles her. Then a quick rush home, to change, to be sitting by the fire when the others come in, as though she'd never been out.

" And then came the revelation of Julia's identity. She breaks her pearls and is terrified they may notice her scar. Later, the Inspector telephones that he's bringing everyone there. No time to think, to rest. Up to her neck in murder now, no mercy killing—or undesirable young man to be put out of the way. Crude plain murder. Is she safe? Yes, so far. And then comes Mitzi—yet *another* danger. Kill Mitzi, stop her tongue! She's beside herself with fear. Not human any longer. Just a dangerous animal."

" But why were you in the broom cupboard, Aunt Jane?" asked Bunch. " Couldn't you have left it to Sergeant Fletcher?"

" It was safer with two of us, my dear. And besides, I knew I could mimic Dora Bunner's voice. If anything could break Charlotte Blacklock down—that would."

" And it did . . . !"

" Yes . . . she went to pieces."

There was a long silence as memory laid hold of them and then, speaking with determined lightness, to ease the strain, Julia said :

" It's made a wonderful difference to Mitzi. She told

274

me yesterday that she was taking a post near Southampton. And she said (Julia produced a very good imitation of Mitzi's accent):

" ' I go there and if they say to me you have to register with the Police—you are an alien, I say to them, " Yes, I will register! The Police, they know me well. I assist the Police! Without me the Police never would they have made the arrest of a very dangerous criminal. I risked my life because I am brave—brave like a lion—I do not care about risks." " Mitzi," they say to me, " you are a *heroine*, you are superb." " Ach! it is nothing, I say." ' "

Julia stopped.

" And a great deal more," she added.

" I think," said Edmund thoughtfully, " that soon Mitzi will have assisted the Police in not one but hundreds of cases!"

" She's softened towards me," said Phillipa. " She actually presented me with the recipe for Delicious Death as a kind of wedding present. She added that I was on no account to divulge the secret to Julia, because Julia had ruined her omelette pan."

" Mrs. Lucas," said Edmund, " is all over Phillipa now that since Belle Goedler's death, Phillipa and Julia have inherited the Goedler millions. She sent us some silver asparagus tongs as a wedding present. I shall have enormous pleasure in *not* asking her to the wedding!"

" And so they lived happily ever after," said Patrick. " Edmund and Phillipa—and Julia and Patrick?" he added, tentatively.

" Not with me, you won't live happily ever after," said Julia. " The remarks that Inspector Craddock improvised to address to Edmund apply far more aptly to you. You *are* the sort of soft young man who would like a rich wife. Nothing doing!"

" There's gratitude for you," said Patrick. " After all I did for that girl."

" Nearly landed me in prison on a murder charge—that's what your forgetfulness nearly did for me," said Julia. " I shall never forget that evening when your sister's letter came. I really thought I was for it. I couldn't see any way out.

" As it is," she added musingly, " I think I shall go on the stage."

" What? You, too?" groaned Patrick.

" Yes. I might go to Perth. See if I can get your Julia's place in the rep there. Then, when I've learnt my job, I shall go into theatre management—and put on Edmund's plays, perhaps."

" I thought you wrote novels," said Julian Harmon.

" Well, so did I," said Edmund. " I began writing a novel. Rather good it was. Pages about an unshaven man getting out of bed and what he smelt like, and the grey streets, and a horrible old woman with dropsy and a vicious young tart who dribbled down her chin—and they all talked interminably about the state of the world and wondered what they were alive for. And suddenly I began to wonder too . . . And then a rather comic idea occurred to me . . . and I jotted it down—and then I worked up rather a good little scene . . . All very obvious stuff. But somehow, I got interested . . . And before I knew what I was doing I'd finished a roaring farce in three acts."

" What's it called?" asked Patrick. " *What the butler saw?*"

" Well, it easily might be . . . As a matter of fact I've called it *Elephants Do Forget*. What's more, it's been accepted and it's going to be produced !"

" Elephants Do Forget," murmured Bunch. " I thought they didn't?"

276

The Rev. Julian Harmon gave a guilty start.

" My goodness. I've been so interested. My *sermon*!"

" Detective stories again," said Bunch. " Real life ones this time."

" You might preach on Thou Shall Do No Murder," suggested Patrick.

" No," said Julian Harmon quietly. " I shan't take that as my text."

" No," said Bunch. " You're quite right, Julian. I know a much nicer text, a happy text." She quoted in a fresh voice, " For lo the Spring is here and the Voice of the Turtle is heard in the Land—I haven't got it quite right—but you know the one I mean. Though why a *turtle* I can't think. I shouldn't think turtles have got nice voices at all."

" The word turtle," explained the Rev. Julian Harmon, " is not very happily translated. It doesn't mean a reptile but the turtle dove. The Hebrew word in the original is——"

Bunch interrupted him by giving him a hug and saying :

" I know one thing—*You* think that the Ahasuerus of the Bible is Artaxerxes the Second, but between you and me it was Artaxerxes the Third."

As always, Julian Harmon wondered why his wife should think that story so particularly funny . . .

" Tiglath Pileser wants to go and help you," said Bunch. " He ought to be a very proud cat. *He* showed us how the lights fused."

"WE ought to order some papers," said Edmund to Phillipa upon the day of their return to Chipping Cleghorn after the honeymoon. "Let's go along to Totman's."

Mr. Totman, a heavy-breathing, slow-moving man, received them with affability.

"Glad to see you back, sir. *And* madam."

"We want to order some papers."

"Certainly, sir. And your mother is keeping well, I hope? Quite settled down at Bournemouth?"

"She loves it," said Edmund, who had not the faintest idea whether this was so or not, but like most sons, preferred to believe that all was well with those loved, but frequently irritating beings, parents.

"Yes, sir. Very agreeable place. Went there for my holiday last year. Mrs. Totman enjoyed it very much."

"I'm glad. About papers, we'd like——"

"And I hear you have a play on in London, sir. Very amusing, so they tell me."

"Yes, it's doing very well."

"Called *Elephants Do Forget*, so I hear. You'll excuse me, sir, asking you, but I always thought that they *didn't* —forget, I mean."

"Yes—yes, exactly—I've begun to think it was a mistake calling it that. So many people have said just what you say."

"A kind of natural history fact, I've always understood."

"Yes—yes. Like earwigs making good mothers."

"Do they indeed, sir? Now, that's a fact I *didn't* know."

"About the papers——"

"*The Times*, sir, I think it was?" Mr. Totman paused with pencil uplifted.

"*The Daily Worker*," said Edmund firmly. "And the *Daily Telegraph*," said Phillipa. "And the *New Statesman*," said Edmund. "*The Radio Times*," said Phillipa. "*The Spectator*," said Edmund. "*The Gardener's Chronicle*," said Phillipa.

They both paused to take breath.

"Thank you, sir," said Mr. Totman. "*And* the *Gazette*, I suppose?"

"No," said Edmund.

"No," said Phillipa.

"Excuse me, you *do* want the *Gazette*?"

"No."

"No."

"You mean "—Mr. Totman liked to get things perfectly clear—" You *don't* want the *Gazette*!"

"No, we don't."

"Certainly not."

"You don't want the *North Benham News and the Chipping Cleghorn Gazette*?"

"No."

"You don't want me to send it along to you every week?"

"*No*." Edmund added: "Is that quite clear now?"

"Oh, yes, sir—yes."

Edmund and Phillipa went out, and Mr. Totman padded into his back parlour.

"Got a pencil, Mother?" he said. "My pen's run out."

"Here you are," said Mrs. Totman, seizing the order book. "I'll do it. What do they want?"

" *Daily Worker, Daily Telegraph, Radio Times, New Statesman, Spectator*—let me see—*Gardener's Chronicle*."

" *Gardener's Chronicle*," repeated Mrs. Totman, writing busily. " And the *Gazette*."

" They don't want the *Gazette*."

" What ?"

" They don't want the *Gazette*. They said so."

"Nonsense," said Mrs. Totman. "You don't hear properly. Of course they want the *Gazette*! Everybody has the *Gazette*. How else would they know what's going on round here?"

After the Funeral

FOR JAMES
IN MEMORY OF HAPPY DAYS
AT ABNEY

CONTENTS

Chapter I	285
Chapter II	292
Chapter III	294
Chapter IV	302
Chapter V	315
Chapter VI	328
Chapter VII	336
Chapter VIII	344
Chapter IX	353
Chapter X	364
Chapter XI	370
Chapter XII	379
Chapter XIII	386
Chapter XIV	390
Chapter XV	399
Chapter XVI	406
Chapter XVII	411
Chapter XVIII	415
Chapter XIX	423
Chapter XX	431
Chapter XXI	436
Chapter XXII	443
Chapter XXIII	454
Chapter XXIV	460
Chapter XXV	469

CHAPTER I

OLD LANSCOMBE moved totteringly from room to room, pulling up the blinds. Now and then he peered with screwed up rheumy eyes through the windows.

Soon they would be coming back from the funeral. He shuffled along a little faster. There were so many windows.

Enderby Hall was a vast Victorian house built in the Gothic style. In every room the curtains were of rich faded brocade or velvet. Some of the walls were still hung with faded silk. In the green drawing-room, the old butler glanced up at the portrait above the mantelpiece of old Cornelius Abernethie for whom Enderby Hall had been built. Cornelius Abernethie's brown beard stuck forward aggressively, his hand rested on a terrestrial globe, whether by desire of the sitter, or as a symbolic conceit on the part of the artist, no one could tell.

A very forceful looking gentleman, so old Lanscombe had always thought, and was glad that he himself had never known him personally. Mr. Richard had been *his* gentleman. A good master, Mr. Richard. And taken very sudden, he'd been, though of course the doctor had been attending him for some little time. Ah, but the master had never recovered from the shock of young Mr. Mortimer's death. The old man shook his head as he hurried through a connecting door into the White Boudoir. Terrible, that had been, a real catastrophe. Such a fine upstanding young gentleman, so strong and healthy. You'd never have thought such a thing likely to happen to him. Pitiful, it had been, quite pitiful. And Mr. Gordon killed in the war. One thing on top of another. That was the way things went nowadays. Too much for the master, it had been. And yet he'd seemed almost himself a week ago.

The third blind in the White Boudoir refused to go up as it should. It went up a little way and stuck. The springs were weak—that's what it was—very old, these blinds were, like everything else in the house. And you couldn't get these old things mended nowadays. Too old-fashioned, that's what they'd say, shaking their heads in that silly superior way—as if the old things weren't a great deal better than the new ones! *He* could tell them that! Gimcrack, half the new stuff was—came to pieces in your hand. The material wasn't good, or the craftsmanship either. Oh yes, *he* could tell them.

Couldn't do anything about this blind unless he got the steps. He didn't like climbing up the steps much, these days, made him come over giddy. Anyway, he'd leave the blind for now. It didn't matter, since the White Boudoir didn't face the front of the house where it would be seen as the cars came back from the funeral—and it wasn't as though the room was ever used nowadays. It was a lady's room, this, and there hadn't been a lady at Enderby for a long while now. A pity Mr. Mortimer hadn't married. Always going off to Norway for fishing and to Scotland for shooting and to Switzerland for those winter sports, instead of marrying some nice young lady and settling down at home with children running about the house. It was a long time since there had been any children in the house.

And Lanscombe's mind went ranging back to a time that stood out clearly and distinctly—much more distinctly than the last twenty years or so, which were all blurred and confused and he couldn't really remember who had come and gone or indeed what they looked like. But he could remember the old days well enough.

More like a father to those young brothers and sisters of his, Mr. Richard had been. Twenty-four when his father had died, and he'd pitched in right away to the business, going off every day as punctual as clockwork, and keeping the house running and everything as lavish as it could be. A very happy household with all those young ladies and gentlemen growing up. Fights and quarrels now and again, of course, and those governesses had had a bad time of it ! Poor spirited creatures, governesses, Lanscombe had always despised them. Very spirited the young ladies had been. Miss Geraldine in particular. Miss Cora, too, although she was so much younger. And now Mr. Leo was dead, and Miss Laura gone too. And Mr. Timothy such a sad invalid. And Miss Geraldine dying somewhere abroad. And Mr. Gordon killed in the war. Although he was the eldest, Mr. Richard himself turned out the strongest of the lot. Outlived them all, he had—at least not quite because Mr. Timothy was still alive and little Miss Cora who'd married that unpleasant artist chap. Twenty-five years since he'd seen her and she'd been a pretty young girl when she went off with that chap, and now he'd hardly have known her, grown so stout—and so arty-crafty in her dress ! A Frenchman her husband had been, or nearly a

Frenchman—and no good ever came of marrying one of *them* ! But Miss Cora had always been a bit—well, *simple like* you'd call it if she'd lived in a village. Always one of them in a family.

She'd remembered *him* all right. " Why, it's Lanscombe ! " she'd said and seemed ever so pleased to see him. Ah, they'd all been fond of him in the old days and when there was a dinner party they'd crept down to the pantry and he'd given them jelly and Charlotte Russe when it came out of the dining-room. They'd all known old Lanscombe, and now there was hardly anyone who remembered. Just the younger lot whom he could never keep clear in his mind and who just thought of him as a butler who'd been there a long time. A lot of strangers, he had thought, when they all arrived for the funeral—and a seedy lot of strangers at that !

Not Mrs. Leo—she was different. She and Mr. Leo had come here off and on ever since Mr. Leo married. She was a nice lady, Mrs. Leo—a *real* lady. Wore proper clothes and did her hair well and looked what she was. And the master had always been fond of her. A pity that she and Mr. Leo had never had any children. . . .

Lanscombe roused himself ; what was he doing standing here and dreaming about old days with so much to be done ? The blinds were all attended to on the ground floor now, and he'd told Janet to go upstairs and do the bedrooms. He and Janet and the cook had gone to the funeral service in the church but instead of going on to the Crematorium they'd driven back to the house to get the blinds up and the lunch ready. Cold lunch, of course, it had to be. Ham and chicken and tongue and salad. With cold lemon soufflé and apple tart to follow. Hot soup first—and he'd better go along and see that Marjorie had got it on ready to serve, for they'd be back in a minute or two now for certain.

Lanscombe broke into a shuffling trot across the room. His gaze, abstracted and uncurious, just swept up to the picture over this mantelpiece—the companion portrait to the one in the green drawing-room. It was a nice painting of white satin and pearls. The human being round whom they were draped and clasped was not nearly so impressive. Meek features, a rosebud mouth, hair parted in the middle. A woman both modest and unassuming. The only thing really worthy of note about Mrs. Cornelius Abernethie had been her name—Coralie.

For over sixty years after their original appearance, Coral Cornplasters and the allied " Coral " foot preparations still held their own. Whether there had ever been anything out-standing about Coral Cornplasters nobody could say—but they had appealed to the public fancy. On a foundation of Coral Cornplasters there had arisen this neo-Gothic palace, its acres of gardens, and the money that had paid out an in-come to seven sons and daughters and had allowed Richard Abernethie to die three days ago a very rich man.

2

Looking into the kitchen with a word of admonition, Lanscombe was snapped at by Marjorie, the cook. Marjorie was young, only twenty-seven, and was a constant irritation to Lanscombe as being so far removed from what his conception of a proper cook should be. She had no dignity and no proper appreciation of his, Lanscombe's, position. She frequently called the house " a proper old mausoleum " and complained of the immense area of the kitchen, scullery and larder, saying that it was a " day's walk to get round them all." She had been at Enderby two years and only stayed because in the first place the money was good, and in the second because Mr. Abernethie had really appreciated her cooking. She cooked very well. Janet, who stood by the kitchen table, refreshing herself with a cup of tea, was an elderly housemaid who, although enjoying frequent acid disputes with Lans-combe, was nevertheless usually in alliance with him against the younger generation as represented by Marjorie. The fourth person in the kitchen was Mrs. Jacks, who " came in " to lend assistance where it was wanted and who had much enjoyed the funeral.

" Beautiful it was," she said with a decorous sniff as she replenished her cup. " Nineteen cars and the church quite full and the Canon read the service beautiful, I thought. A nice fine day for it, too. Ah, poor dear Mr. Abernethie, there's not many like him left in the world. Respected by all, he was."

There was the note of a horn and the sound of a car coming up the drive, and Mrs. Jacks put down her cup and exclaimed : " Here they are."

Marjorie turned up the gas under her large saucepan of creamy chicken soup. The large kitchen range of the days of Victorian grandeur stood cold and unused, like an altar to the past.

The cars drove up one after the other and the people issuing

288

from them in their black clothes moved rather uncertainly across the hall and into the big green drawing-room. In the big steel grate a fire was burning, tribute to the first chill of the autumn days and calculated to counteract the further chill of standing about at a funeral.

Lanscombe entered the room, offering glasses of sherry on a silver tray.

Mr. Entwhistle, senior partner of the old and respected firm of Bollard, Entwhistle, Entwhistle and Bollard, stood with his back to the fireplace warming himself. He accepted a glass of sherry, and surveyed the company with his shrewd lawyer's gaze. Not all of them were personally known to him, and he was under the necessity of sorting them out, so to speak. Introductions before the departure for the funeral had been hushed and perfunctory.

Appraising old Lanscombe first, Mr. Entwhistle thought to himself, " Getting very shaky, poor old chap—going on for ninety I shouldn't wonder. Well, he'll have that nice little annuity. Nothing for *him* to worry about. Faithful soul. No such thing as old-fashioned service nowadays. Household helps and baby sitters, God help us all ! A sad world. Just as well, perhaps, poor Richard didn't last his full time. He hadn't much to live for."

To Mr. Entwhistle, who was seventy-two, Richard Abernethie's death at sixty-eight was definitely that of a man dead before his time. Mr. Entwhistle had retired from active business two years ago, but as executor of Richard Abernethie's will and in respect for one of his oldest clients who was also a personal friend, he had made the journey to the North.

Reflecting in his own mind on the provisions of the will, he mentally appraised the family.

Mrs. Leo, Helen, he knew well, of course. A very charming woman for whom he had both liking and respect. His eyes dwelt approvingly on her now as she stood near one of the windows. Black suited her. She had kept her figure well. He liked the clear cut features, the springing line of grey hair back from her temples and the eyes that had once been likened to cornflowers and which were still quite vividly blue.

How old was Helen now ? About fifty-one or -two, he supposed. Strange that she had never married again after Leo's death. An attractive woman. Ah, but they had been very devoted, those two.

His eyes went on to Mrs. Timothy. He had never known her very well. Black didn't suit her—country tweeds were her wear. A big sensible capable-looking woman. She'd

always been a good devoted wife to Timothy. Looking after
his health, fussing over him—fussing over him a bit too much,
probably. Was there really anything the matter with
Timothy ? Just a hypochondriac, Mr. Entwhistle suspected.
Richard Abernethie had suspected so, too. " Weak chest, of
course, when he was a boy," he had said. " But blest if
I think there's much wrong with him now." Oh well, everybody had to have some hobby. Timothy's hobby was the all
absorbing one of his own health. Was Mrs. Tim taken in ?
Probably not—but women never admitted that sort of thing.
Timothy must be quite comfortably off. He'd never been
a spendthrift. However, the extra would not come amiss—
not in these days of taxation. He'd probably had to retrench
his scale of living a good deal since the war.

Mr. Entwhistle transferred his attention to George Crossfield, Laura's son. Dubious sort of fellow Laura had married.
Nobody had ever known much about him. A stockbroker
he had called himself. Young George was in a solicitor's
office—not a very reputable firm. Good-looking young
fellow—but something a little shifty about him. He couldn't
have too much to live on. Laura had been a complete fool
over her investments. She'd left next to nothing when she
died five years ago. A handsome romantic girl, she'd been,
but no money sense.

Mr. Entwhistle's eyes went on from George Crossfield.
Which of the two girls was which ? Ah yes, that was Rosamund, Geraldine's daughter, looking at the wax flowers on
the malachite table. Pretty girl, beautiful, in fact—rather a
silly face. On the stage. Repertory companies or some
nonsense like that. Had married an actor, too. Good-
looking fellow. " *And* knows he is," thought Mr. Entwhistle,
who was prejudiced against the stage as a profession. "Wonder
what sort of a background *he* has and where he comes from."

He looked disapprovingly at Michael Shane with his fair
hair and his haggard charm.

Now Susan, Gordon's daughter, would do much better on
the stage than Rosamund. More personality. A little too
much personality for everyday life, perhaps. She was quite
near him and Mr. Entwhistle studied her covertly. Dark hair,
hazel—almost golden-eyes, a sulky attractive mouth. Beside
her was the husband she had just married—a chemist's
assistant, he understood. Really, a chemist's assistant ! In
Mr. Entwhistle's creed girls did not marry young men who
served behind a counter. But now of course, they married
anybody ! The young man, who had a pale nondescript face

290

and sandy hair, seemed very ill at ease. Mr. Entwhistle wondered why, but decided charitably that it was the strain of meeting so many of his wife's relations.

Last in his survey Mr. Entwhistle came to Cora Lansquenet. There was a certain justice in that, for Cora had decidedly been an afterthought in the family. Richard's youngest sister, she had been born when her mother was just on fifty, and that meek woman had not survived her tenth pregnancy (three children had died in infancy). Poor little Cora! All her life, Cora had been rather an embarrassment. growing up tall and gawky, and given to blurting out remarks that had always better have remained unsaid. All her elder brothers and sisters had been very kind to Cora, atoning for her deficiencies and covering her social mistakes. It had never really occurred to anyone that Cora would marry. She had not been a very attractive girl, and her rather obvious advances to visiting young men had usually caused the latter to retreat in some alarm. And then, Mr. Entwhistle mused, there had come the Lansquenet business—Pierre Lansquenet, half French, whom she had come across in an Art school where she had been having very correct lessons in painting flowers in water colours. But somehow she had got into the Life class and there she had met Pierre Lansquenet and had come home and announced her intention of marrying him. Richard Abernethie had put his foot down—he hadn't liked what he saw of Pierre Lansquenet and suspected that the young man was really in search of a rich wife. But whilst he was making a few researches into Lansquenet's antecedents, Cora had bolted with the fellow and married him out of hand. They had spent most of their married life in Brittany and Cornwall and other painters' conventional haunts. Lansquenet had been a very bad painter and not, by all accounts, a very nice man, but Cora had remained devoted to him and had never forgiven her family for their attitude to him. Richard had generously made his young sister an allowance and on that they had, so Mr. Entwhistle believed, lived. He doubted if Lansquenet had ever earned any money at all. He must have been dead now twelve years or more, thought Mr. Entwhistle. And now here was his widow, rather cushion-like in shape and dressed in wispy artistic black with festoons of jet beads, back in the home of her girlhood, moving about and touching things and exclaiming with pleasure when she recalled some childish memory. She made very little pretence of grief at her brother's death. But then, Mr. Entwhistle reflected, Cora had never pretended.

Re-entering the room Lanscombe murmured in muted tones suitable to the occasion :

" Luncheon is served."

CHAPTER II

AFTER THE delicious chicken soup, and plenty of cold viands accompanied by an excellent *chablis*, the funeral atmosphere lightened. Nobody had really felt any deep grief for Richard Abernethie's death since none of them had had any close ties with him. Their behaviour had been suitably decorous and subdued (with the exception of the uninhibited Cora who was clearly enjoying herself) but it was now felt that the decencies had been observed and that normal conversation could be resumed. Mr. Entwhistle encouraged this attitude. He was experienced in funerals and knew exactly how to set correct funeral timing.

After the meal was over, Lanscombe indicated the library for coffee. This was his feeling for niceties. The time had come when business—in other words, The Will—would be discussed. The library had the proper atmosphere for that with its bookshelves and its heavy red velvet curtains. He served coffee to them there and then withdrew, closing the door.

After a few desultory remarks, everyone began to look tentatively at Mr. Entwhistle. He responded promptly after glancing at his watch.

" I have to catch the 3.30 train," he began.

Others, it seemed, also had to catch that train.

"As you know," said Mr. Entwhistle, " I am the executor of Richard Abernethie's will——"

He was interrupted.

" *I* didn't know," said Cora Lansquenet brightly. " Are you ? Did he leave me anything ? "

Not for the first time, Mr. Entwhistle felt that Cora was too apt to speak out of turn.

Bending a repressive glance at her he continued :

" Up to a year ago, Richard Abernethie's will was very simple. Subject to certain legacies he left everything to his son Mortimer."

" Poor Mortimer," said Cora. " I do think all this infantile paralysis is *dreadful*."

" Mortimer's death, coming so suddenly and tragically, was a great blow to Richard. It took him some months to rally from it. I pointed out to him that it might be advisable for him to make new testamentary dispositions."

Maude Abernethie asked in her deep voice :

" What would have happened if he *hadn't* made a new will ? Would it—would it all have gone to Timothy—as the next of kin, I mean ? "

Mr. Entwhistle opened his mouth to give a disquisition on the subject of next of kin, thought better of it, and said crisply :

" On my advice, Richard decided to make a new will. First of all, however, he decided to get better acquainted with the younger generation."

" He had us up on appro," said Susan with a sudden rich laugh. " First George and then Greg and I, and then Rosamund and Michael."

Gregory Banks said sharply, his thin face flushing :

" I don't think you ought to put it like that, Susan. On appro, indeed ! "

" But that was what it was, wasn't it, Mr. Entwhistle ? "

" Did he leave *me* anything ? " repeated Cora.

Mr. Entwhistle coughed and spoke rather coldly :

" I propose to send you all copies of the will. I can read it to you in full now if you like but its legal phraseology may seem to you rather obscure. Briefly it amounts to this : After certain small bequests and a substantial legacy to Lanscombe to purchase an annuity, the bulk of the estate—a very considerable one—is to be divided into six equal portions. Four of these, after all duties are paid, are to go to Richard's brother Timothy, his nephew George Crossfield, his niece Susan Banks, and his niece Rosamund Shane. The other two portions are to be held upon trust and the income from them paid to Mrs. Helen Abernethie, the widow of his brother Leo ; and to his sister Mrs. Cora Lansquenet, during their lifetime. The capital after their death to be divided between the other four beneficiaries or their issue.

" That's *very* nice ! " said Cora Lansquenet with real appreciation. " An income ! How much ? "

" I—er—can't say exactly at present. Death duties, of course will be heavy and——"

" Can't you give me any idea ? "

Mr. Entwhistle realised that Cora must be appeased.

" Possibly somewhere in the neighbourhood of three to four thousand a year."

" Goody ! " said Cora. " I shall go to Capri."

Helen Abernethie said softly :

" How very kind and generous of Richard. I do appreciate his affection towards me."

" He was very fond of you," said Mr. Entwhistle. " Leo was his favourite brother and your visits to him were always much appreciated after Leo died."

Helen said regretfully :

" I wish I had realised how ill he was—I came up to see him not long before he died, but although I knew he *had* been ill, I did not think it was serious."

" It was always serious," said Mr. Entwhistle. " But he did not want it talked about and I do not believe that anybody expected the end to come as soon as it did. The doctor was quite surprised, I know."

" ' *Suddenly, at his residence*,' that's what it said in the paper," said Cora, nodding her head. " I wondered, then."

" It was a shock to all of us," said Maude Abernethie. " It upset poor Timothy dreadfully. So sudden, he kept saying. So *sudden*."

" Still, it's been hushed up very nicely, hasn't it ? " said Cora.

Everybody stared at her and she seemed a little flustered.

" I think you're all quite right," she said hurriedly. " *Quite* right. I mean—it can't do any good—making it public. Very unpleasant for everybody. It should be kept strictly in the family."

The faces turned towards her looked even more blank.

Mr. Entwhistle leaned forward :

" Really, Cora, I'm afraid I don't quite understand what you mean."

Cora Lansquenet looked round at the family in wide-eyed surprise. She tilted her head on one side with a bird-like movement.

" But he *was* murdered, wasn't he ? " she said.

CHAPTER III

TRAVELLING TO London in the corner of a first-class carriage Mr. Entwhistle gave himself up to somewhat uneasy thought over that extraordinary remark made by Cora Lansquenet. Of course Cora was a rather unbalanced and excessively stupid woman, and she had been noted, even as a girl, for the embarrassing manner in which she had blurted out unwelcome truths. At least, he didn't mean *truths*—that was *quite* the

294

wrong word to use. Awkward statements—that was a much better term.

In his mind he went back over the immediate sequence to that unfortunate remark. The combined stare of many startled and disapproving eyes had roused Cora to a sense of the enormity of what she had said.

Maude had exclaimed, " *Really*, Cora ! " George had said, " My dear Aunt Cora." Somebody else had said, " What *do* you mean ? "

And at once Cora Lansquenet, abashed, and convicted of enormity, had burst into fluttering phrases.

" Oh I'm sorry—I didn't mean—oh, of course, it was very stupid of me, but I did think from what he said—— Oh, of course I know it's quite all right, but his death was so *sudden*—please forget that I said anything at all—— I didn't mean to be so stupid—I know I'm always saying the wrong thing."

And then the momentary upset had died down and there had been a practical discussion about the disposition of the late Richard Abernethie's personal effects. The house and its contents, Mr. Entwhistle supplemented, would be put up for sale.

Cora's unfortunate *gaffe* had been forgotten. After all, Cora had always been, if not subnormal, at any rate embarrassingly *naïve*. She had never had any idea of what should or should not be said. At nineteen it had not mattered so much. The mannerisms of an *enfant terrible* can persist to then, but an *enfant terrible* of nearly fifty is decidedly disconcerting. To blurt out unwelcome truths—

Mr. Entwhistle's train of thought came to an abrupt check. It was the second time that that disturbing word had occurred. *Truths*. And why was it so disturbing ? Because, of course, that had always been at the bottom of the embarrassment that Cora's outspoken comments had caused. It was because her *naïve* statements had been either true or had contained some grain of truth that they had been so embarrassing !

Although in the plump woman of forty-nine, Mr. Entwhistle had been able to see little resemblance to the gawky girl of earlier days, certain of Cora's mannerisms had persisted—the slight bird-like twist of the head as she brought out a particularly outrageous remark—a kind of air of pleased expectancy. In just such a way had Cora once commented on the figure of the kitchen-maid. " Mollie can hardly get near the kitchen table, her stomach sticks out so. It's only been like that' the last month or two. I wonder *why* she's getting so fat ? "

295

Cora had been quickly hushed. The Abernethie household **was** Victorian in tone. The kitchen-maid had disappeared from the premises the next day, and after due inquiry the second gardener had been ordered to make an honest woman of her and had been presented with a cottage in which to do so.

Far-off memories—but they had their point . . .

Mr. Entwhistle examined his uneasiness more closely. What was there in Cora's ridiculous remarks that had remained to tease his subconscious in this manner ? Presently he isolated two phrases. " I did think from what he said—" and " his death was so sudden. . . ."

Mr. Entwhistle examined that last remark first. Yes, Richard's death could, in a fashion, be considered sudden. Mr. Entwhistle had discussed Richard's health both with Richard himself and with his doctor. The latter had indicated plainly that a long life could not be expected. If Mr. Aber-nethie took reasonable care of himself he might live two or even three years. Perhaps longer—but that was unlikely. In any case the doctor had anticipated no collapse in the near future.

Well, the doctor had been wrong—but doctors, as they were the first to admit themselves, could never be sure about the individual reaction of a patient to disease. Cases given up, unexpectedly recovered. Patients on the way to recovery, relapsed and died. So much depended on the vitality of the patient. On his own inner urge to live.

And Richard Abernethie, though a strong and vigorous man, had had no great incentive to live.

For six months previously his only surviving son, Mortimer, had contracted infantile paralysis and had died within a week. His death had been a shock greatly augmented by the fact that he had been such a particularly strong and vital young man. A keen sportsman, he was also a good athlete and was one of those people of whom it was said that he had never had a day's illness in his life. He was on the point of becoming engaged to a very charming girl and his father's hopes for the future were centred in this dearly loved and thoroughly satis-factory son of his.

Instead had come tragedy. And besides the sense of per-sonal loss, the future had held little to stir Richard Aber-nethie's interest. One son had died in infancy, the second without issue. He had no grandchildren. There was, in fact, no one of the Abernethie name to come after him, and he was the holder of a vast fortune with wide business interests which he himself still controlled to a certain extent. Who was to succeed to that fortune and to the control of those interests ?

That this had worried Richard deeply, Entwhistle knew. His only surviving brother was very much of an invalid. There remained the younger generation. It had been in Richard's mind, the lawyer thought, though his friend had not actually said so, to choose one definite successor, though minor legacies would probably have been made. Anyway, as Entwhistle knew, within the last six months Richard Abernethie had invited to stay with him, in succession, his nephew George, his niece Susan and her husband, his niece Rosamund and her husband, and his sister-in-law, Mrs. Leo Abernethie. It was amongst the first three, so the lawyer thought, that Abernethie had looked for his successor. Helen Abernethie, he thought, had been asked out of personal affection and even possibly as someone to consult, for Richard had always held a high opinion of her good sense and practical judgment. Mr. Entwhistle also remembered that sometime during that six months period Richard had paid a short visit to his brother Timothy.

The net result had been the will which the lawyer now carried in his brief-case. An equable distribution of property. The only conclusion that could be drawn, therefore, was that he had been disappointed both in his nephew, and in his nieces —or perhaps in his nieces' husbands.

As far as Mr. Entwhistle knew, he had not invited his sister, Cora Lansquenet, to visit him—and that brought the lawyer back to that first disturbing phrase that Cora had let slip so incoherently—" but I did think from what he *said*——"

What had Richard Abernethie said ? And when had he said it ? If Cora had not been to Enderby, then Richard Abernethie must have visited her at the artistic village in Berkshire where she had a cottage. Or was it something that Richard had said in a letter ?

Mr. Entwhistle frowned. Cora, of course, was a very stupid woman. She could easily have misinterpreted a phrase, and twisted its meaning. But he did wonder what the phrase could have been. . . .

There was enough uneasiness in him to make him consider the possibility of approaching Mrs. Lansquenet on the subject. Not too soon. Better not make it seem of importance. But he *would* like to know just what it was that Richard Abernethie had said to her which had led her to pipe up so briskly with that outrageous question :

" *But he was murdered, wasn't he ?* "

2

In a third-class carriage, farther along the train, Gregory Banks said to his wife :

" That aunt of yours must be completely bats ! "

" Aunt Cora ? " Susan was vague. " Oh, yes, I believe she was always a bit simple or something."

George Crossfield, sitting opposite, said sharply :

" She really ought to be stopped from going about saying things like that. It might put ideas into people's heads."

Rosamund Shane, intent on outlining the cupid's bow of her mouth with lipstick, murmured vaguely :

" I don't suppose anyone would pay any attention to what a frump like that says. The most peculiar clothes and lashings and lashings of jet——"

" Well, I think it ought to be stopped," said George.

" All right, darling," laughed Rosamund, putting away her lipstick and contemplating her image with satisfaction in the mirror. " You stop it."

Her husband said unexpectedly :

" I think George is right. It's so easy to set people talking."

" Well, would it matter ? " Rosamund contemplated the question. The cupid's bow lifted at the corners in a smile. " It might really be rather fun."

" Fun ? " Four voices spoke.

" Having a murder in the family," said Rosamund. " Thrilling, you know ! "

It occurred to that nervous and unhappy young man Gregory Banks that Susan's cousin, setting aside her attractive exterior, might have some faint points of resemblance to her Aunt Cora. Her next words rather confirmed his impression.

" If he was murdered," said Rosamund, " who do you think did it ? "

Her gaze travelled thoughtfully round the carriage.

" His death has been awfully convenient for all of us," she said thoughtfully. " Michael and I are absolutely on our beam ends. Mick's had a really good part offered to him in the Sandborne show if he can afford to wait for it. Now we'll be in clover. We'll be able to back our own show if we want to. As a matter of fact there's a play with a simply wonderful part——"

Nobody listened to Rosamund's ecstatic disquisition. Their attention had shifted to their own immediate future.

" Touch and go," thought George to himself. " Now I can

298

put that money back and nobody will ever know. . . . But it's been a near shave."

Gregory closed his eyes as he lay back against the seat. Escape from bondage.

Susan said in her clear rather hard voice, " I'm very sorry, of course, for poor old Uncle Richard. But then he *was* very old, and Mortimer had died, and he'd nothing to live for and it would have been awful for him to go on as an invalid year after year. *Much* better for him to pop off suddenly like this with no fuss."

Her hard confident young eyes softened as they watched her husband's absorbed face. She adored Greg. She sensed vaguely that Greg cared for her less than she cared for him— but that only strengthened her passion. Greg was hers, she'd do anything for him. Anything at all. . . .

3

Maude Abernethie, changing her dress for dinner at Enderby, (for she was staying the night) wondered if she ought to have offered to stay longer to help Helen out with the sorting and clearing of the house. There would be all Richard's personal things . . . There might be letters . . . All important papers, she supposed, had already been taken possession of by Mr. Entwhistle. And it really was necessary for her to get back to Timothy as soon as possible. He fretted so when she was not there to look after him. She hoped he would be pleased about the will and not annoyed. He had expected, she knew, that most of Richard's fortune would come to *him*. After all, he was the only surviving Abernethie. Richard could surely have trusted *him* to look after the younger generation. Yes, she was afraid Timothy *would* be annoyed. . . . And that was so bad for his digestion. And really, when he was annoyed, Timothy could become quite unreasonable. There were times when he seemed to lose his sense of proportion . . . She wondered if she ought to speak to Dr. Barton about it . . . Those sleeping pills—Timothy had been taking far too many of them lately—he got so angry when she wanted to keep the bottle for him. But they could be dangerous—Dr. Barton had said so—you could get drowsy and forget you'd taken them—and then take more. And then anything might happen ! There certainly weren't as many left in the bottle as there ought to be . . . Timothy was really very naughty about medicines. He wouldn't listen to her . . . He was very difficult sometimes.

She sighed—then brightened. Things were going to be much easier now. The garden, for instance——

4

Helen Abernethie sat by the fire in the green drawing-room waiting for Maude to come down to dinner.

She looked round her, remembering old days here with Leo and the others. It had been a happy house. But a house like this needed *people*. It needed children and servants and big meals and plenty of roaring fires in winter. It had been a sad house when it had been lived in by one old man who had lost his son. . . .

Who would buy it, she wondered ? Would it be turned into an hotel, or an institute, or perhaps one of those hostels for young people ? That was what happened to these vast houses nowadays. No one would buy them to live in. It would be pulled down, perhaps, and the whole estate built over. It made her sad to think of that, but she pushed the sadness aside resolutely. It did one no good to dwell on the past. This house, and happy days here, and Richard, and Leo, all that was good, but it was over. She had her own activities and friends and interests. Yes, her interests. . . . And now, with the income Richard had left her, she would be able to keep on the villa in Cyprus and do all the things she had planned to do.

How worried she had been lately over money—taxation— all those investments going wrong. . . . Now, thanks to Richard's money, all that was over. . . .

Poor Richard. To die in his sleep like that had been really a great mercy. . . . *Suddenly on the 22nd*—she supposed that that was what had put the idea into Cora's head. Really Cora was outrageous ! She always had been. Helen remembered meeting her once abroad, soon after her marriage to Pierre Lansquenet. She had been particularly foolish and fatuous that day, twisting her head sideways and making dogmatic statements about painting, and particularly about her husband's painting, which must have been most uncomfortable for him. No man could like his wife appearing such a fool. And Cora was a fool ! Oh, well, poor thing, she couldn't help it, and that husband of hers hadn't treated her too well.

Helen's gaze rested absently on a bouquet of wax flowers that stood on a round malachite table. Cora had been sitting

beside it when they had all been sitting round waiting to start
for the church. She had been full of reminiscences and
delighted recognitions of various things and was clearly so
pleased at being back in her old home that she had completely
lost sight of the reason for which they were assembled.

" But perhaps," thought Helen, " she was just less of a
hypocrite than the rest of us. . . ."

Cora had never been one for observing the conventions.
Look at the way she had plumped out that question : " But
he *was* murdered, wasn't he ? "

The faces all round, startled, shocked, staring at her !
Such a variety of expressions there must have been on those
faces. . . .

And suddenly, seeing the picture clearly in her mind,
Helen frowned. . . . There was something wrong with that
picture. . . .

Something . . . ?
Somebody . . . ?

Was it an expression on someone's face ? Was that it ?
Something that—how could she put it ?—ought not to have
been there . . . ?

She didn't know . . . she couldn't place it . . . but there had
been something—somewhere—*wrong*.

5

Meanwhile, in the buffet at Swindon, a lady in wispy
mourning and festoons of jet was eating bath buns and
drinking tea and looking forward to the future. She had no
premonitions of disaster. She was happy.

These cross-country journeys were certainly tiring. It
would have been easier to get back to Lytchett St. Mary via
London—and not so very much more expensive. Ah, but
expense didn't matter now. Still, she would have had to
travel with the family—probably having to talk all the way.
Too much of an effort.

No, better to go home cross-country. These bath buns
were really excellent. Extraordinary how hungry a funeral
made you feel. The soup at Enderby had been delicious—
and so was the cold soufflé.

How smug people were—and what hypocrites ! All those
faces—when she'd said that about murder ! The way they'd
all looked at her !

Well, it had been the right thing to say. She nodded her

head in satisfied approval of herself. Yes, it had been the right thing to do.

She glanced up at the clock. Five minutes before her train went. She drank up her tea. Not very good tea. She made a grimace.

For a moment or two she sat dreaming. Dreaming of the future unfolding before her. . . . She smiled like a happy child.

She was really going to enjoy herself at last . . . She went out to the small branch line train busily making plans. . . .

CHAPTER IV

MR. ENTWHISTLE passed a very restless night. He felt so tired and so unwell in the morning that he did not get up.

His sister who kept house for him, brought up his breakfast on a tray and explained to him severely how wrong he had been to go gadding off to the North of England at his age and in his frail state of health.

Mr. Entwhistle contented himself with saying that Richard Abernethie had been a very old friend.

" Funerals ! " said his sister with deep disapproval. " Funerals are absolutely fatal for a man of your age ! You'll be taken off as suddenly as your precious Mr. Abernethie was if you don't take more care of yourself."

The word " suddenly " made Mr. Entwhistle wince. It also silenced him. He did not argue.

He was well aware of what had made him flinch at the word *suddenly*.

Cora Lansquenet ! What she had suggested was definitely quite impossible, but all the same he would like to find out exactly why she had suggested it. Yes, he would go down to Lytchett St. Mary and see her. He could pretend that it was business connected with probate, that he needed her signature. No need to let her guess that he had paid any attention to her silly remark. But he would go down and see her—and he would do it soon.

He finished his breakfast and lay back on his pillows and read *The Times*. He found *The Times* very soothing.

It was about a quarter to six that evening when his telephone rang.

He picked it up. The voice at the other end of the wire

302

was that of Mr. James Parrott, the present second partner of
Bollard, Entwhistle, Entwhistle and Bollard.

" Look here, Entwhistle," said Mr. Parrott, " I've just
been rung up by the police from a place called Lytchett St.
Mary."

" Lytchett St. Mary ? "

" Yes. It seems——" Mr. Parrott paused a moment. He
seemed embarrassed. " It's about a Mrs. Cora Lansquenet.
Wasn't she one of the heirs of the Abernethie estate ? "

" Yes, of course. I saw her at the funeral yesterday."

" Oh ? She was at the funeral, was she ? "

" Yes. What about her ? "

" Well," Mr. Parrot sounded apologetic. " She's—it's
really *most* extraordinary—she's been well—*murdered.*"

Mr. Parrott said the last word with the uttermost depreca-
tion. It was not the sort of word, he suggested, that ought to
mean anything to the firm of Bollard, Entwhistle, Entwhistle
and Bollard.

" *Murdered ?* "

" Yes—yes—I'm afraid so. Well, I mean, there's no
doubt about it."

" How did the police get on to us ? "

" Her companion, or housekeeper, or whatever she is—a
Miss Gilchrist. The police asked for the name of her nearest
relative or of her solicitors. And this Miss Gilchrist seemed
rather doubtful about relatives and their addresses, but she
knew about us. So they got through at once."

" What makes them think she was murdered ? " demanded
Mr. Entwhistle.

Mr. Parrott sounded apologetic again.

" Oh well, it seems there can't be any doubt about *that*—I
mean it was a hatchet or something of that kind—a very
violent sort of crime."

" Robbery ? "

" That's the idea. A window was smashed and there are
some trinkets missing and drawers pulled out and all that,
but the police seem to think there might be something—well—
phony about it."

" What time did it happen ? "

" Sometime between two and four-thirty this afternoon."

" Where was the housekeeper ? "

" Changing library books in Reading. She got back about
five o'clock and found Mrs. Lansquenet dead. The police
want to know if we've any idea of who could have been
likely to attack her. I said," Mr. Parrott's voice sounded

303

outraged, " that I thought it was a most unlikely thing to happen."

" Yes, of course."

" It *must* be some half-witted local oaf—who thought there might be something to steal and then lost his head and attacked her. That must be it—eh, don't you think so, Entwhistle ? "

" Yes, yes . . ." Mr. Entwhistle spoke absentmindedly.

Parrott was right, he told himself. That was what must have happened. . . .

But uncomfortably he heard Cora's voice saying brightly : " *He* was *murdered, wasn't he ?* "

Such a fool, Cora. Always had been. Rushing in where angels fear to tread . . . Blurting out unpleasant truths . . . *Truths !*

That blasted word again. . . .

2

Mr. Entwhistle and Inspector Morton looked at each other appraisingly.

In his neat precise manner Mr. Entwhistle had placed at the Inspector's disposal all the relevant facts about Cora Lansquenet. Her upbringing, her marriage, her widowhood, her financial position, her relatives.

" Mr. Timothy Abernethie is her only surviving brother and her next of kin, but he is a recluse and an invalid, and is quite unable to leave home. He has empowered me to act for him and to make all such arrangements as may be necessary."

The Inspector nodded. It was a relief for him to have this shrewd elderly solicitor to deal with. Moreover he hoped that the lawyer might be able to give him some assistance in solving what was beginning to look like a rather puzzling problem.

He said :

" I understand from Miss Gilchrist that Mrs. Lansquenet had been North, to the funeral of an elder brother, on the day before her death ? "

" That is so, Inspector. I myself was there."

" There was nothing unusual in her manner—nothing strange—or apprehensive ? "

Mr. Entwhistle raised his eyebrows in well-simulated surprise.

" Is it customary for there to be something strange in the manner of a person who is shortly to be murdered ? " he asked.

The Inspector smiled rather ruefully.

" I'm not thinking of her being ' fey ' or having a premonition. No, I'm just hunting around for something—well, something out of the ordinary."

" I don't think I quite understand you, Inspector," said Mr. Entwhistle.

" It's not a very easy case to understand, Mr. Entwhistle. Say someone watched the Gilchrist woman come out of the house at about two o'clock and go along to the village and the bus stop. This someone then deliberately takes the hatchet that was lying by the woodshed, smashes the kitchen window with it, gets into the house, goes upstairs, attacks Mrs Lansquenet with the hatchet—and attacks her savagely. Six or eight blows were struck." Mr. Entwhistle flinched— " Oh, yes, quite a brutal crime. Then the intruder pulls out a few drawers, scoops up a few trinkets—worth perhaps a tenner in all, and clears off."

" She was in bed ? "

" Yes. It seems she returned late from the North the night before, exhausted and very excited. She'd come into some legacy as I understand ? "

" Yes."

" She slept very badly and woke with a terrible headache. She had several cups of tea and took some dope for her head and then told Miss Gilchrist not to disturb her till lunch-time. She felt no better and decided to take two sleeping pills. She then sent Miss Gilchrist into Reading by the bus to change some library books. She'd have been drowsy, if not already asleep, when this man broke in. He could have taken what he wanted by means of threats, or he could easily have gagged her. A hatchet, deliberately taken up with him from outside, seems excessive."

" He may just have meant to threaten her with it,' Mr. Entwhistle suggested. " If she showed fight then——'

" According to the medical evidence there is no sigr that she did. Everything seems to show that she was lying on her side sleeping peacefully when she was attacked."

Mr. Entwhistle shifted uneasily in his chair.

" One does hear of these brutal and rather senseless murders," he pointed out.

" Oh yes, yes, that's probably what it will turn out to be. There's an alert out, of course, for any suspicious character.

305

Nobody local is concerned, we're pretty sure of that. The locals are all accounted for satisfactorily. Most people are at work at that time of day. Of course her cottage is up a lane outside the village proper. Anyone could get there easily without being seen. There's a maze of lanes all round the village. It was a fine morning and there has been no rain for some days, so there aren't any distinctive car tracks to go by—in case anyone came by car."

" You think someone came by car ? " Mr. Entwhistle asked sharply.

The Inspector shrugged his shoulders. " I don't know. All I'm saying is there are curious features about the case. These, for instance——" He shoved across his desk a handful of things—a trefoil-shaped brooch with small pearls, a brooch set with amethysts, a small string of seed pearls, and a garnet bracelet.

" Those are the things that were taken from her jewel box. They were found just outside the house shoved into a bush."

" Yes—yes, that *is* rather curious. Perhaps if her assailant was frightened at what he had done——"

" Quite. But he would probably then have left them upstairs in her room. . . . Of course a panic may have come over him between the bedroom and the front gate."

Mr. Entwhistle said quietly :

" Or they may, as you are suggesting, have only been taken as a blind."

" Yes, several possibilities . . . Of course this Gilchrist woman may have done it. Two women living alone together —you never know what quarrels or resentments or passions may have been aroused. Oh yes, we're taking that possibility into consideration as well. But it doesn't seem very likely. From all accounts they were on quite amicable terms." He paused before going on. " According to you, nobody stands to gain by Mrs. Lansquenet's death ? "

The lawyer shifted uneasily.

" I didn't quite say that."

Inspector Morton looked up sharply.

" I thought you said that Mrs. Lansquenet's source of income was an allowance made to her by her brother and that as far as you knew she had no property or means of her own."

" That is so. Her husband died a bankrupt, and from what I knew of her as a girl and since, I should be surprised if she had ever saved or accumulated any money."

" The cottage itself is rented, not her own, and the few

sticks of furniture aren't anything to write home about, even in these days. Some spurious ' cottage oak ' and some arty painted stuff. Whoever she's left them to won't gain much —if she's made a will, that is to say."

Mr. Entwhistle shook his head.

" I know nothing about her will. I had not seen her for many years, you must understand."

" Then what exactly did you mean just now ? You had something in mind, I think ? "

" Yes. Yes, I did. I wished to be strictly accurate."

" Were you referring to the legacy you mentioned ? The one that her brother left her ? Had she the power to dispose of that by will ? "

" No, not in the sense you mean. She had no power to dispose of the capital. Now that she is dead, it will be divided amongst the five other beneficiaries of Richard Abernethie's will. That is what I meant. All five of them will benefit automatically by her death."

The Inspector looked disappointed.

" Oh, I thought we were on to something. Well, there certainly seems no motive there for anyone to come and swipe her with a hatchet. Looks as though it's some chap with a screw loose—one of these adolescent criminals, perhaps—a lot of them about. And then he lost his nerve and bushed the trinkets and ran . . . Yes, it must be that. Unless it's the highly respectable Miss Gilchrist, and I must say that seems unlikely."

" When did she find the body ? "

" Not until just about five o'clock. She came back from Reading by the 4.50 bus. She arrived back at the cottage, let herself in by the front door, and went into the kitchen and put the kettle on for tea. There was no sound from Mrs. Lansquenet's room, but Miss Gilchrist assumed that she was still sleeping. Then Miss Gilchrist noticed the kitchen window; the glass was all over the floor. Even then, she thought at first it might have been done by a boy with a ball or a catapult. She went upstairs and peeped very gently into Mrs. Lansquenet's room to see if she were asleep or if she was ready for some tea. Then of course, she let loose, shrieked, and rushed down the lane to the nearest neighbour. Her story seems perfectly consistent and there was no trace of blood in her room or in the bathroom, or on her clothes. No, I don't think Miss Gilchrist had anything to do with it. The doctor got there at half-past five. He puts the time of death not later than four-thirty—and probably much nearer two o'clock, so it looks as though whoever it was, was hanging round waiting for Miss Gilchrist to leave the cottage.

The lawyer's face twitched slightly. Inspector Morton went on : " You'll be going to see Miss Gilchrist, I suppose ? "

" I thought of doing so."

" I should be glad if you would. She's told us, I think, everything that she can, but you never know. Sometimes, in conversation, some point or other may crop up. She's a trifle old-maidish—but quite a sensible, practical woman—and she's really been most helpful and efficient."

He paused and then said :

" The body's at the mortuary. If you would like to see it——"

Mr. Entwhistle assented, though with no enthusiasm.

Some few minutes later he stood looking down at the mortal remains of Cora Lansquenet. She had been savagely attacked and the henna dyed fringe was clotted and stiffened with blood. Mr. Entwhistle's lips tightened and he looked away queasily.

Poor little Cora. How eager she had been the day before yesterday to know whether her brother had left her anything. What rosy anticipations she must have had of the future. What a lot of silly things she could have done—and enjoyed doing—with the money.

Poor Cora. . . . How short a time those anticipations had lasted.

No one had gained by her death—not even the brutal assailant who had thrust away those trinkets as he fled. Five people had a few thousands more of capital—but the capital they had already received was probably more than sufficient for them. No, there could be no motive there.

Funny that murder should have been running in Cora's mind the very day before she herself was murdered.

" *He was murdered, wasn't he ?* "

Such a ridiculous thing to say. Ridiculous ! Quite ridiculous ! Much too ridiculous to mention to Inspector Morton.

Of course, after he had seen Miss Gilchrist . . .

Supposing that Miss Gilchrist, although it was unlikely, could throw any light on what Richard had said to Cora.

" *I thought from what he said——*" What *had* Richard said ?

" I must see Miss Gilchrist at once," said Mr. Entwhistle to himself.

3

Miss Gilchrist was a spare faded-looking woman with short, iron-grey hair. She had one of those indeterminate faces that women around fifty so often acquire.

She greeted Mr. Entwhistle warmly.

" I'm *so* glad you have come, Mr. Entwhistle. I really know *so little* about Mrs. Lansquenet's family, and of course I've never, never had anything to do with a *murder* before. It's too dreadful ! "

Mr. Entwhistle felt quite sure that Miss Gilchrist had never before had anything to do with murder. Indeed, her reaction to it was very much that of his partner.

" One *reads* about them, of course," said Miss Gilchrist, relegating crimes to their proper sphere." And even *that* I'm not very fond of doing. So *sordid*, most of them."

Following her into the sitting-room Mr. Entwhistle was looking sharply about him. There was a strong smell of oil paint. The cottage was overcrowded, less by furniture, which was much as Inspector Morton had described it, than by pictures. The walls were covered with pictures, mostly very dark and dirty oil paintings. But there were water-colour sketches as well, and one or two still lifes. Smaller pictures were stacked on the window-seat.

" Mrs. Lansquenet used to buy them at sales," Miss Gilchrist explained. " It was a great interest to her, poor dear. She went to all the sales round about. Pictures go so cheap, nowadays, a mere song. She never paid more than a pound for any of them, sometimes only a few shillings, and there was a wonderful chance, she always said, of picking up something worth while. She used to say that this was an Italian Primitive that might be worth a lot of money."

Mr. Entwhistle looked at the Italian Primitive pointed out to him dubiously. Cora, he reflected, had never really known anything about pictures. He'd eat his hat if any of these daubs were worth a five pound note !

" Of course," said Miss Gilchrist, noticing his expression, and quick to sense his reaction. " I don't know much myself, though my father was a painter—not a very successful one, I'm afraid. But I used to do water-colours myself as a girl and I heard a lot of talk about painting and that made it nice for Mrs. Lansquenet to have someone she could talk to about painting and who'd understand. Poor dear soul, she cared so much about artistic things."

" You were fond of her ? "

A foolish question, he told himself. Could she possibly answer " no " ? Cora, he thought, must have been a tiresome woman to live with.

" Oh *yes*," said Miss Gilchrist. " We get on *very* well together. In some ways, you know, Mrs. Lansquenet was just like a child. She said anything that came into her head. I don't know that her *judgment* was always very good——"

One does not say of the dead—" She was a thoroughly silly woman "—Mr. Entwhistle said, " She was not in any sense an intellectual woman."

" No—no—perhaps not. But she was very shrewd, Mr. Entwhistle. Really very shrewd. It quite surprised me sometimes—how she managed to hit the nail on the head."

Mr. Entwhistle looked at Miss Gilchrist with more interest. He thought that she was no fool herself.

" You were with Mrs. Lansquenet for some years, I think? "

" Three and a half."

" You—er—acted as companion and also did the—er—well —looked after the house ? "

It was evident that he had touched on a delicate subject. Miss Gilchrist flushed a little.

" Oh yes, indeed. I did most of the cooking—I *quite* enjoy cooking—and did some dusting and light housework. None of the *rough*, of course." Miss Gilchrist's tone expressed a firm principle. Mr. Entwhistle who had no idea what " the rough " was, made a soothing murmur.

" Mrs. Panter from the village came in for that. Twice a week regularly. You see, Mr. Entwhistle, I could not have contemplated being in any way a *servant*. When my little tea-shop failed—such a disaster—it was the war, you know. A delightful place. I called it the Willow Tree and all the china was blue willow pattern—sweetly pretty—and the cakes *really* good—I've always had a hand with cakes and scones. Yes I was doing really well and then the war came and supplies were cut down and the whole thing went bankrupt —a war casualty, that is what I always say, and I try to think of it like that. I lost the little money my father left me that I had invested in it, and of course I had to look round for something to do. I'd never been trained for anything. So I went to one lady but it didn't answer at all—she was so rude and overbearing—and then I did some office work—but I didn't like that at all, and then I came to Mrs. Lansquenet and we suited each other from the start—her husband being an artist and everything." Miss Gilchrist came to a breathless

310

stop and added mournfully : " But how I loved my dear, dear little tea-shop. Such *nice* people used to come to it ! "

Looking at Miss Gilchrist, Mr. Entwhistle felt a sudden stab of recognition—a composite picture of hundreds of lady-like figures approaching him in numerous Bay Trees, Ginger Cats, Blue Parrots, Willow Trees and Cosy Corners, all chastely encased in blue or pink or orange overalls and taking orders for pots of china tea and cakes. Miss Gilchrist had a Spiritual Home—a lady-like tea-shop of Ye Olde Worlde variety with a suitable genteel clientèle. There must, he thought, be large numbers of Miss Gilchrists all over the country, all looking much alike with mild patient faces and obstinate upper lips and slightly wispy grey hair.

Miss Gilchrist went on :

" But really I must not talk about myself. The police have been very kind and considerate. Very kind indeed. An Inspector Morton came over from headquarters and he was *most* understanding. He even arranged for me to go and spend the night at Mrs. Lake's down the lane but I said ' No.' I felt it my duty to stay here with all Mrs. Lansquenet's nice things in the house. They took the—the——" Miss Gilchrist gulped a little—" the body away, of course, and locked up the room, and the Inspector told me there would be a constable on duty in the kitchen all night—because of the broken window—it has been reglazed this morning, I am glad to say —where was I ? Oh yes, so I said I should be *quite* all right in my own room, though I must confess I *did* pull the chest of drawers across the door and put a big jug of water on the window-sill. One never knows—and if by any chance it *was* a maniac—one does hear of such things . . ."

Here Miss Gilchrist ran down. Mr. Entwhistle said quickly :

" I am in possession of all the main facts. Inspector Morton gave them to me. But if it would not distress you too much to give me your own account—— ? "

" Of course, Mr. Entwhistle. I know *just* what you feel. The police are so impersonal, are they not ? Rightly so, of course."

"Mrs. Lansquenet got back from the funeral the night before last," Mr. Entwhistle prompted.

" Yes, her train didn't get in until quite late. I had ordered a taxi to meet it as she told me to. She was very tired, poor dear—as was only natural—but on the whole she was in quite good spirits."

" Yes, yes. Did she talk about the funeral at all ? "

" Just a little. I gave her a cup of hot milk—she didn't

311

want anything else—and she told me that the church had been
quite full and lots and lots of flowers—oh! and she said that
she was sorry not to have seen her other brother—Timothy—
was it ? "

" Yes, Timothy."

" She said it was over twenty years since she had seen him
and that she hoped he would have been there, but she quite
realised he would have thought it better not to come under
the circumstances, but that his wife was there and that she'd
never been able to stand Maude—oh dear, I *do* beg your pardon,
Mr. Entwhistle—it just slipped out—I never meant——"

" Not at all. Not at all," said Mr. Entwhistle encouragingly.
" I am no relation, you know. And I believe that Cora and
her sister-in-law never hit it off very well."

" Well, she almost said as much. ' I always knew Maude
would grow into one of those bossy interfering women,' is
what she said. And then she was very tired and said she'd
go to bed at once—I'd got her hot-water bottle in all ready—
and she went up."

" She said nothing else that you can remember specially? "

" She had no *premonition*, Mr. Entwhistle, if that is what
you mean. I'm sure of that. She was really, you know, in
remarkably good spirits—apart from tiredness and the—the
sad occasion. She asked me how I'd like to go to Capri. To
Capri ! Of course I said it would be too wonderful—it's a
thing I'd never dreamed I'd ever do—and she said, ' We'll
go ! ' Just like that. I gathered—of course it wasn't actually
mentioned—that her brother had left her an annuity or something of the kind."

Mr. Entwhistle nodded.

" Poor dear. Well, I'm glad she had the pleasure of planning—at all events." Miss Gilchrist sighed and murmured
wistfully, " I don't suppose I shall ever go to Capri now. . . "

" And the next morning ? " Mr. Entwhistle prompted,
oblivious of Miss Gilchrist's disappointments.

" The next morning Mrs. Lansquenet wasn't at all well.
Really, she looked dreadful. She'd hardly slept at all, she
told me. Nightmares. ' It's because you were overtired
yesterday,' I told her, and she said maybe it was. She had
her breakfast in bed, and she didn't get up all the morning,
but at lunch-time she told me that she still hadn't been able
to sleep. ' I feel so restless,' she said. ' I keep thinking of
things and wondering.' And then she said she'd take some
sleeping tablets and try and get a good sleep in the afternoon.
And she wanted me to go over by bus to Reading and change

her two library books, because she'd finished them both on the train journey and she hadn't got anything to read. Usually two books lasted her nearly a week. So I went off just after two and that—and that—was the last time——" Miss Gilchrist began to sniff. " She must have been asleep, you know. She wouldn't have heard anything and the Inspector assures me that she didn't suffer. . . . He thinks the first blow killed her. Oh dear, it makes me quite sick even to *think* of it ! "

" Please, please. I've no wish to take you any further over what happened. All I wanted was to hear what you could tell me about Mrs. Lansquenet before the tragedy."

" Very natural, I'm sure. Do tell her relations that apart from having such a bad night she was really very happy and looking forward to the future."

Mr. Entwhistle paused before asking his next question. He wanted to be careful not to lead the witness.

" She did not mention any of her relations in particular ? "

" No, no, I don't think so." Miss Gilchrist considered. " Except what she said about being sorry not to see her brother Timothy."

" She did not speak at all about her brother's decease ? The—er—cause of it ? Anything like that ? "

" No."

There was no sign of alertness in Miss Gilchrist's face. Mr. Entwhistle felt certain there would have been if Cora had plumped out her verdict of murder.

" He'd been ill for some time, I think," said Miss Gilchrist vaguely, " though I must say I was surprised to hear it. He looked so very vigorous."

Mr. Entwhistle said quickly :

" You saw him—when ? "

" When he came down here to see Mrs. Lansquenet. Let me see—that was about three weeks ago."

" Did he stay here ? "

" Oh—no—just came for luncheon. It was quite a surprise. Mrs. Lansquenet hadn't expected him. I gather there had been some family disagreement. She hadn't seen him for years, she told me."

" Yes, that is so."

" It quite upset her—seeing him again—and probably realising how ill he was——"

" She knew that he was ill ? "

" Oh yes. I remember quite well. Because I wondered— only in my own mind, you understand—if perhaps Mr.

Abernethie might be suffering from softening of the brain.
An aunt of mine——"

Mr. Entwhistle deftly side-tracked the aunt.

" Something Mrs. Lansquenet said caused you to think of
softening of the brain ? "

" Yes. Mrs. Lansquenet said something like ' Poor Richard.
Mortimer's death must have aged him a lot. He sounds quite
senile. All these fancies about persecution and that someone
is poisoning him. Old people get like that.' And of course,
as I knew, that is only too *true*. This aunt that I was telling
you about—was convinced the servants were trying to poison
her in her food and at last would eat only boiled eggs—because,
she said, you couldn't get inside a boiled egg to poison it. We
humoured her, but if it had been nowadays I don't know
what we should have done. With eggs so scarce and mostly
foreign at that, so that boiling is always risky."

Mr. Entwhistle listened to the saga of Miss Gilchirist's
aunt with deaf ears. He was very much disturbed.

He said at last, when Miss Gilchrist had twittered into
silence :

" I suppose Mrs. Lansquenet didn't take all this too seriously ? "

" Oh no, Mr. Entwhislte, she *quite* understood."

Mr. Entwhistle found that remark disturbing too, though
not quite in the sense in which Miss Gilchrist had used it.

Had Cora Lansquenet understood ? Not then, perhaps, but
later. Had she understood only too well ?

Mr. Entwhistle knew that there had been no senility about
Richard Abernethie. Richard had been in full possession of
his faculties. He was not the man to have persecution mania
in any form. He was, as he always had been, a hard-headed
business man—and his illness made no difference in that
respect.

It seemed extraordinary that he should have spoken to his
sister in the terms that he had. But perhaps Cora, with her
odd childlike shrewdness had read between the lines, and had
crossed the t's and dotted the i's of what Richard Abernethie
had actually said.

In most ways, thought Mr. Entwhistle, Cora had been a
complete fool. She had no judgment, no balance, and a crude
childish point of view, but she had also the child's uncanny
knack of sometimes hitting the nail on the head in a way that
seemed quite startling.

Mr. Entwhistle left it at that. Miss Gilchrist, he thought,
knew no more than she had told him. He asked whether she

knew if Cora Lansquenet had left a will. Miss Gilchrist replied promptly that Mrs. Lansquenet's will was at the Bank.

With that and after making certain further arrangements he took his leave. He insisted on Miss Gilchrist's accepting a small sum in cash to defray present expenses and told her he would communicate with her again, and in the meantime he would be grateful if she would stay on at the cottage while she was looking about for a new post. That would be, Miss Gilchrist said, a great convenience and really she was not at all nervous.

He was unable to escape without being shown round the cottage by Miss Gilchrist, and introduced to various pictures by the late Pierre Lansquenet which were crowded into the small dining-room and which made Mr. Entwhistle flinch—they were mostly nudes executed with a singular lack of draughtsmanship but with much fidelity to detail. He was also made to admire various small oil sketches of picturesque fishing ports done by Cora herself.

" Polperro," said Miss Gilchrist proudly. " We were there last year and Mrs. Lansquenet was delighted with its pic-turesqueness."

Mr. Entwhistle, viewing Polperro from the south-west, from the north-west, and presumably from the several other points of the compass, agreed that Mrs. Lansquenet had certainly been enthusiastic.

" Mrs. Lansquenet promised to leave me her sketches," said Miss Gilchrist wistfully. " I admired them so much. One can really see the waves breaking in this one, can't one ? Even if she forgot, I might perhaps have just *one* as a souvenir, do you think ? "

" I'm sure that could be arranged," said Mr. Entwhistle graciously.

He made a few further arrangements and then left to interview the Bank Manager and to have a further consulta-tion with Inspector Morton.

CHAPTER V

" WORN OUT, that's what you are," said Miss Entwhistle in the indignant and bullying tones adopted by devoted sisters towards brothers for whom they keep house. " You shouldn't do it, at your age. What's it all got to do with you, I'd like to know ? You've retired, haven't you ? "

315

Mr. Entwhistle said mildly that Richard Abernethie had been one of his oldest friends.

" I dare say. But Richard Abernethie's dead, isn't he ? So I see no reason for you to go mixing yourself up in things that are no concern of yours and catching your death of cold in these nasty draughty railway trains. And murder, too ! *I* can't see why they sent for you at all."

" They communicated with me because there was a letter in the cottage signed by me, telling Cora the arrangements for the funeral."

" Funerals ! One funeral after another, and that reminds me. Another of these precious Abernethies has been ringing you up—Timothy, I think he said. From somewhere in Yorkshire—and *that's* about a funeral, too ! Said he'd ring again later."

A personal call for Mr. Entwhistle came through that evening. Taking it, he heard Maude Abernethie's voice at the other end.

" Thank goodness I've got hold of you at last ! Timothy has been in the most terrible state. This news about Cora has upset him dreadfully."

" Quite understandable," said Mr. Entwhistle.

" What did you say ? "

" I said it was quite understandable."

" I suppose so." Maude sounded more than doubtful. " Do you mean to say it was really murder ? "

(" *It was murder, wasn't it ?* " Cora had said. But this time there was no hesitation about the answer.)

" Yes, it was murder," said Mr. Entwhistle.

" And with a hatchet, so the papers say ? "

" Yes."

" It seems *quite* incredible to me," said Maude, " that Timothy's sister—his own sister—can have been murdered with a *hatchet* ! "

It seemed no less incredible to Mr. Entwhistle. Timothy's life was so remote from violence that even his relations, one felt, ought to be equally exempt.

" I'm afraid one has to face the fact," said Mr. Entwhistle mildly.

" I am really *very* worried about Timothy. It's so bad for him all this ! I've got him to bed now but he insists on my persuading you to come up and see him. He wants to know a hundred things—whether there will be an inquest, and who ought to attend, and how soon after that the funeral can take place, and where, and what funds there are, and if Cora expressed any wishes about being cremated or what, and if she left a will——"

Mr. Entwhistle interrupted before the catalogue got too long.

"There is a will, yes. She left Timothy her executor."

"Oh dear, I'm afraid Timothy can't undertake any-thing——"

"The firm will attend to all the necessary business. The will's very simple. She left her own sketches and an amethyst brooch to her companion, Miss Gilchrist, and everything else to Susan."

"To Susan ? Now I wonder why Susan ? I don't believe she ever saw Susan—not since she was a baby anyway."

"I imagine that it was because Susan was reported to have made a marriage not wholly pleasing to the family."

Maude snorted.

"Even Gregory is a great deal better than Pierre Lans-quenet ever was ! Of course marrying a man who serves in a shop would have been unheard of in my day—but a chemist's shop is much better than a haberdasher's—and at least Gregory seems quite respectable." She paused and added : "Does this mean that Susan gets the income Richard left to Cora ? "

"Oh no. The capital of that will be divided according to the instructions of Richard's will. No, poor Cora had only a few hundred pounds and the furniture of her cottage to leave. When outstanding debts are paid and the furniture sold I doubt if the whole thing will amount to more than at most five hundred pounds." He went on : "There will have to be an inquest, of course. That is fixed for next Thursday. If Timothy is agreeable, we'll send down young Lloyd to watch the proceedings on behalf of the family." He added apologetically : "I'm afraid it may attract some notoriety owing to the—er—circumstances."

"How very unpleasant ! Have they caught the wretch who did it ? "

"Not yet."

"One of these dreadful half-baked young men who go about the country roving and murdering, I suppose. The police are so incompetent."

"No, no," said Mr. Entwhistle. "The police are by no means incompetent. Don't imagine that, for a moment."

"Well, it all seems to me quite extraordinary. And so bad for Timothy. I suppose you couldn't possibly come down here, Mr. Entwhistle ? I should be most grateful if you

317

could. I think Timothy's mind might be set at rest if you were here to reassure him."

Mr. Entwhistle was silent for a moment. The invitation was not unwelcome.

"There is something in what you say," he admitted. "And I shall need Timothy's signature as executor to certain documents. Yes, I think it might be quite a good thing."

"That is splendid. I am so relieved. To-morrow? And you'll stay the night? The best train is the 11.20 from St. Pancras."

"It will have to be an afternoon train, I'm afraid. I have," said Mr. Entwhistle, "other business in the morning. . . ."

2

George Crossfield greeted Mr. Entwhistle heartily but with, perhaps, just a shade of surprise.

Mr. Entwhistle said, in an explanatory way, although it really explained nothing :

"I've just come up from Lytchett St. Mary."

"Then it really was Aunt Cora? I read about it in the papers and I just couldn't believe it. I thought it must be someone of the same name."

"Lansquenet is not a common name."

"No, of course it isn't. I suppose there is a natural aversion to believing that anyone of one's own family can be murdered. Sounds to me rather like that case last month on Dartmoor."

"Does it ? "

"Yes. Same circumstances. Cottage in a lonely position. Two elderly women living together. Amount of cash taken really quite pitifully inadequate one would think."

"The value of money is always relative," said Mr. Entwhistle. "It is the need that counts."

"Yes—yes, I suppose you're right."

"If you need ten pounds desperately—then fifteen is more than adequate. And inversely also. If your need is for a hundred pounds, forty-five would be worse than useless. And if it's thousands you need, then hundreds are not enough."

George said with a sudden flicker of the eyes : "I'd say *any* money came in useful these days. Everyone's hard up."

"But not *desperate*," Mr. Entwhistle pointed out. "It's the desperation that counts."

"Are you thinking of something in particular ? "

"Oh no, not at all." He paused then went on : "It will

be a little time before the estate is settled; would it be convenient for you to have an advance ? "

" As a matter of fact, I *was* going to raise the subject. However, I saw the Bank this morning and referred them to you and they were quite obliging about an overdraft."

Again there came that flicker in George's eyes, and Mr. Entwhistle, from the depths of his experience, recognised it. George, he felt certain, had been, if not desperate, then in very sore straits for money. He knew at that moment, what he had felt subconsciously all along, that in money matters he would not trust George. He wondered if old Richard Abernethie, who also had had great experience in judging men, had felt that. Mr. Entwhistle was almost sure that after Mortimer's death, Richard Abernethie had formed the intention of making George his heir. George was not an Abernethie, but he was the only male of the younger generation. He was the natural successor to Mortimer. Richard Abernethie had sent for George, had had him staying in the house for some days. It seemed probable that at the end of the visit the older man had not found George satisfactory. Had he felt instinctively, as Mr. Entwhistle felt, that George was not straight ? George's father, so the family had thought, had been a poor choice on Laura's part. A stockbroker who had had other rather mysterious activities. George took after his father rather than after the Abernethies.

Perhaps misinterpreting the old lawyer's silence, George said with an uneasy laugh :

" Truth is, I've not been very lucky with my investments lately. I took a bit of a risk and it didn't come off. More or less cleaned me out. But I'll be able to recoup myself now. All one needs is a bit of capital. Ardens Consolidated are pretty good, don't you think ? "

Mr. Entwhistle neither agreed nor dissented. He was wondering if by any chance George had been speculating with money that belonged to clients and not with his own ? If George had been in danger of criminal prosecution——

Mr. Entwhistle said precisely :

" I tried to reach you the day after the funeral, but I suppose you weren't in the office."

" Did you ? They never told me. As a matter of fact, I thought I was entitled to a day off after the good news ! "

" The good news ? "

George reddened.

" Oh look here, I didn't mean Uncle Richard's death. But knowing you've come into money does give one a bit of a kick. One feels one must celebrate. As a matter of fact I went to Hurst Park. Backed two winners. It never rains but it pours ! If your luck's in, it's in ! Only a matter of fifty quid, but it all helps."

" Oh yes," said Mr. Entwhistle. " It all helps. And there will now be an additional sum coming to you as a result of your Aunt Cora's death."

George looked concerned.

" Poor old girl," he said. " It does seem rotten luck, doesn't it ? Probably just when she was all set to enjoy herself."

" Let us hope the police will find the person responsible for her death," said Mr. Entwhistle.

" I expect they'll get him all right. They're good, our police. They round up all the undesirables in the neighbourhood and go through 'em with a tooth comb—make them account for their actions at the time it happened."

" Not so easy if a little time has elapsed," said Mr. Entwhistle. He gave a wintry little smile that indicated he was about to make a joke. " I myself was in Hatchard's bookshop at 3.30 on the day in question. Should I remember that if I were questioned by the police in ten days' time ? I very much doubt it. And you, George, you were at Hurst Park. Would you remember which day you went to the races in—say—a month's time ? "

" Oh I could fix it by the funeral—the day after."

" True—true. And then you backed a couple of winners. Another aid to memory. One seldom forgets the name of a horse on which one has won money. Which were they, by the way ? "

" Let me see. Gaymarck and Frogg II. Yes, I shan't forget them in a hurry."

Mr. Entwhistle gave his dry little cackle of laughter and took his leave.

3

" It's lovely to see you, of course," said Rosamund without any marked enthusiasm. " But it's frightfully early in the morning."

She yawned heavily.

" It's eleven o'clock," said Mr. Entwhistle.

Rosamund yawned again. She said apologetically :

" We had the hell of a party last night. Far too much to drink. Michael's got a terrible hangover still."

320

Michael appeared at this moment, also yawning. He had a cup of black coffee in his hand and was wearing a very smart dressing-gown. He looked haggard and attractive—and his smile had the usual charm. Rosamund was wearing a black skirt, a rather dirty yellow pullover, and nothing else as far as Mr. Entwhistle could judge.

The precise and fastidious lawyer did not approve at all of the young Shanes' way of living. The rather ramshackle flat on the first floor of a Chelsea house—the bottles and glasses and cigarette ends that lay about in profusion—the stale air, and the general air of dust and dishevelment.

In the midst of this discouraging setting Rosamund and Michael bloomed with their wonderful good looks. They were certainly a very handsome couple and they seemed, Mr. Entwhistle thought, very fond of each other. Rosamund was certainly adoringly fond of Michael.

"Darling," she said. "Do you think just a teeny sip of champagne? Just to pull us together and toast the future. Oh, Mr. Entwhistle, it really is the most marvellous luck Uncle Richard leaving us all that lovely money just now——"

Mr. Entwhistle noted the quick, almost scowling frown that Michael gave, but Rosamund went on serenely :

"Because there's the most wonderful chance of a play. Michael's got an option on it. It's a most wonderful part for him and even a small part for me, too. It's about one of these young criminals, you know, that are really saints—it's absolutely full of the latest modern ideas."

"So it would seem," said Mr. Entwhistle stiffly.

"He robs, you know, and he kills, and he's hounded by the police and by society—and then in the end, he does a miracle."

Mr. Entwhistle sat in outraged silence. Pernicious nonsense these young fools talked ! *And* wrote.

Not that Michael Shane was talking much. There was still a faint scowl on his face.

"Mr. Entwhistle doesn't want to hear all our rhapsodies, Rosamund," he said. "Shut up for a bit and let him tell us why he's come to see us."

"There are just one or two little matters to straighten out," said Mr. Entwhistle. "I have just come back from Lytchett St. Mary."

"Then it *was* Aunt Cora who was murdered ? We saw it in the paper. And I said it must be because it's a very uncommon name. Poor old Aunt Cora. I was looking at her at the funeral that day and thinking what a frump she was and

321

that really one might as well be dead if one looked like that
—and now she *is* dead. They absolutely wouldn't *believe* it
last night when I told them that that murder with the hatchet
in the paper was actually *my aunt* ! They just laughed, didn't
they, Michael ? "

Michael Shane did not reply and Rosamund with every
appearance of enjoyment said :

" Two murders one after another. It's almost too much,
isn't it ? "

" Don't be a fool, Rosamund, your Uncle Richard wasn't
murdered."

" Well, Cora thought he was."

Mr. Entwhistle intervened to ask :

" You came back to London after the funeral, didn't
you ? "

" Yes, we came by the same train as you did."

" Of course . . . of course. I ask because I tried to get
hold of you," he shot a quick glance at the telephone—" on
the following day—several times in fact, and couldn't get an
answer."

" Oh dear—I'm so sorry. What were we doing that day ?
The day before yesterday. We were here until about twelve,
weren't we ? And then you went round to try and get hold of
Rosenheim and you went on to lunch with Oscar and I went
out to see if I could get some nylons and round the shops.
I was to meet Janet but we missed each other. Yes, I had a
lovely afternoon shopping—and then we dined at the *Castile*.
We got back here about ten o'clock, I suppose."

" About that," said Michael. He was looking thoughtfully
at Mr. Entwhistle. " What did you want to get hold of us
for, sir ? "

" Oh ! Just some points that had arisen about Richard
Abernethie's estate—papers to sign—all that."

Rosamund asked : " Do we get the money now, or not for
ages ? "

" I'm afraid," said Mr. Entwhistle, " that the law is prone
to delays."

" But we can get an advance, can't we ? " Rosamund looked
alarmed. " Michael said we could. Actually it's terribly
important. Because of the play."

Michael said pleasantly :

" Oh, there's no real hurry. It's just a question of deciding
whether or not to take up the option."

" It will be quite easy to advance you some money," said
Mr. Entwhistle. " As much as you need."

" Then that's all right." Rosamund gave a sigh of relief. She added as an afterthought : " Did Aunt Cora leave any money ? "

" A little. She left it to your Cousin Susan."

" Why Susan, I should like to know ! Is it much ? "

" A few hundred pounds and some furniture."

" Nice furniture ? "

" No," said Mr. Entwhistle.

Rosamund lost interest. " It's all very odd, isn't it ? " she said. " There was Cora, after the funeral, suddenly coming out with ' He *was* murdered ! ' and then, the very next day, *she* goes and gets *herself* murdered ? I mean, it is *odd*, isn't it ? "

There was a moment's rather uncomfortable silence before Mr. Entwhistle said quietly :

" Yes, it is indeed very odd. . . ."

4

Mr. Entwhistle studied Susan Banks as she leant forward across the table talking in her animated manner.

None of the loveliness of Rosamund here. But it was an attractive face and its attraction lay, Mr. Entwhistle decided, in its vitality. The curves of the mouth were rich and full. It was a woman's mouth and her body was very decidedly a woman's—emphatically so. Yet in many ways Susan reminded him of her uncle, Richard Abernethie. The shape of her head, the line of her jaw, the deep-set reflective eyes. She had the same kind of dominant personality that Richard had had, the same driving energy, the same foresightedness and forthright judgment. Of the three members of the younger generation she alone seemed to be made of the metal that had raised up the vast Abernethie fortunes. Had Richard recognised in this niece a kindred spirit to his own ? Mr. Entwhistle thought he must have done. Richard had always had a keen appreciation of character. Here, surely, were exactly the qualities of which he was in search. And yet, in his will, Richard Abernethie had made no distinction in her favour. Distrustful, as Mr. Entwhistle believed, of George, passing over that lovely dimwit, Rosamund—could he not have found in Susan what he was seeking—an heir of his own mettle ?

If not, the cause must be—yes, it followed logically—the husband. . . .

Mr. Entwhistle's eyes slid gently over Susan's shoulder to where Gregory Banks stood absently whittling at a pencil.

A thin, pale, nondescript young man with reddish sandy hair. So overshadowed by Susan's colourful personality that it was difficult to realise what he himself was really like. Nothing to take hold of in the fellow—quite pleasant, ready to be agreeable—a "yes" man, as the modern term went. And yet that did not seem to describe him satisfactorily. There was something vaguely disquieting about the unobtrusiveness of Gregory Banks. He had been an unsuitable match—yet Susan had insisted on marrying him—had overborne all opposition—why? What had she seen in him?

And now, six months after the marriage—" She's crazy about the fellow," Mr. Entwhistle said to himself. He knew the signs. A large number of wives with matrimonial troubles had passed through the office of Bollard, Entwhistle, Entwhistle and Bollard. Wives madly devoted to unsatisfactory and often what appeared quite unprepossessing husbands, wives contemptuous of, and bored by, apparently attractive and impeccable husbands. What any woman saw in some particular man was beyond the comprehension of the average intelligent male. It just was so. A woman who could be intelligent about everything else in the world could be a complete fool when it came to some particular man. Susan, thought Mr. Entwhistle, was one of those women. For her the world revolved around Greg. And that had its dangers in more ways than one.

Susan was talking with emphasis and indignation.

"—because it *is* disgraceful. You remember that woman who was murdered in Yorkshire last year? Nobody was ever arrested. And the old woman in the sweet shop who was killed with a crowbar. They detained some man, and then they let him go!"

"There has to be evidence, my dear," said Mr. Entwhistle.

Susan paid no attention.

"And that other case—a retired nurse—that was a hatchet or an axe—just like Aunt Cora."

"Dear me, you appear to have made quite a study of these crimes, Susan," said Mr. Entwhistle mildly.

"Naturally one remembers these things—and when someone in one's own family is killed—and in very much the same way —well, it shows that there must be a lot of these sort of people going round the countryside, breaking into places and attacking lonely women—and that the police just don't *bother!*"

324

Mr. Entwhistle shook his head.

" Don't belittle the police, Susan. They are a very shrewd and patient body of men—persistent, too. Just because it isn't still mentioned in the newspapers doesn't mean that a case is closed. Far from it."

" And yet there are hundreds of unsolved crimes every year."

" Hundreds ? " Mr. Entwhistle looked dubious. " A certain number, yes. But there are many occasions when the police know who has committed a crime but where the evidence is insufficient for a prosecution."

" I don't believe it," said Susan. " I believe if you knew definitely *who* committed a crime you could always get the evidence."

" I wonder now." Mr. Entwhistle sounded thoughtful. " I very much wonder . . ."

" Have they any idea *at all*—in Aunt Cora's case—of who might be ? "

" That I couldn't say. Not as far as I know. But they would hardly confide in me—and it's early days yet—the murder took place only the day before yesterday, remember."

" It's definitely got to be a certain kind of person," Susan mused. " A brutal, perhaps slightly half-witted type—a discharged soldier or a gaol bird. I mean, using a hatchet like that."

Looking slightly quizzical, Mr. Entwhistle raised his eyebrows and murmured :

> " Lizzie Borden with an axe
> Gave her father fifty whacks
> When she saw what she had done
> She gave her mother fifty-one."

" Oh," Susan flushed angrily, "C ora hadn't got any relations living with her—unless you mean the companion. And anyway Lizzie Borden was acquitted. Nobody knows for certain she killed her father and stepmother."

" The rhyme is quite definitely libellous," Mr. Entwhistle agreed.

" You mean the companion *did* do it ? Did Cora leave her anything ? "

" An amethyst brooch of no great value and some sketches of fishing villages of sentimental value only."

" One has to have a motive for murder—unless one is half-witted."

Mr. Entwhistle gave a little chuckle.

" As far as one can see, the only person who had a motive is *you*, my dear Susan."

" What's that ? " Greg moved forward suddenly. He was like a sleeper coming awake. An ugly light showed in his eyes. He was suddenly no longer a negligible feature in the background. " What's Sue got to do with it ? What do you mean—saying things like that ? "

Susan said sharply :

" Shut up, Greg. Mr. Entwhistle doesn't mean any-thing——"

" Just my little joke," said Mr. Entwhistle apologetically. " Not in the best taste, I'm afraid. Cora left her estate, such as it was, to you, Susan. But to a young lady who has just inherited several hundred thousand pounds, an estate, amounting at the most to a few hundreds, can hardly be said to represent a motive for murder."

" She left her money to me ? " Susan sounded surprised. " How extraordinary. She didn't even know me ? Why did she do it, do you think ? "

" I think she had heard rumours that there had been a little difficulty—er—over your marriage." Greg, back again at sharpening his pencil, scowled. " There had been a certain amount of trouble over her own marriage—and I think she experienced a fellow feeling."

Susan asked with a certain amount of interest :

" She married an artist, didn't she, whom none of the family liked ? Was he a good artist ? "

Mr. Entwhistle shook his head very decidedly.

" Are there any of his paintings in the cottage ? "

" Yes."

" Then I shall judge for myself," said Susan.

Mr. Entwhistle smiled at the resolute tilt of Susan's chin.

" So be it. Doubtless I am an old fogey and hopelessly old-fashioned in matters of art, but I really don't think you will dispute my verdict."

" I suppose I ought to go down there, anyway ? And look over what there is. Is there anybody there now ? "

" I have arranged with Miss Gilchrist to remain there until further notice."

Greg said : " She must have a pretty good nerve—to stay in a cottage where a murder's been committed."

" Miss Gilchrist is quite a sensible woman, I should say. Besides," added the lawyer dryly, " I don't think she has anywhere else to go until she gets another situation."

326

" So Aunt Cora's death left her high and dry ? Did she—
were she and Aunt Cora—on intimate terms—— ? "

Mr. Entwhistle looked at her rather curiously, wondering
just exactly what was in her mind.

" Moderately so, I imagine," he said. " She never treated
Miss Gilchrist as a servant."

" Treated her a damned sight worse, I dare say," said
Susan. " These wretched so called ' ladies ' are the ones who
get it taken out of them nowadays. I'll try and find her a
decent post somewhere. It won't be difficult. Anyone who's
willing to do a bit of housework and cook is worth their
weight in gold—she does cook, doesn't she ? "

" Oh yes. I gather it is something she called, er, ' the
rough ' that she objected to. I'm afraid I don't quite know
what ' the rough ' is."

Susan appeared to be a good deal amused.

Mr. Entwhistle, glancing at his watch, said :

" Your aunt left Timothy her executor."

" Timothy," said Susan with scorn. " Uncle Timothy is
practically a myth. Nobody ever sees him."

" Quite." Mr. Entwhistle glanced at his watch. " I am
travelling up to see him this afternoon. I will acquaint him
with your decision to go down to the cottage."

" It will only take me a day or two, I imagine. I don't
want to be long away from London. I've got various schemes
in hand. I'm going into business."

Mr. Entwhistle looked round him at the cramped sitting-
room of the tiny flat. Greg and Susan were evidently hard up.
Her father, he knew, had run through most of his money. He
had left his daughter badly off.

" What are your plans for the future, if I may ask ? "

" I've got my eye on some premises in Cardigan Street.
I suppose, if necessary, you can advance me some money ?
I may have to pay a deposit."

" That can be managed," said Mr. Entwhistle. " I rang you
up the day after the funeral several times—but could get no
answer. I thought perhaps you might care for an advance.
I wondered whether you might perhaps have gone out of
Town."

" Oh no," said Susan quickly. " We were in all day. Both
of us. We didn't go out at all."

Greg said gently : " You know, Susan, I think our telephone
must have been out of order that day. You remember how
I couldn't get through to Hard and Co. in the afternoon. I
meant to report it, but it was all right the next morning."

" Telephones," said Mr. Entwhistle, " can be very unreliable sometimes."

Susan said suddenly :

" How did Aunt Cora know about our marriage ? It was at a Registry Office and we didn't tell anyone until afterwards ! "

" I fancy Richard may have told her about it. She remade her will about three weeks ago (it was formerly in favour of the Theosophical Society)—just about the time he had been down to see her."

Susan looked startled.

" Did Uncle Richard go down to see her ? I'd no idea of that ? "

" I hadn't any idea of it myself," said Mr. Entwhistle.

" So that was when——"

" When what ? "

" Nothing," said Susan.

CHAPTER VI

" VERY GOOD of you to come along," said Maude gruffly, as she greeted Mr. Entwhistle on the platform of Bayham Compton station. " I can assure you that both Timothy and I much appreciate it. Of course the truth is that Richard's death was the worst thing possible for Timothy."

Mr. Entwhistle had not yet considered his friend's death from this particular angle. But it was, he saw, the only angle from which Mrs. Timothy Abernethie was likely to regard it.

As they proceeded towards the exit, Maude developed the theme.

" To begin with, it was a *shock*—Timothy was really very attached to Richard. And then unfortunately it put the idea of death into Timothy's head. Being such an invalid has made him rather nervous about himself. He realised that he was the only one of the brothers left alive—and he started saying that he'd be the next to go—and that it wouldn't be long now—all very morbid talk, as I told him."

They emerged from the station and Maude led the way to a dilapidated car of almost fabulous antiquity.

" Sorry about our old rattletrap," she said. " We've wanted a new car for years, but really we couldn't afford it. This has had a new engine twice—and these old cars really stand up to a lot of hard work.

" I hope it will start," she added. " Sometimes one has to wind it."

She pressed the starter several times but only a meaningless whirr resulted. Mr. Entwhistle, who had never wound a car in his life, felt rather apprehensive, but Maude herself descended, inserted the starting handle and with a vigorous couple of turns woke the motor to life. It was fortunate, Mr. Entwhistle reflected, that Maude was such a powerfully built woman.

" That's that," she said. " The old brute's been playing me up lately. Did it when I was coming back after the funeral. Had to walk a couple of miles to the nearest garage and they weren't good for much—just a village affair. I had to put up at the local inn while they tinkered at it. Of course *that* upset Timothy, too. I had to phone through to him and tell him I couldn't be back till the next day. Fussed him terribly. One tries to keep things from him as much as possible—but some things one can't do anything about—Cora's murder, for instance. I had to send for Dr. Barton to give him a sedative. Things like murder are too much for a man in Timothy's state of health. I gather Cora was always a fool."

Mr. Entwhistle digested this remark in silence. The inference was not quite clear to him.

" I don't think I'd seen Cora since our marriage," said Maude. " I didn't like to say to Timothy at the time : ' Your youngest sister's batty,' not just like that. But it's what I *thought*. There she was saying the most extraordinary things ! One didn't know whether to resent them or whether to laugh. I suppose the truth is she lived in a kind of imaginary world of her own—full of melodrama and fantastic ideas about other people. Well, poor soul, she's paid for it now. She didn't have any protégés, did she ? "

" Protégés ? What do you mean ? "

" I just wondered. Some young cadging artist, or musician —or something of that kind. Someone she might have let in that day, and who killed her for her loose cash. Perhaps an adolescent—they're so queer at that age sometimes—especially if they're the neurotic arty type. I mean, it seems so odd to break in and murder her in the middle of the afternoon. If you break into a house surely you'd do it at night."

" There would have been two women there then."

" Oh yes, the companion. But really I can't believe that anyone would deliberately wait until she was out of the way and then break in and attack Cora. What for ? He can't have expected she'd have any cash or stuff to speak of, and

329

there must have been times when both the women were out and
the house was empty. That would have been much safer. It
seems so stupid to go and commit a murder unless it's absolutely necessary."

" And Cora's murder, you feel, was unnecessary ? "

" It all seems so stupid."

Should murder make sense ? Mr. Entwhistle wondered.
Academically the answer was yes. But many pointless crimes
were on record. It depended, Mr. Entwhistle reflected, on the
mentality of the murderer.

What did he really know about murderers and their mental
processes ? Very little. His firm had never had a criminal
practice. He was no student of criminology himself. Murderers, as far as he could judge, seemed to be of all sorts and
kinds. Some had had over-weening vanity, some had had
a lust for power, some, like Seddon, had been mean and
avaricious, others, like Smith and Rowse had had an incredible
fascination for women ; some, like Armstrong, had been
pleasant fellows to meet. Edith Thompson had lived in a
world of violent unreality, Nurse Waddington had put her
elderly patients out of the way with business-like cheerfulness.

Maude's voice broke into his meditations.

" If I could only keep the newspapers from Timothy !
But he will insist on reading them—and then, of course, it
upsets him. You do understand, don't you, Mr. Entwhistle,
that there can be *no question* of Timothy's attending the
inquest ? If necessary, Dr. Barton can write out a certificate
or whatever it is."

" You can set your mind at rest about that."

" Thank goodness ! "

They turned in through the gates of Stansfield Grange,
and up a neglected drive. It had been an attractive small
property once—but had now a doleful and neglected appearance. Maude sighed as she said :

" We had to let this go to seed during the war. Both
gardeners called up. And now we've only got one old man
—and he's not much good. Wages have gone up so terribly.
I must say it's a blessing to realise that we'll be able to spend
a little money on the place now. We're both so fond of it.
I was really afraid that we might have to sell it. . . . Not
that I suggested anything of the kind to Timothy. It would
have upset him—dreadfully."

They drew up before the portico of a very lovely old
Georgian house which badly needed a coat of paint.

" No servants," said Maude bitterly, as she led the way in.

" Just a couple of women who come in. We had a resident maid until a month ago—slightly hunchbacked and terribly adenoidal and in many ways not too bright, but she was *there* which was such a comfort—and quite good at plain cooking. And would you believe it, she gave notice and went to a fool of a woman who keeps six Pekinese dogs (it's a larger house than this and more work) because she was ' so fond of little doggies,' she said. Dogs, indeed ! Being sick and making messes all the time I've no doubt ! Really, these girls are *mental* ! So there we are, and if I have to go out any afternoon, Timothy is left quite alone in the house and if anything should happen, how could he get help ? Though I do leave the telephone close by his chair so that if he felt faint he could dial Dr. Barton immediately."

Maude led the way into the drawing-room where tea was laid ready by the fireplace, and establishing Mr. Entwhistle there, disappeared, presumably to the back regions. She returned in a few minutes' time with a teapot and silver kettle, and proceeded to minister to Mr. Entwhistle's needs. It was a good tea with home-made cake and fresh buns. Mr. Entwhistle murmured :

" What about Timothy ? " and Maude explained briskly that she had taken Timothy his tray before she set out for the station.

" And now," said Maude, " he will have had his little nap and it will be the best time for him to see you. Do try and not let him excite himself too much."

Mr. Entwhistle assured her that he would exercise every precaution.

Studying her in the flickering firelight, he was seized by a feeling of compassion. This big, stalwart matter-of-fact woman, so healthy, so vigorous, so full of common sense, and yet so strangely, almost pitifully, vulnerable in one spot. Her love for her husband was maternal love, Mr. Entwhistle decided. Maude Abernethie had borne no child and she was a woman built for motherhood. Her invalid husband had become her child, to be shielded, guarded, watched over. And perhaps, being the stronger character of the two, she had unconsciously imposed on him a state of invalidism greater than might otherwise have been the case.

" Poor Mrs. Tim," thought Mr. Entwhistle to himself.

331

2

" Good of you to come, Entwhistle."

Timothy raised himself up in his chair as he held out a hand.
He was a big man with a marked resemblance to his brother
Richard. But what was strength in Richard, in Timothy was
weakness. The mouth was irresolute, the chin very slightly
receding, the eyes less deep-set. Lines of peevish irritability
showed on his forehead.

His invalid status was emphasised by the rug across his
knees and a positive pharmacopœia of little bottles and boxes
on a table at his right hand.

" I mustn't exert myself," he said warningly. " Doctor's
forbidden it. Keeps telling me not to worry ! Worry ! If
he'd had a murder in his family he'd do a bit of worrying, I
bet ! It's too much for a man—first Richard's death—then
hearing all about his funeral and his will—what a will !—and
on top of that poor little Cora killed with a hatchet. Hatchet !
Ugh ! This country's full of gangsters nowadays—thugs—
left over from the war ! Going about killing defenceless
women. Nobody's got the guts to put these things down—to
take a strong hand. What's the country coming to, I'd like
to know ? What's the damned country coming to ? "

Mr. Entwhistle was familiar with this gambit. It was a
question almost invariably asked sooner or later by his clients
for the last twenty years and he had his routine for answering
it. The non-committal words he uttered could have been
classified under the heading of soothing noises.

" It all began with that damned Labour Government," said
Timothy. " Sending the whole country to blazes. And the
Government we've got now is no better. Mealy-mouthed,
milk-and-water socialists ! Look at the state we're in ! Can't
get a decent gardener, can't get servants—poor Maude here
has to work herself to a shadow messing about in the kitchen
(by the way, I think a custard pudding would go well with the
sole to-night, my dear—and perhaps a little clear soup first ?).
I've got to keep my strength up—Doctor Barton said so—let
me see, where was I ? Oh yes, Cora. It's a shock, I can tell
you, to a man, when he hears his sister—his own sister—has
been *murdered* ! Why, I had palpitations for twenty minutes !
You'll have to attend to everything for me, Entwhistle. *I*
can't go to the inquest or be bothered by business of any
kind connected with Cora's estate. I want to forget the whole
thing. What happens, by the way, to Cora's share of Richard's
money ? Comes to me, I suppose ? "

332

Murmuring something about clearing away tea, Maude left the room.

Timothy lay back in his chair and said :

" Good thing to get rid of the women. Now we can talk business without any silly interruptions."

" The sum left in trust for Cora," said Mr. Entwhistle, " goes equally to you and the nieces and nephew."

" But look here," Timothy's cheeks assumed a purplish hue of indignation. " Surely I'm her next of kin ? Only surviving brother."

Mr. Entwhistle explained with some care the exact provisions of Richard Abernethie's will, reminding Timothy gently that he had had a copy sent him.

" Don't expect me to understand all that legal jargon, do you ? " said Timothy ungratefully. " You lawyers ! Matter of fact, I couldn't believe it when Maude came home and told me the gist of it. Thought she'd got it wrong. Women are never clear headed. Best woman in the world, Maude—but women don't understand finance. I don't believe Maude even realises that if Richard hadn't died when he did, we might have had to clear out of here. Fact ! "

" Surely if you had applied to Richard——"

Timothy gave a short bark of harsh laughter.

" That's not my style. Our father left us all a perfectly reasonable share of his money—that is, if we didn't want to go into the family concern. I didn't. I've a soul above corn-plasters, Entwhistle ! Richard took my attitude a bit hard. Well, what with taxes, depreciation of income, one thing and another—it hasn't been easy to keep things going. I've had to realise a good deal of capital. Best thing to do these days. I did hint once to Richard that this place was getting a bit hard to run. He took the attitude that we'd be much better off in a smaller place altogether. Easier for Maude, he said, more labour saving—labour saving, what a term ! Oh no, I wouldn't have asked Richard for help. But I can tell you, Entwhistle, that the worry affected my health most unfavourably. A man in my state of health oughtn't to have to worry. Then Richard died and though of course naturally I was cut up about it—my brother and all that—I couldn't help feeling relieved about future prospects. Yes, it's all plain sailing now—and a great relief. Get the house painted—get a couple of really good men on the garden—you can get them at a price. Restock the rose garden completely. And— where was I——"

" Detailing your future plans."

" Yes, yes—but I mustn't bother you with all that. What did hurt me—and hurt me cruelly—were the terms of Richard's will."

" Indeed ? " Mr. Entwhistle looked inquiring. " They were not—as you expected ? "

" I should say they weren't ! Naturally, after Mortimer's death, I assumed that Richard would leave everything to *me*."

" Ah—did he—ever—indicate that to you ? "

" He never said so—not in so many words. Reticent sort of chap, Richard. But he asked himself here—not long after Mortimer's death. Wanted to talk over family affairs generally. We discussed young George—and the girls and their husbands. Wanted to know my views—not that I could tell him much. I'm an invalid and I don't get about, and Maude and I live out of the world. Rotten silly marriages both of those girls made, if you ask me. Well, I ask you, Entwhistle, naturally I thought he was consulting me as the head of the family after he was gone and naturally I thought the control of the money would be mine. Richard could surely trust me to do the right thing by the younger generation. And to look after poor old Cora. Dash it all, Entwhistle, I'm an Abernethie—the last Abernethie. Full control should have been left in my hands."

In his excitement Timothy had kicked aside his rug and had sat up in his chair. There were no signs of weakness or fragility about him. He looked, Mr. Entwhistle thought, a perfectly healthy man, even if a slightly excitable one. Moreover the old lawyer realised very clearly that Timothy Abernethie had probably always been secretly jealous of his brother Richard. They had been sufficiently alike for Timothy to resent his brother's strength of character and firm grasp of affairs. When Richard had died, Timothy had exulted in the prospect of succeeding at this late date to the power to control the destinies of others.

Richard Abernethie had not given him that power. Had he thought of doing so and then decided against it ?

A sudden squalling of cats in the garden brought Timothy up out of his chair. Rushing to the window he threw up the sash, bawled out " Stop it, you ! " and picking up a large book hurled it out at the marauders.

" Beastly cats," he grumbled, returning to his visitor. " Ruin the flower beds and I can't stand that damned yowling."

He sat down again and asked :

334

" Have a drink, Entwhistle ? "

" Not quite so soon. Maude has just given me an excellent tea."

Timothy grunted.

" Capable woman, Maude. But she does too much. Even has to muck about with the inside of that old car of ours—she's quite a mechanic in her way, you know."

" I hear she had a breakdown coming back from the funeral ? "

" Yes. Car conked out. She had the sense to telephone through about it, in case I should be anxious, but that ass of a daily woman of ours wrote down the message in a way that didn't make sense. I was out getting a bit of fresh air—I'm advised by the doctor to take what exercise I can if I feel like it—I got back from my walk to find scrawled on a bit of paper: ' Madam's sorry car gone wrong got to stay night.' Naturally I thought she was still at Enderby. Put a call through and found Maude had left that morning. Might have had the breakdown *anywhere* ! Pretty kettle of fish ! Fool of a daily woman only left me a lumpy macaroni cheese for supper. I had to go down to the kitchen and warm it up *myself—and* make myself a cup of tea—to say nothing of stoking the boiler. I might have had a heart attack—but does that class of woman care ? Not she ? With any decent feelings she'd have come back that evening and looked after me properly. No loyalty any more in the lower classes——"

He brooded sadly.

" I don't know how much Maude told you about the funeral and the relatives," said Mr. Entwhistle. " Cora produced rather an awkward moment. Said brightly that Richard had been murdered, hadn't he ? Perhaps Maude told you."

Timothy chuckled easily.

" Oh yes, I heard about that. Everybody looked down their noses and pretended to be shocked. Just the sort of thing Cora would say ! You know how she always managed to put her foot in it when she was a girl, Entwhistle ? Said something at our wedding that upset Maude, I remember. Maude never cared for her very much. Yes, Maude rang me up that evening after the funeral to know if I was all right and if Mrs. Jones had come in to give me my evening meal and then she told me it had all gone off very well, and I said ' What about the will ? ' and she tried to hedge a bit, but of course I had the truth out of her. I couldn't believe it, and I said she must have made a mistake, but she stuck to it. It hurt me, Entwhistle—it really *wounded* me, if you know what

I mean. If you ask me, it was just *spite* on Richard's part.
I know one shouldn't speak ill of the dead, but, upon my
word——"

Timothy continued on this theme for some time.

Then Maude came back into the room and said firmly :

" I think, dear, Mr. Entwhistle has been with you quite
long enough. You really *must* rest. If you have settled
everything——"

" Oh, we've settled things. I leave it all to you, Entwhistle.
Let me know when they catch the fellow—if they ever do.
I've no faith in the police nowadays—the Chief Constables
aren't the right type. You'll see to the—er—interment—
won't you ? We shan't be able to come, I'm afraid. But
order an expensive wreath—and there must be a proper stone
put up in due course—she'll be buried locally, I suppose ?
No point in bringing her North and I've no idea where
Lansquenet is buried, somewhere in France I believe. I don't
know what one puts on a stone when it's murder. . . . Can't
very well say ' entered into rest ' or anything like that. One
will have to choose a text—something appropriate. R.I.P. ?
No, that's only for Catholics."

" O Lord, thou hast seen my wrong. Judge thou my case,"
murmured Mr. Entwhistle.

The startled glance Timothy bent on him made Mr. Entwhistle smile faintly.

" From Lamentations," he said. " It seems appropriate if
somewhat melodramatic. However, it will be some time
before the question of the Memorial stone comes up. The—er
—ground has to settle, you know. Now don't worry about
anything. We will deal with things and keep you fully
informed."

Mr. Entwhistle left for London by the breakfast train on
the following morning.

When he got home, after a little hesitation, he rang up
a friend of his.

CHAPTER VII

" I CAN'T tell you how much I appreciate your invitation."

Mr. Entwhistle pressed his host's hand warmly.

Hercule Poirot gestured hospitably to a chair by the fire.

Mr. Entwhistle sighed as he sat down.

On one side of the room a table was laid for two.

" I returned from the country this morning," he said.

" And you have a matter on which you wish to consult me ? "

" Yes. It's a long rambling story, I'm afraid."

" Then we will not have it until after we have dined. *Georges* ? "

The efficient George materialised with some *Pâté de Foie Gras* accompanied by hot toast in a napkin.

" We will have our *Pâté* by the fire," said Poirot. "Afterwards we will move to the table."

It was an hour and a half later that Mr. Entwhistle stretched himself comfortably out in his chair and sighed a contented sigh.

" You certainly know how to do yourself well, Poirot. Trust a Frenchman."

" I am a Belgian. But the rest of your remark applies. At my age the chief pleasure, almost the *only* pleasure that still remains, is the pleasure of the table. Mercifully I have an excellent stomach."

" Ah," murmured Mr. Entwhistle.

They had dined off *Sole Veronique*, followed by *Escalope de Veau Milanaise*, proceeding to *Poire Flambée* with ice-cream.

They had drunk a *Pouilly Fuisse* followed by a *Corton*, and a very good port now reposed at Mr. Entwhistle's elbow. Poirot, who did not care for port, was sipping *Crème de Cacao*.

" I don't know," murmured Mr. Entwhistle reminiscently, " how you manage to get hold of an escalope like that ! It melted in the mouth ! "

" I have a friend who is a Continental butcher. For him I solve a small domestic problem. He is appreciative—and ever since then he is most sympathetic to me in the matters of the stomach."

" A domestic problem." Mr. Entwhistle sighed. " I wish you had not reminded me . . . This is such a perfect moment . . ."

" Prolong it, my friend. We will have presently the *demi tasse* and the fine brandy, and then, when digestion is peacefully under way, *then* you shall tell why you need my advice."

The clock struck the half hour after nine before Mr. Entwhistle stirred in his chair. The psychological moment had come. He no longer felt reluctant to bring forth his perplexities—he was eager to do so.

" I don't know," he said, " whether I'm making the most colossal fool of myself. In any case I don't see that there's

337

anything that can possibly be done. But I'd like to put the facts before you, and I'd like to know what you think."

He paused for a moment or two, then in his dry meticulous way, he told his story. His trained legal brain enabled him to put the facts clearly, to leave nothing out, and to add nothing extraneous. It was a clear succinct account, and as such appreciated by the little elderly man with the egg-shaped head who sat listening to him.

When he had finished there was a pause. Mr. Entwhistle was prepared to answer questions, but for some few moments no question came. Hercule Poirot was reviewing the evidence.

He said at last :

" It seems very clear. You have in your mind the suspicion that your friend, Richard Abernethie, may have been murdered ? That suspicion, or assumption, rests on the basis of one thing only—*the words spoken by Cora Lansquenet at Richard Abernethie's funeral*. Take those away—and there is nothing left. The fact that she herself was murdered the day afterwards *may* be the purest coincidence. It is true that Richard Abernethie died suddenly, but he was attended by a reputable doctor who knew him well, and that doctor had no suspicions and gave a death certificate. Was Richard buried or cremated ? "

" Cremated—according to his own request."

" Yes, that is the law. And it means that a second doctor signed the certificate—but there would be no difficulty about that. So we come back to the essential point, *what Cora Lansquenet said*. You were there and you heard her. She said : ' But he *was* murdered, wasn't he ? ' "

" Yes."

" And the real point is—that you believe she was speaking the truth."

The lawyer hesitated for a moment, then he said :

" Yes, I do."

" Why ? "

" Why ? " Entwhistle repeated the word, slightly puzzled.

" But yes, *why* ? Is it because, already, deep down, you had an uneasiness about the manner of Richard's death ? "

The lawyer shook his head. " No, no, not in the least."

" Then it is because of *her*—of Cora herself. You knew her well ? "

" I had not seen her for—oh—over twenty years."

" Would you have known her if you had met her in the street ? "

Mr. Entwhistle reflected.

338

AFTER THE FUNERAL

" I might have passed her by in the street without recognising her. She was a thin slip of a girl when I saw her last
and she had turned into a stout, shabby, middle-aged woman.
But I think that the moment I spoke to her face to face I
should have recognised her. She wore her hair in the same
way, a bang cut straight across the forehead and she had a
trick of peering up at you through her fringe like a rather shy
animal, and she had a very characteristic, abrupt way of
talking, and a way of putting her head on one side and then
coming out with something quite outrageous. She had
character, you see, and character is always highly individual."

" She was, in fact, the same Cora you had known years ago.
And she still said outrageous things ! The things, the outrageous things, she had said in the past—were they usually—
justified ? "

" That was always the awkward thing about Cora. When
truth would have been better left unspoken, she spoke it."

" And that characteristic remained unchanged. Richard
Abernethie was murdered—so Cora at once mentioned the
fact."

Mr. Entwhistle stirred.

" You think he *was* murdered ? "

" Oh, no, no, my friend, we cannot go so fast. We agree
on this—Cora *thought* he had been murdered. She was quite
sure he had been murdered. It was, to her, more a certainty
than a surmise. And so, we come to this, *she must have had
some reason for the belief*. We agree, by your knowledge of
her, that it was not just a bit of mischief making. Now tell
me—when she said what she did, there was, at once, a kind
of chorus of protest—that is right ? "

" Quite right."

" And she then became confused, abashed, and retreated
from the position—saying—as far as you can remember,
something like ' But I thought—from what he told me——' "

The lawyer nodded.

" I wish I could remember more clearly. But I am fairly
sure of that. She used the words ' he told me ' or ' he
said '——"

" And the matter was then smoothed over and everyone
spoke of something else. You can remember, looking back,
no special expression on anyone's face ? Anything that
remains in your memory as—shall we say—*unusual* ? "

" No."

" And the very next day, *Cora is killed*—and you ask
yourself : ' Can it be cause and effect ? ' "

339

The lawyer stirred.

" I suppose that seems to you quite fantastic ? "

" Not at all," said Poirot. " Given that the original assumption is correct, it is logical. The perfect murder, the murder of Richard Abernethie, has been committed, all has gone off smoothly—and suddenly it appears that there is one person who has a knowledge of the truth ! Clearly that person must be silenced *as quickly as possible.*"

" Then you do think that—it was murder ? "

Poirot said gravely :

" I think, *mon cher*, exactly as you thought—that there is a case for investigation. Have you taken any steps ? You have spoken of these matters to the police ? "

" No." Mr. Entwhistle shook his head. " It did not seem to me that any good purpose could be achieved. My position is that I represent the family. If Richard Abernethie was murdered, there seems only one method by which it could be done.

" By poison ? "

" Exactly. *And the body has been cremated.* There is now no evidence available. But I decided that I, myself, *must* be satisfied on the point. That is why, Poirot, I have come to *you.*"

" Who was in the house at the time of his death ? "

" An old butler who has been with him for years, a cook and a housemaid. It would seem, perhaps, as though it must necessarily be one of them——"

" Ah ! do not try to pull the wool upon my eyes. This Cora, she knows Richard Abernethie was killed, yet she acquiesces in the hushing up. She says ' I think you are all quite right.' Therefore it *must* be one of the family who is concerned, someone whom the victim himself might prefer not to have openly accused. Otherwise, since Cora was fond of her brother, she would not agree to let the sleeping murderer lie. You agree to that, yes ? "

" It was the way I reasoned—yes," confessed Mr. Entwhistle. " Though how any of the family could possibly——"

Poirot cut him short.

" Where poison is concerned there are all sorts of possibilities. It must, presumably, have been a narcotic of some sort if he died in his sleep and if there were no suspicious appearances. Possibly he was already having some narcotic administered to him."

" In any case," said Mr. Entwhistle, " the *how* hardly matters. We shall never be able to prove anything."

340

" In the case of Richard Abernethie, no. But the murder of Cora Lansquenet is different. Once we know ' who ' then evidence ought to be possible to get." He added with a sharp glance, " You have, perhaps, already done something."

" Very little. My purpose was mainly, I think, *elimination*. It is distasteful to me to think that one of the Abernethie family is a murderer. I still can't quite believe it. I hoped that by a few apparently idle questions I could exonerate certain members of the family beyond question. Perhaps, who knows, *all* of them ? In which case, Cora would have been wrong in her assumption and her own death could be ascribed to some casual prowler who broke in. After all, the issue is very simple. What were the members of the Abernethie family doing on the afternoon that Cora Lansquenet was killed ? "

" *Eh bien,*" said Poirot, " what were they doing ? "

" George Crossfield was at Hurst Park races. Rosamund Shane was out shopping in London. Her husband—for one must include husbands——"

" Assuredly."

" Her husband was fixing up a deal about an option on a play, Susan and Gregory Banks were at home all day. Timothy Abernethie, who is an invalid, was at his home in Yorkshire, and his wife was driving herself home from Enderby."

He stopped.

Hercule Poirot looked at him and nodded comprehendingly.

" Yes, that is what they *say*. And is it all true ? "

" I simply don't know, Poirot. Some of the statements are capable of proof or disproof—but it would be difficult to do so without showing one's hand pretty plainly. In fact to do so would be tantamount to an accusation. I will simply tell you certain conclusions of my own. George *may* have been at Hurst Park races, but I do not think he was. He was rash enough to boast that he had backed a couple of winners. It is my experience that so many offenders against the law ruin their own case by saying too much. I asked him the name of the winners, and he gave the names of two horses without any apparent hesitation. Both of them, I found, had been heavily tipped on the day in question and one had duly won. The other, though an odds on favourite, had unaccountably failed even to get a place."

" Interesting. Had this George any urgent need for money at the time of his uncle's death ? "

" It is my impression that his need was very urgent. I have no evidence for saying so, but I strongly suspect that

341

he has been speculating with his clients' funds and that he was in danger of prosecution. It is only my impression but I have some experience in these matters. Defaulting solicitors, I regret to say, are not entirely uncommon. I can only tell you that I would not have cared to entrust my own funds to George, and I suspect that Richard Abernethie, a very shrewd judge of men, was dissatisfied with his nephew and placed no reliance on him.

" His mother," the lawyer continued, " was a good-looking, rather foolish girl and she married a man of what I should call dubious character." He sighed. " The Abernethie girls were not good choosers."

He paused and then went on :

" As for Rosamund, she is a lovely nitwit. I really cannot see her smashing Cora's head in with a hatchet ! Her husband, Michael Shane, is something of a dark horse—he's a man with ambition and also a man of overweening vanity I should say. But really I know very little about him. I have no reason to suspect him of a brutal crime or of a carefully planned poisoning, but until I know that he really was doing what he says he was doing I cannot rule him out."

" But you have no doubts about the wife ? "

" No—no—there is a certain rather startling callousness . . . but no, I really cannot envisage the hatchet. She is a fragile looking creature."

" And beautiful ! " said Poirot with a faint cynical smile. " And the other niece ? "

" Susan ? She is a very different type from Rosamund—a girl of remarkable ability, I should say. She and her husband were at home together that day. I said (falsely) that I had tried to get them on the telephone on the afternoon in question. Greg said very quickly that the telephone had been out of order all day. He had tried to get someone and failed."

" So again it is not conclusive. . . . You cannot eliminate as you hoped to do. . . . What is the husband like ? "

" I find him hard to make out. He has a somewhat unpleasing personality though one cannot say exactly why he makes this impression. As for Susan——"

" Yes ? "

" Susan reminds me of her uncle. She has the vigour, the drive, the mental capacity of Richard Abernethie. It may be my fancy that she lacks some of the kindliness and the warmth of my old friend."

" Women are never kind," remarked Poirot. " Though they can sometimes be tender. She loves her husband ? "

342

" Devotedly, I should say. But really, Poirot, I can't believe—I *won't* believe for one moment that Susan——"

" You prefer George ? " said Poirot. " It is natural ! As for me, I am not so sentimental about beautiful young ladies. Now tell me about your visit to the older generation ? "

Mr. Entwhistle described his visit to Timothy and Maude at some length. Poirot summarised the result.

" So Mrs. Abernethie is a good mechanic. She knows all about the inside of a car. And Mr. Abernethie is not the invalid he likes to think himself. He goes out for walks and is, according to you, capable of vigorous action. He is also a bit of an ego maniac and he resented his brother's success and superior character."

" He spoke very affectionately of Cora."

" And ridiculed her silly remark after the funeral. What of the sixth beneficiary ? "

" Helen ? Mrs. Leo ? I do not suspect her for a moment. In any case, her innocence will be easy to prove. She was at Enderby. With three servants in the house."

" *Eh bien*, my friend," said Poirot. " Let us be practical. What do you want me to do ? "

" I want to know the truth, Poirot."

" Yes. Yes, I should feel the same in your place."

" And you're the man to find it out for me. I know you don't take cases any more, but I ask you to take this one. This is a matter of business. I will be responsible for your fees. Come now, money is always useful."

Poirot grinned.

" Not if it all goes in the taxes ! But I will admit, your problem interests me ! Because it is not easy. . . . It is all so nebulous. . . . One thing, my friend, had better be done by you. After that, I will occupy myself of everything. But I think it will be best if you yourself seek out the doctor who attended Mr. Richard Abernethie. You know him ? "

" Slightly."

" What is he like ? "

" Middle-aged G.P. Quite competent. On very friendly terms with Richard. A thoroughly good fellow."

" Then seek him out. He will speak more freely to you than to me. Ask him about Mr. Abernethie's illness. Find out what medicines Mr. Abernethie was taking at the time of his death and before. Find out if Richard Abernethie ever said anything to his doctor about fancying himself being poisoned. By the way, this Miss Gilchrist is sure that he used the term *poisoned* in talking to his sister ? "

343

Mr. Entwhistle reflected.

" It was the word she used—but she is the type of witness who often changes the actual words used, because she is convinced she is keeping to the sense of them. If Richard had said he was afraid someone wanted to kill him, Miss Gilchrist might have assumed poison because she connected his fears with those of an aunt of hers who thought her food was being tampered with. I can take up the point with her again some time."

" Yes. Or I will do so." He paused and then said in a different voice : " Has it occurred to you, my friend, that your Miss Gilchrist may be in some danger herself ? "

Mr. Entwhistle looked surprised.

" I can't say that it had."

" But, yes. Cora voiced her suspicions on the day of the funeral. The question in the murderer's mind will be, did she voice them to anybody when she first heard of Richard's death ? And the most likely person for her to have spoken to about them will be Miss Gilchrist. I think, *mon cher*, that she had better not remain alone in that cottage."

" I believe Susan is going down."

" Ah, so Mrs. Banks is going down ? "

" She wants to look through Cora's things."

" I see . . . I see . . . Well, my friend, do what I have asked of you. You might also prepare Mrs. Abernethie—Mrs. Leo Abernethie, for the possibility that I may arrive in the house. We will see. From now on I occupy myself of everything."

And Poirot twirled his moustaches with enormous energy.

CHAPTER VIII

MR. ENTWHISTLE looked at Dr. Larraby thoughtfully.

He had had a lifetime of experience in summing people up. There had been frequent occasions on which it had been necessary to tackle a difficult situation or a delicate subject. Mr. Entwhistle was an adept by now in the art of how exactly to make the proper approach. How would it be best to tackle Dr. Larraby on what was certainly a very difficult subject and one which the doctor might very well resent as reflecting upon his own professional skill ?

Frankness, Mr. Entwhistle thought—or at least a modified frankness. To say that suspicions had arisen because of a haphazard suggestion thrown out by a silly woman would be ill-advised. Dr. Larraby had not known Cora.

Mr. Entwhistle cleared his throat and plunged bravely.

" I want to consult you on a very delicate matter," he said. " You may be offended, but I sincerely hope not. You are a sensible man and you will realise, I'm sure, that a—er—preposterous suggestion is best dealt with by finding a reasonable answer and not by condemning it out of hand. It concerns my client, the late Mr. Abernethie. I'll ask you my question flat out. Are you certain, *absolutely certain*, that he died what is termed a natural death ? "

Dr. Larraby's good-humoured, rubicund middle-aged face turned in astonishment on his questioner.

" What on earth—— Of course he did. I gave a certificate, didn't I ? If I hadn't been satisfied——"

Mr. Entwhistle cut in adroitly :

" Naturally, naturally. I assure you that I am not assuming anything to the contrary. But I would be glad to have your positive assurance—in face of the—er—rumours that are flying around."

" Rumours ? What rumours ? "

" One doesn't know quite how these things start," said Mr. Entwhistle mendaciously. " But my feeling is that they should be stopped—authoritatively, if possible."

" Abernethie was a sick man. He was suffering from a disease that would have proved fatal within, I should say, at the earliest, two years. It might have come much sooner. His son's death had weakened his will to live, and his powers of resistance. I admit that I did not expect his death to come so soon, or indeed so suddenly, but there are precedents—plenty of precedents. Any medical man who predicts exactly when a patient will die, or exactly how long he will live, is bound to make a fool of himself. The human factor is always incalculable. The weak have often unexpected powers of resistance, the strong sometimes succumb."

" I understand all that. I am not doubting your diagnosis. Mr. Abernethie was, shall we say (rather melodramatically, I'm afraid) under sentence of death. All I'm asking you is, is it quite impossible that a man, knowing or suspecting that he is doomed, might of his own accord shorten that period of life ? Or that someone else might do it for him ? "

Dr. Larraby frowned.

" Suicide, you mean ? Abernethie wasn't a suicidal type."

" I see. You can assure me, medically speaking, that such a suggestion is impossible."

The doctor stirred uneasily.

" I wouldn't use the word impossible. After his son's death life no longer held the interest for Abernethie that it had done. I certainly don't feel that suicide is likely—but I can't say that it's *impossible*."

" You are speaking from the psychological angle. When I said *medically*, I really meant ; do the circumstances of his death make such a suggestion impossible ? "

" No, oh no. No, I can't say that. He died in his sleep, as people often do. There was no reason to suspect suicide, no evidence of his state of mind. If one were to demand an autopsy every time a man who is seriously ill died in his sleep——"

The doctor's face was getting redder and redder. Mr. Entwhistle hastened to interpose.

" Of course. Of course. But if there *had* been evidence— evidence of which you yourself were not aware ? If, for instance, he had said something to someone——"

" Indicating that he was contemplating suicide ? Did he ? I must say it surprises me."

" But if it *were* so—my case is purely hypothetical—could you rule out the possibility ? "

Dr. Larraby said slowly :

" No—no—I could not do that. But I say again, I should be very much surprised."

Mr. Entwhistle hastened to follow up his advantage.

" If, then, we assume that his death was *not* natural—all this is *purely* hypothetical—what could have caused it ? What kind of a drug, I mean ? "

" Several. Some kind of a narcotic would be indicated. There was no sign of cyanosis, the attitude was quite peaceful."

" He had sleeping draughts or pills ? Something of that kind."

" Yes. I had prescribed Slumberyl—a very safe and dependable hypnotic. He did not take it every night. And he only had a small bottle of tablets at a time. Three or even four times the prescribed dose would not have caused death. In fact, I remember seeing the bottle on his wash-stand after his death still nearly full."

" What else had you prescribed for him ? "

" Various things—a medicine containing a small quantity of morphia to be taken when he had an attack of pain. Some vitamin capsules. An indigestion mixture."

Mr. Entwhistle interrupted.

" Vitamin capsules ? I think I was once prescribed a course of those. Small round capsules of gelatine."

" Yes. Containing adexoline."

" Could anything else have been introduced into—say—one of those capsules ? "

" Something lethal, you mean ? " The doctor was looking more and more surprised. " But surely no man would ever —look here, Entwhistle, what are you getting at ? My God, man, are you suggesting *murder* ? "

" I don't quite know what I'm suggesting. . . . I just want to know what would be *possible*."

" But what evidence have you for even suggesting such a thing ? "

" I haven't any evidence," said Mr. Entwhistle in a tired voice. " Mr. Abernethie is dead—and the person to whom he spoke is also dead. The whole thing is rumour—vague, unsatisfactory rumour, and I want to scotch it if I can. If you tell me that no one could possibly have poisoned Abernethie in any way whatsoever, I'll be delighted ! It would be a big weight off my mind, I can assure you."

Dr. Larraby got up and walked up and down.

" I can't tell you what you want me to tell you," he said at last. " I wish I could. Of course it could have been done. Anybody could have extracted the oil from a capsule and replaced it with—say—pure nicotine or half a dozen other things. Or something could have been put in his food or drink ? Isn't that more likely ? "

" Possibly. But you see, there were only the servants in the house when he died—and I don't think it was any of them—in fact I'm quite sure it wasn't. So I'm looking for some delayed action possibility. There's no drug, I suppose, that you can administer and then the person dies weeks later ? "

" A convenient idea—but untenable, I'm afraid," said the doctor dryly. " I know you're a responsible person, Entwhistle, but who *is* making this suggestion ? It seems to me wildly far fetched."

" Abernethie never said anything to you ? Never hinted that one of his relations might be wanting him out of the way ? "

The doctor looked at him curiously.

" No, he never said anything to me. Are you sure, Entwhistle, that somebody hasn't been—well, playing up the sensational ? Some hysterical subjects can give an appearance of being quite reasonable and normal, you know."

347

" I hope it was like that. It might well be."

" Let me understand. Someone claims that Abernethie told her—it was a woman, I suppose ? "

" Oh yes, it was a woman."

"—told her that someone was trying to kill him ? "

Cornered, Mr. Entwhistle reluctantly told the tale of Cora's remark at the funeral. Dr. Larraby's face lightened.

" My dear fellow. I shouldn't pay any attention ! The explanation is quite simple. The woman's at a certain time of life—craving for sensation, unbalanced, unreliable—might say anything. They do, you know ! "

Mr. Entwistle resented the doctor's easy assumption. He himself had had to deal with plenty of sensation-hunting and hysterical women.

" You may be quite right," he said, rising. " Unfortunately we can't tackle her on the subject, as she's been murdered herself."

" What's that—murdered ? " Dr. Larraby looked as though he had grave suspicions of Mr. Entwhistle's own stability of mind.

" You've probably read about it in the paper. Mrs. Lansquenet at Lytchett St. Mary in Berkshire."

" Of course—I'd no idea she was a relation of Richard Abernethie's ! " Dr. Larraby was looking quite shaken.

Feeling that he had revenged himself for the doctor's professional superiority, and unhappily conscious that his own suspicions had not been assuaged as a result of the visit, Mr. Entwhistle took his leave.

2

Back at Enderby, Mr. Entwhistle decided to talk to Lanscombe.

He started by asking the old butler what his plans were.

" Mrs. Leo has asked me to stay on here until the house is sold, sir, and I'm sure I shall be very pleased to oblige her. We are all very fond of Mrs. Leo." He sighed. " I feel it very much, sir, if you will excuse me mentioning it, that the house has to be sold. I've known it for so very many years, and seen all the young ladies and gentlemen grow up in it. I always thought that Mr. Mortimer would come after his father and perhaps bring up a family here, too. It was arranged, sir, that I should go to the North Lodge when I got past doing my work here. A very nice little place, the North Lodge—and I looked forward to having it very spick and span. But I suppose that's all over now."

"I'm afraid so, Lanscombe. The estate will all have to be sold together. But with your legacy——"

"Oh I'm not complaining, sir, and I'm very sensible of Mr. Abernethie's generosity. I'm well provided for, but it's not so easy to find a little place to buy nowadays and though my married niece has asked me to make my home with them, well, it won't be quite the same thing as living on the estate."

"I know," said Mr. Entwhistle. "It's a hard new world for us old fellows. I wish I'd seen more of my old friend before he went. How did he seem those last few months ? "

"Well,. he wasn't himself, sir. Not since Mr. Mortimer's death."

"No, it broke him up. And then he was a sick man—sick men have strange fancies sometimes. I imagine Mr. Abernethie suffered from that sort of thing in his last days. He spoke of enemies sometimes, of somebody wishing to do him harm—perhaps ? He may even have thought his food was being tampered with ? "

Old Lanscombe looked surprised—surprised and offended.

"I cannot recall anything of that kind, sir."

Entwhistle looked at him keenly.

"You're a very loyal servant, Lanscombe, I know that. But such fancies on Mr. Abernethie's part would be quite—er —unimportant—a natural symptom in some—er diseases."

"Indeed, sir ? I can only say Mr. Abernethie never said anything like that to me, or in my hearing."

Mr. Entwhistle slid gently to another subject.

"He had some of his family down to stay with him, didn't he, before he died. His nephew and his two nieces and their husbands ? "

"Yes, sir, that is so."

"Was he satisfied with those visits ? Or was he disappointed ? "

Lanscombe's eyes became remote, his old back stiffened.

"I really could not say, sir."

"I think you could, you know," said Mr. Entwhistle gently. "It's not your place to say anything of that kind—that's what you really mean. But there are times when one has to do violence to one's sense of what is fitting. I was one of your master's oldest friends. I cared for him very much. So did you. That's why I'm asking you for your opinion as a *man*, not as a butler."

Lanscombe was silent for a moment, then he said in a colourless voice :

" Is there anything—wrong, sir ? "

Mr. Entwhistle replied truthfully.

" I don't know," he said. " I hope not. I would like to make sure. Have you yourself felt that something was— wrong ? "

" Only since the funeral, sir. And I couldn't say exactly what it is. But Mrs. Leo and Mrs. Timothy, too, they didn't seem quite themselves that evening after the others had gone."

" You know the contents of the will ? "

" Yes, sir. Mrs. Leo thought I would like to know. It seemed to me, if I may permit myself to comment, a very fair will."

" Yes, it was a fair will. Equal benefits. But it is not, I think, the will that Mr. Abernethie originally intended to make after his son died. Will you answer now the question that I asked you just now ? "

" As a matter of personal opinion——"

" Yes, yes, that is understood."

" The master, sir, was very much disappointed after Mr. George had been here. . . . He had hoped, I think, that Mr. George might resemble Mr. Mortimer. Mr. George, if I may say so, did not come up to standard. Miss Laura's husband was always considered unsatisfactory, and I'm afraid Mr. George took after him." Lanscombe paused and then went on, " Then the young ladies came with their husbands. Miss Susan he took to at once—a very spirited and handsome young lady, but it's my opinion he couldn't abide her husband. Young ladies make funny choices nowadays, sir."

" And the other couple ? "

" I couldn't say much about that. A very pleasant and good-looking young pair. I think the master enjoyed having them here—but I don't think——" The old man hesitated.

" Yes, Lanscombe ? "

" Well, the master had never had much truck with the stage. He said to me one day, ' I can't understand why anyone gets stage-struck. It's a foolish kind of life. Seems to deprive people of what little sense they have. I don't know what it does to your moral sense. You certainly lose your sense of proportion.' Of course he wasn't referring directly——"

" No, no, I quite understand. Now after these visits, Mr. Abernethie himself went away—first to his brother, and afterwards to his sister Mrs. Lansquenet."

" That I did not know, sir. I mean he mentioned to me that he was going to Mr. Timothy and afterwards to Something St. Mary."

" That is right. Can you remember anything he said on his return in regard to those visits ? "

Lanscombe reflected.

" I really don't know—nothing direct. He was glad to be back. Travelling and staying in strange houses tired him very much—that I do remember his saying."

" Nothing else ? Nothing about either of them ? "

Lanscombe frowned.

" The master used to—well, to *murmur*, if you get my meaning—speaking to me and yet more to himself—hardly noticing I was there—because he knew me so well."

" Knew you and trusted you, yes."

" But my recollection is very vague as to what he said—something about he couldn't think what he'd done with his money—that was Mr. Timothy, I take it. And then he said something about ' Women can be fools in ninety-nine different ways but be pretty shrewd in the hundredth.' Oh yes, and he said, ' You can only say what you really think to someone of your own generation. They don't think you're fancying things as the younger ones do.' And later he said—but I don't know in what connection— 'It's not very nice to have to set traps for people, but I don't see what else I can do.' But I think it possible, sir, that he may have been thinking of the second gardener—a question of the peaches being taken.

But Mr. Entwhistle did not think that it was the second gardener who had been in Richard Abernethie's mind. After a few more questions he let Lanscombe go and reflected on what he had learned. Nothing, really—nothing, that is, that he had not deduced before. Yet there were suggestive points. It was not his sister-in-law, Maude, but his sister Cora of whom he had been thinking when he made the remark about women who were fools and yet shrewd. And it was to her he had confided his " fancies." And he had spoken of setting a trap. For whom ?

351

3

Mr. Entwhistle had meditated a good deal over how much he should tell Helen. In the end he decided to take her wholly into his confidence.

First he thanked her for sorting out Richard's things and for making various household arrangements. The house had been advertised for sale and there were one or two prospective buyers who would be shortly coming to look over it.

" Private buyers ? "

" I'm afraid not. The Y.W.C.A. are considering it, and there is a young people's club, and the Trustees of the Jefferson Trust are looking for a suitable place to house their Collection."

" It seems sad that the house will not be lived in, but of course it is not a practicable proposition nowadays."

" I am going to ask you if it would be possible for you to remain here until the house is sold. Or would it be a great inconvenience ? "

" No—actually it would suit me very well. I don't want to go to Cyprus until May, and I much prefer being here than to being in London as I had planned. I love this house, you know ; Leo loved it, and we were always happy when we were here together."

" There is another reason why I should be grateful if you would stay on. There is a friend of mine, a man called Hercule Poirot——"

Helen said sharply : " Hercule Poirot ? Then you think——"

" You know of him ? "

" Yes. Some friends of mine—but I imagined that he was dead long ago."

" He is very much alive. Not young, of course."

" No, he could hardly be young."

She spoke mechanically. Her face was white and strained. She said with an effort :

" You think—that Cora was right ? That Richard was—*murdered* ? "

Mr. Entwhistle unburdened himself. It was a pleasure to unburden himself to Helen with her clear calm mind.

When he had finished she said :

" One ought to feel it's fantastic—but one doesn't. Maude and I, that night after the funeral—it was in both our minds, I'm sure. Saying to ourselves what a silly woman Cora was—and yet being uneasy. And then—Cora was killed—and

352

I told myself it was just coincidence—and of course it may be—
but oh ! if one can only be sure. It's all so difficult."

" Yes, it's difficult. But Poirot is a man of great originality
and he has something really approaching genius. He under-
stands perfectly what we need—assurance that the whole
thing is a mare's nest."

" And suppose it isn't ? "

" What makes you say that ? " asked Mr. Entwhistle
sharply.

" I don't know. I've been uneasy . . . Not just about what
Cora said that day—something else. Something that I felt
at the time to be wrong."

" Wrong ? In what way ? "

" That's just it. I don't know."

" You mean it was something about one of the people in
the room ? "

" Yes—yes—something of that kind. But I don't know
who or what . . . Oh that sounds absurd——"

" Not at all. It is interesting—very interesting. You are
not a fool, Helen. If you noticed something, that something
has significance."

" Yes, but I can't remember what it *was*. The more I
think——"

" Don't think. That is the wrong way to bring anything
back. Let it go. Sooner or later it will flash into your mind.
And when it does—let me know—at once."

" I will."

CHAPTER IX

MISS GILCHRIST pulled her black felt hat down firmly on her
head and tucked in a wisp of grey hair. The inquest was set
for twelve o'clock and it was not quite twenty-past eleven.
Her grey coat and skirt looked quite nice, she thought, and
she had bought herself a black blouse. She wished she could
have been all in black, but that would have been far beyond
her means. She looked round the small neat bedroom and at
the walls hung with representations of Brixham harbour,
Cockington Forge, Anstey's Cove, Kyance Cove, Polflexan
harbour, Babbacombe Bay, etc., all signed in a dashing way,
Cora Lansquenet. Her eyes rested with particular fondness
on Polflexan harbour. On the chest of drawers a faded
photograph carefully framed represented the Willow Teashop.
Miss Gilchrist looked at it lovingly and sighed.

She was disturbed from her reverie by the sound of the door bell below.

" Dear me," murmured Miss Gilchrist, " I wonder who——"

She went out of her room and down the rather rickety stairs. The bell sounded again and there was a sharp knock.

For some reason Miss Gilchrist felt nervous. For a moment or two her steps slowed up, then she went rather unwillingly to the door, adjuring herself not to be so silly.

A young woman dressed smartly in black and carrying a small suitcase was standing on the step. She noticed the alarmed look on Miss Gilchrist's face and said quickly :

" Miss Gilchrist ? I am Mrs. Lansquenet's niece—Susan Banks."

" Oh dear, yes, of course. I didn't know. Do come in, Mrs. Banks. Mind the hall-stand—it sticks out a little. In here, yes. I didn't know you were coming down for the inquest. I'd have had something ready—some coffee or something."

Susan Banks said briskly :

" I don't want anything. I'm so sorry if I startled you."

" Well, you know you *did*, in a way. It's very silly of me. I'm not usually nervous. In fact I told the lawyer that I *wasn't* nervous, and that I wouldn't be nervous staying on here alone, and really I'm *not* nervous. Only—perhaps it's just the inquest and—and thinking of things, but I have been jumpy all this morning. Just about half an hour ago the bell rang and I could hardly bring myself to open the door—which was really very stupid and so unlikely that a murderer would come *back*—and why should he ?—and actually it was only a nun, collecting for an orphanage—and I was so relieved I gave her two shillings although I'm *not* a Roman Catholic and indeed have no sympathy with the Roman Church and all these monks and nuns though I believe the Little Sisters of the Poor do really do good work. But do please sit down, Mrs.—Mrs.——"

" Banks."

" Yes, of course, Banks. Did you come down by train ? "

" No, I drove down. The lane seemed so narrow I ran the car on a little way and found a sort of old quarry I backed it into."

" This lane is very narrow, but there's hardly ever any traffic along here. It's rather a lonely road."

Miss Gilchrist gave a little shiver as she said those last words.

Susan Banks was looking round the room.

354

" Poor old Aunt Cora," she said. " She left what she had to me, you know."

" Yes, I know. Mr. Entwhistle told me. I expect you'll be glad of the furniture. You're newly married, I understand, and furnishing is such an expense nowadays. Mrs. Lansquenet had some very nice things."

Susan did not agree. Cora had had no taste for the antique. The contents varied between " modernistic " pieces and the " arty " type.

" I shan't want any of the furniture," she said. " I've got my own, you know. I shall put it up for auction. Unless —is there any of it you would like ? I'd be very glad . . ."

She stopped, a little embarrassed. But Miss Gilchrist was not at all embarrassed. She beamed.

" Now really, that's *very* kind of you, Mrs. Banks—yes, very kind indeed. I really do appreciate it. But actually, you know, I have my own things. I put them in store in case —some day—I should need them. There are some pictures my father left too. I had a small tea-shop at one time, you know—but then the war came—it was all very unfortunate. But I didn't sell up everything, because I did hope to have my own little home again one day, so I put the best things in store with my father's pictures and some relics of our old home. But I *would* like very much, if you *really* wouldn't mind, to have that little painted tea table of dear Mrs. Lansquenet's. Such a pretty thing and we always had tea on it."

Susan, looking with a slight shudder at a small green table painted with large purple clematis, said quickly that she would be delighted for Miss Gilchrist to have it.

" Thank you *very* much, Mrs. Banks. I feel a little greedy. I've got all her beautiful pictures, you know, and a lovely amethyst brooch, but I feel that perhaps I ought to give *that* back to you."

" No, no, indeed."

" You'll want to go through her things ? After the inquest, perhaps ? "

" I thought I'd stay here a couple of days, go through things, and clear everything up."

" Sleep here, you mean ? "

" Yes. Is there any difficulty ? "

" Oh no, Mrs. Banks, of course not. I'll put fresh sheets on my bed, and I can doss down here on the couch quite well."

" But there's Aunt Cora's room, isn't there ? I can sleep in that ? "

355

" You—you wouldn't mind ? "

" You mean because she was murdered there ? Oh no, I wouldn't mind. I'm very tough, Miss Gilchrist. It's been —I mean—it's all right again ? "

Miss Gilchrist understood the question.

" Oh *yes*, Mrs. Banks. All the blankets sent away to the cleaners and Mrs. Panter and I scrubbed the whole room out thoroughly. And there are plenty of spare blankets. But come up and see for yourself."

She led the way upstairs and Susan followed her.

The room where Cora Lansquenet had died was clean and fresh and curiously devoid of any sinister atmosphere. Like the sitting-room it contained a mixture of modern utility and elaborately painted furniture. It represented Cora's cheerful tasteless personality. Over the mantelpiece an oil painting showed a buxom young woman about to enter her bath.

Susan gave a slight shudder as she looked at it and Miss Gilchrist said :

" That was painted by Mrs. Lansquenet's husband. There are a lot of more of his pictures in the dining-room downstairs."

" How terrible."

" Well, I don't care very much for that style of painting *myself*—but Mrs. Lansquenet was very proud of her husband as an artist and thought that his work was sadly unappreciated."

" Where are Aunt Cora's own pictures ? "

" In my room. Would you like to see them ? "

Miss Gilchrist displayed her treasures proudly.

Susan remarked that Aunt Cora seemed to have been fond of sea coast resorts.

" Oh yes. You see, she lived for many years with Mr. Lansquenet at a small fishing village in Brittany. Fishing boats are always so picturesque, are they not ? "

" Obviously," Susan murmured. A whole series of picture postcards could, she thought, have been made from Cora Lansquenet's paintings which were faithful to detail and very highly coloured. They gave rise to the suspicion that they might actually have been painted from picture postcards.

But when she hazarded this opinion Miss Gilchrist was indignant. Mrs. Lansquenet *always* painted from Nature ! Indeed, once she had had a touch of the sun from reluctance to leave a subject when the light was just right.

" Mrs. Lansquenet was a real artist," said Miss Gilchrist reproachfully.

She glanced at her watch and Susan said quickly :

" Yes, we ought to start for the inquest. Is it far? Shall I get the car? "

It was only five minutes' walk, Miss Gilchrist assured her. So they set out together on foot. Mr. Entwhistle, who had come down by train, met them and shepherded them into the Village Hall.

There seemed to be a large number of strangers present. The inquest was not sensational. There was evidence of identification of the deceased. Medical evidence as to the nature of the wounds that had killed her. There were no signs of a struggle. Deceased was probably under a narcotic at the time she was attacked and would have been taken quite unawares. Death was unlikely to have occurred later than four-thirty. Between two and four-thirty was the nearest approximation. Miss Gilchrist testified to finding the body. A police constable and Inspector Morton gave their evidence. The Coroner summed up briefly. The jury made no bones about the verdict, "*Murder by some person or persons unknown.*"

It was over. They came out again into the sunlight. Half a dozen cameras clicked. Mr. Entwhistle shepherded Susan and Miss Gilchrist into the King's Arms, where he had taken the precaution to arrange for lunch to be served in a private room behind the bar.

" Not a very good lunch, I am afraid," he said apologetically.

But the lunch was not at all bad. Miss Gilchrist sniffed a little and murmured that " it was all so dreadful," but cheered up and tackled the Irish stew with appetite after Mr. Entwhistle had insisted on her drinking a glass of sherry. He said to Susan :

" I'd no idea you were coming down to-day, Susan. We could have come together."

" I know I said I wouldn't. But it seemed rather mean for none of the family to be there. I rang up George but he said he was very busy and couldn't possibly make it, and Rosamund had an audition and Uncle Timothy, of course, is a crock. So it had to be me."

" Your husband didn't come with you? "

" Greg had to settle up with his tiresome shop."

Seeing a startled look in Miss Gilchrist's eye, Susan said : " My husband works in a chemist's shop."

A husband in retail trade did not quite square with Miss Gilchrist's impression of Susan's smartness, but she said valiantly : " Oh yes, just like Keats."

" Greg's no poet," said Susan.

She added :

" We've got great plans for the future—a double-barrelled establishment—Cosmetics and Beauty parlour and a laboratory for special preparations."

" That will be much nicer," said Miss Gilchrist approvingly. " Something like Elizabeth Arden who is really a Countess, so I have been told—or is that Helena Rubinstein ? In any case," she added kindly, " a pharmacist's is not in the least like an ordinary shop—a *draper*, for instance, or a *grocer*."

" You kept a tea-shop, you said, didn't you ? "

" Yes, indeed," Miss Gilchrist's face lit up. That the Willow Tree had ever been " trade " in the sense that a shop was trade, would never have occurred to her. To keep a tea-shop was in her mind the essence of gentility. She started telling Susan about the Willow Tree.

Mr. Entwhistle, who had heard about it before, let his mind drift to other matters. When Susan had spoken to him twice without his answering he hurriedly apologised.

" Forgive me, my dear, I was thinking, as a matter of fact, about your Uncle Timothy. I am a little worried."

" About Uncle Timothy ? I shouldn't be. I don't believe really there's anything the matter with him. He's just a hypochondriac."

" Yes—yes, you may be right. I confess it was not his health that was worrying me. It's Mrs. Timothy. Apparently she's fallen downstairs and twisted her ankle. She's laid up and your uncle is in a terrible state."

" Because he'll have to look after her instead of the other way about ? Do him a lot of good," said Susan.

" Yes—yes, I dare say. But will your poor aunt *get* any looking after ? That is really the question. With no servants in the house."

" Life is really hell for elderly people," said Susan. " They live in a kind of Georgian Manor house, don't they ? "

Mr. Entwhistle nodded.

They came rather warily out of the King's Arms, but the Press seemed to have dispersed.

A couple of reporters were lying in wait for Susan by the cottage door. Shepherded by Mr. Entwhistle she said a few necessary and non-committal words. Then she and Miss Gilchrist went into the cottage and Mr. Entwhistle returned to the King's Arms where he had booked a room. The funeral was to be on the following day.

" My car's still in the quarry," said Susan. " I'd forgotten about it. I'll drive it along to the village later."

Miss Gilchrist said anxiously :

" Not too late. You won't go out after dark, will you ? '
Susan looked at her and laughed.

" You don't think there's a murderer still hanging about,
do you ? "

" No—no, I suppose not." Miss Gilchrist looked embarrassed.

" But it's exactly what she does think," thought Susan.
" How amazing ! "

Miss Gilchrist had vanished towards the kitchen.

" I'm sure you'd like tea early. In about half an hour,
do you think, Mrs. Banks ? "

Susan thought that tea at half-past three was overdoing
it, but she was charitable enough to realise that " a nice cup
of tea " was Miss Gilchrist's idea of restoration for the nerves
and she had her own reasons for wishing to please Miss Gilchrist,
so she said :

" Whenever you like, Miss Gilchrist."

A happy clatter of kitchen implements began and Susan
went into the sitting-room. She had only been there a few
minutes when the bell sounded and was succeeded by a very
precise little rat-tat-tat.

Susan came out into the hall and Miss Gilchrist appeared
at the kitchen door wearing an apron and wiping floury hands
on it.

" Oh dear, who do you think that can be ? "

" More reporters, I expect,' said Susan.

" Oh dear, how annoying for you, Mrs. Banks."

" Oh well, never mind, I'll attend to it."

" I was just going to make a few scones for tea."

Susan went towards the front door and Miss Gilchrist
hovered uncertainly. Susan wondered whether she thought
a man with a hatchet was waiting outside.

The visitor, however proved to be an elderly gentleman
who raised his hat when Susan opened the door and said,
beaming at her in avuncular style.

" Mrs. Banks, I think ? "

" Yes."

" My name is Guthrie—Alexander Guthrie. I was a friend
—a very old friend, of Mrs. Lansquenet's. You, I think, are
her niece, formerly Miss Susan Abernethie ? "

" That's quite right."

" Then since we know who we are, I may come in ? "

" Of course."

Mr. Guthrie wiped his feet carefully on the mat, stepped
inside, divested himself of his overcoat, laid it down with his

hat on a small oak chest and followed Susan into the sitting-room.

"This is a melancholy occasion," said Mr. Guthrie, to whom melancholy did not seem to come naturally, his own inclination being to beam. "Yes, a very melancholy occasion. I was in this part of the world and I felt the least I could do was to attend the inquest—and of course the funeral. Poor Cora—poor foolish Cora. I have known her, my dear Mrs. Banks, since the early days of her marriage. A high-spirited girl—and she took art very seriously—took Pierre Lansquenet seriously, too—as an artist, I mean. All things considered he didn't make her too bad a husband. He strayed, if you know what I mean, yes, he strayed—but fortunately Cora took it as part of the artistic temperament. He was an artist and therefore immoral! In fact, I'm not sure she didn't go further: he was immoral and therefore he must be an artist! No kind of sense in artistic matters, poor Cora—though in other ways, mind you, Cora had a lot of sense—yes, a surprising lot of sense."

"That's what everybody seems to say," said Susan. "I didn't really know her."

"No, no, cut herself off from her family because they didn't appreciate her precious Pierre. She was never a pretty girl—but she had *something*. She was good company! You never knew what she'd say next and you never knew if her *naiveté* was genuine or whether she was doing it deliberately. She made us all laugh a good deal. The eternal child—that's what we always felt about her. And really the last time I saw her (I have seen her from time to time since Pierre died) she struck me as still behaving very much like a child."

Susan offered Mr. Guthrie a cigarette, but the old gentleman shook his head.

"No thank you, my dear. I don't smoke. You must wonder why I've come? To tell you the truth I was feeling rather conscience-stricken. I promised Cora to come and see her some weeks ago. I usually called upon her once a year, and just lately she'd taken up the hobby of buying pictures at local sales, and wanted me to look at some of them. My profession is that of art critic, you know. Of course most of Cora's purchases were horrible daubs, but take it all in all, it isn't such a bad speculation. Pictures go for next to nothing at these country sales and the frames alone are worth more than you pay for the picture. Naturally any important sale is attended by dealers and one isn't likely to get hold of masterpieces. But only the other day, a small Cuyp was

360

knocked down for a few pounds at a farmhouse sale. The history of it was quite interesting. It had been given to an old nurse by the family she had served faithfully for many years—they had no idea of its value. Old nurse gave it to farmer nephew who liked the horse in it but thought it was a dirty old thing ! Yes, yes, these things sometimes happen, and Cora was convinced that she had an eye for pictures. She hadn't, of course. Wanted me to come and look at a Rembrandt she had picked up last year. A Rembrandt ! Not even a respectable copy of one ! But she had got hold of a quite nice Bartolozzi engraving—damp spotted unfortunately. I sold it for her for thirty pounds and of course that spurred her on. She wrote to me with great gusto about an Italian Primitive she had bought at some sale and I promised I'd come along and see it."

" That's it over there, I expect," said Susan, gesturing to the wall behind him.

Mr. Guthrie got up, put on a pair of spectacles, and went over to study the picture.

" Poor dear Cora," he said at last.

" There are a lot more," said Susan.

Mr. Guthrie proceeded to a leisurely inspection of the art treasures acquired by the hopeful Mrs. Lansquenet. Occasionally he said, " Tchk, Tchk," occasionally he sighed.

Finally he removed his spectacles.

" Dirt," he said, " is a wonderful thing, Mrs. Banks ! It gives a patina of romance to the most horrible examples of the painter's art. I'm afraid that Bartolozzi was beginner's luck. Poor Cora. Still it gave her an interest in life. I am really thankful that I did not have to disillusion her."

" There are some pictures in the dining-room," said Susan, " but I think they are all her husband's work."

Mr. Guthrie shuddered slightly and held up a protesting hand.

" Do not force me to look at those again. Life classes have much to answer for ! I always tried to spare Cora's feelings. A devoted wife—a very devoted wife. Well, dear Mrs. Banks, I must not take up more of your time."

" Oh, do stay and have some tea. I think it's nearly ready."

" That is very kind of you." Mr. Guthrie sat down again promptly.

" I'll just go and see."

In the kitchen, Miss Gilchrist was just lifting a last batch of scones from the oven. The tea-tray stood ready and the kettle was just gently rattling its lid.

361

" There's a Mr. Guthrie here, and I've asked him to stay for tea."

" Mr. Guthrie ? Oh, yes, he was a great friend of dear Mrs. Lansquenet's. He's the celebrated art critic. How fortunate ; I've made a nice lot of scones and that's some home-made strawberry jam, and I just whipped up some little drop cakes. I'll just make the tea—I've warmed the pot. Oh, please, Mrs. Banks, don't carry that heavy tray. I can manage *everything*."

However, Susan took in the tray and Miss Gilchrist followed with teapot and kettle, greeted Mr. Guthrie, and they set to.

" Hot scones, that *is* a treat," said Mr. Guthrie, " and what delicious jam ! Really, the stuff one buys nowadays."

Miss Gilchrist was flushed and delighted. The little cakes were excellent and so were the scones, and everyone did justice to them. The ghost of the Willow Tree hung over the party. Here, it was clear, Miss Gilchrist was in her element.

" Well, thank you, perhaps I will," said Mr. Guthrie as he accepted the last cake, pressed upon him by Miss Gilchrist. " I do feel rather guilty, though—enjoying my tea here, where poor Cora was so brutally murdered."

Miss Gilchrist displayed an unexpected Victorian reaction to this.

" Oh, but Mrs. Lansquenet would have wished you to take a good tea. You've got to keep your strength up."

" Yes, yes, perhaps you are right. The fact is, you know, that one cannot really bring oneself to believe that someone you knew—actually knew—*can* have been murdered ! "

" I agree," said Susan. " It just seems—fantastic."

" And certainly not by some casual tramp who broke in and attacked her. I *can* imagine, you know, reasons why Cora might have been murdered——"

Susan said quickly, " Can you ? What reasons ? "

" Well, she wasn't discreet," said Mr. Guthrie. " Cora was never discreet. And she enjoyed—how shall I put it—showing how sharp she could be ? Like a child who's got hold of some-body's secret. If Cora got hold of a secret she'd want to talk about it. Even if she promised not to, she'd still do it. She wouldn't be able to help herself."

Susan did not speak. Miss Gilchrist did not either. She looked worried. Mr. Guthrie went on :

" Yes, a little dose of arsenic in a cup of tea—*that* would not have surprised me, or a box of chocolates by post. But sordid robbery and assault—that seems highly incongruous. I may be wrong but I should have thought she had very little to take that would be worth a burglar's while. She didn't keep much money in the house, did she ? "

Miss Gilchrist said, " Very little."

Mr. Guthrie sighed and rose to his feet.

" Ah ! well, there's a lot of lawlessness about since the war. Times have changed."

Thanking them for the tea he took a polite farewell of the two women. Miss Gilchrist saw him out and helped him on with his overcoat. From the window of the sitting-room, Susan watched him trot briskly down the front path to the gate.

Miss Gilchrist came back into the room with a small parcel in her hand.

" The postman must have been while we were at the inquest. He pushed it through the letter-box and it had fallen in the corner behind the door. Now I wonder—why, of course, it must be wedding cake."

Happily Miss Gilchrist ripped off the paper. Inside was a small white box tied with silver ribbon.

" It is ! " She pulled off the ribbon, inside was a modest wedge of rich cake with almond paste and white icing. " How nice ! Now who——" She consulted the card attached. " *John and Mary*. Now who *can* that be ? How silly to put no surname."

Susan, rousing herself from contemplation, said vaguely :

" It's quite difficult sometimes with people just using Christian names. I got a postcard the other day signed Joan. I counted up I knew eight Joans—and with telephoning so much, one often doesn't know their handwriting."

Miss Gilchrist was happily going over the possible Johns or Marys of her acquaintance.

" It might be Dorothy's daughter—*her* name was Mary, but I hadn't heard of an engagement, still less of a marriage. Then there's little John Banfield—I suppose he's grown up and old enough to be married—or the Enfield girl—no, her name was Margaret. No address or anything. Oh well, I dare say it will come to me . . ."

She picked up the tray and went out to the kitchen.

Susan roused herself and said :

" Well—I suppose I'd better go and put the car somewhere."

CHAPTER X

SUSAN RETRIEVED the car from the quarry where she had left it and drove it into the village. There was a petrol pump but no garage and she was advised to take it to the King's Arms. They had room for it there and she left it by a big Daimler which was preparing to go out. It was chauffeur driven and inside it, very much muffled up, was an elderly foreign gentleman with a large moustache.

The boy to whom Susan was talking about the car was staring at her with such rapt attention the he did not seem to be taking in half of what she said.

Finally he said in an awe-stricken voice :

" You're her niece, aren't you ? "

" What ? "

" You're the victim's niece," the boy repeated with relish.

" Oh—yes—yes, I am."

" Ar ! Wondered where I'd seen you before."

" Ghoul," thought Susan as she retraced her steps to the cottage.

Miss Gilchrist greeted her with :

" Oh, you're safely back," in tones of relief which further annoyed her. Miss Gilchrist added anxiously :

" You *can* eat spaghetti, can't you ? I thought for to-night——"

" Oh yes, anything. I don't want much."

" I really flatter myself that I can make a very tasty spaghetti *au gratin*."

The boast was not an idle one. Miss Gilchrist, Susan reflected, was really an excellent cook. Susan offered to help wash up but Miss Gilchrist, though clearly gratified by the offer, assured Susan that there was very little to do.

She came in a little while later with coffee. The coffee was less excellent, being decidedly weak. Miss Gilchrist offered Susan a piece of the wedding cake which Susan refused.

" It's really very good cake," Miss Gilchrist insisted, tasting it. She had settled to her own satisfaction that it must have been sent by someone whom she alluded to as " dear Ellen's daughter who I know was engaged to be married but I can't remember her name."

Susan let Miss Gilchrist chirrup away into silence before starting her own subject of conversation. This moment, after supper, sitting before the fire, was a companionable one.

364

She said at last :

" My Uncle Richard came down here before he died, didn't he ? "

" Yes, he did."

" When was that exactly ? "

" Let me see—it must have been one, two—nearly three weeks before his death was announced."

" Did he seem—ill ? "

" Well, no, I wouldn't say he seemed exactly ill. He had a very hearty vigorous manner. Mrs. Lansquenet was very surprised to see him. She said, ' Well, really, Richard, after all these years ! ' And he said, ' I came to see for myself exactly how things are with you.' And Mrs. Lansquenet said, ' I'm all right.' I think, you know, she was a teeny bit offended by his turning up so casually—after the long break. Anyway Mr. Abernethie said, ' No use keeping up old griev-ances. You and I and Timothy are the only ones left—and nobody can talk to Timothy except about his own health.' And he said, ' Pierre seems to have made you happy, so it seems I was in the wrong. There, will that content you ? ' Very nicely he said it. A handsome man, though elderly, of course."

" How long was he here ? "

" He stayed for lunch. Beef olives, I made. Fortunately it was the day the butcher called."

Miss Gilchrist's memory seemed to be almost wholly culinary.

" They seemed to be getting on well together ? "

" Oh, yes."

Susan paused and then said :

" Was Aunt Cora surprised when—he died ? "

" Oh yes, it was quite sudden, wasn't it ? "

" Yes, it was sudden . . . I meant—she *was* surprised. He hadn't given her any indication how ill he was."

" Oh—I see what you mean." Miss Gilchrist paused a moment. " No, no, I think perhaps you are right. She did say that he had got very old—I think she said senile . . ."

" But *you* didn't think he was senile ? "

" Well, not to *look* at. But I didn't talk to him much, naturally I left them alone together."

Susan looked at Miss Gilchrist speculatively. Was Miss Gilchrist the kind of woman who listened at doors ? She was honest, Susan felt sure, she wouldn't ever pilfer, or cheat over the housekeeping, or open letters. But inquisitiveness can drape itself in a mantle of rectitude. Miss Gilchrist might have found it necessary to garden near an open window, or to dust the hall . . . That would be within the permitted lengths. And then, of course, she could not have helped hearing something. . . .

" You didn't hear any of their conversation ? " Susan asked.

Too abrupt. Miss Gilchrist flushed angrily.

" No, indeed, Mrs. Banks. It has never been my custom to listen at doors ! "

That means she does, thought Susan, otherwise she'd just say " No."

Aloud she said : " I'm so sorry, Miss Gilchrist. I didn't mean it that way. But sometimes, in these small flimsily built cottages, one simply can't help hearing nearly everything that goes on, and now that they are both dead, it's really rather important to the family to know just what was said at that meeting between them."

The cottage was anything but flimsily built—it dated from a sturdier era of building, but Miss Gilchrist accepted the bait, and rose to the suggestion held out.

" Of course what you say is quite true, Mrs. Banks—this *is* a very small place and I do appreciate that you would want to know what passed between them, but really I'm afraid I can't help very much. I think they were talking about Mr. Abernethie's health—and certain—well, *fancies* he had. He didn't look it, but he must have been a sick man and as is so often the case, he put his ill-health down to *outside agencies*. A common symptom, I believe. My aunt——"

Miss Gilchrist described her aunt.

Susan, like Mr. Entwhistle, side-tracked the aunt.

" Yes," she said. " That is just what we thought. My uncle's servants were all very attached to him and naturally they are upset by his thinking——" She paused.

" Oh, of course ! Servants are *very* touchy about anything of that kind. I remember that my aunt——"

Again Susan interrupted.

" It *was* the servants he suspected, I suppose ? Of poisoning him, I mean ? "

" I don't know . . . I—really——"

Susan noted her confusion.

" It wasn't the servants. Was it one particular person ? "

" I don't know, Mrs. Banks. Really I don't know——"

But her eye avoided Susan's. Susan thought to herself that Miss Gilchrist knew more than she was willing to admit.

It was possible that Miss Gilchrist knew a good deal . . .

366

Deciding not to press the point for the moment, Susan said :
" What are your own plans for the future, Miss Gilchrist ? "
" Well, really, I was going to speak to you about that,
Mrs. Banks. I told Mr. Entwhistle I would be willing to stay
on until everything here was cleared up."
" I know. I'm very grateful."
" And I wanted to ask you how long that was likely to be,
because, of course, I must start looking about for another
post."
Susan considered.
" There's really not very much to be done here. In a
couple of days I can get things sorted and notify the auc-
tioneer."
" You have decided to sell up everything, then ? "
" Yes. I don't suppose there will be any difficulty in
letting the cottage ? "
" *Oh, no*—people will queue up for it, I'm sure. There are
so few cottages to rent. One nearly always has to buy."
" So it's all very simple, you see." Susan hesitated a
moment before saying, " I wanted to tell you—that I hope
you'll accept three months' salary."
" That's very generous of you, I'm sure, Mrs. Banks. I do
appreciate it. And you would be prepared to—I mean I
could ask you—if necessary—to—to recommend me ? To
say that I had been with a relation of yours and that I had
—proved satisfactory ? "
" Oh, of course."
" I don't know whether I ought to ask it." Miss Gilchrist's
hands began to shake and she tried to steady her voice. " But
would it be possible not to—to mention the circumstances—
or even the *name* ? "
Susan stared.
" I don't understand."
" That's because you haven't thought, Mrs. Banks. It's
murder. A murder that's been in the papers and that everybody has read about. Don't you see ? People might think.
' Two women living together, and one of them is killed—and
perhaps the companion did it.' Don't you see, Mrs. Banks ?
I'm sure that if *I* was looking for someone, I'd—well, I'd
think twice before engaging myself—if you understand what
I mean. Because one never *knows* ! It's been worrying me
dreadfully, Mrs. Banks ; I've been lying awake at night
thinking that perhaps I'll never get another job—not of this
kind. And what else is there that I can do ? "
The question came out with unconscious pathos. Susan

felt suddenly stricken. She realised the desperation of this pleasant-spoken commonplace woman who was dependent for existence on the fears and whims of employers. And there was a lot of truth in what Miss Gilchrist had said. You wouldn't, if you could help it, engage a woman to share domestic intimacy who had figured, however innocently, in a murder case.

Susan said : " But if they find the man who did it——"

" Oh *then*, of course, it will be quite all right. But will they find him ? I don't think, myself, the police have the *least idea*. And if he's *not* caught—well, that leaves me as—as not quite the most likely person, but as a person who *could* have done it."

Susan nodded thoughtfully. It was true that Miss Gilchrist did not benefit from Cora Lansquenet's death—but who was to know that ? And besides, there were so many tales—ugly tales—of animosity arising between women who lived together—strange pathological motives for sudden violence. Someone who had not known them might imagine that Cora Lansquenet and Miss Gilchrist had lived on those terms. . . .

Susan spoke with her usual decision.

" Don't worry, Miss Gilchrist," she said, speaking briskly and cheerfully. " I'm sure I can find you a post amongst my friends. There won't be the least difficulty."

" I'm afraid," said Miss Gilchrist, regaining some of her customary manner, " that I couldn't undertake any really *rough* work. Just a little plain cooking and housework——"

The telephone rang and Miss Gilchrist jumped.

" Dear me, I wonder who *that* can be."

" I expect it's my husband," said Susan, jumping up. " He said he'd ring me to-night."

She went to the telephone.

" Yes ?—yes, this is Mrs. Banks speaking personally . . ." There was a pause and then her voice changed. It became soft and warm. " Hallo, darling—yes, it's me . . . Oh, quite well . . . Murder by someone unknown . . . the usual thing . . . Only Mr. Entwhistle . . . What ? . . . it's difficult to say, but I think so . . . Yes, just as we thought . . . Absolutely according to plan . . . I shall sell the stuff. There's nothing *we'd* want . . . Not for a day or two . . . Absolutely frightful . . . Don't fuss. I know what I'm doing . . . Greg, you didn't . . . You were careful to . . . No, it's nothing. Nothing at all. Good night, darling."

She rang off. The nearness of Miss Gilchrist had hampered her a little. Miss Gilchrist could probably hear from the kitchen, where she had tactfully retired, exactly what went on. There were things she had wanted to ask Greg, but she hadn't liked to.

She stood by the telephone, frowning abstractedly. Then suddenly an idea came to her.

" Of course," she murmured. " Just the thing."

Lifting the receiver she asked for Trunk Enquiry.

Some quarter of an hour later a weary voice from the exchange was saying :

" I'm afraid there's no reply."

" Please go on ringing them."

Susan spoke autocratically. She listened to the far off buzzing of a telephone bell. Then, suddenly it was interrupted and a man's voice, peevish and slightly indignant, said :

" Yes, yes, what is it ? "

" Uncle Timothy ? "

" What's that ? I can't hear you."

" Uncle Timothy ? I'm Susan Banks."

" Susan who ? "

" Banks. Formerly Abernethie. Your niece Susan."

" Oh, you're Susan, are you ? What's the matter ? What are you ringing up for at this time of night ? "

" It's quite early still."

" It isn't. I was in bed."

" You must go to bed very early. How's Aunt Maude ? "

" Is that all you rang up to ask ? Your aunt's in a good deal of pain and she can't do a thing. Not a thing. She's helpless. We're in a nice mess, I can tell you. That fool of a doctor says he can't even get a nurse. He wanted to cart Maude off to hospital. I stood out against *that*. He's trying to get hold of someone for us. *I* can't do anything—I daren't even try. There's a fool from the village staying in the house to-night—but she's murmuring about getting back to her husband. Don't know *what* we're going to do."

" That's what I rang up about. Would you like Miss Gilchrist ? "

" Who's she ? Never heard of her."

" Aunt Cora's companion. She's very nice and capable."

" Can she cook ? "

" Yes, she cooks very well, and she could look after Aunt Maude."

" That's all very well, but when could she come ? Here I am, all on my own, with only these idiots of village women popping in and out at odd hours, and it's not good for me. My heart's playing me up."

369

" I'll arrange for her to get off to you as soon as possible.
The day after to-morrow, perhaps ? "

" Well, thanks very much," said the voice rather grudgingly.
" You're a good girl, Susan—er—thank you."

Susan rang off and went into the kitchen.

" Would you be willing to go up to Yorkshire and look after
my aunt ? She fell and broke her ankle and my uncle is quite
useless. He's a bit of a pest but Aunt Maude is a very good
sort. They have help in from the village, but you could cook
and look after Aunt Maude."

Miss Gilchrist dropped the coffee pot in her agitation.

" Oh, thank you, thank you—that really is kind. I think
I can say of myself that I am really good in the sickroom, and
I'm sure I can manage your uncle and cook him nice little
meals. It's really very kind of you, Mrs. Banks, and I *do*
appreciate it."

CHAPTER XI

SUSAN LAY in bed and waited for sleep to come. It had been
a long day and she was tired. She had been quite sure that she
would go to sleep at once. She never had any difficulty in
going to sleep. And yet here she lay, hour after hour, wide
awake, her mind racing.

She had said she did not mind sleeping in this room, in this
bed. This bed where Cora Abernethie——

No, no, she must put all that out of her mind. She had
always prided herself on having no nerves. Why think of
that afternoon less than a week ago ? Think ahead—the
future. Her future and Greg's. Those premises in Cardigan
Street—just what they wanted. The business on the ground
floor and a charming flat upstairs. The room out at the back
a laboratory for Greg. For purposes of income tax it would
be an excellent set-up. Greg would get calm and well again.
There would be no more of those alarming brain-storms.
The times when he looked at her without seeming to know
who she was. Once or twice she'd been quite frightened . . .
And old Mr. Cole—he'd hinted—threatened : " If this
happens again . . ." And it might have happened again—it
would have happened again. If Uncle Richard hadn't died
just when he did . . .

Uncle Richard—but really why look at it like that ? He'd
nothing to live for. Old and tired and ill. His son dead.

370

It was a mercy really. To die in his sleep quietly like that. Quietly . . . in his sleep. . . . If only she could sleep. It was so stupid lying awake hour after hour . . . hearing the furniture creak, and the rustling of trees and bushes outside the window and the occasional queer melancholy hoot—an owl, she supposed. How sinister the country was, somehow. So different from the big noisy indifferent town. One felt so safe there—surrounded by people—never alone. Whereas here . . .

Houses where a murder had been committed were sometimes haunted. Perhaps this cottage would come to be known as the haunted cottage. Haunted by the spirit of Cora Lansquenet . . . Aunt Cora. Odd, really, how ever since she had arrived she had felt as though Aunt Cora were quite close to her . . . within reach. All nerves and fancy. Cora Lansquenet was dead, to-morrow she would be buried. There was no one in the cottage except Susan herself and Miss Gilchrist. Then why did she feel that there was someone in this room, someone close beside her . . .

She had lain on this bed when the hatchet fell. . . . Lying there trustingly asleep . . . Knowing nothing till the hatchet fell . . . And now she wouldn't let Susan sleep. . . .

The furniture creaked again . . . was that a stealthy step? Susan switched on the light. Nothing. Nerves, nothing but nerves. Relax . . . close your eyes . . .

Surely that was a groan—a groan or a faint moan . . . Someone in pain—someone dying . . .

"I mustn't imagine things, I mustn't, I mustn't," Susan whispered to herself.

Death was the end—there was no existence after death. Under no circumstances could anyone come back. Or was she reliving a scene from the past—a dying woman groaning. . . .

There it was again . . . stronger . . . someone groaning in acute pain . . .

But—this was real. Once again Susan switched on the light, sat up in bed and listened. The groans were real groans and she was hearing them through the wall. They came from the room next door.

Susan jumped out of bed, flung on a dressing-gown and crossed to the door. She went out on to the landing, tapped for a moment on Miss Gilchrist's door and then went in. Miss Gilchrist's light was on. She was sitting up in bed. She looked ghastly. Her face was distorted with pain.

"Miss Gilchrist, what's the matter? Are you ill?"

"Yes. I don't know what—I—" she tried to get out of

371

bed, was seized with a fit of vomiting and then collapsed back on the pillows.

She murmured: "Please—ring up doctor. Must have eaten something. . . ."

" I'll get you some bicarbonate. We can get the doctor in the morning if you're not better."

Miss Gilchrist shook her head.

" No, get doctor now. I—I feel dreadful."

" Do you know his number ? Or shall I look in the book ? "

Miss Gilchrist gave her the number. She was interrupted by another fit of retching.

Susan's call was answered by a sleepy male voice.

" Who ? Gilchrist ? In Mead's Lane. Yes, I know. I'll be right along."

He was as good as his word. Ten minutes later Susan heard his car draw up outside and she went to open the door to him.

She explained the case as she took him upstairs. " I think," she said, " she must have eaten something that disagreed with her. But she seems pretty bad."

The doctor had had the air of one keeping his temper in leash and who has had some experience of being called out unnecessarily on more than one occasion. But as soon as he examined the moaning woman his manner changed. He gave various curt orders to Susan and presently came down and telephoned. Then he joined Susan in the sitting-room.

" I've sent for an ambulance. Must get her into hospital."

" She's really bad then ? "

" Yes. I've given her a shot of morphia to ease the pain. But it looks——" He broke off. " What's she eaten ? "

" We had macaroni *au gratin* for supper and a custard pudding. Coffee afterwards."

" You have the same things ? "

" Yes."

" And you're all right ? No pain or discomfort ? "

" No."

" She's taken nothing else ? No tinned fish ? Or sausages?"

" No. We had lunch at the King's Arms—after the inquest."

" Yes, of course. You're Mrs. Lansquenet's niece ? "

" Yes."

" That was a nasty business. Hope they catch the man who did it."

" Yes, indeed."

The ambulance came. Miss Gilchrist was taken away and the doctor went with her. He told Susan he would ring her

up in the morning. When he had left she went upstairs to bed.
This time she fell asleep as soon as her head touched the
pillow.

2

The funeral was well attended. Most of the village had
turned out. Susan and Mr. Entwhistle were the only mourners,
but various wreaths had been sent by the other members of
the family. Mr. Entwhistle asked where Miss Gilchrist was,
and Susan explained the circumstances in a hurried whisper.
Mr. Entwhistle raised his eyebrows.

" Rather an odd occurrence ? "

" Oh, she's better this morning. They rang up from the
hospital. People do get these bilious turns. Some make more
fuss than others."

Mr. Entwhistle said no more. He was returning to London
immediately after the funeral.

Susan went back to the cottage. She found some eggs and
made herself an omelette. Then she went up to Cora's room
and started to sort through the dead woman's things.

She was interrupted by the arrival of the doctor.

The doctor was looking worried. He replied to Susan's
inquiry by saying that Miss Gilchrist was much better.

" She'll be out and around in a couple of days," he said.
" But it was lucky I got called in so promptly. Otherwise—it
might have been a near thing."

Susan stared. " Was she really so bad ? "

" Mrs. Banks, will you tell me again exactly what Miss
Gilchrist had to eat and drink yesterday. Everything."

Susan reflected and gave a meticulous account. The doctor
shook his head in a dissatisfied manner.

" There must have been something she had and you
didn't ? "

" I don't think so . . . Cakes, scones, jam, tea—and then
supper. No, I can't remember anything."

The doctor rubbed his nose. He walked up and down the
room.

" Was it definitely something she ate ? Definitely food
poisoning ? "

The doctor threw her a sharp glance. Then he seemed to
come to a decision.

" It was arsenic," he said.

" Arsenic ? " Susan stared. " You mean somebody gave
her arsenic ? "

373

" That's what it looks like."

" Could she have taken it herself ?   Deliberately, I mean ? "

" Suicide ?   She says not and she should know.   Besides, if she wanted to commit suicide she wouldn't be likely to choose arsenic.   There are sleeping pills in this house.   She could have taken an overdose of them."

" Could the arsenic have got into something by accident ? "

" That's what I'm wondering.   It seems very unlikely, but such things have been known.   But if you and she ate the same things——"

Susan nodded.   She said, " It all seems impossible—" then she gave a sudden gasp.   " Why, of course, the wedding cake ! "

" What's that ?   Wedding cake ? "

Susan explained.   The doctor listened with close attention.

" Odd.   And you say she wasn't sure who sent it ?   Any of it left ?   Or is the box it came in lying around ? "

" I don't know.   I'll look."

They searched together and finally found the white cardboard box with a few crumbs of cake still in it lying on the kitchen dresser.   The doctor packed it away with some care.

" I'll take charge of this.   Any idea where the wrapping paper it came in might be ? "

Here they were not successful and Susan said that it had probably gone into the Ideal boiler.

" You won't be leaving here just yet, Mrs. Banks ? "

His tone was genial, but it made Susan feel a little uncomfortable.

" No, I have to go through my aunt's things.   I shall be here for a few days."

" Good.   You understand the police will probably want to ask some questions.   You don't know of anyone who—well, might have had it in for Miss Gilchrist ? "

Susan shook her head.

" I don't really know much about her.   She was with my aunt for some years—that's all I know."

" Quite, quite.   Always seemed a pleasant unassuming woman—quite ordinary.   Not the kind, you'd say, to have enemies or anything melodramatic of that kind.   Wedding cake through the post.   Sounds like some jealous woman— but who'd be jealous of Miss Gilchrist ?   Doesn't seem to fit."

" No."

" Well, I must be on my way.   I don't know what's happening to us in quiet little Lytchett St. Mary.   First a brutal

374

murder and now attempted poisoning through the post. Odd, the one following the other."

He went down the path to his car. The cottage felt stuffy and Susan left the door standing open as she went slowly upstairs to resume her task.

Cora Lansquenet had not been a tidy or methodical woman. Her drawers held a miscellaneous assortment of things. There were toilet accessories and letters and old handkerchiefs and paint brushes mixed up together in one drawer. There were a few old letters and bills thrust in amongst a bulging drawer of underclothes. In another drawer under some woollen jumpers was a cardboard box holding two false fringes. There was another drawer full of old photographs and sketching books. Susan lingered over a group taken evidently at some French place many years ago and which showed a younger, thinner Cora clinging to the arm of a tall lanky man with a straggling beard dressed in what seemed to be a velveteen coat and whom Susan took to be the late Pierre Lansquenet.

The photographs interested Susan, but she laid them aside, sorted all the papers she had found into a heap and began to go through them methodically. About a quarter way through she came on a letter. She read it through twice and was still staring at it when a voice speaking behind her caused her to give a cry of alarm.

" And what may you have got hold of there, Susan ? Hallo, what's the matter ? "

Susan reddened with annoyance. Her cry of alarm had been quite involuntary and she felt ashamed and anxious to explain.

" George ? How you startled me ! "

Her cousin smiled lazily.

" So it seems."

" How did you get here ? "

" Well, the door downstairs was open, so I walked in. There seemed to be nobody about on the ground floor, so I came up here. If you mean how did I get to this part of the world, I started down this morning to come to the funeral."

" I didn't see you there ? "

" The old bus played me up. The petrol feed seemed choked. I tinkered with it for some time and finally it seemed to clear itself. I was too late for the funeral by then, but I thought I might as well come on down. I knew you were here."

He paused and then went on :

" I rang you up, as a matter of fact—and Greg told me you'd come down to take possession, as it were. I thought I might give you a hand."

Susan said, " Aren't you needed in the office ? Or can you take days off whenever you like ? "

" A funeral has always been a recognised excuse for absenteeism. And this funeral is indubitably genuine. Besides, a murder always fascinates people. Anyway, I shan't be going much to the office in future—not now that I'm a man of means. I shall have better things to do."

He paused and grinned, " Same as Greg," he said.

Susan looked at George thoughtfully. She had never seen much of this cousin of hers and when they did meet she had always found him rather difficult to make out.

She asked, " Why did you really come down here, George ? "

" I'm not sure it wasn't to do a little detective work. I've been thinking a good deal about the last funeral we attended. Aunt Cora certainly threw a spanner into the works that day. I've wondered whether it was sheer irresponsibility and auntly *joie de vivre* that prompted her words, or whether she really had something to go upon. What actually is in that letter that you were reading so attentively when I came in ? "

Susan said slowly, " It's a letter that Uncle Richard wrote to Cora after he'd been down here to see her."

How very black George's eyes were. She'd thought of them as brown but they were black, and there was something curiously impenetrable about black eyes. They concealed the thoughts that lay behind them.

George drawled slowly, " Anything interesting in it ? "

" No, not exactly . . . "

" Can I see ? "

She hesitated for a moment, then put the letter into his outstretched hand.

He read it, skimming over the contents in a low monotone.

" *Glad to have seen you again after all these years . . . looking very well . . . had a good journey home and arrived back not too tired. . . .*"

His voice changed suddenly, sharpened :

" *Please don't say anything to anyone about what I told you. It may be a mistake. Your loving brother, Richard.*"

He looked up at Susan. " What does that mean ? "

" It might mean anything . . . It might be just about his health. Or it might be some gossip about a mutual friend."

" Oh yes, it might be a lot of things. It isn't conclusive—

but it's suggestive. . . . What did he tell Cora ? Does anyone know what he told her ? "

" Miss Gilchrist might know," said Susan thoughtfully. " I think she listened."

" Oh, yes, the companion help. Where is she, by the way ? "

" In hospital, suffering from arsenic poisoning."

George stared.

" You don't mean it ? "

" I do. Someone sent her some poisoned wedding cake."

George sat down on one of the bedroom chairs and whistled.

" It looks," he said, " as though Uncle Richard was not mistaken."

3

On the following morning Inspector Morton called at the cottage.

He was a quiet middle-aged man with a soft country burr in his voice. His manner was quiet and unhurried, but his eyes were shrewd.

" You realise what this is about, Mrs. Banks ? " he said. " Dr. Proctor has already told you about Miss Gilchrist. The few crumbs of wedding cake that he took from here have been analysed and show traces of arsenic."

" So somebody deliberately wanted to poison her ? "

" That's what it looks like. Miss Gilchrist herself doesn't seem able to help us. She keeps repeating that it's impossible—that nobody would do such a thing. But somebody did. *You* can't throw any light on the matter ? "

Susan shook her head.

" I'm simply dumbfounded," she said. " Can't you find out anything from the postmark ? Or the handwriting ? "

" You've forgotten—the wrapping paper was presumably burnt. And there's a little doubt whether it came through the post at all. Young Andrews, the driver of the postal van, doesn't seem able to remember delivering it. He's got a big round, and he can't be sure—but there it is—there's a doubt about it."

" But—what's the alternative ? "

" The alternative, Mrs. Banks, is that an old piece of brown paper was used that already had Miss Gilchrist's name and address on it and a cancelled stamp, and that the package was pushed through the letter box or deposited inside the door by hand to create the impression that it had come by post."

He added dispassionately :

" It's quite a clever idea, you know, to choose wedding cake. Lonely middle-aged women are sentimental about wedding cake, pleased at having been remembered. A box of sweets, or something of that kind *might* have awakened suspicion."

Susan said slowly :

" Miss Gilchrist speculated a good deal about who could have sent it, but she wasn't at all suspicious—as you say, she was pleased and yes—flattered."

She added : " Was there enough poison in it to—kill ? "

" That's difficult to say until we get the quantitative analysis. It rather depends on whether Miss Gilchrist ate the whole of the wedge. She seems to think that she didn't. Can you remember ? "

" No—no, I'm not sure. She offered me some and I refused and then she ate some and said it was a very good cake, but I don't remember if she finished it or not."

" I'd like to go upstairs if you don't mind, Mrs. Banks."

" Of course."

She followed him up to Miss Gilchrist's room. She said apologetically :

" I'm afraid it's in a rather disgusting state. But I didn't have time to do anything about it with my aunt's funeral and everything, and then after Dr. Proctor came I thought perhaps I ought to leave it as it was."

" That was very intelligent of you, Mrs. Banks. It's not everyone who would have been so intelligent."

He went to the bed and slipping his hand under the pillow raised it carefully. A slow smile spread over his face.

" There you are," he said.

A piece of wedding cake lay on the sheet looking somewhat the worse for wear.

" How extraordinary," said Susan.

" Oh no, it's not. Perhaps your generation doesn't do it. Young ladies nowadays mayn't set so much store on getting married. But it's an old custom. Put a piece of wedding cake under your pillow and you'll dream of your future husband."

" But surely Miss Gilchrist——"

" She didn't want to tell us about it because she felt foolish doing such a thing at her age. But I had a notion that's what it might be." His face sobered. " And if it hadn't been for an old maid's foolishness, Miss Gilchrist mightn't be alive to-day."

378

" But who could have possibly wanted to kill her ? "

His eyes met hers, a curious speculative look in them that made Susan feel uncomfortable.

" You don't know ? " he asked.

" No—of course I don't."

" It seems then as though we shall have to find out," said Inspector Morton.

CHAPTER XII

Two ELDERLY MEN sat together in a room whose furnishings were of the most modern kind. There were no curves in the room. Everything was square. Almost the only exception was Hercule Poirot himself who was full of curves. His stomach was pleasantly rounded, his head resembled an egg in shape, and his moustaches curved upwards in a flamboyant flourish.

He was sipping a glass of *sirop* and looking thoughtfully at Mr. Goby.

Mr. Goby was small and spare and shrunken. He had always been refreshingly nondescript in appearance and he was now so nondescript as practically not to be there at all. He was not looking at Poirot because Mr. Goby never looked at anybody.

Such remarks as he was now making seemed to be addressed to the left-hand corner of the chromium-plated fireplace curb.

Mr. Goby was famous for the acquiring of information. Very few people knew about him and very few employed his services—but those few were usually extremely rich. They had to be, for Mr. Goby was very expensive. His speciality was the acquiring of information quickly. At the flick of Mr. Goby's double jointed thumb, hundreds of patient questioning plodding men and women, old and young, of all apparent stations in life, were despatched to question, and probe, and achieve results.

Mr. Goby had now practically retired from business. But he occasionally " obliged " a few old patrons. Hercule Poirot was one of these.

" I've got what I could for you," Mr. Gob told the fire curb in a soft confidential whisper. " I sent the boys out. They do what they can—good lads—good lads all of them, but not what they used to be in the old days. They don't come that way nowadays. Not willing to learn, that's what it is. Think they know everything after they've only been a couple of years on the job. And they work to time. Shocking the way they work to time."

He shook his head sadly and shifted his gaze to an electric plug socket.

"It's the Government," he told it. " And all this education racket. It gives them ideas. They come back and tell us what they think. They *can't* think, most of them, anyway. All they know is things out of books. That's no good in our business. Bring in the answers—that's all that's needed—no thinking."

Mr. Goby flung himself back in his chair and winked at a lampshade.

"Mustn't crab the Government, though! Don't know really what we'd do without it. I can tell you that nowadays you can walk in most anywhere with a notebook and pencil, dressed right, and speaking B.B.C., and ask people all the most intimate details of their daily lives and all their back history, and what they had for dinner on November 23rd because that was a test day for middle-class incomes—or whatever it happens to be (making it a grade above to butter them up!)—ask 'em any mortal thing you can ; and nine times out of ten they'll come across pat, and even the tenth time though they may cut up rough, they won't doubt for a minute that you're what you say you are—and that the Government really wants to know—for some completely unfathomable reason ! I can tell you, M. Poirot," said Mr. Goby, still talking to the lampshade, " that it's the best line we've ever had ; much better than taking the electric meter or tracing a fault in the telephone—yes, or than calling as nuns, or the Girl Guides or the Boy Scouts asking for subscriptions—though we use all those too. Yes, Government snooping is God's gift to investigators and long may it continue ! "

Poirot did not speak. Mr. Goby had grown a little garrulous with advancing years, but he would come to the point in his own good time.

" Ar," said Mr. Goby and took out a very scrubby little notebook. He licked his finger and flicked over the pages. " Here we are. Mr. George Crossfield. We'll take him first. Just the plain facts. You won't want to know how I got them. He's been in Queer Street for quite a while now. Horses, mostly, and gambling—he's not a great one for women. Goes over to France now and then, and Monte too. Spends a lot of time at the Casino. Too downy to cash cheques there, but gets hold of a lot more money than his travelling allowance would account for. I didn't go into that, because it wasn't what you want to know. But he's not scrupulous about evading the law—and being a lawyer he knows how to do it. Some reason to believe that he's been using trust funds entrusted to him to invest. Plunging pretty wildly of late—on the Stock Exchange *and* on the gee-gees ! Bad judgment and bad luck. Been off his feed badly for three months. Worried, bad-tempered and irritable in the office. *But* since his uncle's death that's all changed. He's like the breakfast eggs (if we had 'em). Sunny side up !

" Now, as to particular information asked for. Statement that he was at Hurst Park races on day in question almost certainly untrue. Almost invariably places bets with one or other of two bookies on the course. They didn't see him that day. Possible that he left Paddington by train for destination unknown. Taxi-driver who took fare to Paddington made doubtful identification of his photograph. But I wouldn't bank on it. He's a very common type—nothing outstanding about him. No success with porters, etc., at Paddington. Certainly didn't arrive at Cholsey Station—which is nearest for Lytchett St. Mary. Small station, strangers noticeable. Could have got out at Reading and taken bus. Buses there crowded, frequent and several routes go within a mile or so of Lytchett St. Mary as well as the bus service that goes right into the village. He wouldn't take that—not if he meant business. All in all, he's a downy card. Wasn't seen in Lytchett St. Mary but he needn't have been. Other ways of approach than through the village. Was in the OUDS at Oxford, by the way. If he went to the cottage that day he mayn't have looked quite like the usual George Crossfield. I'll keep him in my book, shall I ? There's a black market angle I'd like to play up."

" You may keep him in," said Hercule Poirot.

Mr. Goby licked his finger and turned another page of his notebook.

" Mr. Michael Shane. He's thought quite a lot of in the profession. Has an even better idea of himself than other people have. Wants to star and wants to star quickly. Fond of money and doing himself well. Very attractive to women. They fall for him right and left. He's partial to them himself —but business comes first, as you might say. He's been running around with Sorrel Dainton who was playing the lead in the last show he was in. He only had a minor part but made quite a hit in it, and Miss Dainton's husband doesn't like him. His wife doesn't know about him and Miss Dainton. Doesn't

know much about anything, it seems. Not much of an actress
I gather, but easy on the eye. Crazy about her husband.
Some rumour of a bust-up likely between them not long ago,
but that seems out now. Out since Mr. Richard Abernethie's
death."

Mr. Goby emphasised the last point by nodding his head
significantly at a cushion on the sofa.

" On the day in question, Mr. Shane says he was meeting
a Mr. Rosenheim and a Mr. Oscar Lewis to fix up some stage
business. He didn't meet them. Sent them a wire to say he
was terribly sorry he couldn't make it. What he *did* do was
to go to the Emeraldo Car people, who hire out ' drive
yourself ' cars. He hired a car about twelve o'clock and drove
away in it. He returned it about six in the evening. According
to the speedometer it had been driven just about the right
number of miles for what we're after. No confirmation from
Lytchett St. Mary. No strange car seems to have been
observed there that day. Lots of places it could be left
unnoticed a mile or so away. And there's even a disused
quarry a few hundred yards down the lane from the cottage.
Three market towns within walking distance where you can
park in side streets, without the police bothering about you.
All right, we keep Mr. Shane in ? "

" Most certainly."

" Now Mrs. Shane." Mr. Goby rubbed his nose and told
his left cuff about Mrs. Shane. " She says she was shopping.
Just shopping . . ." Mr. Goby raised his eyes to the ceiling.
" Women who are shopping—just scatty, that's what they
are. And she'd heard she'd come into money the day before.
Naturally there'd be no holding her. She has one or two
charge accounts but they're overdrawn and they've been
pressing her for payment and she didn't put any more on the
sheet. It's quite on the cards that she went in here and there
and everywhere, trying on clothes, looking at jewellery,
pricing this, that, and the other—and as likely as not, not
buying anything ! She's easy to approach—I'll say that.
I had one of my young ladies who's knowledgeable on the
theatrical line do a hook up. Stopped by her table in a
restaurant and exclaimed the way they do : " Darling, I
haven't seen you since *Way Down Under*. You were *wonderful* in that ! Have you seen Hubert lately ? " That was
the producer and Mrs. Shane was a bit of a flop in the
play—but that makes it go all the better. They're chatting
theatrical stuff at once, and my girl throws the right names
about, and then she says, ' I believe I caught a glimpse of

you at so and so, on so and so, giving the day—and most ladies fall for it and say, ' Oh no, I was——' whatever it may be. But not Mrs. Shane. Just looks vacant and says, ' Oh, I dare say.' What can you do with a lady like that ? " Mr. Goby shook his head severely at the radiator.

" Nothing," said Hercule Poirot with feeling. " Do I not have cause to know it ? Never shall I forget the killing of Lord Edgware. I was nearly defeated—yes, I, Hercule Poirot—by the extremely simple cunning of a vacant brain. The very simple minded have often the genius to commit an uncomplicated crime and then leave it alone. Let us hope that our murderer—if there is a murderer in this affair—is intelligent and superior and thoroughly pleased with himself and unable to resist painting the lily. *Enfin*—but continue."

Once more Mr. Goby applied himself to his little book.

" Mr. and Mrs. Banks—who said they were at home all day. *She* wasn't, anyway ! Went round to the garage, got out her car, and drove off in it about 1 o'clock. Destination unknown. Back about five. Can't tell about mileage because she's had it out every day since and it's been nobody's business to check.

" As to Mr. Banks, we've dug up something curious. To begin with, I'll mention that on the day in question we don't know *what* he did. He didn't go to work. Seems he'd already asked for a couple of days off on account of the funeral. And since then he's chucked his job—with no consideration for the firm. Nice, well-established small pharmacy it is. They're not too keen on Master Banks. Seems he used to get into rather queer excitable states.

" Well, as I say, we don't know what he was doing on the day of Mrs. L.'s death. He didn't go with his wife. It *could* be that he stopped in their little flat all day. There's no porter there, and nobody knows whether tenants are in or out. But his back history is interesting. Up till about four months ago—just before he met his wife, he was in a Mental Home. Not certified—just what they call a mental breakdown. Seems he made some slip up in dispensing a medicine. (He was working with a Mayfair firm then.) The woman recovered, and the firm were all over themselves apologising, and there was no prosecution. After all, these accidental slips do occur, and most decent people are sorry for a poor young chap who's done it—so long as there's no permanent harm done, that is. The firm didn't sack him, but he resigned—said it had shaken his nerve. But afterwards, it seems, he got into a very low state and told the doctor he was obsessed by guilt—that it

383

had all been deliberate—the woman had been overbearing and rude to him when she came into the shop, had complained that her last prescription had been badly made up—and that he had resented this and had deliberately added a near lethal dose of some drug or other. He said ' She had to be punished for daring to speak to me like that ! ' And then wept and said he was too wicked to live and a lot of things like that. The medicos have a long word for that sort of thing—guilt complex or something—and don't believe it was deliberate at all, just carelessness, but that he wanted to make it important and serious."

" *Ça se peut,*" said Hercule Poirot.

" Pardon ? Anyway, he went into this Sanitorium and they treated him and discharged him as cured, and he met Miss Abernethie as she was then. And he got a job in this respectable but rather obscure little chemist's shop. Told them he'd been out of England for a year and a half, and gave them his former reference from some shop in Eastbourne. Nothing against him in that shop, but a fellow dispenser said he had a very queer temper and was odd in his manner sometimes. There's a story about a customer saying once as a joke, ' Wish you'd sell me something to poison my wife, ha ha ! ' And Banks says to him, very soft and quiet : ' I could . . . It would cost you two hundred pounds.' The man felt uneasy and laughed it off. *May* have been all a joke, but it doesn't seem to me that Banks is the joking kind."

" *Mon ami,*" said Hercule Poirot. " It really amazes me how you get your information ! Medical and highly confidential most of it ! "

Mr. Goby's eyes swivelled right round the room and he murmured, looking expectantly at the door, that there were *ways. . . .*

" Now we come to the country department. Mr. and Mrs. Timothy Abernethie. Very nice place they've got, but sadly needing money spent on it. Very straitened they seem to be, very straitened. Taxation and unfortunate investments. Mr. Abernethie enjoys ill health and the emphasis is on the enjoyment. Complains a lot and has everyone running and fetching and carrying. Eats hearty meals, and seems quite strong physically if he likes to make the effort. There's no one in the house after the daily woman goes and no one's allowed into Mr. Abernethie's room unless he rings his bell. He was in a very bad temper the morning of the day after the funeral. Swore at Mrs. Jones. Ate only a little of his breakfast and said he wouldn't have any lunch—he'd had a bad night. He said the supper she had left out for him was unfit to eat and a good deal more. He was alone in the house and unseen by anybody from 9.30 that morning until the following morning."

" And Mrs. Abernethie ? "

" She started off from Enderby by car at the time you mentioned. Arrived on foot at a small local garage in a place called Cathstone and explained her car had broken down a couple of miles away.

" A mechanic drove her out to it, made an investigation and said they'd have to tow it in and it would be a long job—couldn't promise to finish it that day. The lady was very put out, but went to a small inn, arranged to stay the night, and asked for some sandwiches as she said she'd like to see something of the countryside—it's on the edge of the moorland country. She didn't come back to the inn till quite late that evening. My informant said he didn't wonder. It's a sordid little place ! "

" And the times ? "

" She got the sandwiches at eleven. If she'd walked to the main road, a mile, she could have hitch-hiked into Wallcaster and caught a special South Coast express which stops at Reading West. I won't go into details of buses etcetera. It *could* just have been done if you could make the—er—attack fairly late in the afternoon.

" I understand the doctor stretched the time limit to possibly 4.30."

" Mind you," said Mr. Goby, " I shouldn't say it was likely. She seems to be a nice lady, liked by everybody. She's devoted to her husband, treats him like a child."

" Yes, yes, the maternal complex."

" She's strong and hefty, chops the wood and often hauls in great baskets of logs. Pretty good with the inside of a car, too."

" I was coming to that. What exactly *was* wrong with the car ? "

" Do you want the exact details, M. Poirot ? "

" Heaven forbid. I have no mechanical knowledge."

" It was a difficult thing to spot. And also to put right. And it *could* have been done maliciously by someone without very much trouble. By someone who was familiar with the insides of a car."

" *C'est magnifique !* " said Poirot with bitter enthusiasm. " All so convenient, all so possible. *Bon dieu*, can we eliminate *nobody* ? And Mrs. Leo Abernethie ? "

385

" She's a very nice lady, too. Mr. Abernethie deceased was very fond of her. She came there to stay about a fortnight before he died."

" After he had been to Lytchett St. Mary to see his sister ? "

" No, just before. Her income is a good deal reduced since the war. She gave up her house in England and took a small flat in London. She has a villa in Cyprus and spends part of the year there. She has a young nephew whom she is helping to educate, and there seems to be one or two young artists whom she helps financially from time to time."

" St. Helen of the blameless life," said Poirot, shutting his eyes. " And it was quite impossible for her to have left Enderby that day without the servants knowing ? Say that that is so, I implore you ! "

Mr. Goby brought his glance across to rest apologetically on Poirot's polished patent leather shoe, the nearest he had come to a direct encounter, and murmured :

" I'm afraid I can't say that, M. Poirot. Mrs. Abernethie went to London to fetch some extra clothes and belongings as she had agreed with Mr. Entwhistle to stay on and see to things."

" *Il ne manquait que ça !* " said Poirot with strong feeling.

CHAPTER XIII

WHEN THE CARD of Inspector Morton of the Berkshire County Police was brought to Hercule Poirot, his eyebrows went up.

" Show him in, Georges, show him in. And bring—what is it that the police prefer ? "

" I would suggest beer, sir."

" How horrible ! But how British. Bring beer, then."

Inspector Morton came straight to the point.

" I had to come to London," he said. " And I got hold of your address, M. Poirot. I was interested to see you at the inquest on Thursday."

" So you saw me there ? "

" Yes. I was surprised—and, as I say, interested. You won't remember me but I remember you very well. In that Pangbourne Case."

" Ah, you were connected with that ? "

" Only in a very junior capacity. It's a long time ago but I've never forgotten you."

" And you recognised me at once the other day ? "

386

" That wasn't difficult, sir." Inspector Morton repressed a slight smile. " Your appearance is—rather unusual."

His gaze took in Poirot's sartorial perfection and rested finally on the curving moustaches.

" You stick out in a country place," he said.

" It is possible, it is possible," said Poirot with complacency.

" It interested me *why* you should be there. That sort of crime—robbery—assault—doesn't usually interest you."

" Was it the usual ordinary brutal type of crime ? "

" That's what I've been wondering."

" You have wondered from the beginning, have you not ? "

" Yes, M. Poirot. There were some unusual features. Since then we've worked along the routine lines. Pulled in one or two people for questioning, but everyone has been able to account quite satisfactorily for his time that afternoon. It wasn't what you'd call an ' ordinary ' crime, M. Poirot—we're quite sure of that. The Chief Constable agrees. It was done by someone who wished to make it appear that way. It could have been the Gilchrist woman, but there doesn't seem to be any motive—and there wasn't any emotional background. Mrs. Lansquenet was perhaps a bit mental—or ' simple,' if you like to put it that way, but it was a household of mistress and dogsbody with no feverish feminine friendship about it. There are dozens of Miss Gilchrists about, and they're not usually the murdering type."

He paused.

" So it looks as though we'd have to look farther afield. I came to ask if you could help us at all. *Something* must have brought you down there, M. Poirot."

" Yes, yes, something did. An excellent Daimler car. But not only that."

" You had—information ? "

" Hardly in your sense of the word. Nothing that could be used as evidence."

" But something that could be—a pointer ? "

" Yes."

" You see, M. Poirot, there have been developments."

Meticulously, in detail, he told of the poisoned wedge of wedding cake.

Poirot took a deep hissing breath.

" Ingenious—yes, ingenious . . . I warned Mr. Entwhistle to look after Miss Gilchrist. An attack on her was always a possibility. But I must confess that I did *not* expect poison. I anticipated a repetition of the hatchet *motif*. I merely thought that it would be inadvisable for her to walk alone in unfrequented lanes after dark."

" But *why* did you anticipate an attack on her ? I think M. Poirot, you ought to tell me that."

Poirot nodded his head slowly.

" Yes, I will tell you. Mr. Entwhistle will not tell you, because he is a lawyer and lawyers do not like to speak of suppositions, of inferences made from the character of a dead woman, or from a few irresponsible words. But he will not be averse to *my* telling you—no, he will be relieved. He does not wish to appear foolish or fanciful, but he wants you to know what may—only *may*—be the facts."

Poirot paused as George entered with a tall glass of beer.

" Some refreshment, Inspector. No, no, I insist."

" Won't you join me ? "

" I do not drink the beer. But I will myself have a glass of *sirop de cassis*—the English they do not care for it, I have noticed."

Inspector Morton looked gratefully at his beer.

Poirot, sipping delicately from his glass of dark purple fluid, said :

" It begins, all this, at a funeral. Or rather, to be exact, *after* the funeral."

Graphically, with many gestures, he set forth the story as Mr. Entwhistle had told it to him, but with such embellishments as his exuberant nature suggested. One almost felt that Hercule Poirot had himself been an eye-witness of the scene.

Inspector Morton had an excellent clear-cut brain. He seized at once on what were, for his purposes, the salient points.

" This Mr. Abernethie may have been poisoned ? "

" It is a possibility."

" And the body has been cremated and there is no evidence? "

" Exactly."

Inspector Morton ruminated.

" Interesting. There's nothing in it for *us*. Nothing, that is, to make Richard Abernethie's death worth investigating. It would be waste of time."

" Yes."

" But there are the *people*—the people who were there—the people who heard Cora Lansquenet say what she did, and one of whom *may* have thought that she might say it again and with more detail."

" As she undoubtedly would have. There are, Inspector, as you say, *the people*. And now you see why I was at the inquest, why I interest myself in the case—because it is, always, *people* in whom I interest myself."

" Then the attack on Miss Gilchrist——"

" Was always indicated. Richard Abernethie had been down to the cottage. He had talked to Cora. He had, perhaps, actually mentioned a *name*. The only person who might possibly have known or overheard something was Miss Gilchrist. After Cora is silenced, the murderer might continue to be anxious. Does the other woman know something— anything ? Of course, if the murderer is wise he will let well alone, but murderers, Inspector, are seldom wise. Fortunately for us. They brood, they feel uncertain, they desire to make sure—quite sure. They are pleased with their own cleverness. And so, in the end, they protrude their necks, as you say."

Inspector Morton smiled faintly.

Poirot went on :

" This attempt to silence Miss Gilchrist, already it is a mistake. For now there are *two* occasions about which you make inquiry. There is the handwriting on the wedding label also. It is a pity the wrapping paper was burnt."

" Yes, I could have been certain, then, whether it came by post or whether it didn't."

" You have reason for thinking the latter, you say ? "

" It's only what the postman thinks—he's not sure. If the parcel had gone through a village post office, it's ten to one the postmistress would have noticed it, but nowadays the mail is delivered by van from Market Keynes and of course the young chap does quite a round and delivers a lot of things. He thinks it was letters only and no parcel at the cottage—but he isn't sure. As a matter of fact he's having a bit of girl trouble and he can't think about anything else. I've tested his memory and he isn't reliable in any way. If he *did* deliver it, it seems to me odd that the parcel shouldn't have been noticed until after this Mr.—whatshisname—Guthrie——"

" Ah, Mr. Guthrie."

Inspector Morton smiled.

" Yes, M. Poirot. We're checking up on him. After all, it would be easy, wouldn't it, to come along with a plausible tale of having been a friend of Mrs. Lansquenet's. Mrs. Banks wasn't to know if he was or he wasn't. He could have dropped that little parcel, you know. It's easy to make a thing look as though it's been through the post. Lamp black a little smudged, makes quite a good postmark cancellation mark over a stamp."

He paused and then added :

" And there are other possibilities."

Poirot nodded.

" You think—— ? "

" Mr. George Crossfield was down in that part of the world —but not until the next day. Meant to attend the funeral, but had a little engine trouble on the way. Know anything about him, M. Poirot ? "

" A little. But not as much as I would like to know."

" Like that, is it ? Quite a little bunch interested in the late Mr. Abernethie's will, I understand. I hope it doesn't mean going after all of them."

" I have accumulated a little information. It is at your disposal. Naturally *I* have no authority to ask these people questions. In, fact it would not be wise for me to do so."

" I shall go slowly myself. You don't want to fluster your bird too soon. But when you do fluster it, you want to fluster it well."

" A very sound technique. For you then, my friend, the routine—with all the machinery you have at your disposal. It is slow—but sure. For myself——"

" Yes, M. Poirot ? "

" For myself, I go North. As I have told you, it is *people* in whom I interest myself. Yes—a little preparatory *camouflage*—and I go North.

" I intend," added Hercule Poirot, " to purchase a country mansion for foreign refugees. I represent U.N.A.R.C.O."

" Ane what's U.N.A.R.C.O. ? "

" United Nations Aid for Refugee Centres Organisation. It sounds well, do you not think ? "

Inspector Morton grinned.

CHAPTER XIV

HERCULE POIROT said to a grim-faced Janet :

" Thank you very much. You have been most kind."

Janet, her lips still fixed in a sour line, left the room. These foreigners ! The questions they asked. Their impertinence ! All very well to say that he was a specialist interested in un-suspected heart conditions such as Mr. Abernethie must have suffered from. That was very likely true—gone very sudden the master had, and the doctor had been surprised. But what business was it of some foreign doctor coming along and nosing around ?

All very well for Mrs. Leo to say : " Please answer Monsieur Pontarlier's questions. He has a good reason for asking."

Questions. Always questions. Sheets of them sometimes to fill in as best you could—and what did the Government or anyone else want to know about your private affairs for ? Asking your age at that census—downright impertinent and she hadn't told them, either ! Cut off five years she had. Why not ? If she only felt fifty-four, she'd *call* herself fifty-four !

At any rate Monsieur Pontarlier hadn't wanted to know her age. He'd had *some* decency. Just questions about the medicines the master had taken, and where they were kept, and if, perhaps, he might have taken too much of them if he was feeling not quite the thing—or if he'd been forgetful. As though she could remember all that rubbish—the master knew what he was doing ! And asking if any of the medicines he took were still in the house. Naturally they'd all been thrown away. Heart condition—and some long word he'd used. Always thinking of something new they were, these doctors. Look at them telling old Rogers he had a disc or some such in his spine. Plain lumbago, that was all that was the matter with him. Her father had been a gardener and *he'd* suffered from lumbago. Doctors !

The self-appointed medical man sighed and went downstairs in search of Lanscombe. He had not got very much out of Janet but he had hardly expected to do so. All he had really wanted to do was to check such information as could unwillingly be extracted from her with that given him by Helen Abernethie and which had been obtained from the same source—but with much less difficulty, since Janet was ready to admit that Mrs. Leo had a perfect right to ask such questions and indeed Janet herself had enjoyed dwelling at length on the last few weeks of her master's life. Illness and death were congenial subjects to her.

Yes, Poirot thought, he could have relied on the information that Helen had got for him. He had done so really. But by nature and long habit he trusted nobody until he himself had tried and proved them.

In any case the evidence was slight and unsatisfactory. It boiled down to the fact that Richard Abernethie had been prescribed vitamin oil capsules. That these had been in a large bottle which had been nearly finished at the time of

391

his death. Anybody who had wanted to, could have operated on one or more of those capsules with a hypodermic syringe and could have rearranged the bottle so that the fatal dose would only be taken some weeks after that somebody had left the house. Or someone might have slipped into the house on the day before Richard Abernethie died and have doctored a capsule then—or, which was more likely—have substituted something else for a sleeping tablet in the little bottle that stood beside the bed. Or again might have quite simply tampered with the food or drink.

Hercule Poirot had made his own experiments. The front door was kept locked, but there was a side door giving on the garden which was not locked until evening. At about quarter-past one, when the gardeners had gone to lunch and when the household was in the dining-room, Poirot had entered the grounds, come to the side door, and mounted the stairs to Richard Abernethie's bedroom without meeting anybody. As a variant he had pushed through a baize door and slipped into the larder. He had heard voices from the kitchen at the end of the passage but no one had seen him.

Yes, it could have been done. But had it been done ? There was nothing to indicate that that was so. Not that Poirot was really looking for evidence—he wanted only to satisfy himself as to possibilities. The murder of Richard Abernethie could only be a hypothesis. It was Cora Lansquenet's murder for which evidence was needed. What he wanted was to study the people who had been assembled for the funeral that day, and to form his own conclusions about them. He already had his plan, but first he wanted a few more words with old Lanscombe.

Lanscombe was courteous but distant. Less resentful than Janet, he nevertheless regarded this upstart foreigner as the materialisation of the Writing on the Wall. This was What We are Coming to !

He put down the leather with which he was lovingly polishing the Georgian teapot and straightened his back.

" Yes, sir ? " he said politely.

Poirot sat down gingerly on a pantry stool.

" Mrs. Abernethie tells me that you hoped to reside in the lodge by the north gate when you retired from service here ? "

" That is so, sir. Naturally all that is changed now. When the property is sold——"

Poirot interrupted deftly :

" It might still be possible. There are cottages for the gardeners. The lodge is not needed for the guests or their

392

attendants. It might be possible to make an arrangement of some kind."

" Well, thank you, sir, for the suggestion. But I hardly think—— The majority of the—guests would be foreigners, I presume ? "

" Yes, they will be foreigners. Amongst those who fled from Europe to this country are several who are old and infirm. There can be no future for them if they return to their own countries, for these persons, you understand, are those whose relatives there have perished. They cannot earn their living here as an able-bodied man or woman can do. Funds have been raised and are being administered by the organisation which I represent to endow various country homes for them. This place is, I think, eminently suitable. The matter is practically settled."

Lanscombe sighed.

" You'll understand, sir, that it's sad for me to think that this won't be a private dwelling-house any longer. But I know how things are nowadays. None of the family could afford to live here—and I don't think the young ladies and gentlemen would even want to do so. Domestic help is too difficult to obtain these days, and even if obtained is expensive and unsatisfactory. I quite realise that these fine mansions have served their turn." Lanscombe sighed again. " If it has to be an—an institution of some kind, I'll be glad to think that it's the kind you're mentioning. We were Spared in This Country, sir, owing to our Navy and Air Force and our brave young men and being fortunate enough to be an island. If Hitler had landed here we'd all have turned out and given him short shrift. My sight isn't good enough for shooting, but I could have used a pitchfork, sir, and I intended to do so if necessary. We've always welcomed the unfortunate in this country, sir, it's been our pride. We shall continue so to do."

" Thank you, Lanscombe," said Poirot gently. " Your master's death must have been a great blow to you."

" It was, sir. I'd been with the master since he was quite a young man. I've been very fortunate in my life, sir. No one could have had a better master."

" I have been conversing with my friend and—er colleague, Dr. Larraby. We were wondering if your master could have had any extra worry—any unpleasant interview—on the day before he died ? You do not remember if any visitors came to the house that day ? "

" I think not, sir. I do not recall any."

" No one called at all just about that time ? "

" The vicar was here to tea the day before. Otherwise—some nuns called for a subscription—and a young man came to the back door and wanted to sell Marjorie some brushes and saucepan cleaners. Very persistent he was. Nobody else."

A worried expression had appeared on Lanscombe's face. Poirot did not press him further. Lanscombe had already unburdened himself to Mr. Entwhistle. He would be far less forthcoming with Hercule Poirot.

With Marjorie, on the other hand, Poirot had had instant success. Marjorie had none of the conventions of " good service." Marjorie was a first-class cook and the way to her heart lay through her cooking. Poirot had visited her in the kitchen, praised certain dishes with discernment, and Marjorie, realising that here was someone who knew what he was talking about, hailed him immediately as a fellow spirit. He had no difficulty in finding out exactly what had been served the night before Richard Abernethie had died. Marjorie, indeed, was inclined to view the matter as " It was the night I made that chocolate soufflé that Mr. Abernethie died. Six eggs I'd saved up for it. The dairyman he's a friend of mine. Got hold of some cream too. Better not ask how. Enjoyed it, Mr. Abernethie did." The rest of the meal was likewise detailed. What had come out from the dining-room had been finished in the kitchen. Ready as Marjorie was to talk, Poirot had learned nothing of value from her.

He went now to fetch his overcoat and a couple of scarves, and thus padded against the North Country air he went out on the terrace and joined Helen Abernethie, who was clipping some late roses.

" Have you found out anything fresh ? " she asked.

" Nothing. But I hardly expected to do so."

" I know. Ever since Mr. Entwhistle told me you were coming, I've been ferreting round, but there's really been nothing."

She paused and said hopefully :

" Perhaps it *is* all a mare's nest ? "

" To be attacked with a hatchet ? "

" I wasn't thinking of Cora."

" But it is of Cora that I think. Why was it necessary for someone to kill her ? Mr. Entwhistle has told me that on that day, at the moment that she came out suddenly with her *gaffe*, you yourself felt that something was wrong. That is so ? "

" Well—yes, but I don't know——"

Poirot swept on.

394

" How ' wrong ' ? Unexpected ? Surprising ? Or—what shall we say—uneasy ? Sinister ? "

" Oh no, not sinister. Just something that wasn't—oh, I don't know. I can't remember and it wasn't important."

" But why cannot you remember—because something else put it out of your head—something more important ? "

" Yes—yes—I think you're right there. It was the mention of murder, I suppose. That swept away everything else."

" It was, perhaps, the reaction of some particular person to the word ' murder ' ? "

" Perhaps . . . But I don't remember looking at anyone in particular. We were all staring at Cora."

" It may have been something you heard—something dropped perhaps . . . or broken . . ."

Helen frowned in an effort of remembrance.

" No . . . I don't think so. . . ."

" Ah well, someday it will come back. And it may be of no consequence. Now tell me, Madame, of those here, who knew Cora best ? "

Helen considered.

" Lanscombe, I suppose. He remembers her from a child. The housemaid, Janet, only came after she had married and gone away."

" And next to Lanscombe ? "

Helen said thoughtfully : " I suppose—*I* did. Maude hardly knew her at all."

" Then, taking you as the person who knew her best, why do you think she asked that question as she did ? "

Helen smiled.

" It was very characteristic of Cora ! "

" What I mean is, was it a *bêtise* pure and simple ? Did she just blurt out what was in her mind without thinking ? Or was she being malicious—amusing herself by upsetting everyone ? "

Helen reflected.

" You can't ever be quite sure about a person, can you ? I never have known whether Cora was just ingenuous—or whether she counted, childishly, on making an effect. That's what you mean, isn't it ? "

" Yes. I was thinking : Suppose this Mrs. Cora says to herself ' What fun it would be to ask if Richard was murdered and see how they all look ! ' That would be like her, yes ? "

Helen looked doubtful.

" It might be. She certainly had an impish sense of humour as a child. But what difference does it make ? "

" It would underline the point that it is unwise to make jokes about murder," said Poirot dryly.

Helen shivered.

" Poor Cora."

Poirot changed the subject.

" Mrs. Timothy Abernethie stayed the night after the funeral ? "

" Yes."

" Did she talk to you at all about what Cora had said ? "

" Yes, she said it was outrageous and just like Cora ! "

" She didn't take it seriously ? "

"Oh, no. No, I'm sure she didn't."

The second " no," Poirot thought, had sounded suddenly doubtful. But was not that almost always the case when you went back over something in your mind ?

" And you, Madame, did you take it seriously ? "

Helen Abernethie, her eyes looking very blue and strangely young under the sideways sweep of crisp grey hair, said thoughtfully :

" Yes, M. Poirot, I think I did."

" Because of your feeling that something was wrong ? "

" Perhaps."

He waited—but as she said nothing more, he went on :

" There had been an estrangement, lasting many years, between Mrs. Lansquenet and her family ? "

" Yes. None of us liked her husband and she was offended about it, and so the estrangement grew."

" And then, suddenly, your brother-in-law went to see her. Why ? "

"I don't know—I suppose he knew, or guessed, that he hadn't very long to live and wanted to be reconciled—but I really don't know."

" He didn't tell you ? "

" Tell *me* ? "

"Yes. You were here, staying with him, just before he went there. He didn't even mention his intention to you ? "

He thought a slight reserve came into her manner.

" He told me that he was going to see his brother Timothy —which he did. He never mentioned Cora at all. Shall we go in ? It must be nearly lunch-time."

She walked beside him carrying the flowers she had picked. As they went in by the side door, Poirot said :

" You are sure, quite sure, that during your visit, Mr. Abernethie said nothing to you about any member of the family which might be relevant ? "

A faint resentment in her manner, Helen said :

" You are speaking like a policeman."

" I *was* a policeman—once. I have no status—no right to question you. But you want the truth—or so I have been led to believe ? "

They entered the green drawing-room. Helen said with a sigh :

" Richard was disappointed in the younger generation. Old men usually are. He disparaged them in various ways— but there was nothing—*nothing*, do you understand—that could possibly suggest a motive for murder."

" Ah," said Poirot. She reached for a Chinese bowl, and began to arrange the roses in it. When they were disposed to her satisfaction she looked round for a place to put it.

" You arrange flowers admirably, Madame," said Hercule. " I think that anything you undertook you would manage to do with perfection."

" Thank you. I am fond of flowers. I think this would look well on that green malachite table."

There was a bouquet of wax flowers under a glass shade on the malachite table. As she lifted it off, Poirot said casually :

" Did anyone tell Mr. Abernethie that his niece Susan's husband had come near to poisoning a customer when making up a prescription ? Ah, *pardon* ! "

He sprang forward.

The Victorian ornament had slipped from Helen's fingers. Poirot's spring forward was not quick enough. It dropped on the floor and the glass shade broke. Helen gave an expression of annoyance.

" How careless of me. However, the flowers are not damaged. I can get a new glass shade made for it. I'll put it away in the big cupboard under the stairs."

It was not until Poirot had helped her to lift it on to a shelf in the dark cupboard and had followed her back to the drawing-room that he said :

" It was my fault. I should not have startled you."

" What was it that you asked me ? I have forgotten."

" Oh, there is no need to repeat my question. Indeed—I have forgotten what it was."

Helen came up to him. She laid her hand on his arm.

" M. Poirot, is there anyone whose life would really bear close investigation ? *Must* people's lives be dragged into this when they have nothing to do with—with——"

" With the death of Cora Lasquenet ? Yes. Because one has to examine *everything*. Oh ! it is true enough—it is an

397

old maxim—*everyone has something to hide.* It is true of all of us—it is perhaps true of you, too, Madame. But I say to you, nothing can be ignored. That is why your friend, Mr. Entwhistle, he has come to me. For I am not the police. I am discreet and what I learn does not concern me. But I have to *know.* And since in this matter is not so much *evidence* as *people*—then it is *people* with whom I occupy myself. I need, Madame, to meet everyone who was here on the day of the funeral. And it would be a great convenience—yes, and it would be strategically satisfactory—if I could meet them *here.*"

" I'm afraid," Helen said slowly, " that that would be too difficult——"

" Not so difficult as you think. Already I have devised a means. The house, it is sold. So Mr. Entwhistle will declare. (*Entendu,* sometimes these things fall through !) He will invite the various member of the family to assemble here and to choose what they will from the furnishings before it is all put up to auction. A suitable week-end can be selected for that purpose."

He paused and then said :

" You see, it is easy, is it not ? "

Helen looked at him. The blue eyes were cold—almost frosty.

" Are you laying a trap for someone, M. Poirot ? "

" Alas ! I wish I knew enough. No, I have still the open mind."

" There may," Hercule Poirot added thoughtfully, " be certain tests . . ."

" Tests ? What kind of tests ? "

" I have not yet formulated them to myself. And in any case, Madame, it would be better that you should not know them."

" So that I can be tested too ? "

" You, Madame, have been taken behind the scenes. Now there is one thing that is doubtful. The young people will, I think, come readily. But it may be difficult, may it not, to secure the presence here of Mr. Timothy Abernethie. I hear that he never leaves home."

Helen smiled suddenly.

" I believe you may be lucky there, M. Poirot. I heard from Maude yesterday. The workmen are in painting the house and Timothy is suffering terribly from the smell of the paint. He says that it is seriously affecting his health. I think that he and Maude would both be pleased to come here—perhaps for a week or two. Maude is still not able to get about very well—you know she broke her ankle ? "

" I had not heard. How unfortunate."

" Luckily they have got Cora's companion, Miss Gilchrist. It seems that she has turned out a perfect treasure."

" What is that ? " Poirot turned sharply on Helen. " Did *they* ask for Miss Gilchrist to go to them ? Who suggested it ? "

" I think Susan fixed it up. Susan Banks."

" Aha," said Poirot in a curious voice. " So it was the little Susan who suggested it. She is fond of making the arrangements."

" Susan struck me as being a very competent girl."

" Yes. She is competent. Did you hear that Miss Gilchrist had a narrow escape from death with a piece of poisoned wedding cake ? "

" No ! " Helen looked startled. " I do remember now that Maude said over the telephone that Miss Gilchrist had just come out of hospital but I'd no idea why she had been in hospital. Poisoned ? But, M. Poirot—*why* ? "

" Do you really ask that ? "

Helen said with sudden vehemence :

" Oh ! get them all here ! Find out the truth ! There mustn't be any more murders."

" So you will co-operate ? "

" Yes—I will co-operate."

CHAPTER XV

" THAT LINOLEUM does look nice, Mrs. Jones. What a hand you have with lino. The teapot's on the kitchen table, so go and help yourself. I'll be there as soon as I've taken up Mr. Abernethie's elevenses."

Miss Gilchrist trotted up the staircase, carrying a daintily set out tray. She tapped on Timothy's door, interpreted a growl from within as an invitation to enter, and tripped briskly in.

" Morning coffee and biscuits, Mr. Abernethie. I do hope you're feeling brighter to-day. Such a lovely day."

Timothy grunted and said suspiciously :

" Is there skim on that milk ? "

" Oh no, Mr. Abernethie. I took it off very carefully, and anyway I've brought up the little strainer in case it should form again. Some people like it, you know, they say it's the *cream*—and so it is really."

" Idiots ! " said Timothy. " What kind of biscuits are those ? "

" They're those nice digestive biscuits."

" Digestive tripe. Ginger-nuts are the only biscuits worth eating."

" I'm afraid the grocer hadn't got any this week. But these are really *very* nice. You try them and see."

" I know what they're like, thank you. Leave those curtains alone, can't you ? "

" I thought you might like a little sunshine. It's such a nice sunny day."

" I want the room kept dark. My head's terrible. It's this paint. I've always been sensitive to paint. It's poisoning me."

Miss Gilchrist sniffed experimentally and said brightly :

" One really can't smell it much in here. The workmen are over on the other side."

" You're not sensitive like I am. Must I have *all* the books I'm reading taken out of my reach ? "

" I'm so sorry, Mr. Abernethie, I didn't know you were reading all of them."

" Where's my wife ? I haven't seen her for over an hour."

" Mrs. Abernethie's resting on the sofa."

" Tell her to come and rest up here."

" I'll tell her, Mr. Abernethie. But she may have dropped off to sleep. Shall we say in about a quarter of an hour ? "

" No, tell her I want her now. Don't monkey about with that rug. It's arranged the way I like it."

" I'm so sorry. I thought it was slipping off the far side."

" I like it slipping off. Go and get Maude. I want her."

Miss Gilchrist departed downstairs and tiptoed into the drawing-room where Maude Abernethie was sitting with her leg up reading a novel.

" I'm so sorry, Mrs. Abernethie," she said apologetically. " Mr. Abernethie is asking for you."

Maude thrust aside her novel with a guilty expression.

" Oh dear," she said, " I'll go up at once."

She reached for her stick.

Timothy burst out as soon as his wife entered the room :

" So there you are at last ! "

" I'm so sorry, dear, I didn't know you wanted me."

" That woman you've got into the house will drive me mad.

400

Twittering and fluttering round like a demented hen. Real typical old maid, that's what she is."

" I'm sorry she annoys you. She tries to be kind, that's all."

" I don't want anybody kind. I don't want a blasted old maid always chirruping over me. She's so damned arch, too——"

" Just a little, perhaps."

" Treats me as though I was a confounded kid ! It's maddening."

" I'm sure it must be. But please, *please*, Timothy, do try not to be rude to her. I'm really very helpless still—and you yourself say she cooks well."

" Her cooking's all right," Mr. Abernethie admitted grudgingly. " Yes, she's a decent enough cook. But keep her in the kitchen, that's all I ask. Don't let her come fussing round me."

" No, dear, of course not. How are you feeling ? "

" Not at all well. I think you'd better send for Barton to come and have a look at me. This paint affects my heart. Feel my pulse—the irregular way it's beating."

Maude felt it without comment.

" Timothy, shall we go to an hotel until the house painting is finished ? "

" It would be a great waste of money."

" Does that matter so much—now ? "

" You're just like all women—hopelessly extravagant ! Just because we've come into a ridiculously small part of my brother's estate, you think we can go and live indefinitely at the Ritz."

" I didn't quite say that, dear."

" I can tell you that the difference Richard's money will make will be hardly appreciable. This bloodsucking Government will see to that. You mark my words, the whole lot will go in taxation."

Mrs. Abernethie shook her head sadly.

" This coffee's cold," said the invalid, looking with distaste at the cup which he had not as yet tasted. " Why can't I ever get a cup of really hot coffee ? "

" I'll take it down and warm it up."

In the kitchen Miss Gilchrist was drinking tea and conversing affably, though with slight condescension, with Mrs. Jones.

" I'm so anxious to spare Mrs. Abernethie all I can," she said. " All this running up and down stairs is so painful for her."

401

" Waits on him hand and foot, she does," said Mrs. Jones, stirring the sugar in her cup.

" It's very sad his being such an invalid."

" Not such an invalid either," Mrs. Jones said darkly. " Suits him very well to lie up and ring bells and have trays brought up and down. But he's well able to get up and go about. Even seen him out in the village, I have, when *she's* been away. Walking as hearty as you please. Anything he *really* needs—like his tobacco or a stamp—he can come and get. And that's why when *she* was off at that funeral and got held up on the way back, and *he* told me I'd got to come in and stay the night again, I refused. ' I'm sorry, sir,' I said, ' but I've got my husband to think of. Going out to oblige in the mornings is all very well, but I've got to be there to see to him when he comes back from work.' Nor I wouldn't budge, I wouldn't. Do him good, I thought, to get about the house and look after himself for once. Might make him see what a lot he gets done for him. So I stood firm, I did. He didn't half create."

Mrs. Jones drew a deep breath and took a long satisfying drink of sweet inky tea. " Ar," she said.

Though deeply suspicious of Miss Gilchrist, and considering her as a finicky thing and a " regular fussy old maid," Mrs. Jones approved of the lavish way in which Miss Gilchrist dispensed her employer's tea and sugar ration.

She set down the cup and said affably :

" I'll give the kitchen floor a nice scrub down and then I'll be getting along. The potatoes is all ready peeled, dear, you'll find them by the sink."

Though slightly affronted by the " dear," Miss Gilchrist was appreciative of the goodwill which had divested an enormous quantity of potatoes of their outer coverings.

Before she could say anything the telephone rang and she hurried out in the hall to answer it. The telephone, in the style of fifty odd years ago, was situated inconveniently in a draughty passage behind the staircase.

Maude Abernethie appeared at the top of the stairs while Miss Gilchrist was still speaking. The latter looked up and said :

" It's Mrs.—Leo—is it ?—Abernethie speaking."

" Tell her I'm just coming."

Maude descended the stairs slowly and painfully.

Miss Gilchrist murmured, " I'm so sorry you've had to come down again, Mrs. Abernethie. Has Mr. Abernethie finished his elevenses ? I'll just nip up and get the tray."

402

AFTER THE FUNERAL

She trotted up the stairs as Mrs. Abernethie said into the receiver.

" Helen ? This is Maude here."

The invalid received Miss Gilchrist with a baleful glare. As she picked up the tray he asked fretfully :

" Who's that on the telephone ? "

" Mrs. Leo Abernethie."

" Oh ? Suppose they'll go gossiping for about an hour. Women have no sense of time when they get on the phone. Never think of the money they're wasting."

Miss Gilchrist said brightly that it would be Mrs. Leo who had to pay, and Timothy grunted.

" Just pull that curtain aside, will you ? No, not that one, the *other* one. I don't want the light slap in my eyes. That's better. No reason because I'm an invalid that I should have to sit in the dark all day."

He went on :

" And you might look in that bookcase over there for a green—— What's the matter *now* ? What are you rushing off for ? "

" It's the front door, Mr. Abernethie."

" *I* didn't hear anything. You've got that woman downstairs, haven't you ? Let her go and answer it."

" Yes, Mr. Abernethie. What was the book you wanted me to find ? "

The invalid closed his eyes.

" I can't remember now. You've put it out of my head. You'd better go."

Miss Gilchrist seized the tray and hurriedly departed. Putting the tray on the pantry table she hurried into the front hall, passing Mrs. Abernethie who was still at the telephone.

She returned in a moment to ask in a muted voice :

" I'm so sorry to interrupt. It's a nun. Collecting. The Heart of Mary Fund, I think she said. She has a book. Half a crown or five shillings most people seem to have given."

Maude Abernethie said :

" Just a moment, Helen," into the telephone, and to Miss Gilchrist, " I don't subscribe to Roman Catholics. We have our own Church charities."

Miss Gilchrist hurried away again.

Maude terminated her conversation after a few minutes with the phrase, " I'll talk to Timothy about it."

She replaced the receiver and came into the front hall. Miss Gilchrist was standing quite still by the drawing-room

403

door. She was frowning in a puzzled way and jumped when Maude Abernethie spoke to her.

" There's nothing the matter, is there, Miss Gilchrist ? "

" Oh no, Mrs. Abernethie, I'm afraid I was just wool gathering. So stupid of me when there's so much to be done."

Miss Gilchrist resumed her imitation of a busy ant and Maude Abernethie climbed the stairs slowly and painfully to her husband's room.

" That was Helen on the telephone. It seems that the place is definitely sold—some Institution for Foreign Refugees——"

She paused whilst Timothy expressed himself forcefully on the subject of Foreign Refugees, with side issues as to the house in which he had been born and brought up. " No decent standards left in this country. My old home ! I can hardly bear to think of it."

Maude went on.

" Helen quite appreciates what you—we—will feel about it. She suggests that we might like to come there for a visit before it goes. She was very distressed about your health and the way the painting is affecting it. She thought you might prefer coming to Enderby to going to an hotel. The servants are there still, so you could be looked after comfortably."

Timothy, whose mouth had been open in outraged protests half-way through this, had closed it again. His eyes had become suddenly shrewd. He now nodded his head approvingly.

" Thoughtful of Helen," he said. " Very thoughtful. I don't know, I'm sure, I'll have to think it over. . . . There's no doubt that this paint is poisoning me—there's arsenic in paint, I believe. I seem to have heard something of the kind. On the other hand the exertion of moving might be too much for me. It's difficult to know what would be the best."

" Perhaps you'd prefer an hotel, dear," said Maude. " A good hotel is very expensive, but where your health is concerned——"

Timothy interrupted.

" I wish I could make you understand, Maude, that we *are not millionaires*. Why go to an hotel when Helen has very kindly suggested that we should go to Enderby ? Not that it's really for her to suggest ! The house isn't hers. I don't understand legal subtleties, but I presume it belongs to us equally until it's sold and the proceeds divided. Foreign Refugees ! It would have made old Cornelius turn in his grave. Yes," he sighed, " I should like to see the old place again before I die."

404

Maude played her last card adroitly.

" I understand that Mr. Entwhistle has suggested that the members of the family might like to choose certain pieces of furniture or china or something—before the contents are put up for auction."

Timothy heaved himself briskly upright.

" We must certainly go. There must be a very exact valuation of what is chosen by each person. Those men the girls have married—I wouldn't trust either of them from what I've heard. There might be some sharp practice. Helen is far too amiable. As the head of the family, it is my duty to be present ! "

He got up and walked up and down the room with a brisk vigorous tread.

" Yes, it is an excellent plan. Write to Helen and accept. What I am really thinking about is you, my dear. It will be a nice rest and change for you. You have been doing far too much lately. The decorators can get on with the painting while we are away and that Gillespie woman can stay here and look after the house."

" Gilchrist," said Maude.

Timothy waved a hand and said that it was all the same.

2

" I can't do it," said Miss Gilchrist.

Maude looked at her in surprise.

Miss Gilchrist was trembling. Her eyes looked pleadingly into Maude's.

" It's stupid of me, I know . . . But I simply can't. Not stay here all alone in the house. If there was anyone who could come and—and sleep here too ? "

She looked hopefully at the other woman, but Maude shook her head. Maude Abernethie knew only too well how difficult it was to get anyone in the neighbourhood to " live in."

Miss Gilchrist went on, a kind of desperation in her voice.

" I know you'll think it nervy and foolish—and I wouldn't have dreamed once that I'd ever feel like this. I've never been a nervous woman—or fanciful. But now it all seems different. I'd be terrified—yes, literally terrified—to be all alone here."

" Of course," said Maude. " It's stupid of me. After what happened at Lytchett St. Mary."

" I suppose that's it . . . It's not logical, I know. And I

405

didn't feel it at first. I didn't mind being alone in the cottage after—after it had happened. The feeling's grown up gradually. You'll have no opinion of me at all, Mrs. Abernethie, but even since I've been here I've been feeling it—*frightened*, you know. Not of anything in particular—but just *frightened*. . . . It's so silly and I really am ashamed. It's just as though all the time I was expecting something awful to happen . . . Even that nun coming to the door startled me. Oh dear, I *am* in a bad way . . ."

"I suppose it's what they call delayed shock," said Maude vaguely.

"Is it? I don't know. Oh dear, I'm so sorry to appear so—so ungrateful, and after all your kindness. What you will think——"

Maude soothed her.

"We must think of some other arrangement," she said.

CHAPTER XVI

GEORGE CROSSFIELD paused irresolutely for a moment as he watched a particular feminine back disappear through a doorway. Then he nodded to himself and went in pursuit.

The doorway in question was that of a double-fronted shop —a shop that had gone out of business. The plate-glass windows showed a disconcerting emptiness within. The door was closed, but George rapped on it. A vacuous faced young man with spectacles opened it and stared at George.

"Excuse me," said George. "But I think my cousin just came in here."

The young man drew back and George walked in.

"Hallo, Susan," he said.

Susan, who was standing on a packing-case and using a foot-rule, turned her head in some surprise.

"Hallo, George. Where did you spring from?"

"I saw your back. I was sure it was yours."

"How clever of you. I suppose backs are distinctive."

"Much more so than faces. Add a beard and pads in your cheeks and do a few things to your hair and nobody will know you when you come face to face with them—but beware of the moment when you walk away."

"I'll remember. Can you remember seven feet five inches until I've got time to write it down."

"Certainly. What is this, book shelves?"

406

" No, cubicle space. Eight feet nine—and three seven . . ."

The young man with the spectacles who had been fidgeting from one foot to the other, coughed apologetically.

" Excuse me, Mrs. Banks, but if you want to be here for some time——"

" I do, rather," said Susan. " If you leave the keys, I'll lock the door and return them to the office when I go past. Will that be all right ? "

" Yes, thank you. If it weren't that we're short staffed this morning——"

Susan accepted the apologetic intent of the half-finished sentence and the young man removed himself to the outer world of the street.

" I'm glad we've got rid of him," said Susan. " House agents are a bother. They will keep talking just when I want to do sums."

" Ah," said George. " Murder in an empty shop. How exciting it would be for the passers-by to see the dead body of a beautiful young woman displayed behind plate glass. How they would goggle. Like goldfish."

" There wouldn't be any reason for you to murder me, George."

" Well, I should get a fourth part of your share of our esteemed uncle's estate. If one were sufficiently fond of money that should be a reason."

Susan stopped taking measurements and turned to look at him. Her eyes opened a little.

" You look a different person, George. It's really—extraordinary."

" Different ? How different ? "

" Like an advertisement. *This is the same man that you saw overleaf, but now he has taken Uppington's Health Salts.*"

She sat down on another packing-case and lit a cigarette.

" You must have wanted your share of old Richard's money pretty badly, George ? "

" Nobody could honestly say that money isn't welcome these days."

George's tone was light.

Susan said : " You were in a jam, weren't you ? "

" Hardly your business, is it, Susan ? "

" I was just interested."

" Are you renting this shop as a place of business ? "

" I'm buying the whole house."

" With possession ? "

" Yes. The two upper floors were flats. One's empty and

407

went with the shop. The other I'm buying the people out."

" Nice to have money, isn't it, Susan ? "

There was a malicious tone in George's voice. But Susan merely took a deep breath and said :

" As far as I'm concerned, it's wonderful. An answer to prayer."

" Does prayer kill off elderly relatives ? "

Susan paid no attention.

" This place is exactly *right*. To begin with, it's a very good piece of period architecture. I can make the living part upstairs something quite unique. There are two lovely moulded ceilings and the rooms are a beautiful shape. This part down here which has already been hacked about I shall have completely modern."

" What is this ? A dress business ? "

" No. Beauty culture. Herbal preparations. Face creams ! "

" The full racket ? "

" The racket as before. It pays. It always pays. What you need to put it over is personality. I can do it."

George looked at his cousin appreciatively. He admired the slanting planes of her face, the generous mouth, the radiant colouring. Altogether an unusual and vivid face. And he recognised in Susan that odd, indefinable quality, the quality of success.

" Yes," he said, " I think you've got what it takes, Susan. You'll get back your outlay on this scheme and you'll get places with it."

" It's the right neighbourhood, just off a main shopping street *and* you can park a car right in front of the door."

Again George nodded.

" Yes, Susan, you're going to succeed. Have you had this in mind for a long time ? "

" Over a year ? "

" Why didn't you put it up to old Richard ? He might have staked you ? "

" I did put it up to him."

" And he didn't see his way ? I wonder why. I should have thought he'd have recognised the same mettle that he himself was made of."

Susan did not answer, and into George's mind there leapt a swift bird's eye view of another figure. A thin, nervous, suspicious-eyed young man.

" Where does—what's his name—Greg—come in on all

408

this ? " he asked. " He'll give up dishing out pills and powders, I take it ? "

" Of course. There will be a laboratory built out at the back. We shall have our own formulas for face creams and beauty preparations."

George suppressed a grin. He wanted to say : " So baby is to have his play pen," but he did not say it. As a cousin he did not mind being spiteful, but he had an uneasy sense that Susan's feeling for her husband was a thing to be treated with care. It had all the qualities of a dangerous explosive. He wondered, as he had wondered on the day of the funeral, about that queer fish, Gregory. Something odd about the fellow. So nondescript in appearance—and yet, in some way, not nondescript . . .

He looked again at Susan, calmly and radiantly triumphant.

" You've got the true Abernethie touch," he said. " The only one of the family who has. Pity as far as old Richard was concerned that you're a woman. If you'd been a boy, I bet he'd have left you the whole caboodle."

Susan said slowly : " Yes, I think he would."

She paused and then went on :

" He didn't like Greg, you know . . ."

" Ah." George raised his eyebrows. " His mistake."

" Yes."

" Oh, well. Anyway, things are going well now—all going according to plan."

As he said the words he was struck by the fact that they seemed particularly applicable to Susan.

The idea made him, just for a moment, a shade uncomfortable.

He didn't really like a woman who was so cold-bloodedly efficient.

Changing the subject he said :

" By the way, did you get a letter from Helen ? About Enderby ? "

" Yes, I did. This morning. Did you ? "

" Yes. What are you going to do about it ? "

" Greg and I thought of going up the week-end after next —if that suits everyone else. Helen seemed to want us all together."

George laughed shrewdly.

" Or somebody might choose a more valuable piece of furniture than somebody else ? "

Susan laughed.

" Oh, I suppose there is a proper valuation. But a valuation for probate will be much lower than the things would be in the open market. And besides, I'd quite like to have a few relics of the founder of the family fortunes. Then I think it would be amusing to have one or two really absurd and charming specimens of the Victorian age in this place. Make a kind of *thing* of them! That period's coming in now. There was a green malachite table in the drawing-room. You could build quite a colour scheme around it. And perhaps a case of stuffed humming birds—or one of those crowns made of waxed flowers. Something like that—just as a key-note—can be very effective."

" I trust your judgment."

" You'll be there, I suppose ? "

" Oh, I shall be there—to see fair play if nothing else." Susan laughed.

" What do you bet there will be a grand family row ? " she asked.

" Rosamund will probably want your green malachite table for a stage set ! "

Susan did not laugh. Instead she frowned.

" Have you seen Rosamund lately ? "

" I have not seen beautiful Cousin Rosamund since we all came back third-class from the funeral."

" I've seen her once or twice . . . She—she seemed rather odd——"

" What was the matter with her ? Trying to think ? "

" No. She seemed—well—upset."

" Upset about coming into a lot of money and being able to put on some perfectly frightful play in which Michael can make an ass of himself ? "

" Oh, that's going ahead and it *does* sound frightful—but all the same, it may be a success. Michael's good, you know. He can put himself across the footlights—or whatever the term is. He's not like Rosamund, who's just beautiful and ham."

" Poor beautiful ham Rosamund."

" All the same Rosamund is not quite so dumb as one might think. She says things that are quite shrewd, sometimes. Things that you wouldn't have imagined she'd even noticed. It's—it's quite disconcerting."

" Quite like our Aunt Cora——"

" Yes . . ."

A momentary uneasiness descended on them both—conjured up it seemed, by the mention of Cora Lansquenet.

Then George said with a rather elaborate air of unconcern :

" Talking of Cora—what about that companion woman of hers ? I rather think something ought to be done about her."

" Done about her ? What do you mean ? "

" Well, it's up to the family, so to speak. I mean I've been thinking Cora was our Aunt—and it occurred to me that this woman mayn't find it easy to get another post."

" That occurred to you, did it ? "

" Yes. People are so careful of their skins. I don't say they'd actually think that this Gilchrist female would take a hatchet to them—but at the back of their minds they'd feel that it might be unlucky. People are superstitious."

" How odd that you should have thought of all that, George ? How would you know about things like that ? "

George said dryly :

" You forget that I'm a lawyer. I see a lot of the queer, illogical side of people. What I'm getting at is, that I think we might do something about the woman, give her a small allowance or something, to tide her over, or find some office post for her if she's capable of that sort of thing. I feel rather as though we ought to keep in touch with her."

" You needn't worry," said Susan. Her voice was dry and ironic. " I've seen to things. She's gone to Timothy and Maude."

George looked startled.

" I say, Susan—is that wise ? "

" It was the best thing I could think of—at the moment."

George looked at her curiously.

" You're very sure of yourself, aren't you, Susan ? You know what you're doing and you don't have—regrets."

Susan said lightly :

" It's a waste of time—having regrets."

CHAPTER XVII

MICHAEL TOSSED the letter across the table to Rosamund.

" What about it ? "

" Oh, we'll go. Don't you think so ? "

Michael said slowly :

" It might be as well."

" There might be some jewellery . . . Of course all the things in the house are quite hideous—stuffed birds and wax flowers—ugh ! "

" Yes. Bit of a mausoleum. As a matter of fact I'd like

411

to make a sketch or two—particularly in that drawing-room. The mantelpiece, for instance, and that very odd shaped couch. They'd be just right for *The Baronet's Progress*—if we revive it."

He got up and looked at his watch.

" That reminds me. I must go round and see Rosenheim. Don't expect me until rather late this evening. I'm dining with Oscar and we're going into the question of taking up that option and how it fits in with the American offer."

" Darling Oscar. He'll be pleased to see you after all this time. Give him my love."

Michael looked at her sharply. He no longer smiled and his face had an alert predatory look.

" What do you mean—after all this time ? Anyone would think I hadn't seen him for months."

" Well, you haven't, have you ? " murmured Rosamund.

" Yes, I have. We lunched together only a week ago."

" How funny. He must have forgotten about it. He rang up yesterday and said he hadn't seen you since the first night of *Tilly Looks West*."

" The old fool must be off his head."

Michael laughed. Rosamund, her eyes wide and blue, oked at him without emotion.

" You think I'm a fool, don't you, Mick ? "

Michael protested.

" Darling, of course I don't."

" Yes, you do. But I'm not an absolute nitwit. You didn't go near Oscar that day. I know where you did go."

" Rosamund darling—what do you mean ? "

" I mean I know where you really were . . ."

Michael, his attractive face uncertain, stared at his wife. She stared back at him, placid, unruffled.

How very disconcerting, he suddenly thought, a really empty stare could be.

He said rather unsuccessfully :

" I don't know what you're driving at . . ."

" I just meant it's rather silly telling me a lot of lies."

" Look here, Rosamund——"

He had started to bluster—but he stopped, taken aback as his wife said softly :

" We do want to take up this option and put this play on, don't we ? "

" Want to ? It's the part I've always dreamed must exist somewhere."

" Yes—that's what I mean."

412

" Just what do you mean ? "

" Well—it's worth a good deal, isn't it ? But one mustn't take *too* many risks."

He stared at her and said slowly :

" It's your money—I know that. If you don't want to risk it——"

" It's *our* money, darling." Rosamund stressed it. " I think that's rather important."

" Listen, darling. The part of Eileen—it would bear writing up."

Rosamund smiled.

" I don't think—really—I want to play it."

" My dear girl." Michael was aghast. " What's come over you ?:"

" Nothing."

" Yes, there is, you've been different lately—moody— nervous, what is it ? "

" Nothing. I only want you to be—careful, Mick."

" Careful about what ? I'm always careful."

" No, I don't think you are. You always think you can get away with things and that everyone will believe whatever you want them to. You were stupid about Oscar that day."

Michael flushed angrily.

" And what about you ? You said you were going shopping with Jane. You didn't. Jane's in America, has been for weeks."

" Yes," said Rosamund. " That was stupid, too. I really just went for a walk—in Regent's Park."

Michael looked at her curiously.

" Regent's Park ? You never went for a walk in Regent's Park in your life. What's it all about ? Have you got a boy friend ? You may say what you like, Rosamund, you *have* been different lately. Why ? "

" I've been—thinking about things. About what to do . . .."

Michael came round the table to her in a satisfying spontaneous rush. His voice held fervour as he cried :

" Darling—you know I love you madly ! "

She responded satisfactorily to the embrace, but as they drew apart he was struck again disagreeably by the odd calculation in those beautiful eyes.

" Whatever I'd done, you'd always forgive me, wouldn't you ? " he demanded.

" I suppose so," said Rosamund vaguely. " That's not the point. You see, it's all different now. We've got to think and plan."

413

" Think and plan—what ? "

Rosamund, frowning, said :

" Things aren't over when you've done them. It's really a sort of beginning and then one's got to arrange what to do next, and what's important and what is not."

" Rosamund . . ."

She sat, her face perplexed, her wide gaze on a middle distance in which Michael, apparently, did not feature.

At the third repetition of her name, she started slightly and came out of her reverie.

" What did you say ? "

" I asked you what you were thinking about . . ."

" Oh ? Oh yes, I was wondering if I'd go down to—what is it ?—Lytchett St. Mary, and see that Miss Somebody—the one who was with Aunt Cora."

" But why ? "

" Well, she'll be going away soon, won't she ? To relatives or someone. I don't think we ought to let her go away until we've asked her."

" Asked her what ? "

" Asked her who killed Aunt Cora ? "

Michael stared.

" You mean—you think she *knows* ? "

Rosamund said rather absently :

" Oh yes, I expect so . . . She lived there, you see."

" But she'd have told the police."

" Oh, I don't mean she knows *that* way—I just mean that she's probably quite sure. Because of what Uncle Richard said when he went down there." He did go down there, you know, Susan told me so.

" But she wouldn't have heard what he said."

" Oh yes, she would, darling." Rosamund sounded like someone arguing with an unreasonable child.

" Nonsense, I can hardly see old Richard Abernethie discussing his suspicions of his family before an outsider."

" Well, of course. She'd have heard it through the door."

" Eavesdropping, you mean ? "

" I expect so—in fact I'm sure. It must be so deadly dull shut up, two women in a cottage and nothing ever happening except washing up and the sink and putting the cat out and things like that. Of course she listened and read letters—anyone would."

Michael looked at her with something faintly approaching dismay.

" Would you ? " he demanded bluntly.

" I wouldn't go and be a companion in the country."
Rosamund shuddered. " I'd rather die."

" I meant—would you read letters and—and all that ? "

Rosamund said calmly :

" If I wanted to know, yes. Everybody does, don't you
think so ? "

The limpid gaze met his.

" One just wants to know," said Rosamund. " One doesn't
want to do anything about it. I expect that's how *she* feels
—Miss Gilchrist, I mean. But I'm certain she *knows*."

Michael said in a stifled voice :

" Rosamund, who do you think killed Cora ? And old
Richard ? "

Once again that limpid blue gaze met his.

" Darling—don't be absurd . . . You know as well as I do.
But it's much, much better *never* to mention it. So we
won't."

CHAPTER XVIII

FROM HIS SEAT by the fireplace in the library, Hercule Poirot
looked at the assembled company.

His eyes passed thoughtfully over Susan, sitting upright,
looking vivid and animated, over her husband, sitting near her,
his expression rather vacant and his fingers twisting a loop of
string ; they went on to George Crossfield, debonair and
distinctly pleased with himself, talking about card sharpers
on atlantic cruises to Rosamund, who said mechanically,
" How extraordinary, darling. But why ? " in a completely
uninterested voice ; went on to Michael with his very individual
type of haggard good looks and his very apparent charm ; to
Helen, poised and slightly remote ; to Timothy, comfortably
settled in the best armchair with an extra cushion at his back ;
and Maude, sturdy and thick-set, in devoted attendance, and
finally to the figure sitting with a tinge of apology just
beyond the range of the family circle—the figure of Miss
Gilchrist wearing a rather peculiar "dressy" blouse. Presently, he judged, she would get up, murmur an excuse and
leave the family gathering and go up to her room. Miss
Gilchrist, he thought, knew her place. She had learned it the
hard way.

Hercule Poirot sipped his after-dinner coffee and between
half-closed lids made his appraisal.

He had wanted them there—all together, and he had got them. And what, he thought to himself, was he going to do with them now ? He felt a sudden weary distaste for going on with the business. Why was that, he wondered ? Was it the influence of Helen Abernethie ? There was a quality of passive resistance about her that seemed unexpectedly strong. Had she, while apparently graceful and unconcerned, managed to impress her own reluctance upon him ? She was averse to this raking up of the details of old Richard's death, he knew that. She wanted it left alone, left to die out into oblivion. Poirot was not surprised by that. What did surprise him was his own disposition to agree with her.

Mr. Entwhistle's account of the family had, he realised, been admirable. He had described all these people shrewdly and well. With the old lawyer's knowledge and appraisal to guide him, Poirot had wanted to see for himself. He had fancied that, meeting these people intimately, he would have a very shrewd idea—not of *how* and *when*—(those were questions with which he did not propose to concern himself. Murder had been possible—that was all he needed to know !)— but of *who*. For Hercule Poirot had a lifetime of experience behind him, and as a man who deals with pictures can recognise the artist, so Poirot believed he could recognise a likely type of the amateur criminal who will—if his own particular need arises—be prepared to kill.

But it was not to be so easy.

Because he could visualise almost all of those people as a possible—though not a probable—murderer. George might kill—as the cornered rat kills. Susan calmly—efficiently—to further a plan. Gregory because he had that queer morbid streak which discounts and invites, almost craves, punishment. Michael because he was ambitious and had a murderer's cock-sure vanity. Rosamund because she was frighteningly simple in outlook. Timothy because he had hated and resented his brother and had craved the power his brother's money would give. Maude because Timothy was her child and where her child was concerned she would be ruthless. Even Miss Gilchrist, he thought, might have contemplated murder if it could have restored to her the Willow Tree in its lady-like glory !

And Helen ? He could not see Helen as committing murder. She was too civilised—too removed from violence. And she and her husband had surely loved Richard Abernethie.

Poirot sighed to himself. There were to be no short cuts to the truth. Instead he would have to adopt a longer, but a reasonably sure method. There would have to be conversation. Much conversation. For in the long run, either through a lie, or through truth, people were bound to give themselves away. . . .

He had been introduced by Helen to the gathering, and had set to work to overcome the almost universal annoyance caused by his presence—a foreign stranger !—in this family gathering. He had used his eyes and his ears. He had watched and listened—openly and behind doors ! He had noticed affinities, antagonisms, the unguarded words that arose as always when property was to be divided. He had engineered adroitly tête-à-têtes, walks upon the terrace, and had made his deductions and observations. He had talked with Miss Gilchrist about the vanished glories of her tea-shop and about the correct composition of *brioches* and chocolate *éclairs* and had visited the kitchen garden with her to discuss the proper use of herbs in cooking. He had spent some long half-hours listening to Timothy talking about his own health and about the effect upon it of paint.

Paint ? Poirot frowned. Somebody else had said something about paint—Mr. Entwhistle ?

There had also been discussion of a different kind of painting. Pierre Lansquenet as a painter. Cora Lansquenet's paintings, rapturised over by Miss Gilchrist, dismissed scornfully by Susan. " Just like picture postcards," she had said. " She did them from postcards, too."

Miss Gilchrist had been quite upset by that and had said sharply that dear Mrs. Lansquenet always painted from Nature.

" But I bet she cheated," said Susan to Poirot when Miss Gilchrist had gone out of the room. " In fact I know she did, though I won't upset the old pussy by saying so."

" And how do you know ? "

Poirot watched the strong confident line of Susan's chin.

" She will always be sure, this one," he thought. " And perhaps sometime, she will be too sure . . ."

Susan was going on.

" I'll tell you, but don't pass it on to the Gilchrist. One picture is of Polflexan, the cove and the lighthouse and the pier—the usual aspect that all amateur artists sit down and sketch. But the pier was blown up in the war, and since Aunt Cora's sketch was done a couple of years ago, it can't very well be from Nature, can it ? But the postcards they sell there still show the pier as it used to be. There was one in her bedroom drawer. So Aunt Cora started her ' rough sketch ' down there, I expect, and then finished it surreptitiously later at home from a postcard! It's funny, isn't it, the way people get caught out?"

"Yes, it is, as you say, funny." He paused, and then thought that the opening was a good one.

"You do not remember me, Madame," he said, "but I remember you. This is not the first time that I have seen you."

She stared at him. Poirot nodded with great gusto.

"Yes, yes, it is so. I was inside an automobile, well wrapped up and from the window I saw you. You were talking to one of the mechanics in the garage. You do not notice me—it is natural—I am inside the car—an elderly muffled-up foreigner! But I notice you, for you are young and agreeable to look at and you stand there in the sun. So when I arrive here, I say to myself, ' Tiens! what a coincidence!'"

"A garage? Where? When was this?"

"Oh, a little time ago—a week—no, more. For the moment," said Poirot disingenuously and with a full recollection of the King's Arms garage in his mind, "I cannot remember where. I travel so much all over this country."

"Looking for a suitable house to buy for your refugees?"

"Yes. There is so much to take into consideration, you see. Price—neighbourhood—suitability for conversion."

"I suppose you'll have to pull the house about a lot? Lots of horrible partitions."

"In the bedrooms, yes, certainly. But most of the ground floor rooms we shall not touch." He paused before going on. "Does it sadden you, Madame, that this old family mansion of yours should go this way—to strangers?"

"Of course not." Susan looked amused. "I think it's an excellent idea. It's an impossible place for anybody to think of living in as it is. And I've nothing to be sentimental about. It's not my old home. My mother and father lived in London. We just came here for Christmas sometimes. Actually I've always thought it quite hideous—an almost indecent temple to wealth."

"The altars are different now. There is the building in, and the concealed lighting and the expensive simplicity. But wealth still has its temples, Madame. I understand—I am not, I hope, indiscreet—that you yourself are planning such an edifice? Everything de luxe—and no expense spared."

Susan laughed.

"Hardly a temple—it's just a place of business."

418

" Perhaps the name does not matter. . . . But it will cost much money—that is true, is it not ? "

" Everything's wickedly expensive nowadays. But the initial outlay will be worth while, I think."

" Tell me something about these plans of yours. It amazes me to find a beautiful young woman so practical, so competent. In my young days—a long time ago, I admit—beautiful women thought only of their pleasures, of cosmetics, of *la toilette*."

" Women still think a great deal about their faces—that's where I come in."

" Tell me."

And she had told him. Told him with a wealth of detail and with a great deal of unconscious self-revelation. He appreciated her business acumen, her boldness of planning and her grasp of detail. A good bold planner, sweeping all side issues away. Perhaps a little ruthless as all those who plan boldly must be. . . .

Watching her, he had said :

" Yes, you will succeed. You will go ahead. How fortunate that you are not restricted, as so many are, by poverty. One cannot go far without the capital outlay. To have had these creative ideas and to have been frustrated by lack of means— that would have been unbearable."

" I couldn't have borne it ! But I'd have raised money somehow or other—got someone to back me."

" Ah ! of course. Your uncle, whose house this was, was rich. Even if he had not died, he would, as you express it, have ' staked ' you."

" Oh no, he wouldn't. Uncle Richard was a bit of a stick-in-the-mud where women were concerned. If I'd been a man——" A quick flash of anger swept across her face. " He made me very angry."

" I see—yes, I see . . ."

" The old shouldn't stand in the way of the young. I—oh, I beg your pardon."

Hercule Poirot laughed easily and twirled his moustache.

" I am old, yes. But I do not impede youth. There is no one who needs to wait for my death."

" What a horrid idea."

" But you are a realist, Madame. Let us admit without more ado that the world is full of the young—or even the middle-aged—who wait, patiently or impatiently, for the death of someone whose decease will give them if not affluence —then opportunity."

419

" Opportunity ! " Susan said, taking a deep breath. "That's what one needs."

Poirot who had been looking beyond her, said gaily :

" And here is your husband come to join our little discussion. . . . We talk, Mr. Banks, of opportunity. Opportunity the golden—opportunity who must be grasped with both hands. How far in conscience can one go ? Let us hear your views ? "

But he was not destined to hear the views of Gregory Banks on opportunity or on anything else. In fact he had found it next to impossible to talk to Gregory Banks at all. Banks had a curious fluid quality. Whether by his own wish, or by that of his wife, he seemed to have no liking for tête-à-têtes or quiet discussions. No, " conversation " with Gregory had failed.

Poirot had talked with Maude Abernethie—also about paint (the smell of) and how fortunate it had been that Timothy had been able to come to Enderby, and how kind it had been of Helen to extend an invitation to Miss Gilchrist also.

" For really she is *most* useful. Timothy so often feels like a snack—and one cannot ask too much of other people's servants but there is a gas ring in a little room off the pantry, so that Miss Gilchrist can warm up Ovaltine or Benger's there without disturbing anybody. And she's so willing about fetching things, she's quite willing to run up and down stairs a dozen times a day. Oh yes, I feel that it was really quite Providential that she should have lost her nerve about staying alone in the house as she did, though I admit it vexed me at the time."

" Lost her nerve ? " Poirot was interested.

He listened whilst Maude gave him an account of Miss Gilchrist's sudden collapse.

" She was frightened, you say ? And yet could not exactly say why ? That is interesting. Very interesting."

" I put it down myself to delayed shock."

" Perhaps."

" Once, during the war, when a bomb dropped about a mile away from us, I remember Timothy——"

Poirot abstracted his mind from Timothy.

" Had anything particular happened that day ? " he asked.

" On what day ? " Maude looked blank.

" The day that Miss Gilchrist was upset."

" Oh, *that*—no, I don't think so. It seems to have been coming on ever since she left Lychett St. Mary, or so she said. She didn't seem to mind when she was there."

And the result, Poirot thought, had been a piece of poisoned wedding cake. Not so very surprising that Miss Gilchrist was frightened after that. . . . And even when she had removed herself to the peaceful country round Stansfield Grange, the fear had lingered. More than lingered. Grown. Why grown? Surely attending on an exacting hypochondriac like Timothy must be so exhausting that nervous fears would be likely to be swallowed up in exasperation?

But something in that house had made Miss Gilchrist afraid. What? Did she know herself?

Finding himself alone with Miss Gilchrist for a brief space before dinner, Poirot had sailed into the subject with an exaggerated foreign curiosity.

"Impossible, you comprehend, for me to mention the matter of murder to members of the family. But I am intrigued. Who would not be? A brutal crime—a sensitive artist attacked in a lonely cottage. Terrible for her family. But terrible, also, I imagine, for *you*. Since Mrs. Timothy Abernethie gives me to understand that you were there at the time?"

"Yes, I was. And if you'll excuse me, M. Pontarlier, I don't want to talk about it."

"I understand—oh yes, I completely understand."

Having said this, Poirot waited. And, as he had thought, Miss Gilchrist immediately *did* begin to talk about it.

He heard nothing from her that he had not heard before, but he played his part with perfect sympathy, uttering little cries of comprehension and listening with an absorbed interest which Miss Gilchrist could not but help enjoy.

Not until she had exhausted the subject of what she herself had felt, and what the doctor had said, and how kind Mr. Entwhistle had been, did Poirot proceed cautiously to the next point.

"You were wise, I think, not to remain alone down in that cottage."

"I couldn't have done it, M. Pontarlier. I really couldn't have done it."

"No. I understand even that you were afraid to remain alone in the house of Mr. Timothy Abernethie whilst they came here?"

Miss Gilchrist looked guilty.

"I'm terribly ashamed about that. So foolish really. It was just a kind of panic I had—I really don't know *why*."

"But of course one knows why. You had just recovered from a dastardly attempt to poison you——"

421

Miss Gilchrist here sighed and said she simply couldn't understand it. Why should anyone try to poison her ?

" But obviously, my dear lady, because this criminal, this assassin, thought that you knew something that might lead to his apprehension by the police."

" But what could *I* know ? Some dreadful tramp, or semi-crazed creature."

" If it *was* a tramp. It seems to me unlikely——"

" Oh, please, M. Pontarlier——" Miss Gilchrist became suddenly very upset. " Don't suggest such things. I don't want to believe it."

" You do not want to believe what ? "

" I don't want to believe that it wasn't—I mean—that it was——"

She paused, confused.

" And yet," said Poirot shrewdly, " you *do* believe."

" Oh, I don't. I *don't* ! "

" But I think you do. That is why you are frightened . . . You are still frightened, are you not ? "

" Oh, no, not since I came here. So many people. And such a nice family atmosphere. Oh, no, everything seems quite all right here."

" It seems to me—you must excuse my interest—I am an old man, somewhat infirm and a great part of my time is given to idle speculation on matters which interest me—it seems to me that there must have been some definite occurrence at Stansfield Grange which, so to speak, brought your fears to a *head*. Doctors recognise nowadays how much takes place in our subconscious."

" Yes, yes—I know they say so."

" And I think your subconscious fears might have been brought to a point by some small concrete happening, something, perhaps, quite extraneous, serving, shall we say, as a focal point."

Miss Gilchrist seemed to lap this up eagerly.

" I'm sure you are right," she said.

" Now what, should you think, was this—er—extraneous circumstance ? "

Miss Gilchrist pondered a moment, and then said, unexpectedly :

" I think, you know, M. Pontarlier, it was the *nun*."

Before Poirot could take this up, Susan and her husband came in, closely followed by Helen.

" A nun," thought Poirot . . . " Now where, in all this, have I heard something about a nun ? "

422

He resolved to lead the conversation on to nuns sometime in the course of the evening.

CHAPTER XIX

THE FAMILY had all been polite to M. Pontarlier, the representative of U.N.A.R.C.O. And how right he had been to have chosen to designate himself by initials. Everyone had accepted U.N.A.R.C.O. as a matter of course—had even pretended to know all about it! How averse human beings were ever to admit ignorance! An exception had been Rosamund, who had asked him wonderingly : " But what *is* it ? I never heard of it ? " Fortunately no one else had been there at the time. Poirot had explained the organisation in such a way that anyone but Rosamund would have felt abashed at having displayed ignorance of such a well-known, world-wide institution. Rosamund, however, had only said vaguely, " Oh ! refugees all over *again.* I'm so *tired* of refugees." Thus voicing the unspoken reaction of many, who were usually too conventional to express themselves so frankly.

M. Pontarlier was, therefore, now accepted—as a nuisance but also as a nonentity. He had become, as it were, a piece of foreign *décor.* The general opinion was that Helen should have avoided having him here this particular week-end, but as he was here they must make the best of it. Fortunately this queer little foreigner did not seem to know much English. Quite often he did not understand what you said to him, and when everyone was speaking more or less at once he seemed completely at sea. He appeared to be interested only in refugees and post-war conditions, and his vocabulary only included those subjects. Ordinary chit-chat appeared to bewilder him. More or less forgotten by all, Hercule Poirot leant back in his chair, sipped his coffee and observed, as a cat may observe, the twitterings, and comings and goings of a flock of birds. The cat is not ready yet to make its spring.

After twenty-four hours of prowling round the house and examining its contents, the heirs of Richard Abernethie were ready to state their preferences, and, if need be, to fight for them.

The subject of conversation was, first, a certain Spode dinner dessert service off which they had just been eating dessert.

" I don't suppose I have long to live," said Timothy in a

faint melancholy voice. " And Maude and I have no children. It is hardly worth while our burdening ourselves with useless possessions. But for sentiment's sake I *should* like to have the old dessert service. I remember it in the dear old days. It's out of fashion, of course, and I understand dessert services have very little value nowadays—but there it is. I shall be *quite* content with that—and perhaps the Boule Cabinet in the White Boudoir."

" You're too late, Uncle," George spoke with debonair insouciance. " I asked Helen to mark off the Spode service to me this morning."

Timothy became purple in the face.

" Mark it off—mark it off ? What do you mean ? Nothing's been settled yet. And what do *you* want with a dessert service. You're not married."

" As a matter of fact I collect Spode. And this is really a splendid specimen. But it's quite all right about the Boule Cabinet, Uncle. I wouldn't have that as a gift."

Timothy waved aside the Boule Cabinet.

" Now look here, young George. You can't go butting in, in this way. I'm an older man than you are—and I'm Richard's only surviving brother. That dessert service is *mine*."

" Why not take the Dresden service, Uncle ? A very fine example and I'm sure just as full of sentimental memories. Anyway, the Spode's mine. First come, first served."

" Nonsense—nothing of the kind ! " Timothy spluttered.

Maude said sharply :

" Please don't upset your uncle, George. It's very bad for him. Naturally he will take the Spode if he wants to ! The first choice is *his*, and you young people must come afterwards. He was Richard's brother, as he says, and you are only a nephew."

" And I can tell you this, young man." Timothy was seething with fury. " If Richard had made a proper will, the disposal of the contents of this place would have been entirely in my hands. That's the way the property *should* have been left, and if it wasn't, I can only suspect *undue influence*. Yes —and I repeat it—*undue influence*."

Timothy glared at his nephew.

" A preposterous will," he said. " Preposterous ! "

He leant back, placed a hand to his heart, and groaned :

" This is very bad for me. If I could have—a little brandy."

Miss Gilchrist hurried to get it and returned with the restorative in a small glass.

"Here you are, Mr. Abernethie. Please—please don't excite yourself. Are you sure you oughtn't to go up to bed?"

"Don't be a fool." Timothy swallowed the brandy. "Go to bed? I intend to protect my interests."

"Really, George, I'm surprised at you," said Maude. "What your uncle says is perfectly true. His wishes come first. If he wants the Spode dessert service he shall have it!"

"It's quite hideous anyway," said Susan.

"Hold your tongue, Susan," said Timothy.

The thin young man who sat beside Susan raised his head. In a voice that was a little shriller than his ordinary tones, he said:

"Don't speak like that to my wife!"

He half rose from his seat.

Susan said quickly: "It's all right, Greg. I don't mind."

"But *I* do."

Helen said: "I think it would be graceful on your part, George, to let your uncle have the dessert service."

Timothy spluttered indignantly: "There's no 'letting' about it!"

But George, with a slight bow to Helen said, "Your wish is law, Aunt Helen. I abandon my claim."

"You didn't really want it, anyway, did you?" said Helen.

He cast a sharp glance at her, then grinned:

"The trouble with you, Aunt Helen, is that you're too sharp by half! You see more than you're meant to see. Don't worry, Uncle Timothy, the Spode is yours. Just my idea of fun."

"Fun, indeed." Maude Abernethie was indignant. "Your uncle might have had a heart attack!"

"Don't you believe it," said George cheerfully. "Uncle Timothy will probably outlive us all. He's what is known as a creaking gate."

Timothy leaned forward balefully.

"I don't wonder," he said, "that Richard was disappointed in *you*."

"What's that?" The good humour went out of George's face.

"You came up here after Mortimer died, expecting to step into his shoes—expecting that Richard would make you his heir, didn't you? But my poor brother soon took *your* measure. He knew where the money would go if you had control of it. I'm surprised that he even left you a part of his fortune. He knew where it would go. Horses, Gambling,

Monte Carlo, foreign Casinos. Perhaps worse. He suspected you of not being straight, didn't he ? "

George, a white dint appearing each side of his nose, said quietly :

" Hadn't you better be careful of what you are saying ? "

" I wasn't well enough to come here for the funeral," said Timothy slowly, " but Maude told me what *Cora said*. Cora always was a fool—but there *may* have been something in it ! And if so, I know who *I'd* suspect——"

" Timothy ! " Maude stood up, solid, calm, a tower of forcefulness. " You have had a very trying evening. You must consider your health. I can't have you getting ill again. Come up with me. You must take a sedative and go straight to bed. Timothy and I, Helen, will take the Spode dessert service and the Boule Cabinet as momentoes of Richard. There is no objection to that, I hope ? "

Her glance swept round the company. Nobody spoke, and she marched out of the room supporting Timothy with a hand under his elbow, waving aside Miss Gilchrist who was hovering half-heartedly by the door.

George broke the silence after they had departed.

" *Femme formidable !* " he said. " That describes Aunt Maude exactly. I should hate ever to impede her triumphal progress."

Miss Gilchrist sat down again rather uncomfortably and murmured :

" Mrs. Abernethie is always so kind."

The remark fell rather flat.

Michael Shane laughed suddenly and said : " You know, I'm enjoying all this ! ' The Voysey Inheritance ' to the life. By the way, Rosamund and I want that malachite table in the drawing-room."

" Oh, no," cried Susan. " *I* want that."

" Here we go again," said George, raising his eyes to the ceiling.

" Well, we needn't get angry about it," said Susan. " The reason I want it is for my new Beauty shop. Just a note of colour—and I shall put a great bouquet of wax flowers on it. It would look wonderful. I can find wax flowers easily enough, but a green malachite table isn't so common."

" But, darling," said Rosamund, " that's just why *we* want it. For the new set. As you say, a note of colour—and so *absolutely* period. And either wax flowers or stuffed humming birds. It will be absolutely *right*."

" I see what you mean, Rosamund," said Susan. " But

426

I don't think you've got as good a case as I have. You could easily have a painted malachite table for the stage—it would look just the same. But for my *salon* I've *got* to have the genuine thing."

" Now, ladies," said George. " What about a sporting decision ? Why not toss for it ? Or cut the cards ? All quite in keeping with the period of the table."

Susan smiled pleasantly.

" Rosamund and I will talk about it to-morrow," she said.

She seemed, as usual, quite sure of herself. George looked with some interest from her face to that of Rosamund. Rosamund's face had a vague, rather far-away expression.

" Which one will you back, Aunt Helen ? " he asked. " An even money chance, I'd say. Susan has determination, but Rosamund is so wonderfully single-minded."

" Or perhaps *not* humming birds," said Rosamund. " One of those big Chinese vases would make a lovely lamp, with a gold shade."

Miss Gilchrist hurried into placating speech.

" This house is full of so many beautiful things," she said. " That green table would look wonderful in your new establishment, I'm sure, Mrs. Banks. I've never seen one like it. It must be worth a lot of money."

" It will be deducted from my share of the estate, of course," said Susan.

" I'm so sorry—I didn't mean——" Miss Gilchrst was covered with confusion.

" It may be deducted from *our* share of the estate," Michael pointed out. " With the wax flowers thrown in."

" They look so right on that table," Miss Gilchrist murmured. " Really artistic. Sweetly pretty."

But nobody was paying any attention to Miss Gilchrist's well-meant trivialities.

Greg said, speaking again in that high nervous voice :

" Susan *wants* that table."

There was a momentary stir of unease, as though, by his words, Greg had set a different musical key.

Helen said quickly :

" And what do you really want, George ? Leaving out the Spode service."

George grinned and the tension relaxed.

" Rather a shame to bait old Timothy," he said. " But he really is quite unbelievable. He's had his own way in everything so long that he's become quite pathological about it."

" You have to humour an invalid, Mr. Crossfield," said Miss Gilchrist.

" Ruddy old hypochondriac, that's what he is," said George.

" Of course he is," Susan agreed. " I don't believe there's anything whatever the matter with him, do you, Rosamund? "

" What ? "

" Anything the matter with Uncle Timothy."

" No—no, I shouldn't think so." Rosamund was vague. She apologised. " I'm sorry. I was thinking about what lighting would be right for the table."

" You see ? " said George. " A woman of one idea. Your wife's a dangerous woman, Michael. I hope you realise it."

" I realise it," said Michael rather grimly.

George went on with every appearance of enjoyment.

" The Battle of the Table ! To be fought to-morrow— politely—but with grim determination. We ought all to take sides. I back Rosamund who looks so sweet and yielding and isn't. Husbands, presumably back their own wives. Miss Gilchrist ? On Susan's side, obviously."

" Oh, really, Mr. Crossfield, I wouldn't venture to——"

" Aunt Helen ? " George paid no attention to Miss Gilchrist's flutterings. " You have the casting vote. Oh, er —I forgot. M. Pontarlier ? "

" *Pardon ?* " Hercule Poirot looked blank.

George considered explanations, but decided against it. The poor old boy hadn't understood a word of what was going on. He said : " Just a family joke."

" Yes, yes, I comprehend." Poirot smiled amiably.

" So yours is the casting vote, Aunt Helen. Whose side are you on ? "

Helen smiled.

" Perhaps I want it myself, George."

She changed the subject deliberately, turning to her foreign guest.

" I'm afraid this is all very dull for you, M. Pontarlier ? "

" Not at all, Madame. I consider myself privileged to be admitted to your family life—" he bowed. " I would like to say—I cannot quite express my meaning—my regret that this house had to pass out of your hands into the hands of strangers. It is without doubt—a great sorrow."

" No, indeed, we don't regret at all," Susan assured him.

" You are very amiable, Madame. It will be, let me tell you, perfection here for my elderly sufferers of persecution. What a haven ! What peace ! I beg you to remember that, when the harsh feelings come to you as assuredly they must. I hear that there was also the question of a school coming here—not a regular school, a convent—run by *religeuses*—by ' nuns,' I think you say ? You would have preferred that, perhaps ? "

" Not at all," said George.

" The Sacred Heart of Mary," continued Poirot. " Fortunately, owing to the kindness of an unknown benefactor we were able to make a slightly higher offer." He addressed Miss Gilchrist directly. " You do not like nuns, I think ? "

Miss Gilchrist flushed and looked embarrassed.

" Oh, really, Mr. Pontarlier, you mustn't—I mean, it's nothing *personal*. But I never do see that it's right to shut yourself up from the world in that way—not necessary, I mean, and really almost selfish, though not teaching ones, of course, or the ones that go about amongst the poor—because I'm sure they're thoroughly unselfish women and do a lot of good."

" I simply can't imagine wanting to be a nun," said Susan.

" It's very becoming," said Rosamund. " You remember —when they revived *The Miracle* last year. Sonia Wells looked absolutely too glamorous for *words*."

" What beats me," said George, " is why it should be pleasing to the Almighty to dress oneself up in medieval dress. For after all, that's all a nun's dress is. Thoroughly cumbersome, unhygienic and impractical."

" And it makes them look so alike, doesn't it ? " said Miss Gilchrist. " It's silly, you know, but I got quite a turn when I was at Mrs. Abernethie's and a nun came to the door, collecting. I got it into my head she was the same as a nun who came to the door on the day of the inquest on poor Mrs. Lansquenet at Lychett St. Mary. I felt, you know, almost as though she had been following me round ! "

" I thought nuns always collected in couples," said George. " Surely a detective story hinged on that point once ? "

" There was only one this time," said Miss Gilchrist. " Perhaps they've got to economise," she added vaguely. " And anyway it couldn't have been the same nun, for the other one was collecting for an organ for St.—Barnabas, I think—and this one was for something quite different—something to do with children."

" But they both had the same type of features ? " Hercule Poirot asked. He sounded interested. Miss Gilchrist turned to him.

" I suppose that must be it. The upper lip—almost as though she had a moustache. I think you know, that *that* is really what alarmed me—being in a rather nervous state at the time, and remembering those stories during the war of nuns who were really men and in the Fifth Column and landed by parachute. Of course it was very foolish of me. I knew that afterwards."

" A nun would be a good disguise," said Susan thoughtfully. " It hides your feet."

" The truth is," said George, " that one very seldom looks properly at anyone. That's why one gets such wildly differing accounts of a person from different witnesses in court. You'd be surprised. A man is often described as tall—short ; thin —stout ; fair—dark ; dressed in a dark—light—suit ; and so on. There's usually *one* reliable observer, but one has to make up one's mind who that is."

" Another queer thing," said Susan, " is that you sometimes catch sight of yourself in a mirror unexpectedly and don't know who it is. It just looks vaguely familiar. And you say to yourself, ' That's somebody I know quite well . . .' and then suddenly realise it's yourself ! "

George said : " It would be more difficult still if you could really see yourself—and not a mirror image."

" Why ? " asked Rosamund, looking puzzled.

" Because, don't you see, nobody ever sees themselves—*as they appear to other people*. They always see themselves in a *glass*—that is—as a reversed image."

" But does that look any different ? "

" Oh, yes," said Susan quickly. " It must. Because people's faces aren't the same both sides. Their eyebrows are different, and their mouths go up one side, and their noses aren't really straight. You can see with a pencil—who's got a pencil ? "

Somebody produced a pencil, and they experimented, holding a pencil each side of the nose and laughing to see the ridiculous variation in angle.

The atmosphere now had lightened a good deal. Everybody was in a good humour. They were no longer the heirs of Richard Abernethie gathered together for a division of property. They were a cheerful and normal set of people gathered together for a week-end in the country.

Only Helen Abernethie remained silent and abstracted.

With a sigh, Hercule Poirot rose to his feet and bade his hostess a polite good night.

" And perhaps, Madame, I had better say good-bye. My train departs itself at nine o'clock to-morrow morning. That is very early. So I will thank you now for all your kindness and hospitality. The date of possession—that will be arranged

430

with the good Mr. Entwhistle. To suit your convenience, of course."

" It can be any time you please, M. Pontarlier. I—I have finished all that I came here to do."

" You will return now to your villa at Cyprus ? "

" Yes." A little smile curved Helen Abernethie's lips.

Poirot said :

" You are glad, yes. You have no regrets ? "

" At leaving England ? Or leaving here, do you mean ? "

" I meant—leaving here ? "

" No—no. It's no good, is it, to cling on to the past ? One must leave that behind one."

" If one can." Blinking his eyes innocently Poirot smiled apologetically round on the group of polite faces that surrounded him.

" Sometimes, is it not, the Past will not be left, will not suffer itself to pass into oblivion ? It stands at one's elbow— it says ' *I am not done with yet.*' "

Susan gave a rather doubtful laugh. Poirot said :

" But I am serious—yes."

" You mean," said Michael, " that your refugees when they come here will not be able to put their past sufferings completely behind them ? "

" I did not mean my Refugees."

" He meant us, darling," said Rosamund. " He means Uncle Richard and Aunt Cora and the hatchet, and all that."

She turned to Poirot.

" Didn't you ? "

Poirot looked at her with a blank face. Then he said :

" Why do you think that, Madame ? "

" Because you're a detective, aren't you ? That's why you're here. N.A.R.C.O., or whatever you call it, is just nonsense, isn't it ? "

CHAPTER XX

THERE WAS a moment of extraordinary tenseness. Poirot felt it, though he himself did not remove his eyes from Rosamund's lovely placid face.

He said with a little bow, " You have great perspicacity, Madame."

" Not really," said Rosamund. " You were pointed out to me once in a restaurant. I remembered."

" But you have not mentioned it—until now ? "

" I thought it would be more fun not to," said Rosamund.
Michael said in an imperfectly controlled voice :

" My—dear girl."

Poirot shifted his gaze then to look at him.

Michael was angry. Angry and something else—apprehensive ?

Poirot's eyes went slowly round all the faces. Susan's, angry and watchful ; Gregory's dead and shut in ; Miss Gilchrist's, foolish, her mouth wide open ; George, wary ; Helen, dismayed and nervous. . . .

All those expressions were normal ones under the circumstances. He wished he could have seen their faces a split second earlier, when the words " a detective " fell from Rosamund's lips. For now, inevitably, it could not be quite the same. . . .

He squared his shoulders and bowed to them. His language and his accent became less foreign.

" Yes," he said. " I am a detective."

George Crossfield said, the white dints showing once more each side of his nose, " Who sent you here ? "

" I was commissioned to inquire into the circumstances of Richard Abernethie's death."

" By whom ? "

" For the moment, that does not concern you. But it would be an advantage, would it not, if you could be assured *beyond any possible doubt* that Richard Abernethie died a natural death ? "

" Of course he died a natural death. Who says anything else ? "

" Cora Lansquenet said so. And Cora Lansquenet is dead herself."

A little wave of uneasiness seemed to sigh through the room like an evil breeze.

" She said it here—in this room," said Susan. " But I didn't really think——"

" Didn't you, Susan ? " George Crossfield turned his sardonic glance upon her. " Why pretend any more ? You won't take M. Pontarlier in ? "

" We all thought so really," said Rosamund. " And his name isn't Pontarlier—it's Hercules something."

" Hercule Poirot—at your service."

Poirot bowed.

There were no gasps of astonishment or of apprehension. His name seemed to mean nothing at all to them.

They were less alarmed by it than they had been by the single word "*detective*."

" May I ask what conclusions you have come to ? " asked George.

" He won't tell you, darling," said Rosamund. " Or if he does tell you, what he says won't be true."

Alone of the company she appeared to be amused.

Hercule Poirot looked at her thoughtfully.

2

Hercule Poirot did not sleep well that night. He was perturbed, and he was not quite sure *why* he was perturbed. Elusive snatches of conversation, various glances, odd movements—all seemed fraught with a tantalising significance in the loneliness of the night. He was on the threshold of sleep, but sleep would not come. Just as he was about to drop off, something flashed into his mind and woke him up again. Paint—Timothy and paint. Oil paint—the smell of oil paint—connected somehow with Mr. Entwhistle. Paint and Cora. Cora's paintings—picture postcards. . . . Cora was deceitful about her painting . . . No, back to Mr. Entwhistle—something Mr. Entwhistle had said—or was it Lanscombe ? A nun who came to the house on the day that Richard Abernethie died. A nun with a moustache. A nun at Stansfield Grange —and at Lytchett St. Mary. Altogether too many nuns ! Rosamund looking glamorous as a nun on the stage. Rosamund—saying that he was a detective—and everyone staring at her when she said it. That was the way that they must all have stared at Cora that day when she said " But he was murdered, wasn't he ? " What was it Helen Abernethie had felt to be " wrong " on that occasion ? Helen Abernethie —leaving the past behind—going to Cyprus . . . Helen dropping the wax flowers with a crash when he had said— *what* was it he had said ? He couldn't quite remember. . . .

He slept then, and as he slept he dreamed . . .

He dreamed of the green malachite table. On it was the glass-covered stand of wax flowers—only the whole thing had been painted over with thick crimson oil paint. Paint the colour of blood. He could smell the paint, and Timothy was groaning, was saying " I'm dying—dying . . . this is the end." And Maude, standing by, tall and stern, with a large knife in her hand was echoing him, saying " Yes, it's the end. . . ."

433

The end—a deathbed, with candles and a nun praying. If he could just see the nun's face, he would know. . . .

Hercule Poirot woke up—and he did know !

Yes, it *was* the end. . . .

Though there was still a long way to go.

He sorted out the various bits of the mosaic.

Mr. Entwhistle, the smell of paint, Timothy's house and something that must be in it—or might be in it . . . the wax flowers . . . Helen . . . Broken glass . . .

3

Helen Abernethie, in her room, took some time in going to bed. She was thinking.

Sitting in front of her dressing-table, she stared at herself unseeingly in the glass.

She had been forced into having Hercule Poirot in the house. She had not wanted it. But Mr. Entwhistle had made it hard for her to refuse. And now the whole thing had come out into the open. No question any more of letting Richard Abernethie lie quiet in his grave. All started by those few words of Cora's. . . .

That day after the funeral . . . How had they all looked, she wondered ? How had they looked to Cora ? How had she herself looked ?

What was it George had said ? About seeing oneself ?

There was some quotation, too. *To see ourselves as others see us.* . . . As others see us.

The eyes that were staring into the glass unseeingly suddenly focused. She was seeing herself—but not really herself—not herself as others saw her—not as Cora had seen her that day.

Her right—no, her left eyebrow was arched a little higher than the right. The mouth ? No, the curve of the mouth was symmetrical. If she met herself she would surely not see much difference from this mirror image. Not like Cora.

Cora—the picture came quite clearly . . . Cora, on the day of the funeral, her head tilted sideways—asking her question—looking at Helen . . .

Suddenly Helen raised her hands to her face. She said to herself. "*It doesn't make sense . . . it can't make sense . . .*

4

Miss Entwhistle was aroused from a delightful dream in which she was playing Piquet with Queen Mary, by the ringing of the telephone.

She tried to ignore it—but it persisted. Sleepily she raised her head from the pillow and looked at the watch beside her bed. Five minutes to seven—who on earth could be ringing up at that hour? It must be a wrong number.

The irritating ding-ding continued. Miss Entwhistle sighed, snatched up a dressing-gown and marched into the sitting-room.

" This is Kensington 675498," she said with asperity as she picked up the receiver.

" This is Mrs. Abernethie speaking. Mrs. *Leo* Abernethie. Can I speak to Mr. Entwhistle? "

" Oh, good morning, Mrs. Abernethie." The " good morning " was not cordial. " This is Miss Entwhistle. My brother is still asleep I'm afraid. I was asleep myself."

" I'm so sorry," Helen was forced to the apology. " But it's very important that I should speak to your brother at once."

" Wouldn't it do later? "

" I'm afraid not."

" Oh, very well then."

Miss Entwhistle was tart.

She tapped at her brother's door and went in.

" Those Abernethies again! " She said bitterly.

" Eh! The Abernethies? "

" Mrs. Leo Abernethie. Ringing up before seven in the morning! Really! "

" Mrs. Leo, is it? Dear me. How remarkable. Where is my dressing-gown? Ah, thank you."

Presently he was saying :

" Entwhistle speaking. Is that you, Helen? "

" Yes. I'm terribly sorry to get you out of bed like this. But you did tell me once to ring you up at once if I remembered what it was that struck me as having been wrong somehow on the day of the funeral when Cora electrified us all by suggesting that Richard had been murdered."

" Ah! You *have* remembered? "

Helen said in a puzzled voice :

" Yes, but it doesn't make sense."

435

" You must allow me to be the judge of that. Was it something you noticed about one of the people ? "

" Yes."

" Tell me."

" It seems absurd." Helen's voice sounded apologetic. " But I'm quite sure of it. It came to me when I was looking at myself in the glass last night. Oh . . ."

The little startled half cry was succeeded by a sound that came oddly through the wires—a dull heavy sound that Mr. Entwhistle couldn't place at all.

He said urgently :

" Hallo—hallo—are you there ? Helen, are you there ? . . . Helen . . ."

CHAPTER XXI

IT WAS NOT until nearly an hour later that Mr. Entwhistle, after a great deal of conversation with supervisors and others, found himself at last speaking to Hercule Poirot.

" Thank heaven ! " said Mr. Entwhistle with pardonable exasperation. " The Exchange seems to have had the greatest difficulty in getting the number."

" That is not surprising. The receiver was off the hook."

There was a grim quality in Poirot's voice which carried through to the listener.

Mr. Entwhistle said sharply :

" Has something happened ? "

" Yes. Mrs. Leo Abernethie was found by the housemaid about twenty minutes ago lying by the telephone in the study. She was unconscious. A serious concussion."

" Do you mean she was struck on the head ? "

" I think so. It is *just* possible that she fell and struck her head on a marble doorstop, but me I do not think so, and the doctor, he does not think so either."

" She was telephoning to me at the time. I wondered when we were cut off so suddenly."

" So it was to you she was telephoning ? What did she say?"

" She mentioned to me some time ago that on the occasion when Cora Lansquenet suggested her brother had been murdered, she herself had a feeling of something being wrong —odd—she did not quite know how to put it—unfortunately she could not remember *why* she had that impression."

" And suddenly, she did remember ? "

436

" Yes."

" And rang you up to tell you ? "

" Yes."

" *Eh bien ?* "

" There's no *eh bien* about it," said Mr. Entwhistle testily. " She started to tell me, but was interrupted."

" How much had she said ? "

" Nothing pertinent."

" You will excuse me, *mon ami*, but *I* am the judge of that, not you. What exactly did she say ? "

" She reminded me that I had asked her to let me know at once if she remembered what it was that had struck her as peculiar. She said she had remembered—but that it ' didn't make sense.'

" I asked her if it was something about one of the people who were there that day, and she said, yes, it was. She said it had come to her when she was looking in the glass——"

" Yes ? "

" That was all."

" She gave no hint as to—which of the people concerned it was ? "

" I should hardly fail to let you know if she had told me *that*," said Mr. Entwhistle acidly.

" I apologise, *mon ami*. Of course you would have told me."

Mr. Entwhistle said :

" We shall just have to wait until she recovers consciousness before we know."

Poirot said gravely :

" That may not be for a very long time. Perhaps never."

" Is it as bad as that ? " Mr. Entwhistle's voice shook a little.

" Yes, it is as bad as that."

" But—that's terrible, Poirot."

" Yes, it is terrible. And it is why we cannot afford to wait. For it shows that we have to deal with someone who is either completely ruthless or so frightened that it comes to the same thing."

" But look here, Poirot, what about Helen ? I feel worried. Are you sure she will be safe at Enderby ? "

" No, she would not be safe. So she is not at Enderby. Already the ambulance has come and is taking her to a nursing home where she will have special nurses and where *no one*, family or otherwise, will be allowed in to see her."

Mr. Entwhistle sighed.

437

" You relieve my mind ! She might have been in danger."
" She assuredly would have been in danger ! "
Mr. Entwhistle's voice sounded deeply moved.
" I have a great regard for Helen Abernethie. I always
have had. A woman of very exceptional character. She may
have had certain—what shall I say ?—reticences in her life."
" Ah, there were reticences ? "
" I have always had an idea that such was the case."
" Hence the villa in Cyprus. Yes, that explains a good
deal. . . ."
" I don't want you to begin thinking——"
" You cannot stop me thinking. But now, there is a little
commission that I have for you. One moment."
There was a pause, then Poirot's voice spoke again.
" I had to make sure that nobody was listening. All is
well. Now here is what I want you to do for me. You must
prepare to make a journey."
" A journey ? " Mr. Entwhistle sounded faintly dismayed.
" Oh, I see—you want me to come down to Enderby ? "
" Not at all. *I* am in charge here. No, you will not have
to travel so far. Your journey will not take you very far
from London. You will travel to Bury St. Edmunds—(*Ma
foi !* what names your English towns have !) and there you
will hire a car and drive to Forsdyke House. It is a Mental
Home. Ask for Dr. Penrith and inquire of him particulars
about a patient who was recently discharged."
" What patient ? Anyway, surely——"
Poirot broke in :
" The name of the patient is Gregory Banks. Find out for
what form of insanity he was being treated."
" Do you mean that Gregory Banks is insane ? "
" Sh ! Be careful what you say. And now—I have not yet
breakfasted and you, too, I suspect have not breakfasted ? "
" Not yet. I was too anxious——"
" Quite so. Then, I pray you, eat your breakfast, repose
yourself. There is a good train to Bury St. Edmunds at twelve
o'clock. If I have any more news I will telephone you before
you start."
" Be careful of *yourself*, Poirot," said Mr. Entwhistle with
some concern.
" Ah that, yes ! Me, I do not want to be hit on the head
with a marble doorstop. You may be assured that I will take
every precaution. And now—for the moment—good-bye."
Poirot heard the sound of the receiver being replaced at
the other end, then he heard a very faint second click—and

438

smiled to himself. Somebody had replaced the receiver on the telephone in the hall.

He went out there. There was no one about. He tiptoed to the cupboard at the back of the stairs and looked inside. At that moment Lanscombe came through the service door carrying a tray with toast and a silver coffee pot. He looked slightly surprised to see Poirot emerge from the cupboard.

"Breakfast is ready in the dining-room, sir," he said.

Poirot surveyed him thoughtfully.

The old butler looked white and shaken.

"Courage," said Poirot, clapping him on the shoulder. "All will yet be well. Would it be too much trouble to serve me a cup of coffee in my bedroom?"

"Certainly, sir. I will send Janet up with it, sir."

Lanscombe looked disapprovingly at Hercule Poirot's back as the latter climbed the stairs. Poirot was attired in an exotic silk dressing-gown with a pattern of triangles and squares.

"Foreigners!" thought Lanscombe bitterly. "Foreigners in the house! And Mrs. Leo with concussion! I don't know what we're coming to. Nothing's the same since Mr. Richard died."

Hercule Poirot was dressed by the time he received his coffee from Janet. His murmurs of sympathy were well received, since he stressed the shock her discovery must have given her.

"Yes, indeed, sir, what I felt when I opened the door of the study and came in with the Hoover and saw Mrs. Leo lying there I never shall forget. There she lay—and I made sure she was dead. She must have been taken faint as she stood at the phone—and fancy her being up at that time in the morning! I've never known her do such a thing before."

"Fancy, indeed!" He added casually: "No one else was up, I suppose?"

"As it happens, sir, Mrs. Timothy was up and about. She's a very early riser always—often goes for a walk before breakfast."

"She is of the generation that rises early," said Poirot nodding his head. "The younger ones, now—*they* do not get up so early?"

"No, indeed, sir, all fast asleep when I brought them their tea—and very late I was, too, what with the shock and getting the doctor to come and having to have a cup first to steady myself."

She went off and Poirot reflected on what she had said.

Maude Abernethie had been up and about, and the younger generation had been in bed—but that, Poirot reflected, meant nothing at all. Anyone could have heard Helen's door open and close, and have followed her down to listen—and would afterwards have made a point of being fast asleep in bed.

" But if I am right," thought Poirot. " And after all, it is natural to me to be right—it is a habit I have !—then there is no need to go into who was here and who was there. First, I must seek a proof where I have deduced the proof may be. And then—I make my little speech. And I sit back and see what happens . . ."

As soon as Janet had left the room, Poirot drained his coffee cup, put on his overcoat and his hat, left his room, ran nimbly down the back stairs and left the house by the side door. He walked briskly the quarter-mile to the post office where he demanded a trunk call. Presently he was once more speaking to Mr. Entwhistle.

" Yes, it is I yet again ! Pay no attention to the commission with which I entrusted you. *C'était une blague !* Someone was listening. Now, *mon vieux*, to the real commission. You must, as I said, take a train. But not to Bury St. Edmunds. I want you to proceed to the house of Mr. Timothy Abernethie."

" But Timothy and Maude are at Enderby."

" Exactly. There is no one in the house but a woman by the name of Jones who has been persuaded by the offer of considerable *largesse* to guard the house whilst they are absent. What I want you to do is to take something out of that house! "

" My dear Poirot ! I really can't stoop to burglary ! "

" It will not seem like burglary. You will say to the excellent Mrs. Jones who knows you, that you have been asked by Mr. or Mrs. Abernethie to fetch this particular object and take it to London. She will not suspect anything amiss."

" No, no, probably not. But I don't like it." Mr. Entwhistle sounded most reluctant. " Why can't you go and get whatever it is yourself."

" Because, my friend, I should be a stranger of foreign appearance and as such a suspicious character, and Mrs. Jones would at once raise the difficulties ! With you, she will not."

" No, no—I see that. But what on earth are Timothy and Maude going to think when they hear about it ? I have known them for forty odd years."

" And you knew Richard Abernethie for that time also ! And you knew Cora Lansquenet when she was a little girl ! "

In a martyred voice Mr. Entwhistle asked :

" You're sure this is really *necessary*, Poirot ? "

" The old question they asked in the wartime on the posters. *Is your journey really necessary ?* I say to you, it *is* necessary. It is vital ! "

" And what is this object I've got to get hold of ? "

Poirot told him.

" But really, Poirot, I don't see———"

" It is not necessary for *you* to see. *I* am doing the seeing."

" And what do you want me to do with the damned thing ? "

" You will take it to London, to an address in Elm Park Gardens. If you have a pencil, note it down."

Having done so, Mr. Entwhistle said, still in his martyred voice :

" I hope you know what you are doing, Poirot ? "

He sounded very doubtful—but Poirot's reply was not doubtful at all.

" Of course I know what I am doing. We are nearing the end."

Mr. Entwhistle sighed :

" If we could only guess what Helen was going to tell me."

" No need to guess. I *know*."

" You know ? But my dear Poirot———"

" Explanations must wait. But let me assure you of this. *I know what Helen Abernethie saw when she looked in her mirror.*"

2

Breakfast had been an uneasy meal. Neither Rosamund nor Timothy had appeared, but the others were there and had talked in rather subdued tones, and eaten a little less than they normally would have done.

George was the first one to recover his spirits. His temperament was mercurial and optimistic.

" I expect Aunt Helen will be all right," he said. " Doctors always like to pull a long face. After all, what's concussion ? Often clears up completely in a couple of days."

" A woman I knew had concussion during the war," said Miss Gilchrist conversationally. " A brick or something hit her as she was walking down Tottenham Court Road—it was during fly bomb time—and she never felt *anything* at all. Just went on with what she was doing—and collapsed in a train to Liverpool twelve hours later. And would you believe it, she had no recollection at all of going to the station and

441

catching the train or *anything*. She just couldn't understand it when she woke up in hospital. She was there for nearly three weeks."

" What I can't make out," said Susan, " is what Helen was doing telephoning at that unearthly hour, and who she was telephoning to ? "

" Felt ill," said Maude with decision. " Probably woke up feeling queer and came down to ring up the doctor. Then had a giddy fit and fell. That's the only thing that makes sense."

" Bad luck hitting her head on that doorstop," said Michael. " If she'd just pitched over on to that thick pile carpet she'd have been all right."

The door opened and Rosamund came in, frowning.

" I can't find those wax flowers," she said. " I mean the ones that were standing on the malachite table the day of Uncle Richard's funeral." She looked accusingly at Susan. " *You* haven't taken them ? "

" Of course I haven't ! Really, Rosamund, you're not *still* thinking about malachite tables with poor old Helen carted off to hospital with concussion ? "

" I don't see why I shouldn't think about them. If you've got concussion you don't know what's happening and it doesn't matter to you. We can't do anything for Aunt Helen, and Michael and I have got to get back to London by to-morrow lunch-time because we're seeing Jackie Lygo about opening dates for *The Baronet's Progress*. So I'd like to fix up definitely about the table. But I'd like to have a look at those wax flowers again. There's a kind of Chinese vase on the table now—nice—but not nearly so period. I do wonder where they are—perhaps Lanscombe knows."

Lanscombe had just looked in to see if they had finished breakfast.

" We're all through, Lanscombe," said George getting up. " What's happened to our foreign friend ? "

" He is having his coffee and toast served upstairs, sir."

" *Petit dejeuner* for N.A.R.C.O."

" Lanscombe, do you know where those wax flowers are that used to be on that green table in the drawing-room ? " asked Rosamund.

" I understand Mrs. Leo had an accident with them, m'am. She was going to have a new glass shade made, but I don't think she has seen about it yet."

" Then where is the thing ? "

" It would probably be in the cupboard behind the staircase, m'am. That is where things are usually placed when awaiting repair. Shall I ascertain for you ? "

" I'll go and look myself. Come with me, Michael sweetie. It's dark there, and I'm not going in any dark corners by myself after what happened to Aunt Helen."

Everybody showed a sharp reaction. Maude demanded in her deep voice :

" What *do* you mean, Rosamund ? "

" Well, she was coshed by someone, wasn't she ? "

Gregory Banks said sharply :

" She was taken suddenly faint and fell."

Rosamund laughed.

" Did she tell you so ? Don't be silly, Greg, of course she was coshed."

George said sharply :

" You shouldn't say things like that, Rosamund."

" Nonsense," said Rosamund. " She *must* have been. I mean, it all adds up. A detective in the house looking for clues, and Uncle Richard poisoned, and Aunt Cora killed with a hatchet, and Miss Gilchrist given poisoned wedding cake, and now Aunt Helen struck down with a blunt instrument. You'll see, it will go on like that. One after another of us will be killed and the one that's left will be It—the murderer, I mean. But it's not going to be *me*—who's killed, I mean."

" And why should anyone want to kill you, beautiful Rosamund ? " asked George lightly.

Rosamund opened her eyes very wide.

" Oh," she said. " Because I know too much, of course."

" What do you know ? " Maude Abernethie and Gregory Banks spoke almost in unison.

Rosamund gave her vacant and angelic smile.

" Wouldn't you all like to know ? " she said agreeably. " Come on, Michael."

CHAPTER XXII

AT ELEVEN O'CLOCK, Hercule Poirot called an informal meeting in the library. Everyone was there and Poirot looked thoughtfully round the semi-circle of faces.

" Last night," he said, " Mrs. Shane announced to you that I was a private detective. For myself, I hoped to retain my —*camouflage*, shall we say ?—a little longer. But no matter !

To-day—or at most the day after—I would have told you the truth. Please listen carefully now to what I have to say.

" I am in my own line a celebrated person—I may say a *most* celebrated person. My gifts, in fact, are unequalled ! "

George Crossfield grinned and said :

" That's the stuff, M. Pont—no, it's M. Poirot, isn't it ? Funny, isn't it, that I've never even heard of you ? "

" It is not funny," said Poirot severely. " It is lamentable ! Alas, there is no proper education nowadays. Apparently one learns nothing but economics—and how to set Intelligence Tests ! But to continue. I have been a friend for many years of Mr. Entwhistle's———"

" So *he's* the nigger in the wood pile ! "

" If you like to put it that way, Mr. Crossfield. Mr. Entwhistle was greatly upset by the death of his old friend, Mr. Richard Abernethie. He was particularly perturbed by some words spoken on the day of the funeral by Mr. Abernethie's sister, Mrs. Lansquenet. Words spoken in this very room."

" Very silly—and just like Cora," said Maude. " Mr. Entwhistle should have had more sense than to pay attention to them ! "

Poirot went on :

" Mr. Entwhistle was even more perturbed after the—the coincidence, shall I say ?—of Mrs. Lansquenet's death. He wanted one thing only—to be assured that that death *was* a coincidence. In other words he wanted to feel assured that Richard Abernethie had died a natural death. To that end he commissioned me to make the necessary investigations."

There was a pause.

" I have made them . . ."

Again there was a pause. No one spoke.

Poirot threw back his head.

" *Eh bien*, you will all be delighted to hear that as a result of my investigations—*there is absolutely no reason to believe that Mr. Abernethie died anything but a natural death*. There is no reason *at all* to believe that he was murdered ! " He smiled. He threw out his hands in a triumphant gesture.

" That is good news, is it not ? "

It hardly seemed to be, by the way they took it. They stared at him and in all but the eyes of one person there still seemed to be doubt and suspicion.

The exception was Timothy Abernethie, who was nodding his head in violent agreement.

" Of course Richard wasn't murdered," he said angrily.

" Never could understand why anybody ever even thought of such a thing for a moment ! Just Cora up to her tricks, that was all. Wanting to give you all a scare. Her idea of being funny. Truth is that although she was my own sister, she was always a bit mental, poor girl. Well, Mr. whatever your name is, I'm glad you've had the sense to come to the right conclusion, though if you ask me, I call it damned cheek of Entwhistle to go commissioning you to come prying and poking about. And if he thinks he's going to charge the estate with your fee, I can tell you he won't get away with it ! Damned cheek, and most uncalled for ! Who's Entwhistle to set himself up ? If the family's satisfied——"

" But the family wasn't, Uncle Timothy," said Rosamund.

" Hey—what's that ? "

Timothy peered at her under beetling brows of displeasure.

" We weren't satisfied. And what about Aunt Helen this morning ? "

Maude said sharply :

" Helen's just the age when you're liable to get a stroke. That's all there is to that."

" I see," said Rosamund. " Another coincidence, you think ? "

She looked at Poirot.

" Aren't there rather too many coincidences ? "

" Coincidences," said Hercule Poirot, " do happen."

" Nonsense," said Maude. " Helen felt ill, came down and rang up the doctor, and then——"

" But she didn't ring up the doctor," said Rosamund. " I asked him——"

Susan said sharply :

" Who did she ring up ? "

" I don't know," said Rosamund, a shade of vexation passing over her face. " But I dare say I can find out," she added hopefully.

2

Hercule Poirot was sitting in the Victorian summer-house. He drew his large watch from his pocket and laid it on the table in front of him.

He had announced that he was leaving by the twelve o'clock train. There was still half an hour to go. Half an hour for someone to make up their minds and come to him. Perhaps more than one person. . . .

445

The summer-house was clearly visible from most of the windows of the house. Surely, soon, someone would come?

If not, his knowledge of human nature was deficient, and his main premises incorrect.

He waited—and above his head a spider in its web waited for a fly.

It was Miss Gilchrist who came first. She was flustered and upset and rather incoherent.

"Oh, Mr. Pontarlier—I can't remember your other name," she said. "I had to come and speak to you although I *don't* like doing it—but really I feel I *ought* to. I mean, after what happened to poor Mrs. Leo this morning—and I think myself Mrs. Shane was *quite right*—and *not* coincidence, and certainly not a *stroke*—as Mrs. Timothy suggested, because my own father had a stroke and it was quite a different appearance, and anyway the doctor *said* concussion quite clearly!"

She paused, took breath and looked at Poirot with appealing eyes.

"Yes," said Poirot gently and encouragingly. "You want to tell me something?"

"As I say, I don't like doing it—because she's been so kind. She found me the position with Mrs. Timothy and everything. She's been really *very* kind. That's why I feel so ungrateful. And even gave me Mrs. Lansquenet's musquash jacket which is really *most* handsome and fits beautifully because it never matters if fur is a little on the large side. And when I wanted to return her the amethyst brooch she wouldn't *hear* of it——"

"You are referring," said Poirot gently, "to Mrs. Banks?"

"Yes, you see——" Miss Gilchrist looked down, twisting her fingers unhappily. She looked up and said with a sudden gulp:

"You see, I *listened*!"

"You mean you happened to overhear a conversation——"

"No." Miss Gilchrist shook her head with an air of heroic determination. "I'd rather speak the truth. And it's not so bad telling you because you're not English."

Hercule Poirot understood her without taking offence.

"You mean that to a foreigner it is natural that people should listen at doors and open letters, or read letters that are left about?"

"Oh, I'd never open anybody else's letters," said Miss Gilchrist in a shocked tone. "Not *that*. But I *did* listen that day—the day that Mr. Richard Abernethie came down to see his sister. I was curious, you know, about his turning up

446

suddenly after all those years. And I did wonder why—and—and—you see when you haven't much life of your own or very many friends, you do tend to get interested—when you're living *with* anybody, I mean."

" Most natural," said Poirot.

" Yes, I do think it was natural . . . Though not, of course, at all *right*. But I did it ! And I heard what he said ! "

" You heard what Mr. Abernethie said to Mrs. Lansquenet? "

" Yes. He said something like—' It's no good talking to Timothy. He pooh-poohs everything. Simply won't listen. But I thought I'd like to get it off my chest to you, Cora. We three are the only ones left. And though you've always liked to play the simpleton you've got a lot of common sense. So what would *you* do about it, if you were me ? '

" I couldn't quite hear what Mrs. Lansquenet said, but I caught the word *police*—and then Mr. Abernethie burst out quite loud, and said, ' I can't do that. Not when it's a question of *my own niece.*' And then I had to run in the kitchen for something boiling over and when I got back Mr. Abernethie was saying, ' Even if I die an unnatural death I don't want the police called in, if it can possibly be avoided. You understand that, don't you, my dear girl ? But don't worry. Now that I *know*, I shall take all possible precautions.' And he went on, saying he'd made a new will, and that she, Cora, would be quite all right. And then he said about her having been happy with her husband and how perhaps he'd made a mistake over that in the past."

Miss Gilchrist stopped.

Poirot said : " I see—I see . . ."

" But I never wanted to say—to tell. I didn't think Mrs. Lansquenet would have·wanted me to . . . But now—after Mrs. Leo being attacked this morning—and then you saying so calmly it was coincidence. But, oh, M. Pontarlier, it *wasn't* coincidence ! "

Poirot smiled. He said :

" No, it wasn't coincidence. . . . Thank you, Miss Gilchrist, for coming to me. It was very necessary that you should."

3

He had a little difficulty in getting rid of Miss Gilchrist, and it was urgent that he should, for he hoped for further confidences.

His instinct was right. Miss Gilchrist had hardly gone before Gregory Banks, striding across the lawn, came impetuously into the summer-house. His face was pale and there were beads of perspiration on his forehead. His eyes were curiously excited.

" At last ! " he said. " I thought that stupid woman would never go. You're all wrong in what you said this morning. You're wrong about everything. Richard Abernethie *was* killed. *I* killed him."

Hercule Poirot let his eyes move up and down over the excited young man. He showed no surprise.

" So you killed him, did you ? How ? "

Gregory Banks smiled.

" It wasn't difficult for *me*. You can surely realise that. There were fifteen or twenty different drugs I could lay my hands on that would do it. The method of administration took rather more thinking out, but I hit on a very ingenious idea in the end. The beauty of it was that *I* didn't need to be anywhere near at the time."

" Clever," said Poirot.

" Yes." Gregory Banks cast his eyes down modestly. He seemed pleased. " Yes—I *do* think it was ingenious."

Poirot asked with interest :

" Why did you kill him ? For the money that would come to your wife ? "

" No. No, of course not." Greg was suddenly excitedly indignant. " I'm not a money grubber. I didn't marry Susan for her *money* ! "

" Didn't you, Mr. Banks ? "

" That's what *he* thought," Greg said with sudden venom. " Richard Abernethie ! He liked Susan, he admired her, he was proud of her as an example of Abernethie blood ! But he thought she'd married beneath her—he thought *I* was no good—he despised me ! I dare say I hadn't the right accent—I didn't wear my clothes the right way. He was a snob—a filthy snob ! "

" I don't think so," said Poirot mildly. " From all I have heard, Richard Abernethie was no snob."

" He was. He was." The young man spoke with something approaching hysteria. " He thought nothing of me. He sneered at me—always very polite but underneath I could *see* that he didn't like me ! "

" Possibly."

" People can't treat me like that and get away with it ! They've tried it before ! A woman who used to come and

448

have her medicines made up. She was rude to me. Do you know what I did ? "

" Yes," said Poirot.

Gregory looked startled.

" So you know that ? "

" Yes."

" She nearly died." He spoke in a satisfied manner. " That shows you I'm not the sort of person to be trifled with ! Richard Abernethie despised me—and what happened to him ? He died."

" A most successful murder," said Poirot with grave congratulation.

He added : " But why come and give yourself away—to me ? "

" Because you said you were through with it all ! You said he *hadn't* been murdered. I had to show you that you're not as clever as you think you are—and besides—besides——"

" Yes," said Poirot. " And besides ? "

Greg collapsed suddenly on to the bench. His face changed. It took on a sudden ecstatic quality.

" It was wrong—wicked . . . I must be punished . . . I must go back there—to the place of punishment . . . to atone . . . Yes, to *atone* ! Repentance ! Retribution ! "

His face was alight now with a kind of glowing ecstasy. Poirot studied him for a moment or two curiously.

Then he asked :

" How badly do you want to get away from your wife ? "

Gregory's face changed.

" Susan ? Susan is wonderful—wonderful ! "

" Yes. Susan is wonderful. That is a grave burden. Susan loves you devotedly. That is a burden, too ? "

Gregory sat looking in front of him. Then he said, rather in the manner of a sulky child :

" Why couldn't she let me alone ? "

He sprang up.

" She's coming now—across the lawn. I'll go now. But you'll tell her what I told you ? Tell her I've gone to the police station. To confess."

4

Susan came in breathlessly.

" Where's Greg ? He was here ! I saw him."

" Yes." Poirot paused a moment—before saying : " He

449

came to tell me that it was he who poisoned Richard Abernethie. . . ."

" What absolute *nonsense* ! You didn't believe him, I
hope ? "

" Why should I not believe him ? "

" He wasn't even near this place when Uncle Richard died ! "

" Perhaps not. Where was he when Cora Lansquenet died ? "

" In London. We both were."

Hercule Poirot shook his head.

" No, no, that will not do. You, for instance, took out
your car that day and were away all the afternoon. I think
I know where you went. You went to Lytchett St. Mary."

" I did no such thing ! "

Poirot smiled.

" When I met you here, Madame, it was not, as I told you,
the first time I had seen you. After the inquest on Mrs. Lansquenet you were in the garage of the King's Arms. You talk
there to a mechanic and close by you is a car containing an
elderly foreign gentleman. You did not notice him, but he
noticed you."

" I don't see what you mean. That was the day of the
inquest."

" Ah, but remember what that mechanic said to you ! He
asked you if you were a relative of the victim, and you said
you were her niece."

" He was just being a ghoul. They're all ghouls."

" And his next words were, ' Ah, wondered where I'd seen
you before.' Where did he see you before, Madame ? It
must have been in Lytchett St. Mary, since in his mind his
seeing you before was accounted for by your being Mrs.
Lansquenet's niece. Had he seen you near her cottage ?
And when ? It was a matter, was it not, that demands
inquiry. And the result of the inquiry is, that you were
there—in Lytchett St. Mary—on the afternoon Cora Lansquenet died. You parked your car in the same quarry where
you left it the morning of the inquest. The car was seen and
the number was noted. By this time Inspector Morton knows
whose car it was."

Susan stared at him. Her breath came rather fast, but she
showed no signs of discomposure.

" You're talking nonsense, M. Poirot. And you're making
me forget what I came here to say—I wanted to try and find
you alone——"

" To confess to me that it was you and not your husband
who committed the murder ? "

450

" No, of course not. What kind of a fool do you think I am ? And I've already told you that Gregory never left London that day."

" A fact which you cannot possibly know since you were away yourself. Why did you go down to Lytchett St. Mary, Mrs. Banks ? "

Susan drew a deep breath.

" All right, if you must have it ! What Cora said at the funeral worried me. I kept on thinking about it. Finally I decided to run down in the car and see her, and ask her what had put the idea into her head. Greg thought it a silly idea, so I didn't even tell him where I was going. I got there about three o'clock, knocked and rang, but there was no answer, so I thought she must be out or gone away. That's all there is to it. I didn't go round to the back of the cottage. If I had, I might have seen the broken window. I just went back to London without the faintest idea there was anything wrong."

Poirot's face was non-committal. He said :

" Why does your husband accuse himself of the crime ? "

" Because he's——" a word trembled on Susan's tongue and was rejected. Poirot seized on it.

" You were going to say ' because he is batty ' speaking in jest—but the jest was too near the truth, was it not ? "

" Greg's all right. He is. He *is*."

" I know something of his history," said Poirot. " He was for some months in Forsdyke House Mental Home before you met him."

" He was never certified. He was a voluntary patient."

" That is true. He is not, I agree, to be classed as insane. But he is, very definitely, unbalanced. He has a punishment complex—has had it, I suspect, since infancy."

Susan spoke quickly and eagerly :

" You don't understand, M. Poirot. Greg has never had a *chance*. That's why I wanted Uncle Richard's money so badly. Uncle Richard was so matter-of-fact. He couldn't understand. I knew Greg had got to set up for himself. He had got to feel he was *someone*—not just a chemist's assistant, being pushed around. Everything will be different now. He will have his own laboratory. He can work out his own formulas."

" Yes, yes—you will give him the earth—because you love him. Love him too much for safety or for happiness. But you cannot give to people what they are incapable of receiving. At the end of it all, he will still be something that he does not want to be. . . ."

" What's that ? "

451

" *Susan's husband.*"

" How cruel you are ! And what nonsense you talk ! "

" Where Gregory Banks is concerned you are unscrupulous. You wanted your uncle's money—not for yourself—but for your husband. *How badly did you want it ?* "

Angrily, Susan turned and dashed away.

5

" I thought," said Michael Shane lightly, " that I'd just come along and say good-bye."

He smiled, and his smile had a singularly intoxicating quality.

Poirot was aware of the man's vital charm.

He studied Michael Shane for some moments in silence. He felt as though he knew this man least well of all the house party, for Michael Shane only showed the side of himself that he wanted to show.

" Your wife," said Poirot conversationally, " is a very unusual woman."

Michael raised his eyebrows.

" Do you think so ? She's a lovely, I agree. But not, or so I've found, conspicuous for brains."

" She will never try to be too clever," Poirot agreed. " But she knows what she wants." He sighed. " So few people do."

" Ah ! " Michael's smile broke out again. " Thinking of the malachite table ? "

" Perhaps." Poirot paused and added : " *And of what was on it.*"

" The wax flowers, you mean ? "

" The wax flowers."

Michael frowned.

" I don't always quite understand you, M. Poirot. However," the smile was switched on again, " I'm more thankful than I can say that we're all out of the wood. It's unpleasant, to say the least of it, to go around with the suspicion that somehow or other one of us murdered poor old Uncle Richard."

" That is how he seemed to you when you met him ? " Poirot inquired. " Poor old Uncle Richard ? "

" Of course he was very well preserved and all that——"

" And in full possession of his faculties——"

" Oh yes."

" And, in fact, quite *shrewd* ? "

" I dare say."

" A shrewd judge of character."

The smile remained unaltered.

" You can't expect me to agree with *that*, M. Poirot. He didn't approve of *me*."

" He thought you, perhaps, the unfaithful type ? " Poirot suggested.

Michael laughed.

" What an old-fashioned idea ! "

" But it is true, isn't it ? "

" Now I wonder what you mean by *that* ? "

Poirot placed the tips of his fingers together.

" There have been inquiries made, you know," he murmured.

" By you ? "

" Not only by me."

Michael Shane gave him a quick searching glance. His reactions, Poirot noted, were quick. Michael Shane was no fool.

" You mean—the police are interested ? "

" They have never been quite satisfied, you know, to regard the murder of Cora Lansquenet as a casual crime."

" And they've been making inquiries about me ? "

Poirot said primly :

" They are interested in the movements of Mrs. Lansquenet's relations on the day that she was killed."

" That's extremely awkward." Michael spoke with a charming confidential rueful air.

" Is it, Mr. Shane ? "

" More so than you can imagine ! I told Rosamund, you see, that I was lunching with a certain Oscar Lewis on that day."

" When, in actual fact, you were not ? "

" No. Actually I motored down to see a woman called Sorrel Dainton—quite a well-known actress. I was with her in her last show. Rather awkward, you see—for though it's quite satisfactory as far as the police are concerned, it won't go down very well with Rosamund."

" Ah ! " Poirot looked discreet. " There has been a little trouble over this friendship of yours ? "

" Yes . . . In fact—Rosamund made me promise I wouldn't see her any more."

" Yes, I can see that may be awkward . . . *Entre nous*, you had an affair with the lady ? "

" Oh, just one of those things ! It's not as though I cared for the woman at all."

" But she cares for you ? "

453

" Well, she's been rather tiresome . . . Women do cling so. However, as you say, the police at any rate will be satisfied."

" You think so ? "

" Well, I could hardly be taking a hatchet to Cora if I was dallying with Sorrel miles and miles away. She's got a cottage in Kent."

" I see—I see—and this Miss Dainton, she will testify for you ? "

" She won't like it—but as it's murder, I suppose she'll have to do it."

" She will do it, perhaps, even if you were *not* dallying with her."

" What do you mean ? " Michael looked suddenly black as thunder.

" The lady is fond of you. When they are fond, women will swear to what is true—and also to what is untrue."

" Do you mean to say that you don't believe me ? "

" It does not matter if *I* believe you or not. It is not *I* you have to satisfy."

" Who then ? "

Poirot smiled.

" Inspector Morton—who has just come out on the terrace through the side door."

Michael Shane wheeled round sharply.

CHAPTER XXIII

" I HEARD YOU were here, M. Poirot, ' said Inspector Morton.

The two men were pacing the terrace together.

" I came over with Superintendent Parwell from Matchfield. Dr. Larraby rang him up about Mrs. Leo Abernethie and he's come over here to make a few inquiries. The doctor wasn't satisfied."

" And you, my friend," inquired Poirot, " where do you come in ? You are a long way from your native Berkshire."

" I wanted to ask a few questions—and the people I wanted to ask them of seemed very conveniently assembled here." He paused before adding, " Your doing ? "

" Yes, my doing."

" And as a result Mrs. Leo Abernethie gets knocked out."

" You must not blame me for that. If she had come to *me* . . . But she did not. Instead she rang up her lawyer in London."

" And was in process of spilling the beans to him when—
Wonk ! "

" When—as you say—Wonk ! "

" And what had she managed to tell him ? "

" Very little. She had only got as far as telling him that
she was looking at herself in the glass."

" Ah ! well," said Inspector Morton philosophically.
" Women will do it." He looked sharply at Poirot. " That
suggests something to you ? "

" Yes, I think I know what it was she was going to tell
him."

" Wonderful guesser, aren't you ? You always were.
Well, what was it ? "

" Excuse me, are you inquiring into the death of Richard
Abernethie ? "

" Officially, no. Actually, of course, if it has a bearing on
the murder of Mrs. Lansquenet——"

" It has a bearing on that, yes. But I will ask you, my
friend, to give me a few more hours. I shall know by then if
what I have imagined—imagined only, you comprehend—is
correct. If it *is*——"

" Well, if it is ? "

" Then I may be able to place in your hands a piece of
concrete evidence."

" We could certainly do with it," said Inspector Morton
with feeling. He looked askance at Poirot. " What have
you been holding back ? "

" Nothing. Absolutely nothing. Since the piece of evidence
I have imagined may not in fact exist. I have only deduced
its existence from various scraps of conversation. I may,"
said Poirot in a completely unconvinced tone, " be wrong."

Morton smiled.

" But that doesn't often happen to you ? "

" No. Though I will admit—yes, I am forced to admit—
that it *has* happened to me."

" I must say I'm glad to hear it ! To be always right must
be sometimes monotonous."

" I do not find it so," Poirot assured him.

Inspector Morton laughed.

" And you're asking me to hold off with my questioning ? "

" No, no, not at all. Proceed as you had planned to do.
I suppose you were not actually contemplating an arrest ? "

Morton shook his head.

" Much too flimsy for that. We'd have to get a decision
from the Public Prosecutor first—and we're a long way from

455

that. No, just statements from certain parties of their movements on the day in question—in one case with a caution,
perhaps."

" I see. Mrs. Banks ? "

" Smart, aren't you ? Yes. She was there that day. Her
car was parked in that quarry."

" She was not seen actually *driving* the car ? "

" No."

The Inspector added, " It's bad, you know, that she's
never said a word about being down there that day. She's
got to explain that satisfactorily."

" She is quite skilful at explanations," said Poirot dryly.

" Yes. Clever young lady. Perhaps a thought too clever."

" It is never wise to be too clever. That is how murderers
get caught. Has anything more come up about George
Crossfield ? "

" Nothing definite. He's a very ordinary type. There are
a lot of young men like him going about the country in trains
and buses or on bicycles. People find it hard to remember
when a week or so has gone by if it was Wednesday or Thursday when they were at a certain place or noticed a certain
person."

He paused and went on : " We've had one piece of rather
curious information—from the Mother Superior of some
convent or other. Two of her nuns had been out collecting
from door to door. It seems that they went to Mrs. Lansquenet's cottage on the day *before* she was murdered, but
couldn't make anyone hear when they knocked and rang.
That's natural enough—she was up North at the Abernethie
funeral and Gilchrist had been given the day off and had
gone on an excursion to Bournemouth. The point is that
they say *there was someone in the cottage*. They say they heard
sighs and groans. I've queried whether it wasn't a day later
but the Mother Superior is quite definite that that couldn't
be so. It's all entered up in some book. Was there someone
searching for something in the cottage that day, who seized
the opportunity of both the women being away ? And did
that somebody not find what he or she was looking for and
come back the next day ? I don't set much store on the sighs
and still less on the groans. Even nuns are suggestible and
a cottage where murder has occurred positively *asks* for
groans. The point is, was there someone in the cottage who
shouldn't have been there ? And if so, who was it ? All the
Abernethie crowd were at the funeral."

Poirot asked a seemingly irrelevant question :

" These nuns who were collecting in that district, did they return at all at a later date to try again ? "

" As a matter of fact they did come again—about a week later. Actually on the day of the inquest, I believe."

" That fits," said Hercule Poirot. " That fits very well."

Inspector Morton looked at him.

" Why this interest in nuns ? "

" They have been forced on my attention whether I will or no. It will not have escaped your attention, Inspector, that the visit of the nuns was the same day that poisoned wedding cake found its way into that cottage."

" You don't think—— Surely that's a ridiculous idea ? ".

" My ideas are never ridiculous," said Hercule Poirot severely. " And now, *mon cher*, I must leave you to your questions and to the inquiries into the attack on Mrs. Abernethie. I myself must go in search of the late Richard Abernethie's niece."

" Now be careful what you go saying to Mrs. Banks."

" I do not mean Mrs. Banks. I mean Richard Abernethie's other niece."

2

Poirot found Rosamund sitting on a bench overlooking a little stream that cascaded down in a waterfall and then flowed through rhododendron thickets. She was staring into the water.

" I do not, I trust, disturb an Ophelia," said Poirot as he took his seat beside her. " You are, perhaps, studying the *rôle* ? "

" I've never played in Shakespeare," said Rosamund. " Except once in Rep. I was Jessica in *The Merchant*. A lousy part."

" Yet not without pathos. ' *I am never merry when I hear sweet music.*' What a load she carried, poor Jessica, the daughter of the hated and despised Jew. What doubts of herself she must have had when she brought with her her father's ducats when she ran away to her lover. Jessica with gold was one thing—Jessica without gold might have been another."

Rosamund turned her head to look at him.

" I thought you'd gone," she said with a touch of reproach. She glanced down at her wrist-watch. " It's past twelve o'clock."

457

" I have missed my train," said Poirot.

" Why ? "

" You think I missed it for a reason ? "

" I suppose so. You're rather precise, aren't you ? If you wanted to catch a train, I should think you'd catch it."

" Your judgment is admirable. Do you know, Madame, I have been sitting in the little summer-house hoping that you would, perhaps, pay me a visit there ? "

Rosamund stared at him.

" Why should I ? You more or less said good-bye to us all in the library."

" Quite so. And there was nothing—*you* wanted to say to *me* ? "

" No." Rosamund shook her head. " I had a lot I wanted to think about. Important things."

" I see."

" I don't often do much thinking," said Rosamund. " It seems a waste of time. But this *is* important. I think one ought to plan one's life just as one wants it to be."

" And that is what you are doing ? "

" Well, yes . . . I was trying to make a decision about something."

" About your husband ? "

" In a way."

Poirot waited a moment, then he said :

" Inspector Morton has just arrived here." He anticipated Rosamund's question by going on : " He is the police officer in charge of the inquiries about Mrs. Lansquenet's death. He has come here to get statements from you all about what you were doing on the day she was murdered."

" I see. *Alibis*," said Rosamund cheerfully.

Her beautiful face relaxed into an impish glee.

" That will be hell for Michael," she said. " He thinks I don't really know he went off to be with that woman that day."

" How did you know ? "

" It was obvious from the *way* he said he was going to lunch with Oscar. So frightfully casually, you know, and his nose twitching just a tiny bit like it always does when he tells lies."

" How devoutly thankful I am I am not married to you, Madame ! "

" And then, of course, I made sure by ringing up Oscar," continued Rosamund. " Men always tell such silly lies."

458

" He is not, I fear, a very faithful husband ? " Poirot
hazarded.

Rosamund, however, did not reject the statement.

" No."

" But you do not mind ? "

" Well, it's rather fun in a way," said Rosamund. " I mean,
having a husband that all the other women want to snatch
away from you. I should hate to be married to a man that
nobody wanted—like poor Susan. Really Greg is so completely wet ! "

Poirot was studying her.

" And suppose someone did succeed—in snatching your
husband away from you ? "

" They won't," said Rosamund. " Not now," she added.

" You mean——"

" Not now that there's Uncle Richard's money. Michael
falls for these creatures in a way—that Sorrel Dainton woman
nearly got her hooks into him—wanted him for keeps—but
with Michael the show will always come first. He can launch
out now in a big way—put his own shows on. Do some pro-
duction as well as acting. He's ambitious, you know, and he
really is good. Not like me. I adore acting—but I'm ham,
though I look nice. No, I'm not worried about Michael any
more. Because it's my money, you see."

Her eyes met Poirot's calmly. He thought how strange it
was that both Richard Abernethie's nieces should have fallen
deeply in love with men who were incapable of returning that
love. And yet Rosamund was unusually beautiful and Susan
was attractive and full of sex appeal. Susan needed and clung
to the illusion that Gregory loved her. Rosamund, clear-
sighted, had no illusions at all, but knew what she wanted.

" The point is," said Rosamund, " that I've got to make a
big decision—about the future. Michael doesn't know yet."
Her face curved into a smile. " He found out that I wasn't
shopping that day and he's madly suspicious about Regent's
Park."

" What is this about Regent's Park ? " Poirot looked
puzzled.

" I went there, you see, after Harley Street. Just to walk
about and think. Naturally Michael thinks that if I went
there at all, I went to meet some man ! "

Rosamund smiled beatifically and added :

" He didn't like that *at all* ! "

" But why should you not go to Regent's Park ? " asked
Poirot.

" Just to walk there, you mean ? "

" Yes. Have you never done it before ? "

" Never. Why should I ? What is there to go to Regent's Park *for* ? "

Poirot looked at her and said :

" For you—nothing."

He added :

" I think, Madame, that you must cede the green malachite table to your cousin Susan."

Rosamund's eyes opened very wide.

" Why should I ? I *want* it."

" I know. I know. But you—you will keep your husband. And the poor Susan, she will lose hers."

" Lose him ? Do you mean Greg's going off with someone ? I wouldn't have believed it of him. He looks so *wet*."

" Infidelity is not the only way of losing a husband, Madame."

" You don't mean—— ? " Rosamund stared at him. " You're not thinking that Greg poisoned Uncle Richard and killed Aunt Cora and conked Aunt Helen on the head ? That's ridiculous. Even *I* know better than that."

" Who did, then ? "

" George, of course. George is a wrong un, you know, he's mixed up in some sort of currency swindle—I heard about it from some friends of mine who were in Monte. I expect Uncle Richard got to know about it and was just going to cut him out of his will."

Rosamund added complacently :

" I've always known it was George."

CHAPTER XXIV

THE TELEGRAM came about six o'clock that evening.

As specially requested it was delivered by hand, not telephoned, and Hercule Poirot, who had been hovering for some time in the neighbourhood of the front door, was at hand to receive it from Lanscombe as the latter took it from the telegraph boy.

He tore it open with somewhat less than his usual precision. It consisted of three words and a signature.

Poirot gave vent to an enormous sigh of relief.

Then he took a pound note from his pocket and handed it to the dumbfounded boy.

"There are moments," he said to Lanscombe, "when economy should be abandoned."

"Very possibly, sir," said Lanscombe politely.

"Where is Inspector Morton?" asked Poirot.

"One of the police gentlemen," Lanscombe spoke with distaste—and indicated subtly that such things as names for police officers were impossible to remember—"has left. The other is, I believe, in the study."

"Splendid," said Poirot. "I join him immediately."

He once more clapped Lanscombe on the shoulder and said:

"Courage, we are on the point of arriving!"

Lanscombe looked slightly bewildered since departures, and not arrivals, had been in his mind.

He said:

"You do not, then, propose to leave by the nine-thirty train after all, sir?"

"Do not lose hope," Poirot told him.

Poirot moved away, then wheeling round, he asked:

"I wonder, can you remember what were the first words Mrs. Lansquenet said to you when she arrived here on the day of your master's funeral?"

"I remember very well, sir," said Lanscombe, his face lighting up. "Miss Cora—I beg pardon, Mrs. Lansquenet—I always think of her as Miss Cora, somehow——"

"Very naturally."

"She said to me: 'Hallo, Lanscombe. It's a long time since you used to bring us out meringues to the huts.' All the children used to have a hut of their own—down by the fence in the Park. In summer, when there was going to be a dinner party, I used to take the young ladies and gentlemen—the younger ones, you understand, sir—some meringues. Miss Cora, sir, was always very fond of her food."

Poirot nodded.

"Yes," he said, "that was as I thought. Yes, it was very typical, that."

He went into the study to find Inspector Morton and without a word handed him the telegram.

Morton read it blankly.

"I don't understand a word of this."

"The time has come to tell you all."

Inspector Morton grinned.

"You sound like a young lady in a Victorian melodrama. But it's about time you came across with something. I can't hold out on this set-up much longer. That Banks fellow is still insisting that he poisoned Richard Abernethie and boasting

461

that we can't find out how. What beats me is why there's always somebody who comes forward when there's a murder and yells out that they did it ! What do they think there is in it for them ? I've never been able to fathom that."

" In this case, probably shelter from the difficulties of being responsible for oneself—in other words—Forsdyke Sanatorium."

" More likely to be Broadmoor."

" That might be equally satisfactory."

" *Did* he do it, Poirot ? The Gilchrist woman came out with the story she'd already told you and it would fit with what Richard Abernethie said about his niece. If her husband did it, it would involve her. Somehow, you know, I can't visualise that girl committing a lot of crimes. But there's nothing she wouldn't do to try and cover *him*."

" I will tell you all——"

" Yes, yes, tell me all ! And for the Lord's sake hurry up and do it ! "

2

This time it was in the big drawing-room that Hercule Poirot assembled his audience.

There was amusement rather than tension in the faces that were turned towards him. Menace had materialised in the shape of Inspector Morton and Superintendent Parwell. With the police in charge, questioning, asking for statements, Hercule Poirot, private detective, had receded into something closely resembling a joke.

Timothy was not far from voicing the general feeling when he remarked in an audible *sotto voce* to his wife :

" Damned little mountebank ! Entwhistle must be *gaga* ! —that's all I can say."

It looked as though Hercule Poirot would have to work hard to make his proper effect.

He began in a slightly pompous manner.

" For the second time, I announce my departure ! This morning I announced it for the twelve o'clock train. This evening I announce it for the nine-thirty—immediately, that is, after dinner. I go because there is nothing more here for me to do."

" Could have told him that all along." Timothy's commentary was still in evidence. " Never was anything for him to do. The cheek of these fellows ! "

" I came here originally to solve a riddle. The riddle is solved. Let me, first, go over the various points which were brought to my attention by the excellent Mr. Entwhistle.

" First, Mr. Richard Abernethie dies suddenly. Secondly, after his funeral, his sister Cora Lansquenet says, ' He was murdered, wasn't he ? ' Thirdly Mrs. Lansquenet is killed. The question is, are those three things part of a *sequence* ? Let us observe what happens next ? Miss Gilchrist, the dead woman's companion, is taken ill after eating a piece of wedding cake which contains arsenic. That, then, is the *next* step in the sequence.

" Now, as I told you this morning, in the course of my inquiries I have come across nothing—nothing at all, to substantiate the belief that Mr. Abernethie was poisoned. Equally, I may say, I have found nothing to prove conclusively that he was *not* poisoned. But as we proceed, things become easier. Cora Lansquenet undoubtedly asked that sensational question at the funeral. Everyone agrees upon *that*. And undoubtedly, on the following day, Mrs. Lansquenet was murdered—a hatchet being the instrument employed. Now let us examine the fourth happening. The local post van driver is strongly of the belief—though he will not definitely swear to it—that he did not deliver that parcel of wedding cake in the usual way. And if that is so, then the parcel was left by hand and though we cannot exclude a ' person unknown ' —we must take particular notice of those people who were actually on the spot and in a position to put the parcel where it was subsequently found. Those were : Miss Gilchrist herself, of course ; Susan Banks who came down that day for the inquest ; Mr. Entwhistle (but yes, we must consider Mr. Entwhistle ; he was present, remember, when Cora made her disquieting remark !) And there were two other people. An old gentleman who represented himself to be a Mr. Guthrie, an art critic, and a nun or nuns who called early that morning to collect a subscription.

" Now I decided that I would start on the assumption that the postal van driver's recollection was correct. Therefore the little group of people under suspicion must be very carefully studied. Miss Gilchrist did not benefit in any way by Richard Abernethie's death and in only a very minute degree by Mrs. Lansquenet's—in actual fact the death of the latter put her out of employment and left her with the possibility of finding it difficult to get new employment. Also Miss Gilchrist was taken to hospital definitely suffering from arsenical poisoning.

" Susan Banks *did* benefit from Richard Abernethie's
death, and in a small degree from Mrs. Lansquenet's—though
here her motive must almost certainly have been security.
She might have very good reason to believe that Miss Gilchrist
had overheard a conversation between Cora Lansquenet and
her brother which referred to her, and she might therefore
decide that Miss Gilchrist must be eliminated. She herself,
remember, refused to partake of the wedding cake and also
suggested not calling in a doctor until the morning, when
Miss Gilchrist was taken ill in the night.

" Mr. Entwhistle did *not* benefit by either of the deaths—
but he had had considerable control over Mr. Abernethie's
affairs, and the trust funds, and there might well be some
reason why Richard Abernethie should not live too long.
But—you will say—if it is Mr. Entwhistle who was concerned,
why should he come to *me* ?

" And to that I will answer—it is not the first time that
a murderer has been too sure of himself.

" We now come to what I may call the two outsiders.
Mr. Guthrie and a nun. If Mr. Guthrie is really Mr. Guthrie,
the art critic, then that clears him. The same applies to the
nun, if she is really a nun. The question is, are these people
themselves, or are they somebody else ?

" And I may say that there seems to be a curious—*motif*—
one might call it—of a nun running through this business.
A nun comes to the door of Mr. Timothy Abernethie's house
and Miss Gilchrist believes it is the same nun she has seen at
Lychett St. Mary. Also a nun, or nuns, called here the day
before Mr. Abernethie died . . ."

George Crossfield murmured, " Three to one, the nun."

Poirot went on :

" So here we have certain pieces of our pattern—the death
of Mr. Abernethie, the murder of Cora Lansquenet, the poisoned wedding cake, the ' *motif* ' of the ' nun.'

" I will add some other features of the case that engaged
my attention :

" The visit of an art critic, a smell of oil paint, a picture
postcard of Polflexan harbour, and finally a bouquet of wax
flowers standing on that malachite table where a Chinese
vase stands now.

" It was reflecting on these things that led me to the truth
—and I am now about to tell you the truth.

" The first part of it I told you this morning. Richard
Abernethie died suddenly—but there would have been no
reason at all to suspect foul play had it not been for the

words uttered by his sister Cora at his funeral. *The whole case for the murder of Richard Abernethie rests upon those words.* As a result of them, you all believed that murder had taken place, and you believed it, not really because of the words themselves but because of *the character of Cora Lansquenet herself*. For Cora Lansquenet had always been famous for speaking the truth at awkward moments. So the case for Richard's murder rested not only upon what Cora had *said* but upon Cora herself.

" And now I come to the question that I suddenly asked myself :

" *How well did you all know Cora Lansquenet ?* "

He was silent for a moment, and Susan asked sharply, " What do you mean ? "

Poirot went on :

" *Not well at all*—that is the answer ! The younger generation had never seen her at all, or if so, only when they were very young children. There were actually only three people present that day who actually *knew* Cora. Lanscombe, the butler, who is old and very blind ; Mrs. Timothy Abernethie who had only seen her a few times round about the date of her own wedding, and Mrs. Leo Abernethie who had known her quite well, but who had not seen her for over twenty years.

" So I said to myself : ' Supposing it was *not* Cora Lansquenet who came to the funeral that day ? ' "

" Do you mean that Aunt Cora—*wasn't* Aunt Cora ? " Susan demanded incredulously. " Do you mean that it wasn't Aunt Cora who was murdered, but someone else ? "

" No, no, it was Cora Lansquenet who was murdered. *But it was not Cora Lansquenet* who came the day before to her brother's funeral. The woman who came that day came for one purpose only—to exploit, one may say, the fact that Richard died suddenly. And to create in the minds of his relations the belief that he had been murdered. Which she managed to do most successfully ! "

" Nonsense ! Why ? What was the point of it ? " Maude spoke bluffly.

" Why ? *To draw attention away from the other murder.* From the murder of Cora Lansquenet herself. For if Cora says that Richard has been murdered and the next day *she herself is killed*, the two deaths are bound to be at least considered as possible cause and effect. But if Cora is murdered and her cottage is broken into, and if the apparent robbery does not convince the police, then they will look—where ?

465

Close at home, will they not ? Suspicion will tend to fall on the woman who shares the house with her."

Miss Gilchrist protested in a tone that was almost bright :

" Oh come—really—Mr. Pontarlier—you don't suggest I'd commit a murder for an amethyst brooch and a few worthless sketches ? "

" No," said Poirot. " For a little more than that. There was one of those sketches, Miss Gilchrist, that represented Polflexan harbour and which, as Mrs. Banks was clever enough to realise, had been copied from a picture postcard which showed the old pier still in position. But Mrs. Lansquenet painted always from life. I remembered then that Mr. Entwhistle had mentioned there being *a smell of oil paint* in the cottage when he first got there. You can paint, can't you, Miss Gilchrist ? Your father was an artist and you know a good deal about pictures. Supposing that one of the pictures that Cora picked up cheaply at a sale was a valuable picture. Supposing that she herself did not recognise it for what it was, but that you did. You knew she was expecting, very shortly, a visit from an old friend of hers who was a well-known art critic. Then her brother dies suddenly—and a plan leaps into your head. Easy to administer a sedative to her in her early cup of tea that will keep her unconscious for the whole of the day of the funeral whilst you yourself are playing her part at Enderby. You know Enderby well from listening to her talk about it. She has talked, as people do when they get on in life, a great deal about her childhood days. Easy for you to start off by a remark to old Lanscombe about meringues and huts which will make him quite sure of your identity in case he was inclined to doubt. Yes, you used your knowledge of Enderby well that day, with allusions to this and that, and recalling memories. None of them suspected you were not Cora. You were wearing her clothes, slightly padded, and since she wore a false front of hair, it was easy for you to assume that. Nobody had seen Cora for twenty years—and in twenty years people change so much that one often hears the remark : ' I would never have known her ! ' But mannerisms are remembered, and Cora had certain very definite mannerisms, all of which you had practised carefully before the glass.

" And it was there, strangely enough, that you made your first mistake. *You forgot that a mirror image is reversed.* When you saw in the glass the perfect reproduction of Cora's bird-like sidewise tilt of the head, you didn't realise that it was actually the *wrong way round*. You saw, let us say, Cora

466

inclining her head to the *right*—but you forgot that actually
your own head was inclined to the *left* to produce that effect
in the glass.

" That was what puzzled and worried Helen Abernethie at
the moment when you made your famous insinuation. Something seemed to her ' wrong.' I realised myself the other night
when Rosamund Shane made an unexpected remark what
happens on such an occasion. Everybody inevitably looks at
the *speaker*. Therefore, when Mrs. Leo felt something was
' wrong,' it must be that something was wrong with *Cora
Lansquenet*. The other evening, after talk about mirror
images and ' seeing oneself ' I think Mrs. Leo experimented
before a looking-glass. Her own face is not particularly
asymmetrical. She probably thought of Cora, remembered
how Cora used to incline her head to the right, did so, and
looked in the glass—when, of course, the image seemed to her
' wrong ' and she realised, in a flash, just what had been
wrong on the day of the funeral. She puzzled it out—either
Cora had taken to inclining her head in the opposite direction
—most unlikely—or else *Cora had not been Cora*. Neither way
seemed to her to make sense. But she determined to tell
Mr..Entwhistle of her discovery at once. Someone who was
used to getting up early was already about, and followed her
down, and fearful of what revelations she might be about to
make struck her down with a heavy doorstop."

Poirot paused and added :

" I may as well tell you now, Miss Gilchrist, that Mrs.
Abernethie's concussion is not serious. She will soon be able
to tell us her own story."

" I never did anything of the sort," said Miss Gilchrist.
" The whole thing is a wicked lie."

" It *was* you that day," said Michael Shane suddenly. He
had been studying Miss Gilchrist's face. " I ought to have
seen it sooner—I felt in a vague kind of way I had seen you
before somewhere—but of course one never looks much
at——" he stopped.

" No, one doesn't bother to look at a mere companion-help,"
said Miss Gilchrist. Her voice shook a little. " A drudge, a
domestic drudge ! Almost a servant ! But go on, M. Poirot.
Go on with this fantastic piece of nonsense ! "

" The suggestion of murder thrown out at the funeral was
only the first step, of course," said Poirot. " You had more
in reserve. At any moment you were prepared to admit to
having listened to a conversation between Richard and his
sister. What he actually told her, no doubt, was the fact that

467

he had not long to live, and that explains a cryptic phrase in the letter he wrote her after getting home. The ' nun ' was another of your suggestions. The nun—or rather nuns—who called at the cottage on the day of the inquest suggested to you a mention of a nun who was ' following you round,' and you used that when you were anxious to hear what Mrs. Timothy was saying to her sister-in-law at Enderby. And also because you wished to accompany her there and find out for yourself just how suspicions were going. Actually to poison *yourself*, badly but not fatally, with arsenic, is a very old device—and I may say that it served to awaken Inspector Morton's suspicions of you."

" But the picture ? " said Rosamund. " What kind of a picture was it ? "

Poirot slowly unfolded a telegram.

" This morning I rang up Mr. Entwhistle, a responsible person, to go to Stansfield Grange and, acting on authority from Mr. Abernethie himself " (here Poirot gave a hard stare at Timothy) " to look amongst the pictures in Miss Gilchrist's room and select the one of Polflexan Harbour on pretext of having it reframed as a surprise for Miss Gilchrist. He was to take it back to London and call upon Mr. Guthrie whom I had warned by telegram. The hastily painted sketch of Polflexan Harbour was removed and the original picture exposed."

He held up the telegram and read :

" *Definitely a Vermeer. Guthrie.*"

Suddenly, with electrifying effect, Miss Gilchrist burst into speech.

" I knew it was a Vermeer. I *knew* it ! *She* didn't know ! Talking about Rembrandts and Italian Primitives and unable to recognise a Vermeer when it was under her nose ! Always prating about Art—and really knowing nothing about it ! She was a thoroughly stupid woman. Always maundering on about this place—about Enderby, and what they did there as children, and about Richard and Timothy and Laura and all the rest of them. Rolling in money always ! Always the best of everything those children had. You don't know how boring it is listening to somebody going on about the same things, hour after hour and day after day. And saying, ' Oh yes, Mrs. Lansquenet ' and ' Really, Mrs. Lansquenet ? ' Pretending to be interested. And really bored—bored— *bored* . . . And nothing to look forward to . . . And then—a Vermeer ! I saw in the papers that a Vermeer sold the other day for over five thousand pounds ! "

468

" You killed her—in that brutal way—for five thousand pounds ? " Susan's voice was incredulous.

" Five thousand pounds," said Poirot, " would have rented and equipped *a tea-shop* . . ."

Miss Gilchrist turned to him.

" At least," she said. " You *do* understand. It was the only chance I'd ever get. I *had* to have a capital sum." Her voice vibrated with the force and obsession of her dream. " I was going to call it the Palm Tree. And have little camels as menu holders. One can occasionally get quite nice china— export rejects—not that awful white utility stuff. I meant to start it in some nice neighbourhood where nice people would come in. I had thought of Rye . . . Or perhaps Chichester . . . I'm sure I could have made a success of it." She paused a minute, then added musingly, " Oak tables—and little basket chairs with striped red and white cushions. . . ."

For a few moments, the tea-shop that would never be, seemed more real than the Victorian solidity of the drawing-room at Enderby . . .

It was Inspector Morton who broke the spell.

Miss Gilchrist turned to him quite politely.

" Oh, certainly," she said. " At once. I don't want to give any trouble, I'm sure. After all, if I can't have the Palm Tree, nothing really seems to matter very much. . . ."

She went out of the room with him and Susan said, her voice still shaken :

" I've never imagined a *lady-like* murderer. It's horrible. . . ."

CHAPTER XXV

" BUT I DON'T understand about the wax flowers," said Rosamund.

She fixed Poirot with large reproachful blue eyes.

They were at Helen's flat in London. Helen herself was resting on the sofa and Rosamund and Poirot were having tea with her.

" I don't see that *wax flowers* had anything to *do* with it," said Rosamund. " Or the malachite table."

" The malachite table, no. But the wax flowers were Miss Gilchrist's second mistake. She said how nice they looked on the malachite table. And you see, Madame, *she* could not have seen them there. Because they had been broken and put away before she arrived with the Timothy

Abernethies. *So she could only have seen them when she was there as Cora Lansquenet.*"

" That *was* stupid of her, wasn't it ? " said Rosamund.

Poirot shook a forefinger at her.

" It shows you, Madame, the dangers of *conversation.* It is a profound belief of mine that if you can induce a person to talk to you for long enough, *on any subject whatever*, sooner or later they will give themselves away. Miss Gilchrist did."

" I shall have to be careful," said Rosamund thoughtfully. Then she brightened up.

" Did you know ?   I'm going to have a baby."

" Aha !   So that is the meaning of Harley Street and Regent's Park ? "

" Yes. I was so upset, you know, and so surprised—that I just had to go somewhere and *think.*"

" You said, I remember, that that does not very often happen."

" Well, it's much easier not to. But this time I had to decide about the future. And I've decided to leave the stage and just be a mother."

" A *rôle* that will suit you admirably. Already I foresee delightful pictures in the *Sketch* and the *Tatler.*"

Rosamund smiled happily.

" Yes, it's wonderful. Do you know, Michael is *delighted.* I didn't really think he would be."

She paused and added :

" Susan's got the malachite table. I thought, as I was having a baby——"

She left the sentence unfinished.

" Susan's cosmetic business promises well," said Helen. " I think she is all set for a big success."

" Yes, she was born to succeed," said Poirot. She is like her uncle."

" You mean Richard, I suppose," said Rosamund. " Not Timothy ? "

" Assuredly not like Timothy," said Poirot.

They laughed.

" Greg's away somewhere," said Rosamund. " Having a rest cure Susan *says* ? "

She looked inquiringly at Poirot who said nothing.

" I can't think why he kept on saying he'd killed Uncle Richard," said Rosamund. " Do you think it was a form of Exhibitionism ? "

Poirot reverted to the previous topic.

" I received a very amiable letter from Mr. Timothy Abernethie," he said. "He expressed himself as highly satisfied with the services I had rendered the family."

" I do think Uncle Timothy is quite awful," said Rosamund.

" I am going to stay with them next week," said Helen. " They seem to be getting the gardens into order, but domestic help is still difficult."

" They miss the awful Gilchrist, I suppose," said Rosamund. " But I dare say in the end, she'd have killed Uncle Timothy too. What fun if she had ! "

" Murder has always seemed fun to you, Madame."

" Oh ! not really," said Rosamund, vaguely. " But I *did* think it was George." She brightened up. " Perhaps he will do one some day."

" And that will be fun," said Poirot sarcastically.

" Yes, won't it ? " Rosamund agreed.

She ate another éclair from the plate in front of her.

Poirot turned to Helen.

" And you, Madame, are off to Cyprus ? "

" Yes, in a fortnight's time."

" Then let me wish you a happy journey."

He bowed over her hand. She came with him to the door, leaving Rosamund dreamily stuffing herself with cream pastries.

Helen said abruptly :

" I should like you to know, M. Poirot, that the legacy Richard left me meant more to me than theirs did to any of the others."

" As much as that, Madame ? "

" Yes. You see—there is a child in Cyprus . . . My husband and I were very devoted—it was a great sorrow to us to have no children. After he died my loneliness was unbelievable. When I was nursing in London at the end of the war, I met someone . . . He was younger than I was and married, though not very happily. We came together for a little while. That was all. He went back to Canada—to his wife and his children. He never knew about—our child. He would not have wanted it. I did. It seemed like a miracle to me—a middle-aged woman with everything behind her. With Richard's money I can educate my so-called nephew, and give him a start in life." She paused, then added, " I never told Richard. He was fond of me and I of him—but he would not have understood. You know so much about us all that I thought I would like you to know this about me."

471

Once again Poirot bowed over her hand.

He got home to find the armchair on the left of the fireplace occupied.

"Hallo, Poirot," said Mr. Entwhistle. "I've just come back from the Assizes. They brought in a verdict of Guilty, of course. But I shouldn't be surprised if she ends up in Broadmoor. She's gone definitely over the edge since she's been in prison. Quite happy, you know, and *most* gracious. She spends most of her time making the most elaborate plans to run a chain of tea-shops. Her newest establishment is to be the Lilac Bush. She's opening it in Cromer."

"One wonders if she was always a little mad? But me, I think not."

"Good Lord, no! Sane as you and I when she planned that murder. Carried it out in cold blood. She's got a good head on her, you know, underneath the fluffy manner."

Poirot gave a little shiver.

"I am thinking," he said, "of some words that Susan Banks said—that she had never imagined a *lady-like* murderer."

"Why not?" said Mr. Entwhistle. "It takes all sorts."

They were silent—and Poirot thought of murderers he had known . . .

THE END